CRITICAL REACTION

CRITICAL REACTION

A NOVEL

TODD M. JOHNSON

BETHANYHOUSE
a division of Baker Publishing Group
Minneapolis, Minnesota

© 2013 by Todd M. Johnson

Published by Bethany House Publishers
11400 Hampshire Avenue South
Bloomington, Minnesota 55438
www.bethanyhouse.com

Bethany House Publishers is a division of
Baker Publishing Group, Grand Rapids, Michigan

Printed in the United States of America

Library of Congress Cataloging-in-Publication Data
Johnson, Todd M. (Todd Maurice).
    Critical Reaction : A Novel / Todd M. Johnson.
        pages   cm
    Summary: "After surviving an explosion at Hanford Nuclear Facility, two employees seek justice—and discover how far someone is willing to go to bury the truth"—Provided by publisher.
    ISBN 978-0-7642-1015-0 (paperback)
    1. Nuclear reactors—Fiction. 2. Radioactive fallout survival—Fiction. I. Title.
PS3610.O38363C75 2013
813'.6—dc23   2013023312

Cover design by Lookout Design, Inc.

13 14 15 16 17 18 19   7 6 5 4 3 2 1

For my Libby.

"The cost of cleaning nuclear defense sites like Hanford could be so high, and the contamination so great, we may just have to erect a fence around them and call them what they are: national sacrifice zones."

unknown nuclear engineer, late 1980s

CHAPTER 1

Under a moonless sky, he slowed the bay stallion as they neared the top of the slope. The evening breeze, strongest there on the narrow plateau at the peak of the ridge, slipped a gust of chill air through his jacket and down his neck. He pulled his hood up over his head.

Through his jeans, the stallion's thick winter coat warmed his thighs, wrapped bareback around its flanks. He pulled off his gloves and slid his hands up and under its thick overgrown mane, where the heat was captured like a blanket.

As feeling returned to his numbed fingers, the man straightened and gazed far down toward the flats below. A distant object glowed there, dipping and bounding across the dark desert a mile and a half further east—back in the direction from which he'd come. He raised the binoculars slung around his neck, grunting with satisfaction as the magnified object gained definition.

It was sagebrush, moving erratically over the desert surface—like a tiny runaway sun released from the laws of nature and glowing beyond any other source of illumination. Ten to twenty miles per hour, the man judged—propelled by a desert wind. Most people wouldn't have seen the small object from this distance, he thought with a touch of pride, not without the binoculars. And if they could see it, would they believe what they saw? If he denied the proof of his own eyes, he'd feel as untethered as that illuminated brush out there tonight.

The trajectory of the glowing object confirmed their calculations, another source of satisfaction for him. Sliding the binoculars back beneath his jacket, he patted the stallion reassuringly on the withers as the animal pawed the ground, snorting thick clouds that quickly dissipated in the cold air.

He glanced back up as the shape bounded once more, arcing upward before dropping from sight beneath a fold in the ground. It didn't reappear.

The eddies of cold air slowed his will to press on. But the man knew he had to. The Hanford Works buildings stood to the northeast, stalagmites in the desert beyond his sight along the Columbia River. One of those buildings housed Hanford's central security. If he'd been detected on the nuclear reservation grounds tonight, cars could already be dispatched to search him out.

He had raised his heels to kick the stallion into motion when the horse whinnied and backed in alarm. Then he heard it: a ragged boom like a thunderclap from an unseen storm blowing out of the dark from the Hanford buildings. The man shushed the animal, gripping its mane tightly as the sound rolled and echoed off the surrounding hills before fading away.

Another boom followed, even louder, sending a ripple of alarm through the stallion. Then a third.

Thunder on a cold night like this? A landslide? An earthquake?

The last echoes faded off. He listened longer as a breeze whispered through the ground brush. Nothing more.

The horse rolled its head, impatient to go. He reassured the animal gently. But the cold air—so fresh in his lungs a moment ago—now tasted sour in the man's mouth.

His stomach lurched as the bay suddenly reared to full height. The man tightened his grip on its mane to stop a slide toward its hips—just as the animal dropped back on its front hooves and launched itself into the black.

Over the stallion's hammering hoofbeats the man shouted for it to slow. Pulling desperately on the horse's mane to yank its head back and himself forward, the man prayed for even ground and to avoid the ridgeline to their right.

A dozen pounding strides passed before he could center himself on the bay's back. Then he loosened his legs' grip and leaned back, yanking harder on the mane. The animal began to ease its pace.

With the slowing beat of the stallion's strides, for the first time the man could hear what had made the horse lose control. The sound of it set his heart pounding.

Give me whatever you've got left, he whispered, leaning deep into the animal's shoulders again, tightening his legs and mouthing encouragement for speed once more. The animal was confused and hesitated—until he kicked its flanks hard, launching the stallion into a gallop.

Whatever you've got left. Whatever it takes to get off this high, naked butte, where the night currents from Hanford will reach long before settling to the desert floor below.

Behind him, the sound was unmistakable and growing ever clearer, rising up and up, striking a deep chord of fear in the man who feared very little. It was a warning siren screaming from one of the buildings of the shuttered plutonium factory, and even over the distance, it chilled him more than the wind ever could.

Because the piercing cry heralded a radiation release, in a wail as shrill as a tortured soul.

2:46 A.M.
LAB BUILDING 5
HANFORD NUCLEAR RESERVATION

Twenty-five-year-old Kieran Mullaney winced as he crouched to adjust his worn pair of boots. The sharp pain had to be another blister, this one on the sole of his left foot. He pulled his sock tighter. There was little else he could do.

Kieran looked up into the stare of his supervisor, Taylor Christensen. The man was standing impatiently by the entryway to the "dark side" of Lab Building 5. Steve Whalen, the aging supply manager for LB5, chewed his gum indifferently from behind the equipment counter. They each were watching Kieran, waiting for him to follow Taylor through the door to start the night shift.

Maybe he should do just that, Kieran thought. Keep his mouth shut and start his shift. Because if he complained about his boots, they'd think it wasn't such a big deal.

But it was a big deal. It wasn't just the pain he'd endure for another shift from these tight replacement boots Whalen had given him last week. It was that nobody had told him where those boots had picked up the plutonium that made them confiscate them in the first place.

It also was Whalen's smug attitude, like that of so many old-timers, the ones who'd been at Hanford as far back as when the place was still operational. Guys like Whalen looked down their noses at the youngest workers like Kieran. Whalen had been broadcasting his disdain for Kieran the whole two weeks he and Taylor had been substituting here at LB5. He was doing it now.

Whalen treated Kieran's supervisor differently; he'd thrown some respect Taylor's way since they'd arrived as stand-ins for the regular LB5 sampling crew. Kieran got it—Taylor had the look and walk of the third-generation Hanford man he was. Kieran was second generation, but he didn't have the walk. He didn't kowtow to the Whalens of Hanford.

Kieran straightened up to his full height. All right. It was their last night here. He'd push back a little.

"Red, I want my own boots back," he said matter-of-factly, using for the first time the nickname he'd heard others call the tech. "The ones made out of real leather instead of recycled footballs."

The equipment man squinted at Kieran from under gray eyebrows with a look like he was chewing lemons. "Well, aren't you the smart one," Whalen fired back with clipped words. "You can go barefoot if you'd like. But you'll get back your own boots when they're done testing 'em."

"You took them last week and we're heading back to our regular station tomorrow," Kieran kept on. "What happened to 'You'll get them back in twenty-four hours'?"

Red Whalen cut him off with a wave of his left hand, raising a Geiger counter from the equipment shelf in his right as though it were something holy.

"Didn't you hear old Samantha here cry out the other day when I wanded your boots for rads, boy? What do they teach you kids in training these days? That was the voice of a *protective angel of heaven*, shoutin' that the soles of that leather tied to your feet had found some serious radiation on the dark side—heaven knows where. And all you can do is whine about wantin' to get back those Walmart specials and take 'em home with you to Momma? Shame on you. I'll tell you this once more: when they figure out where you got the contamination, the folks at headquarters will clean the rads off the boots and get 'em back to you. End of story."

Some of the smugness had come off the supply manager's face—replaced with stubborn anger. This was feeling good, Kieran thought. He held up his HEPA mask.

"How about my air filter?" he said. "I told you my first day here that this one's too small. Feels like a kid's snorkel. Don't they issue you supply guys adult equipment here at LB5—"

Taylor took a step toward Kieran and grabbed the mask from his outstretched hand. "C'mon," the supervisor growled through his thick moustache, then led the way through the security door for their shift.

With a final glance at Whalen's flushed face, Kieran passed the equipment counter and followed Taylor into the dark side.

He only let his grin surface once he was through the door and out of the supply manager's view.

Looking at his supervisor's hunched shoulders, Kieran feared that he'd ticked off Taylor by baiting Whalen. He didn't want a lecture tonight about how *"nobody complained back when Hanford was making the plutonium that went on the trains to Rocky Flats. Everybody knew how important that mission was. This isn't just another job. . . ."*

Taylor had it in him, that vein of pride that rivaled the old-timers. But he must've known Kieran was just letting off steam, because the lecture never came.

Their boots clopped on the concrete floor of the first-floor corridor of LB5's dark side. Every Hanford building ever used for plutonium production had its dark side—the name everyone used for areas where plutonium was produced before the Department of Energy turned out the lights and closed all these buildings for good. Kieran had heard somebody say they chemically recaptured plutonium here at LB5. He didn't exactly know what that meant. Frankly, he didn't care. He worked for a company whose job was to do monitoring and testing ordered by Covington Nuclear—sampling for radiation in the air; checking the contents of aging storage containers with long-disused chemicals; taking swipes off the walls and floors for leaking contaminants or rads. Whatever else they told him to do. He didn't need a history lesson about the Hanford Nuclear Reservation for this job. Growing up in Sherman next to the place, he'd had enough of those to last a dozen lifetimes.

Kieran glanced at a plaque on one of the locked doors they passed in the empty hallway. At Hanford, that meant somebody had gotten a fatal dose of rads in the room, along with the standard compensation issued to the family. Kill boards the old guys called them—or agony plaques. The nicknames said it all: it was no way to die.

Kieran mouthed the name on the plaque they'd just passed:

Severson Room. Likely he died in the fifties or sixties. That's when most of them went; when production was so rushed that lots of corners were cut. He wondered who the man was, whether he'd had a wife and kids. Probably both. Most of these guys were family men, good providers given the top-notch pay out here.

Providers like Kieran's dad—a thirty-year Hanford man. They never worried about money, always had decent cars. Every Christmas topped the one before it. Trips to Disneyland every couple of years, and that surprise trip to Hawaii. College wouldn't have been a problem, that was for sure.

There was no plaque for his dad out here on the grounds, because he didn't get a sudden big dose of plutonium or tritium or some other rad that took you out in a flash. He got it slowly, sucking it into his lungs on long daytime shifts. Maybe eating what had settled invisibly onto his sandwich on breaks. Then hiding away deep inside him until the cancer surfaced in his bones before migrating to his lungs. Two years of chemo and he was gone the spring of Kieran's junior year of college

Nobody offered a plaque for that kind of death.

They passed a room numbered 140. There was no plaque on this door, just a number. He'd never worked in this building before last week—but the room number struck a chord. In a different Hanford lab building miles away was another room 140—the first room Kieran entered as a Hanford worker two years before. Kieran was Taylor's rookie assistant then, and the supervisor had started him out in a "clean" computer lab—one that wasn't supposed to be too crapped up because they'd never handled radioactive materials in the space.

But before they passed through the door, Taylor'd looked him in the eye and told Kieran to forget about "clean" rooms or "crapped up" ones. It was fine, Taylor had said, to reserve the HEPA mask just for emergencies, *"'cause you can't really do your job with it on anyway."*

"But other'n that," the big man had commanded through that thick brush of lip hair he was so proud of, "you act like every room has the potential to dose you. I know they trained you that turbines in all these buildings pull the air through filters to scrub it—and that's true. But if those filters caught everything, you and I'd be out of a job. Fact is, there's hot dust in the cleanest room and any mote of it could end up in your bones or your thyroid. Think of this place like it's full of black widow spiders: you don't want to touch *anything* you don't have to."

Then, to underline his point, Taylor'd pointed up at the nearest sample of dark tape that lined all the Hanford walls at the eight foot level. "And don't you *ever* let me catch you climbing ladders or standin' on chairs above that line. *Never.* Because the dust on the light fixtures up there's as thick as in your grandmother's attic. You take in a mouthful of that and a girl'd be a fool to ever kiss you again."

Those words rang in Kieran's ears that first shift, making him almost tiptoe into the darkness of "clean" room 140 in that other building. Then Taylor had flipped the light switch behind him and Kieran had stopped like he'd stepped knee deep into soft tar.

Fat computer monitors and plastic keyboards lined tables and desks scattered around the room, each covered with the faintest layer of dust. Tools lay on benches like they'd just dropped from workers' fingers. A calendar from the late 1980s decorated a wall next to lab coats still hung on hooks.

Kieran stood frozen, waiting for a shift of ghostly workers to shoulder past him, each layered in that same frosting of powdered dust, to pull on the old lab coats and take their places before the silent computers and benches.

Taylor had walked past and laughed at Kieran's expression. "Relax. The crews left things like this after their last shift in '89 'cause no one told them they weren't coming back. Nobody knew when, or if, they were coming back. Then the Berlin wall came down and *poof.* Job done."

14

That conversation was two years ago. He still thought about it before every shift.

Kieran's mind returned to the present as Taylor, a step ahead of him, reached the stairwell of LB5. He followed his supervisor up the dimly lit stairs to the third-floor hallway. There they stopped. Taylor smoothed his moustache with a finger and thumb. Then he handed Kieran a clipboard and testing equipment.

"Go check out room 369. It used to be a storage locker. Should be clean. Take air and dust samples then come back to me. I'll be here in room 301," he said, gesturing across the hallway. "Seems like a waste of time for our last night. The permanent crew should be able to handle sampling these corners of the building when they're back tomorrow. But there you are. And let's move it along. This is our last night here, so if we get the checklist done, I'm sending us home early."

Kieran took the clipboard and pouch of air and surface sampling equipment. Taylor had complained a few times the past week about "make work" projects that could've waited for the return of LB5's permanent testing crew—away now on some training exercise. He and Taylor hadn't been assigned to test any of LB5's lower level glove-box rooms, production lines, or anywhere else where plutonium had been handled in abundance—typically the highest priorities. But as Taylor often said, he didn't make up the work lists, he just got 'em done. His comments tonight were the closest Kieran had ever heard Taylor come to complaining.

Lab Building 5 was a long rectangle, its corridors stretching for nearly a hundred yards. Kieran left Taylor behind, trudging the distance toward room 369 at the furthest end of the third-floor hallway. As he walked, he marked his progress by counting off the hallway detectors bolted into the floor every fifty feet, humming as they continuously monitored the air for radioactive contamination. Each was crowned with small lights showing green if the air was safe, red if hazardous. They weren't as sophisticated as the tests the lab would perform on samples taken by Kieran, but they reassured him. Like Christmas bulbs on shin-high pines, the green glow always comforted Kieran as he walked the Hanford corridors.

He was nearly to the hallway's end when Kieran detected a brush of heat on his right ear. Another step and it was gone. He stopped—then backed up. There it was again.

To his right was an interlocking pair of steel pressure doors labeled room 365. He pressed a hand against the metal surface. It was warm to the touch.

The temperature in these old buildings was carefully controlled. Kieran reached for his walkie-talkie to call Taylor. Except, he recalled, his super didn't like being bothered with half information. Kieran set the testing equipment and clipboard beside the door on the hallway floor and turned the knobs to open each of the double doors.

They wouldn't budge. He tried again, leaning into each of the doors and pressing with his legs. This time, they slowly gave way.

As he stepped inside, his equipment belt rattled. The sound echoed in the dark interior—just as a wave of heat and humidity rolled past and out the open doors behind him. An instant sheen of sweat rose on Kieran's forehead.

Startled, he swept the black with his eyes for a sign of fire. There was none.

His fingers found the wall switch and he flicked it on. Light flooded a cavern at least thirty yards deep.

The space was filled with aging industrial vats lining each wall, split by a narrow walkway down the middle of the room. Each of the containers was pierced by a collection of pipes and valves, giving the appearance of a ward of metal giants on life support. Some of the pipes led to adjacent vats; others angled into the floor.

The sight was familiar. Kieran had sampled these rooms in other buildings where he'd worked. This was a mixing chamber.

When this was a working production building, chemicals were stored in these containers for transfer to other vats for mixing, or to be pumped to labs and glove rooms elsewhere in the building.

The heat was coming in waves from deeper in the room. Kieran took cautious steps forward, the sweat thickening on his face the further he walked from the doors.

The slow pace finally brought him near the far wall. Here, to his left, hung a towering vat. It was eight feet tall at least, suspended from the ceiling with thick steel posts. The enormous cylinder looked like the queen of the room, with pipes angling into it from every direction. Among all the pipes stabbing its surface, the largest was a single iron tube that descended from its bottom perpendicularly into the floor. *Vat 17* was stenciled across its girth.

Kieran moved closer. Moisture was dripping in rivulets of sweat on all sides of the huge vat's surface, released, Kieran saw, from pressure valves near the vat's lid.

This had to be the source of the heat and humidity.

Nearly beneath the container, Kieran heard a splash at his feet. He leaned into the shadows under the vat.

The sole of his left boot stood in a puddle of pooled condensation from the vat's sides. Satisfied, Kieran straightened up—only to be jerked back into mid crouch. Startled, he looked down again.

The edge of his T-shirt had caught on another valve attached to the iron pipe extending into the floor. Kieran untangled it, then stood fully upright.

The surface of the vat was only three feet away now. Kieran reached out his bare hand and touched it gently.

His fingers recoiled from the scalding metal. In that same moment, he heard his pulse pounding in his ears. Heat shock, he supposed. Or nerves.

He'd had enough. Kieran reached for the walkie-talkie on his hip.

Only the pounding wasn't in his ears, he suddenly realized—and it was growing, not subsiding. Kieran turned his head to one side. The rhythmic pulsing was coming from Vat 17 itself.

An image flashed through his head of a thin-skinned teakettle expanding like a balloon as it reached a boil.

He was running before he was aware of a decision to flee, sprinting toward the distant doors with fear pricking his skin like a thousand beestings. Maybe he was imagining it, but the thump of the vat seemed to match his pounding steps, growing louder and deeper as he ran.

Please, don't blow; don't blow. The mantra cycled in his head. But he heard it from his lips as well, in rhythm with his breath.

The doors were nearing through his sweat-blurred vision: he was going to make it. He'd leave the room and round the corner into the hall, out of the path of the coming explosion.

Then another voice spoke with equal certainty that he was wrong. Because the doors, still twenty yards away, were arcing slowly shut, edged by the rising pressure in the room. And once they were shut, no power on earth would open them again in the face of that pressure.

His wet left boot slipped, nearly taking him down. He stumbled through two strides before straightening again, the boot squeaking angrily on the concrete floor as he regained his pace.

The voices were silenced as the exit drew near. Kieran leaned forward, vaulting toward the shrinking gap between the doors with outstretched arms. His left shoulder skimmed one door's edge; his right knee scraped the other one hard. Then the steel panels grabbed his outstretched left ankle like a vise as his body slammed to the hallway floor beyond.

He lay face first on the cold surface of the corridor. His left ankle was locked at an angle above him. His ribs knifed with pain where they pressed against the floor.

Kieran strained to look over his shoulder at the foot. The effort hurt his ribs, but he could just make out that his ankle was still wedged between the mixing room doors, as the pounding sound leaked through the gap.

Kieran's muscles lit with panic once more. Sliding back toward the doors, he gathered his right knee to his chest and kicked furiously with his free foot at the nearest panel. The door yielded inches. He kicked again. And again and again and again. The fifth kick burst the door open for an instant and his left foot sprang free, stripped of his shoe and sock and layers of skin. Then the panels sprang instantly shut again, their final boom echoing down the empty corridor.

Kieran huddled on the floor, his muscles twitching, his clothes clinging with sweat. His ankle throbbed and bled. His ribs, forgotten briefly, now ached with pain at each breath.

He didn't care. Kieran sucked in wonderful breaths of cool air. He was safe. Safe in this peaceful space that was anywhere but in the mixing room beyond the heavy steel doors.

Metal groaned. Kieran opened his eyes and rolled to his back to look toward his feet.

The door panels strained on their hinges.

Kieran clambered to his feet, pain knifing the bloody bare one. He struggled into a limping run down the hallway, gripping his ribs with one arm. "Taylor," he tried to shout. The walkie-talkie tapped at his hip like it should mean something, but he kept shouting as he stumbled on.

A distant sixty yards or more away, Taylor emerged into the corridor. Kieran still heard the rising groans from the doors behind him and tried to quicken his pace. The supervisor's hands dropped to his belt, grabbing a HEPA mask hung there. He pulled it across his forehead and over his face.

Without breaking his stumbling stride, Kieran felt for his own mask—then sickened as Taylor lifted a second mask in the air.

It was Kieran's own, taken in the entryway to the dark side.

Still dozens of yards away, Taylor broke into a run toward Kieran with the second mask clutched in one fist. Taylor tried to communicate a command with his other hand—but the big man had made only two strides in Kieran's direction when the hall was swallowed by a roar and a shock wave that rocked the walls and floor, lifting Kieran from his feet as though launched from a spring. He twisted through the air, dust and flying paint filling the world—then his hips and back slammed the hard floor, triggering the screaming rib pain again and squeezing the air from his lungs.

The universe hurtled out of control as another roar shook the hall; then another. Kieran bounced off the floor with each succeeding cataclysm, consciousness slipping away—aware only of a final image locked in his mind like high definition.

It was the radiation monitors lining the walls between Kieran and Taylor's prone body on the hallway floor still a hundred feet away. Through a haze of settling debris, Kieran could see the monitors, unmoved by the explosions, bolted solidly in place.

What made them curious to watch were the changing hues of their light bulbs—solidly green before, but now flicking to red, one after another, like runway lights racing away down the hallway away from him.

3:01 A.M.
LAB BUILDING 5
HANFORD NUCLEAR RESERVATION

"Gin."

Patrick "Poppy" Martin cast a narrow-eyed grin and spread a handful of tattered cards across the edge of the desk. "That puts me out."

"Geez, Poppy, you had my seven," Lewis Vandervork spat, tossing his own cards.

Still grinning, Poppy reached out and patted the younger man's shoulder.

"Of *course* I did."

Outside, tiny droplets slid down the window of the rooftop guard shack surrounding them. Poppy stood and squinted out of the glass.

The rooftop guard shed was located along the north end of Lab Building 5, making Poppy's view from the window a southerly one over the full length of the vast roof expanse. A tall smokestack for LB5 stood apart from the building off to his left. It was difficult to make out now because he could see a thin cotton veil of fog rolling across the tarred roof surface from the desert, the moisture sparkling in the glare of the overhead perimeter lights surrounding the building grounds. "Deal again," he said to Lewis. "Let's play one more hand before we walk the roofline."

Lewis grunted and gathered the cards. "I will," the younger man said. "I got time to clean Beverly before we go?"

Poppy shook his head. "You can clean Beverly at the end of the shift, like always. You treat that rifle better'n I treat my wife."

Lew smiled, shaking his head. "That's the difference between my army training and your navy training, Pops. I know how to treat my weapon—and my woman. So, the building manager downstairs told ya we're done in a few more days here?"

Poppy nodded. "He left me a note with my time card. Said the permanent security detail finishes its training early next week and we're gone."

None too soon, he thought. Even in a place as spread out as the Hanford Reservation, this building was isolated. Coming here added twenty minutes to Poppy's usual daily commute, each way. And LB5's small permanent crew—eight most evenings—were just plain unfriendly when they crossed paths with them. He looked forward to getting back to his job rotation nearer to home.

Poppy listened to the sputtering of the fan on the corner space heater that filled the shack with hot, dry air, then the ripple of cards as his companion shuffled. Through the glass, he could make out the small cafeteria building that perched on a hillock twenty yards beyond LB5's southwest corner. Every evening shift since he and Lewis got transferred here for temporary duty, he'd seen people coming and going from there around this hour—registered on his log as HVAC workers. As though in confirmation, the door on the small building swung open and two figures emerged. Poppy watched as they turned and started down the hill on a sloping driveway that quickly led them out of his sight along LB5's west side.

The sight of the workers reminded Poppy: just four more hours on his own shift tonight. Then it was home in time to see his wife and visiting grandson before heading to bed. Later today, after he was up again, they'd have Suzy's fettuccine. What had she told him to pick up on the way home? Bread and . . . something. She was right: he should have written it down.

He glanced at his watch. It was time to walk the roofline and check in with the front office. Poppy reached for his jacket beside the gun rack. "On second thought, Lew, let's—"

His fingers brushed the jacket collar as the reinforced steel roof rippled under his feet like it'd been hit by some monstrous sledge. Poppy's knees buckled and he grabbed for the desk edge as the window splintered into a fine web. The computer monitor bounced from the desk, shattering on the ground; drawers from the corner file cabinet crashed to the floor; and over a fearful howl from Lewis, Poppy's eardrums were smothered by a piercing explosion to the east.

The sound was coming out of the smokestack, he thought, his ears aching—then he was down completely as a second even more violent wave slammed through the roof, like a tsunami crashing onto its surface. Then the terrifying crescendo of a third concussion rocked the shack, lifting the desk from the ground and heaving the window glass from its frame in a final shattering collapse.

This is it, Poppy thought—surprised that he could think at all, that he wasn't frightened past any sensibility. He looked across the floor at Lewis, twenty-five years younger and terrified, clawing at the shack floor with his fingernails as though it could shield him from the maelstrom boiling up below.

How pointless, he thought with a sharp pang of pity as a tear curled down Lew's cheek.

You might as well accept that no amount of steel's going to save us, 'cause something's gone critical down there, he thought. *And you and me and the poor boys working below are about to go up to God in a hellfire mushroom cloud of heat and blood and radiation.*

With that, his mind began a slide toward resignation and a strange welling of peace about it all. He started to mutter a prayer.

Then, as quickly as he'd begun, Poppy stopped. The world had gone silent and still.

Poppy braced for another inevitable blow; he heard Lewis moan through tightly clenched teeth, his hands now clasping his knees in a huddled ball. But the blow didn't come. The only sound other than Lewis was a breeze rattling the few remaining shards of the pulverized windowpane.

Poppy tried to assemble his thoughts, which drifted like scattered smoke. Then he was swept with a rush of exultation that he was alive.

Poppy pushed himself to his knees. His wife and grandson—he'd see them after the shift. The hunting trip next weekend—he'd still do it. He was alive.

The despair was leaching away, replaced by a different, vague impression. There was something he had to do. Poppy reached out and shook Lewis's shoulder. "Lew," he heard his voice say, through the ringing of his ears. "Lew."

The young man's moans stopped, but his eyes were still glassy. He should call someone for Lewis. No. He couldn't do that. No

23

one should see Lewis like this. And besides, that wasn't what he had to do.

Poppy rose, wobbly, and stepped toward the gun rack. He fumbled with the keys to unlock the padlock, watched himself withdraw an M-16 and a full clip, and forced his fingers to load the weapon. His boot kicked something. He looked down. It was a flashlight. He leaned over carefully and grabbed that too. He pulled on his jacket and stepped outside.

The fog seemed thin in the bright spotlights. Poppy stepped onto the tarred roof surface, surprised that it was still solid beneath his feet.

His head ached and his limbs felt drained, but his thoughts were assembling now. Why was he here? To check the ground along the roof perimeter. What for? Observation. Look for injured. What else? There was something else even more pressing.

Sabotage.

His Hanford training rushed back like an accelerated recording. If there was an explosion, the first duty of this post was to monitor the building exits for saboteurs—while maintaining contact with the central office on the front of LB5. If he observed potential saboteurs, he was to shoot. No, no, no, that wasn't it. He was to shoot . . . to kill.

All strength had been wrung from his legs, but he forced himself into a disjointed jog across the length of the roof toward the southern edge, where the building's rear emergency exit emptied out onto the grounds below. He pushed through the cotton in his mind to tick off the evening personnel log: the night building manager and assistant, front side offices; supply tech, dark side entryway; two sampling techs somewhere inside; HVAC engineer on the front side, second floor, north. Then there were two HVAC maintenance guys on the grounds tonight—probably those guys in the cafeteria building. So the only exits likely to be used were out the north, on the front side.

Poppy shifted the rifle to his left hand and reached for the walkie-talkie on his hip to check in.

The hand closed on air. Poppy slowed. He'd forgotten his gear back in the shed—his walkie-talkie, his mask. Everything except the rifle and flashlight.

Poppy turned—and was startled to look directly into Lewis's flushed face. Beverly was slung over Lewis's shoulder and in his hand he extended a walkie-talkie. The young man's eyes were red and swollen, full now with a different kind of fear.

"Pops—ya can't tell . . ." Lewis pleaded in a hoarse whisper.

Poppy took the walkie-talkie. "Don't know what you're talking about."

Relief flooded Lewis's eyes as Poppy pointed toward the eastern roofline—the only side of the building with emergency exits other than the south, where Poppy was headed. "Check the east. The emergency exit on that side's out of the lower level. Nobody should be down there, so anyone coming out is a presumed target."

Lewis nodded his understanding and then trotted off in that direction, unshouldering his rifle as he went. Poppy punched the Talk switch on the walkie-talkie as he faced back to the south.

"Central, this is Roof 1," he called as he began his run. "Central . . ."

He'd taken only two strides when he saw, through the wisps of fog, a gash of green and orange hovering in the air along the southern end of the building. Poppy slowed, trying to trace it with his eyes and make sense of the image.

It was a garish plume pumping from the top of the smokestack, where it stood now fifty yards to Poppy's left. The plume was pouring out of the tall chimney, drifting like a contrail down onto the roof of LB5, then flowing across the roof surface like an enormous snake, its snout tumbling along the tar in front of Poppy, headed toward his right. At its nearest point, the cloud seemed about twenty feet away from Poppy, but it already formed a barrier between him and his goal of reaching the southern edge of the roof.

He pressed the walkie-talkie switch again. "Central, Centr—"

"We hear you," a voice crackled from the device. "Is the roof intact?"

It sounded like the LB5 night manager, though Poppy'd only met him twice. And what was he talking about? *"Is the roof intact?"* Was that all they were worried about? He pressed the Transmit button.

"The roof—I don't know yet. It looks okay. But we've got another problem. There's a plume—a big one, green and orange. It's coming from the smokestack and heading across the roof in front of me."

Chemicals? Radiation? What was in the thing?

There was a pause over the speaker. "Repeat."

He did so.

Another pause. "Hold on."

As he waited, Poppy gauged the flowing cloud again. Its nearest visible edge still appeared at least twenty feet ahead of him, but now he thought he detected a metallic taste on his lips and a mild sting brushing his cheeks. He took a step backwards and peered more closely at the plume. The thick mass was flattening and broadening on its journey across the roof—dissipating at the edges so that its true depth was disguised in the light fog.

Poppy stepped back another full stride, then glanced to his right. The nose of the plume was now approaching the roofline in that direction, to the west.

The HVAC workers leaving the building on the knoll, he thought. They were walking on that side of the building, into the path of the cloud.

Poppy pivoted right and forced his legs into a stumbling run. His weakness still slowed him, like he was immobilized in a dream. Poppy cursed himself and his inability to accelerate.

"Roof security," the walkie-talkie came to life. "Please repeat. You said a plume?"

How many times did he have to say it? "Yeah," Poppy said, still jogging. He forced out a description of its color and movement between gasping breaths, ending just as a final stride brought him to the western roofline.

Sucking air, he scanned the paved path three stories below, leading from the knoll to the plant entrance.

The workers were visible now, moving slowly and uncertainly—but directly into the path the plume would soon take when it fell from the roof of the building.

Poppy realized that the walkie-talkie had gone silent. His throat felt raspy and he coughed as he pressed the Call button. "Listen, you've got personnel out here. On the west side. Repeat, west side. You've gotta sound the take-cover siren. Repeat, there are personnel out on the grounds."

As he finished, Poppy felt his chest tightening and a thickening in his throat. The plume, he thought; he'd swallowed some of it. He turned his head to spit and clear it. Why weren't they firing up the sirens?

"Do you hear me?" he called again into the walkie-talkie. "Please respond." It crackled with static.

The workers were stopped in confusion—one looking back toward the cafeteria on the knoll, the other pointing the other direction, toward the front of LB5. Their hands were waving hurriedly.

Poppy tried to shout a warning, but his throat caught. *It's settling into my lungs*, he thought, as in that instant, his lungs spasmed. He doubled over in a fit of wracking coughs, so violent he felt as though he were trying to tear his lungs right out of his body. He forced his lids open.

Through eyes drowned in tears, he saw that the men had turned toward LB5's front side and were beginning to pick up speed—still unaware of the plume rolling off the roof and toward their path.

Poppy tried to relax and slow the coughing that tore at his lungs. His mind and chest filled with rage at his impotence to stop the cloud rolling to embrace the men below—or even shout out a warning.

Poppy's breath still came in wheezing gasps too weak to call out, but he felt the coughing taper for a moment. He dropped to his knees, unslung his rifle with arms weak from the convulsive coughing, and pointed it skyward. Another spasm was coming on. He ignored it and cupped the trigger in his finger to squeeze.

There was a crackle of a rifle. Poppy's finger still rested gently on the trigger. He hadn't fired yet.

He twisted to look across the roof to the east. There he saw Lewis, leaning far out over the other edge, his rifle extended past the roof line and pointed toward the ground.

What had Lewis shot at? Because if Lew pulled the trigger, it was nearly a sure thing something went down.

Another wave of retching coughs overtook Poppy. Before they could double him over, he squeezed the trigger three times in succession. Then the barrel came down and the weapon dropped with a clatter onto the roof.

His eyes were misted over, his lungs aching, as Poppy forced himself to look down his own side of the building. The men had stopped and were looking up in his direction, a dozen feet from the cloud splaying across the yard toward the path, widening as it rolled. Poppy waved frantically back away from the plume, toward the knoll and the cafeteria. The men turned and ran an instant before Poppy was down on all fours, shuddering with spasms again.

In the next seconds, just as Poppy gained a moment's break from his retching, two things happened so quickly he could barely tell which came first.

A rising chorus of take-cover sirens screamed from the four corners of the grounds, blasting with such fury that Poppy faltered—barely catching himself from tumbling over the edge to the ground below.

In that same instant, the grounds were plunged into darkness with such suddenness that Poppy felt as though he'd been dropped dizzily into a deep, black hole.

CHAPTER 2

Eight months later
Public Defender's Office, King County Courthouse
Seattle, Washington

"You're not listening."

Startled, Emily Hart dropped her pen on the carpet. "I'm sorry," she answered, quickly retrieving it from the floor.

Seated behind his large oak desk covered with the usual stacks of papers in no discernible order, Frank Porter shook his head. "It's alright. We finished the business end of our talk ten minutes ago. You've just deprived yourself of hearing about my new grandson's Apgar score."

Emily smiled. "Sorry, Frank."

"Forget about it." He dismissed her with a wave of his hand. "Get to work. Or sort out whatever's got you daydreaming today. See if you can plea out the Henderson case like we discussed. And remember what I told you earlier: two years slaving here and you haven't taken a day of vacation. Including your comp time, you're already maxed out on accumulated leave."

She shrugged. "I don't mind waiving some of the time."

"I do," Frank said with a serious glare. "You take it. That's not a request. You're carrying a monster load as it is. Burn out, and I lose my rising star."

30

Emily smiled, then grasped her notepad and left the room. Passing Frank's secretary outside his door, she crossed the hallway into the small, windowless space that served as her office.

She didn't bother to sit down or turn on the light. Pulling the door shut behind her, Emily grabbed her cell from the desk and found the voice message from that morning.

"*Emily,*" the voice began. "*It's Kieran. I know it's been a long time. I'm sorry I haven't been in touch for a while. But right now I've got a big problem.*"

The voice halted and she heard a long roll of coughs in the background.

"*I heard about you finishing your law degree,*" he began again, his voice hoarse and low. "*That's great. And actually that's why I'm calling. I need a lawyer myself, right away.*"

There was a pause. "*I think I've gotten dosed out at Hanford, Emily—with radiation. Like what killed my father. It happened awhile ago, and I started a lawsuit, but my lawyer's withdrawn right before trial and now I don't think I'm going to find out what I got exposed to. It's . . . all getting out of control. Please. I've got no other options. Could you give me a call back?*"

The voicemail went silent. Emily stood in the quiet darkness for a full minute.

She hadn't gotten a message from Kieran in nearly three years. She hadn't heard his voice in four. Yet the only thing unfamiliar about it after all this time was the undertone of fear.

Emily felt a surprising urgency about responding to the message. She scrolled through her cell phone list of contacts until she found the number that she hadn't called in several months. Part of her felt she should get back to Kieran first. Even stronger was a preference to be able to offer immediate reassurance. Still, given whom she was reaching out to, Emily hesitated another full minute before making the call to the number on her contact list.

A recorded voice instructed her to leave a message.

"I've got a problem," she said after a final moment's hesitation. "Could we have lunch today, Dad?"

Ryan Hart paced the empty corridor on the fourth floor of the King County Courthouse. He checked the wall clock. Emily was late. He sighed. He was hungry and not in the mood to run into people he knew—which was bound to happen if he kept standing in the hallway.

His cell phone vibrated silently in his pocket. The text from Emily was a brief apology: her boss had her busy, but she'd be down to meet him for lunch in half an hour.

He slid the phone back into his pocket, reminding himself, despite his impatience, that this was the first time Emily had called him in months.

The door to courtroom 431 opened and a man came out, a muttering of voices escaping with him into the hallway. Ryan hesitated a moment, then approached the door. It was better than standing out here with his hands in his pockets.

He slipped through the door before it closed again.

The courtroom was surprisingly full. The case must be a headliner, he thought. "Barflies" drawn to a good fight. With a glance around the room, he took a seat at the rear corner nearest the door.

"All rise," the bailiff bellowed. Ryan was instantly back on his feet before the rest of the crowd could react.

A black robe billowed around the judge as he swept through the doors from chambers, followed by the entourage of his clerk, a court reporter, and a calendar assistant following. The staff split for their stations around the room as the magistrate dropped into his chair, motioning for the crowd to do the same.

As Ryan and everyone else in the gallery obeyed, a slim young woman to his left fidgeted nervously, bumping his shoulder. Ryan glanced at her before sliding to his right to give her a little more room.

This was a civil, not a criminal, case: only eight jurors occupied the jury box—probably six regulars and two alternates.
A corporate case as well, judging from the expensive suits worn
by the "civilians" crowded with their counsel at the three attorneys' tables. Ryan could usually distinguish the civilians from
their lawyers by their looks of caution, and the blank pads and
pens in front of them.

One attorney stood alone at a podium at the room's center,
waiting for the proceedings to begin. His client was likely the
older man at the table closest to the podium, wearing a sport
coat a size too small and a necktie a decade too large. The
minnow in this shark tank, Ryan thought, likely the plaintiff.
And from the legal legions arrayed against him, as well as this
gallery crowd, this was either a whistleblower or a fraud case.

Judge Francis Tipton adjusted his nameplate, then leaned
forward with a glower, signaling his readiness to devour the
entire room if necessary. "You may begin, Mr. Swinton," he
said with a nod to the lawyer at the podium.

A witness occupied the box to the judge's left, seated in a
swivel chair—middle-aged with a mystified look as though she
were in a perpetual state of surprise. She wore a navy suit, mod-
est jewelry, and little makeup—well costumed, Ryan thought.
Except her dark clothing highlighted a pale face and eyes slightly
over wide, and her hands gripped the wood-framed witness box.
"Clingers," Ryan called them—witnesses who clung to the box
like shipwreck victims in rough seas.

"Miss Galbraith," the lawyer at the podium began, "I'd like
you to set aside the last exhibit we were reviewing before the
break and turn back to Exhibit 41."

The witness looked alarmed, but stirred herself to rustle
through a stack of papers at her elbow.

Ryan didn't know the plaintiff's attorney at the podium. The
defense attorneys at the next table were lawyers from Feldman,
Leif, and Ramsdell. He'd faced the woman before.

His eyes went to the third table, where two senior attorneys from Melander and Stout sat, accompanied by a third, unfamiliar younger associate. They were a nasty crew—and expensive. He could only imagine the transgressions that had led their client to hire them.

The plaintiff's attorney asked questions about the exhibit for several minutes before he grasped the podium in both hands. "Now, Miss Galbraith, please tell the jury: is the handwritten note on the bottom of that page written in your former employer's handwriting?"

Five seconds passed. Miss Galbraith had to blink sometime. When Ryan reached a ten count, the judge turned his cannibalizing scowl on the woman and growled, "You must answer counsel's question."

Her discomfort turned frantic. "It's been a long time since I saw this document—before today," she muttered, glancing toward the Melander and Stout counsel table nearest the jury box. "Could I . . . have a break to think about it?"

Clouds darkened the ridges of the judge's stare. "No, Miss Galbraith. You will answer the question."

The gallery crowd and jury were staring expectantly at the stilled witness when the slightest movement drew Ryan's attention away. He glanced toward the fresh-faced Melander and Stout associate sitting nearest the jury, the table where Miss Galbraith had glanced only a moment before. The young attorney had shifted in his chair until he was sideways to the nervous witness, his fingers perched lightly over the edge of his table. Ryan looked past the young attorney toward Miss Galbraith in the witness box—and saw that she was watching those fingers, too, softly, carefully, from the corners of her eyes.

The fingers began a silent rhythm—tap, tap—the second and third fingers downward; tap, tap—the third and fourth. Three times they traced the rhythm before the hand closed in a gentle fist.

The witness stirred, releasing the witness box and sitting back in her chair. "No. That's definitely *not* his handwriting," she announced confidently.

The moment ended with a shuffling of lawyers' papers, the judge turning away with a slight shrug of surprise, and the jurors settling back to gauge one another's reactions. Except one older, well-dressed juror at the far end of the box. His eyes moved from the witness to the young lawyer with the dancing fingers, and back again.

The attorney at the podium was stunned. Ryan shook his head.

It was one thing to do what it took to win: nobody should expect the Queensbury rules in court. It was another to pull a stunt like this—even for Melander and Stout. This was why he was getting out.

Ryan was beginning to slide off the bench when an elbow hit his ribs. "Oh, I'm so sorry," the slim woman at his left whispered, her eyes distressed.

"That's okay," he answered.

"It's just that the man at the podium is my boss," she persisted quietly. "This witness's testimony was a total surprise. We hadn't even taken a statement because . . . well, she insisted we didn't need one. Miss Galbraith seemed so sincere when she told us what she knew about these documents."

"I'm very sorry," Ryan whispered back.

The woman nodded, looking inconsolable.

Ryan began to leave again, but made the mistake of glancing up at the woman's boss, still mourning at the podium while pretending to search for a document. He'd shy away from more testimony from this turncoat witness, Ryan thought: follow the axiom that you never ask a witness a question unless you know how they'll answer. The young lawyer and his bosses would get away with it.

Ryan tapped the legal assistant's arm, crooking a finger to motion her to follow. She looked puzzled, but slid off the bench to comply.

In the hallway, Ryan waited until he heard the courtroom door thud shut behind them. "Get your boss to ask for a recess," he said hurriedly. "Tell him the young Perry Mason at the table nearest the jury box is signaling the witness how to answer."

The woman's eyes blanked with shock as Ryan went on rapidly.

"This judge may help you, but there's no way you can talk to him without signaling the other side what you know—and then it's too late. Tell your boss to resist letting this witness go, even if he's afraid of what she'll say. Because the older juror with the sport coat is catching on. He's dressed up, paying attention, and at his age likely will get the foreman spot. Tell your boss to keep pushing this witness aggressively—while the youngster keeps signaling her. The sympathetic juror will have a chance to be sure of what he suspects and when it comes time to deliberate, he'll lead the rest of the jury right into your arms."

Ryan turned away and headed down the hall, refusing to care if the woman followed his advice.

Twenty minutes later, standing in the courthouse foyer, Ryan heard heavy footfalls approaching across the marble floor behind him. He turned.

"Mr. Hart, don't see you enough around here these days."

"Your Honor," Ryan answered, nodding, relieved that it was Judge Freyling, with graying hair and a thickening frame. If he had to run into someone today, he'd prefer it be his favorite magistrate in the King County Courthouse.

"Say," the judge went on, "there's a rumor you were sighted in one of the upstairs halls of justice a short while ago watching some real lawyers at work in Tipton's courtroom. This true?"

Ryan had tried half a dozen cases in front of Tipton, so the fact that he'd been recognized wasn't surprising. "Talking to your neighbor in courtroom 431?" he asked.

Judge Freyling shook his head. "No. My bailiff ran into Tipton's clerk in the hall a few minutes ago. I'm informed you left the courtroom with a pretty young lady who came rushing back a few minutes later to whisper in the plaintiff attorney's ear—who then asked the judge for an early lunch recess. Don't know what you told her, but it doesn't matter: Tipton's clerk's taking heavy odds that the jury's going to find against the plaintiff and his attorney—and Tipton's clerk's never wrong."

Ryan thought for a moment about telling Freyling what he'd just witnessed. But there was no point; there was nothing he could do with a third-hand charge like that.

"Tell your bailiff," Ryan responded, "to take those odds with a hundred bucks on the plaintiff."

Judge Freyling's eyebrows lifted with surprise. "You know, Counselor, that would be highly unethical and I'd have to fire her if she did." He paused, then leaned close. "But if you're sure, I'll call Tipton and take the bet myself this afternoon."

Ryan smiled as his tension uncoiled a notch. "Have I mentioned how much I appreciated your taking Emily on for that clerkship?" he said.

"Every time we pass in the hall," the judge said, waving Ryan off. "Which is a lot, given that that was, what—almost three years ago. Is it that long since your daughter finished law school? Anyway, as I've told you, it was no favor—she had the grades and was the best candidate to apply. And I hear she's done a great job in the Public Defender's office these last two years since she left me. She's learning her way around the courtroom fast. Like her old man."

The judge took a step back and surveyed Ryan, his eyes narrowing. "You know, I'm in charge of distributing caseloads this year, and I haven't seen many King County cases with your name on them."

"I've been throttling back," Ryan replied neutrally.

The judge nodded. "Um-hmm. You know, I *still* tell people

about that first trial you had in front of me—against Lester Schmidt. Barely out of law school and you pummeled him. He deserved it. I could never figure out what fueled that man's ego. Whenever I see Schmidt, I figure out a way to remind him about it."

Ryan smiled again, just as the judge's look turned serious. "You're a fine trial lawyer, Ryan. I know this has been a rough few years for you—with Carolyn's passing and all. But I'd hate to see you hang up your spurs. You're too young. What would you do with yourself anyway—a hard charger like you."

Ryan was relieved to see Emily coming down the hall from the elevator bank. This was a subject he wanted to avoid just now.

"Just considering a little break, Judge," Ryan replied in a low voice. "But keep it to yourself."

The judge glanced in the direction of Ryan's look, then nodded knowingly. "All right. Well, I'd better get going. I'm off this afternoon—picking up my nephew at the airport. The boy's expecting me to grill salmon for him. Like they can't buy it in Minneapolis. Have a good lunch."

The judge waved at Emily with a smile, then walked away as she arrived.

Her blond hair usually fell naturally across her shoulders, but today it was pulled back from her face with a clip. It made her look more serious, Ryan thought, especially with her dark suit. Like her mother when she'd dressed for court. He considered mentioning it, but he doubted the intended compliment would be welcomed from him.

She approached, stopping short of an invitation to a hug.

"Thanks for doing this," she said, smiling congenially. As she might to a client, he thought painfully. "I've got to rush, Dad; things are crazy upstairs. How about we go to Ivar's for a quick bite and I can tell you why I called."

❖❖❖

It was unusually cool for mid-June and the wharf around the restaurant was uncrowded. Ryan found an empty bench looking out on the Sound. Emily came out of the shop a moment later with their orders of clam strips; she'd insisted on buying today.

She approached, walking with her mother's grace. "You move like a dancer," he said as she drew close. She barely acknowledged the familiar line he used to tell her at breakfast each morning.

"How's the practice, Dad?" she asked, sitting with her back to the water.

"Great," Ryan replied, looking away. "Just great."

It felt lousy to start their first conversation in months with a lie.

Emily tried, over the next half hour, to ignite a conversation. Their small talk proved desultory and unsatisfying. That's what came from not seeing one another more than quarterly, Ryan thought, saddened.

But then he hadn't reached this place of twilight with his only child by accident. He'd done it by slow neglect. He merited no absolution simply because their final breaking point had resulted from the year and a half he was trying to save Carolyn. Emily had desperately needed him at the time, too. And that period was only the crown on a lifetime of neglect by distraction.

He finally turned the conversation to the point of this surprise invitation to lunch. "So what's the problem?" Ryan asked, starting into the strips.

Emily hesitated a moment, moving a strand of hair that blew across her eyes. "I have a friend from college who needs a lawyer."

"Anyone I know?"

"No," she said, then paused. "I mean, I probably mentioned him. But I never brought him home. I only knew him for a year, when we were juniors at UW, back when Mom had just gotten sick. His father had cancer, too, so he really understood what I was going through. But he left college to help his family before his dad died that spring. We talked and texted after, but I haven't seen him since."

"What's his name?" Ryan asked.

"Kieran Mullaney. He left a message, and it doesn't sound good. I'd heard he was working out at Hanford. You remember that explosion last fall?"

Ryan nodded.

"I think maybe he was in it. All I know so far from his message is that he thinks he was exposed to radiation. Apparently he started a lawsuit and his lawyer's withdrawn right before trial. He's looking for a new lawyer with civil experience—product liability if possible. I'll call him later today, but I wanted to talk to you first."

Ryan looked up at a trio of gulls fluttering only a few feet away. Biding his time, he watched their aerial choreography of begging—then picked up a French fry and flipped it in the air. One gull stabbed at the offering, catching it in its beak.

Emily was waiting for an answer. "I could make a few calls if you'd like," he said carefully.

Her face was stony. It wasn't the response she'd hoped for. "With your experience and all, I wanted to tell him you'd take a look at it, Dad," she said. "He sounded pretty desperate. I know it's tough jumping in so late, but Melissa told me you're not as busy these days."

So Emily's still in touch with Melissa, he thought . . . curious. Then he considered her request. Rescuing a case in the late stages of demise—any trial lawyer's definition of torture. And stepping back into the gladiator ring—his own definition of torture. Besides, despite her words, Emily couldn't imagine the price of jumping into a case like this at the last minute—the hours and the pace. Like zero to sixty in three seconds. And there usually was a good reason a client and lawyer divorced on the courthouse steps: attorneys quitting last minute were one of nature's warning signs to the rest of the bar to stay away.

"You know, Ems," he began, "I'm sure your friend would be better served with an attorney from eastern Washington. They know the judges, the lay of the land. They know opposing counsel."

His daughter's voice was part impatience, part plea. "Dad, I've got a feeling he's tried that. He wouldn't call me out of the blue if he hadn't already tried to land other lawyers himself. Won't you just look at it? You should have heard how he sounded."

She looked him in the eye. "I've got a lot of leave, and Frank told me I've got to take it," she went on. "I could even ask for a leave of absence if that wasn't enough. I thought if you took the case, maybe you and I could work together on it."

The breeze off Puget Sound was chilly, especially as the sun drifted behind a low bank of clouds.

If they'd been in touch, he would already have told her he was easing out of the practice. Carolyn's life insurance made every day in the office a choice, and he was choosing to stay away. If he'd told her that before, she might not have believed him—but it would have been out there. If he raised it now, it would just sound like an excuse not to help her.

He looked back at Emily. Oh, those eyes. Reminding him how little he'd been around. Enticing him with the possibility of a détente between the two of them—or better. Broadcasting a belief, despite her words, that it would be as simple as driving together over the mountains, picking up the file, and marching into the courthouse to save the day.

Ryan pulled his sport coat tighter against the chill. He *did* owe her. Missed family dinners, recitals: the list would stretch to Tacoma. And when he was home, still mentally elsewhere. Then throwing himself into Carolyn's care like it was another case he could win—deserting a daughter to carry the weight of what they both were losing alone.

But Emily was chasing a ghost, expecting him to save the day. He'd been putting his career in the rearview mirror for years now.

Ryan looked into those hopeful eyes, then past Emily to the Bremerton ferry approaching on the choppy waters.

"Let me think about it tonight," he said.

"Great, Dad," Emily said, smiling broadly for the first time and turning back to her plate of clam strips. "That's great."

The small talk immediately improved. Ryan brushed away a flash of guilt. He'd avoided disappointing his girl one more time this afternoon; he'd deal with the cost later. For now, he'd enjoy the smile in her eyes, the water on the Sound, and the best clam strips money could buy.

Ryan reached for another fry and, with a flick of his wrist, sent it into the air amidst the growing flock of expectant gulls.

CHAPTER 3

Four hours later, Ryan strode slowly up the steps to the Queen Anne house that served as office and home. The door was unlocked—Melissa must have still been there. He walked in, threw his coat across the bannister leading to the upstairs apartment, then turned right past the vacant reception desk, past the row of empty offices.

Melissa looked up from her desk beside his corner office with a tired smile. "You're here late, Mel," Ryan said. "Already told you, there's no overtime at Hart and Associates."

The fortyish secretary shook her head with mock disapproval. "After fifteen years, imagine you paying me what I'm worth. But don't worry, I'm just cleaning up. I won't charge you."

Ryan looked at the stack of boxes behind her desk chair. Closing down was more apt. He recognized the Glenwater and Schraeder files. Velder and Proffler. All settled or tried the past three years.

"How was lunch with Emily?" she asked, concerned.

"Fine."

"Wasn't that nice of her to call? I suppose she wanted to get caught up."

The logic of the misinformed, he thought. He told Melissa about the signaling lawyer at the courthouse. His secretary shook her head again, disappointment on her face. "What those lawyers will do to win a case."

Ryan turned toward his office.

"If you're going to your desk to check messages," she said, raising a hand, "I can save you the extra steps: there aren't any. Except a threat of an ethics complaint from the Glenwater case just came through."

That was expected. "All right," he said, picking up a stack of mail on the front of Melissa's desk.

She looked at him with concern. "You can't keep losing your temper at depositions like that, Mr. Hart. You're getting a reputation. And some lawyers don't seem to have a sense of humor about that kind of thing."

Especially silk stocking lawyers from firms like Cochrane, Dickerson and Western, he thought. He looked back at his long-time secretary. "No rules were broken, Mel. Just a little growling."

She smiled consolingly. "Well, you didn't used to growl enough to risk an ethics complaint."

Sure he did. He was just more skilled about it when his heart was still in the game.

Her voice grew more serious. "You think they'll file a complaint against you?"

It was unlikely. Ryan knew he was still drawing on a reservoir of goodwill. "No," he responded. Ryan couldn't continue this conversation. "I'm heading upstairs. You'll lock up on your way out?"

She gave him a last glance. "Don't I always?"

He headed for the staircase.

Upstairs, Ryan crossed the small living room of his apartment, dropping his keys onto the kitchen bar. The light wasn't working under the cupboards, oscillating between light and dark like something out of a horror movie. He'd have to call the contractor to fix it in the morning.

Ryan glanced around at the renovations just completed that week. He'd wanted the apartment different than when he and Carolyn first moved in twenty-five years before when the upstairs had served as their home until they could afford a separate house elsewhere in the city. He had the contractors repair the old plumbing and drafty windows that hadn't troubled newly-weds starting a life and career together. But so far, the change hadn't ended the restless nights that had plagued Ryan in their Magnolia house since Carolyn's death.

He turned to the fridge and grabbed a bottle of iced tea, then rustled through the spare cupboards. Grabbing a box of Wheat Thins, he kicked off his shoes and shuffled through the new carpet smell toward the study, bypassing moving boxes still littering the floor.

He and Carolyn had loved watching the sun as it appeared now through the study window, sinking into the Olympic Mountain range across the Sound, melting into a widening puddle of orange. He opened the window to let in some fresh air.

His eyes were drawn to a box of memorabilia under the sill, topped with his boxer's speed bag. He considered going down to the basement to hang it up where it used to rattle the house to Carolyn's complaints. Instead, he picked up his MacBook Pro from the desk and settled back onto the leather love seat, the Wheat Thins at his side.

His most recent email was from Emily, sent since their lunch. An attachment held the Complaint in her friend's case. "I just got this from Kieran. I really appreciate your taking a look at it," her message read. Ryan nearly closed it out. Instead he enlarged it to fill his computer screen.

Kieran Mullaney v. Covington Nuclear Corporation, the caption read. It was a no-frills pleading with a bare recitation of the facts and a statement of the single claim. The Complaint described Kieran Mullaney being exposed to chemicals and radiation from an explosion on the third floor of a mothballed building on the Hanford Nuclear Reservation called LB5. The claim was that Covington was liable based upon its responsibility for safety, maintenance, and cleanup at the Hanford nuclear site, working under contract with the Department of Energy.

Covington Nuclear. A quick Internet search confirmed that the company operated nuclear plants around the country, as well as DOE superfund cleanup sites like Hanford. At one time, in the Cold War days, the company also had a role in nuclear weapons production.

It was a clean case. So why had the boy's attorney withdrawn? And why was he having a problem finding replacement counsel?

Covington was represented by Eric King, of McNary and King in Sherman, Washington. The lawyer for plaintiff Kieran Mullaney was Pauline Strand. Ryan could find no website for the lawyer—almost unheard of in this day and age. He checked her in the bar directory. She was a solo practitioner, with no photo. Based on her bar admission date, Ryan calculated her to be in her late sixties.

Pretty gutsy for a sixty-year-old solo practitioner to take on a Fortune 500 company all by herself, he thought. Gutsy or stupid.

The room had grown dark. So what would he tell Emily?

In the dim light, his gaze fell on the photo of Carolyn on the study desk. What would Carolyn say to all this? He was having difficulty conjuring her voice in the growing darkness.

Ryan studied the photo, tracing the curve of her cheeks and the smile in her eyes, trying to recall the first time he'd heard Carolyn speak—or at least the first time he'd really paid attention to her. In law school, he'd played the monk, spending three years in serious study with no social life, committed to launching a career as a trial lawyer without any personal baggage. Then, his last semester, his mock trial professor had him present closing arguments in the same slot as a slender blond girl with icy blue Scandinavian eyes.

The day they'd presented, he'd *crushed* his argument for the three volunteer judges. They didn't look away the whole forty-five minutes he spoke. Ryan didn't wonder: he *knew* he'd make the other student's effort pale by comparison.

Then Carolyn had stood up. In a voice both sweet and serious, she had, in less than fifteen minutes and without notes, painted her client with such nobility and tragic grandeur that Ryan expected the judges to rise for a standing ovation.

An hour later, sitting with coffee at the campus Starbucks, he'd heard his name called in that voice again. It was Carolyn. She approached and congratulated him on his presentation. Taunting him, Ryan assured himself. Then she'd sat down as he responded tepidly, "You were great. You were the clear winner today."

She'd looked at him quizzically. "Who told you this was a competition?"

The question was not unkind. Ryan looked at her a moment before responding. "Probably my father. And his father before him."

She laughed. Then, through the rising steam of her coffee, she pierced him with the same gaze that had accompanied her argument. "You were better prepared than I was, you know. Your closing had insights that never even *occurred* to me."

"Just a weak presentation," Ryan finished.

"No," she said softly, brushing charitably past the self-pity that he instantly regretted. "No. But maybe you tried a little too hard to beat the judges into submission. Too much punching; too little wooing. I'm starting to think that this . . . this is seduction. Drawing people into the intimacy of your client's loss. This case we argued, for example, was about a tragic accident that took a young life. The judge or jurors have to *feel* that reality. Knocking them around may get their attention, but you want them to want to *help* your client, to side with your client. That takes an embrace."

He'd never pursued a client or a cause harder than his pursuit of Carolyn those next two months until graduation. That summer, they'd married.

Ryan stirred and looked around him. It had grown late. The unpacked boxes were now darker shadows in the already shadowy room. He shook his head. Those memories weren't helping make a decision.

He had to decide what to tell Emily about her friend Kieran Mullaney. He ought to just get it over with: tell her no, as he should have at lunch. Maybe tell her he was shying away from the body blows and the bloody noses of trial practice—the ache of the responsibility, the back-breaking hours preparing for trial, the injustice of certain attorneys, like that young one he saw in the courthouse today, succeeding.

All the things that hadn't seemed to trouble him before Carolyn's cancer.

But he couldn't just say no to Emily now—not when she was reaching out for his help. It was better for their already distant relationship if he gave the appearance of considering the case. After all, he was still an advocate; he could manage this charade.

Ryan pulled his cell out of his pocket and pressed her number. Voicemail answered. "Emily," he said after the beep. "Give your friend Kieran a call. Set up a meeting. Tell him that I'm willing to come his direction—make it dinner so I can drive. But set it up on a day you can come along. I think it would be a good idea for you to be there."

CHAPTER 4

The stethoscope was icy between Poppy's shoulder blades. "Breathe," Dr. Morgan said from behind him. He complied.

The scope lifted mercifully from his back, and the doctor came around the table. "I can hear the thickness, Mr. Martin." He stepped to a small corner desk and his laptop. "I'd say it's a stubborn irritation from the chemicals you were exposed to last fall. Give it another month or so. In the meantime, I'll send your pharmacy a prescription for something stronger to break it up. And something else for the cough."

Poppy bristled at hearing the same song, third verse. "You know," he said, buttoning his shirt, "it's been eight months. I've been back here five times already to see your partners since the explosion. If these meds don't work, what's the next step?"

The doctor kept tapping on the keys. "Well, we'll cross that bridge if we come to it."

"Do you think," Poppy pushed, "that you might want to run some more tests? For radiation or other chemicals?"

The doctor hit Enter with a flourish and turned to Poppy.

"Mr. Martin, from the chart notes, it looks like you've discussed this every time you've been here. As my partners told you, the most accurate testing would have been soon after the explosion." The doctor clicked again at the laptop, slipping on reading glasses and leaning in as he moved through the digital chart.

"Here it is. I see that blood and urine tests that night were negative for any known significant chemical exposure. Then they did a whole body count for radiation exposure that came up negative."

The doctor looked up. "I'd be satisfied with the testing they did that night, Mr. Martin. Obviously, you got no serious dose of radiation, because you survived. Besides, I'm no specialist in the field, but I doubt there's even a test out there to detect radiation exposure this long after the event."

"Um-hmm." Poppy nodded impatiently. Yeah, he was sitting here, so it was obvious he didn't get a terminal dose. But low doses could kill, too—over time.

"You suppose at least you could just take some blood and urine, store it in case they decide it's worth testing down the road?"

The doctor looked over his glasses at Poppy. "Look, Mr. Martin, I really can't do that. Your employer is Darter Security, a subcontractor to Covington Nuclear out at Hanford, right? And they placed you under Covington Nuclear's self-insured health plan. I'm familiar with that plan. It's a specialized one, with nuclear facilities employees in mind. It permits testing for radiation and chemical exposure—but only if there's evidence you've been exposed to something to test."

The doctor offered a last perfunctory smile and a soft handshake before hurrying from the examination room. Poppy resisted crushing the smooth-skinned fingers—or tossing the desk chair after the man's retreating white coat.

Poppy was being treated like a whining kid. It was a wonder the doctor hadn't offered a lollipop. What'd the guy think? Poppy had been around leaks out at Hanford his whole career—his dosimetry badge had gone red occasionally. A time or two he'd even gotten some mandatory time off to avoid excess accumulated exposure. Each time they'd tested and declared him "fine"—and he hadn't complained or questioned them once. He knew there were more risks working at the Hanford Nuclear Reservation than the Sherman Public Works Department, and he'd always trusted his bosses at Hanford to tell him what was going on.

Until now. *This time was different*, Poppy thought as he stepped into his shoes. It was different because he'd read the summary of Covington's investigation report on the LB5 explosion in the newspaper. Not a word was mentioned about Lew's shot being fired, the lights going out, the late take-cover sirens—even though he'd submitted all those things in his own after-event statement about that night. They hadn't even interviewed him about what he'd put on that page—or answered his emails to Covington HQ.

And now his cough and headaches wouldn't go away.

They could take that investigation report and shove it—like the doctor could shove his advice. He didn't send his emails to whine or complain. He was taking the explosion seriously, like they always had at Hanford during his career. And he had a right to know what was in the cloud that night.

Poppy slipped through the quiet lounge, barely acknowledging the receptionist's "Have a nice day, Mr. Martin." In the lot, he started his GMC Sierra and headed toward the highway leading to Hanford and his night shift.

The pain and congestion weren't easing up, and he didn't have time to fill the new prescription before the night shift started in half an hour. If it wasn't for the twenty days of leave he'd already taken since the explosion, he'd probably turn around and head home again today. But he'd rather bull through it than lie in bed, with pain knifing from behind his eyes and long coughs keeping Suzy awake. Besides, Dave Prior, his manager at PCL 237, was a good man. Dave would let him go home early again if things got too bad.

Poppy passed the Keys Diner, where he and Lewis occasionally had breakfast after the night shift. It reminded him of the strangest part of the explosion: the disappearance of his young partner. Poppy'd never had the chance to hear Lew's story of what happened at LB5 that night. He still didn't know what Lew had seen on the east side of LB5—what he'd fired at or whether he'd hit a target. When Poppy'd recovered enough to return to his regular station at PCL 237, Dave told him that Lewis had gotten an immediate transfer after the explosion—and that he'd also requested confidentiality about where he'd gone.

Maybe Lew did it 'cause he was worried his panic that night would get around. If that's why Lew left, he didn't know his older partner very well. Nobody but Poppy knew about Lew's reaction that night. Nobody ever would.

Of course, all this could've been cleared up if Poppy'd had a chance to ask Lew all his questions the night of the explosion. But the rest of that night was a blur of panicked gasps. Poppy remembered Lewis dragging him from the roof's edge and helping him down the dusty air of the stairwell—then the two of them coming out again into the cool night in the front parking lot. There they'd laid him in the back of a van and raced into town to the hospital, while Poppy struggled to pull in enough air between coughing jags. The stars slipped past an open moon roof as Poppy fought down panic by focusing on the whir of tires, bumps on the road, and the whine of the racing engine. From up front, snatches of Lew's rattled voice filtered back, talking to the stranger behind the wheel: "It happened just like *that* . . ."; "Felt like an earthquake . . ."; "Hope Poppy's gonna be okay." And one word Lew kept repeating: *sabotage*.

In the ER, they'd slapped a mask over Poppy's face until his breathing slowed and his weary chest muscles relaxed. By then, Suzy had arrived and Lew had disappeared—and his partner hadn't returned to work since. It was all too strange.

The night crew's cars and trucks were already in their usual spots by the time Poppy pulled his truck into the lot of PCL

237. He parked where the guys always left him a spot, next to the front side entry. He stood for a moment beside the truck, coughing to clear his lungs until they ached and burned. Then he grabbed a water bottle from the cab, gulping half of it down.

He rubbed a hand across his face to wipe away the cough tears and straightened himself up. He'd stow it all away again, like he did before every night's work. There'd be no complaining on the job, despite what that doctor might think of him. He was a Hanford man, like his dad before him, and he had a shift to get through.

But as Poppy trod the sidewalk to the glass doors, his last thoughts were the same as they'd been every night for the past several months.

What had he swallowed out on that roof that night? And where on God's green earth had his partner disappeared to?

CHAPTER 5

Emily looked out the passenger window of Kieran's ancient Corolla as it bucked and creaked on the rutted dirt road. Her thoughts ran to the smell of boys' cars—an amalgam of the scent of their skin, the leather of their shoes, their soaps and deodorants, gym bags stored in back seats, fast-food wrappers.

This one was different. Absent were the loose MP3 wires and stray clothes, empty energy drink bottles and papers littering the back seat. There was a sense of order about this car past its prime. It spoke of someone less scattered, more centered and solid—qualities she'd liked about Kieran when they met.

Still, there was a touch of isolation about Kieran, an echo of loneliness. Maybe it was the lawsuit; maybe it was the loss of his father. She didn't recall that quality in Kieran years ago.

An hour ago, he'd picked her up at the Winchester Inn, where she'd dropped her own car. It was the Sherman bed and breakfast where her dad had made reservations for the night. At Kieran's suggestion, she'd come into town early to catch up before her father arrived for their dinner meeting.

The past week, she'd thought a lot about her friendship with Kieran at college. It wasn't hard to dredge up old feelings and recollections: Emily had only had two steady boyfriends since, and neither turned serious. Of course, she hadn't actually *dated* Kieran. And those other boys were competing with the blur of law school and Emily's first legal jobs.

But that was all history anyway, and unimportant. She was there to get her father on board with Kieran's lawsuit, not to start a romance. Besides, she wasn't the same girl she'd been her junior year of college. She couldn't imagine Kieran was the same boy.

She looked at him again now, focused on the dusty road ahead. Thick blond hair almost reached broad shoulders, framing a face of quiet reserve. He seemed a little nervous, his expression reminding Emily of her mother's early high school advice: "When it comes to girls, young men can imagine a thousand varieties of rejection. You've got to give them time."

Except Kieran hadn't been quiet during the year they'd been friends at the University of Washington. Even suffering through the slow death of his father, Kieran had been outgoing, nearly an extrovert. It was, of course, a show, given what he was going through—it had to be. But Emily had still been drawn to his refusal to wear his pain on his sleeve—pain Emily understood so well with her own mother's illness.

"We're almost there," Kieran said.

"Still won't say where we're going?"

"Patience," he said with a smile.

At Kieran's direction, she'd arrived at the B&B wearing jeans and a light shirt. He'd picked her up right on time and they'd driven northeast out of Sherman for almost an hour before turning onto this dirt road that took them over a hill and out of sight of the highway. Then they'd settled into the pattern of bumps and jolts for another half an hour, passing through a series of twisting canyons that splashed dust onto the sides of the Corolla like a summer storm of fine brown mist.

At last they rolled through a gap into a small valley. A low ranch house waited directly ahead, fronted by a rose-bordered porch, with outbuildings bracketing either side. A truck and horse trailer were parked alongside the building nearest to Emily's side of the car.

"You kidnapping me?" Emily teased as he turned off the car.

Kieran nodded. "Yeah. If he ever wants to see you alive, your dad has to take my case."

The dust was settling as she followed Kieran's lead and opened her car door into the full heat of the day. This flat ground surveyed by the surrounding hills was vacant and sun bleached, though tall firs crowned the encircling slopes. There was another gap through the hills beyond the building to Emily's right. From that direction, she heard the sound of a stream.

A man stepped from the front door of the house and into the shadow of the porch. His skin was lined and sun worn, his hair pulled back in twin braids. He folded thickly veined forearms across his chest and appraised Emily from under the brim of a black hat with a yellow tassel hanging from the crown.

She smiled and nodded. The man did neither in return. The disapproval in his stare froze Emily as Kieran crossed the dusty yard to the porch.

He didn't greet Kieran either, though his stare mercifully left Emily's face. Kieran spoke in a low voice—too low for Emily to overhear. Still, several nods in her direction convinced Emily that they were talking about her, and that there was disagreement. She stood rooted to her spot until the man turned and disappeared back into the house.

"Everything okay?" she asked as Kieran walked back.

"Just a little misunderstanding," he reassured her with a light smile. He walked to the Corolla and retrieved a tan cowboy hat from the back seat that he set on her head. "Follow me," he said, steering her toward the nearer outbuilding.

"His name is Ted Pollock," Kieran said as they walked. "This is his ranch. He lives here with his wife and granddaughter." Before she could ask anything more, they reached a side door in the building, which Kieran opened and passed through. Emily followed into the dim interior.

From somewhere overhead came the whir of an air conditioner. Then Emily heard the clack of hooves on concrete, just as she caught the unmistakable musk of a stable of horses.

"I remembered you liked to ride," he said, leading her down a row between dozens of stalls.

Emily smiled in the darkness.

In the dusty light at the end of the row, Kieran gestured toward the last two stalls. "Got a preference?"

Her eyes were adjusting now. In the closest stall was a youthful chestnut mare with a thin summer coat and a long mane and tail. Emily glanced to the adjacent stall, which held a larger, thick-necked bay stallion.

It'd been half a dozen years since she'd ridden, and the stallion looked intimidating. "I'll take the mare," she answered.

They tacked the horses together, then walked them out the rear of the barn, where Kieran gave her a leg up into the saddle. Then he led on the stallion, guiding them along a worn path through the gap in the surrounding hills.

They crossed the narrow stream Emily had heard earlier. On the other side was a large corral holding several horses. They rode on by, moving toward open country.

The early afternoon heat atop the horses would have been unbearable except for a softening breeze. Emily was glad she hadn't chosen the stallion: the mare was headstrong and powerful enough. Not a trail horse, she thought. This was no dude ranch—not if these horses were typical.

Kieran motioned her to come alongside. "So tell me everything you've been doing since I saw you last."

"Becoming a lawyer," she said crisply.

"Sounds boring."

She smiled. "Never a dull moment."

"Following in your dad's footsteps?"

"My mom's," she answered immediately, then changed the subject. "How do you know about this place?"

Kieran shrugged. "I met Ted and his wife last winter after the explosion and they told me I could ride if I wanted to. I started coming here the last six months. It was a good escape—the exercise helps clear my lungs."

Emily gestured back toward the barn. "This is no trail ranch."

"No. Ted has some cattle. But he keeps horses and lets them out occasionally to experienced riders. He also catches wild mustangs that wander onto the Hanford Reservation. Hanford security picks them up on their motion detectors or patrols. They'll call Ted, who rounds them up, keeps them in the corral you saw, then ships them east for sale to barns."

Kieran turned away and cleared his throat with a long hard cough. "But you're avoiding my first question," he said, recovering. "Tell me everything I've missed."

Now that they were there, Emily found it hard starting this conversation. At college, their walks on campus or in neighborhoods along Lake Washington, talking through the sinking weight of their stricken parents, had sustained her. Day after day, Kieran had always been there for her.

But then he'd disappeared. It wasn't just that he moved away when his father's illness took a bad turn: that she could understand. But he never came back. His emails and phone calls quickly grew rare and flat and distant—then stopped altogether.

Kieran noticed her silence. "I'm sorry about your mom."

"It's been years," she said flatly.

"Yeah, I know. I should've called a long time ago."

A hawk appeared in the sky circling overhead. Except for wisps of white in the distance, nothing else broke the blue from horizon to horizon.

"What tribe does Ted belong to?" she asked, pushing away again.

"The Yakama."

"This is a long way from their reservation."

Kieran nodded. "He's had this ranch for thirty years. He used to work at Hanford."

The breeze was fading, leaving the heat to pound Emily's neck and arms, unprotected by the hat. Kieran must have felt it too. He reined toward a pocket of trees lining a crest, where they tied their horses to saplings overhanging the hilltop's edge.

"Hanford's that direction." He pointed as he sat down in the shade. "The nearest building's probably twenty miles."

Emily settled beside Kieran, aware of a heavy dampness covering her forehead and shirt. She listened to the hissing of a light breeze through hillside grasses. It was quiet and peaceful. This was truly beautiful. But lonely, she thought. Like Kieran seemed today.

As they cooled in the shadows, they finally talked about what they'd each done the past years since they'd lost touch. He'd taken a series of odd jobs after his father died until he'd landed one at Hanford. "It wasn't my first choice, but the pay is incredible . . . for somebody who never got a degree," he explained. "Especially to save enough to get my mother, my sister, and me out of town."

Emily wondered at that last statement, but Kieran pressed her again, and she told about the back-breaking studying in law school; landing the clerkship with Judge Freyling; then on to the Public Defender's office. Did she like it, the pace and all, he asked. It was hard work, she answered—but she drew satisfaction from representing people who really needed her.

Kieran smiled. "That's the Emily I remember."

Kieran tried once to steer onto the ground of her loss, but Emily wasn't sure she wanted to go back there, and the personal conversation faltered, drifting into silences just long enough to be awkward. She began to ask herself whether the bridges that used to link them were lost or fallen. It saddened her—she'd believed they were built of much sterner stuff. Still, she shied away from defaulting to talk about the explosion and lawsuit, the impersonal ground of lawyer to client. That would taste too bitter, like a final surrender of their friendship. Besides, there would be plenty of time for that over dinner with her dad.

The breeze began to pick up again just as Kieran looked at his watch.

"We'd better get going," he said. "I told Ted I'd have the horses back in a couple of hours."

Back in the saddle, Kieran took the lead as they headed away from the slope, back the way they'd come. The sun was throwing long shadows to their front when Emily recognized the approaching hills as they neared the ranch. In that moment, she heard a sound that drew her attention back to Kieran.

He raised a hand to his chest, then suddenly lurched forward in his saddle and plunged into deep, violent coughs. Emily watched with growing concern as the stallion halted and the spasms crescendoed—growing so powerful she thought he might fall out of the saddle. She nudged the mare next to the stallion and reached out, grasping Kieran's shoulder.

The coughing relented, tapering to silence. Kieran sat quietly for a moment, sucking in deep breaths, his face red and his eyes watery. At last he weakly nudged the stallion forward again.

"You okay?" she asked gently.

Kieran nodded.

"How often does that happen?"

"That bad, every couple of days," he said with a raspy voice. "It builds up."

The horses were walking side by side now. "You know," he said, "the cough isn't why I sued. That's chemical stuff and it's bad—but they tell me it's getting better, and at least I know what it is. It's not knowing how much radiation I absorbed that made me sue. I watched my dad die of leukemia. I couldn't go through the next ten years wondering what the chances were of that happening to me."

They passed over the stream and into the valley. Emily felt

the mare pick up the pace, sensing the approach of home, but she reined her back to keep the horses close.

She saw the barn. Waiting beside the open door was Ted, his hat pulled low and hands thrust into his jeans pockets.

She sensed Kieran stiffen at the sight of the man. Then he kicked his horse hard. She nudged the mare to follow, though the more powerful stallion kept pulling away.

It seemed a fitting reminder, she thought as the mare gathered speed, of how the men in her life always seemed to leave her behind.

CHAPTER 6

The corner booth table at the Atomic Café was carved with decades of initials and names, artifacts preserved beneath thick layers of polyurethane. Over the tables, black-and-white photos lined the walls. Ryan saw that the nearest ones depicted nuclear reactors B and D under construction, workers smiling at the perimeter of a huge cooling tank, and a Cold War era billboard reading "Loose Talk—*A Chain Reaction for Espionage!*" A little further along, the wall was festooned with pennants and team photos from the Sherman High School athletic teams, depicting their mascot: a blossoming mushroom cloud.

Ryan shook his head. He only wished the food had been half as interesting as the décor.

Emily sat at Ryan's side, looking at Kieran and his sister across the table of empty plates. Emily was too quiet. He wondered what she could be thinking: after the boy's description of the explosion over dinner, she didn't look the least deterred about his case.

Could she really be blind to the pitfalls? Nothing he shared seemed to faze her.

Kieran was all right, Ryan admitted. A good-looking kid. A lot smarter than Ryan had expected. Careful with his words. Clearly trying hard to not seem overly anxious about Ryan's interest in his case. He liked him—he really did. But he had no interest in restarting his practice on the back of this case.

Kieran's teenage sister, Laura, seated at his side with black hair draped across her shoulders, was less subtle than her brother. "So are you going to take Kieran's case?" she asked Ryan over an unwavering stare.

Ryan nodded congenially at the young woman who so clearly adored her brother. The loyalty he could admire, but the question he chose to ignore for the moment.

The waitress came and cleared their dishes. As she moved away, Ryan thought about this aging restaurant at the southern extreme of Sherman, where the last businesses and homes gave way to the desert. From his seat, Ryan could see through the front window the fading road sign declaring Atomic Café, arced over a blue mushroom cloud. It fronted this building that was so sun wearied it could've been built out of wood scraps collected from the surrounding desert.

This place was a world apart from the drizzling rain Ryan had left in Seattle that morning. He'd driven up into the foggy landscape of rocks and trees in the Cascades, broken by the occasional white flush of a stream. The peak was marked by a sudden break from the fog into bright sunshine—like bursting through a curtain. Then he descended into more green and gray that finally gave way to the yellows and browns of the foothills east of the Cascades. He'd passed the city of Yakima, then Union Gap—a narrow pass between tall cliffs leading west to the Yakama Indian Reservation. Then east again through hard, unyielding land only occasionally spotted with vineyards and hops fields.

This was Hanford country: dry flats with only a few isolated ranches challenging the natural loneliness of the landscape. Four hours and a galaxy of change from the lush, populous seaboard of the West Coast, where he'd grown up. Vacant and lonely.

Until the town of Sherman. Within a half a mile of the freeway he was surrounded by a sprawling suburb. On each side of the road were fast food restaurants, hotel chains, movie theaters, and even a regional airport. An unexpected oasis in a desert on the Columbia River over a hundred miles from the nearest major city.

Ryan looked at his daughter again, with her studied calmness, and felt a small anger kindle in him. She absolutely refused by word or expression to acknowledge the obvious faults with Kieran's case. His patience was slipping away, and with it his last restraint.

Okay. Emily wasn't interested in seeing the obvious. Was it because of the boy? He'd just have to make it *more* obvious.

"So, trial's coming up in a couple months," Ryan finally asked Kieran.

"Yes," Kieran answered.

"And your attorney wanted out of the case."

Kieran nodded.

"Well, I read the Complaint. You claim Covington was responsible for keeping that vat in LB5 safe. You claim the explosion exposed you to chemicals and radiation."

"That's right."

"Do you know what caused the vat to explode?"

Kieran blinked. "No."

"What does Covington say."

"They say the chemicals in the vat I was near became reactive from evaporation and exploded."

"Anything else?"

"They say it's not their fault."

"I understand there was an investigation by Covington."

"Yes. My attorney . . . my former attorney has a copy of their report."

"What's it say. Exactly."

"I don't know. She hasn't sent me a copy."

"Has your lawyer hired experts who say the explosion was Covington's fault?"

Kieran nodded. "Pauline said she's got some expert help, yes."

"What has she told you about your expert's opinions."

64

"Not much yet. Just that her expert says Covington's responsible."

"That's all?"

"Yes."

"Alright. And LB5 wasn't the place you usually worked."

Kieran nodded. "That's right. My supervisor and I were moved to LB5 from our regular station for two weeks just before the explosion. We were covering for the regular stabilizing engineers out there."

"Where were the regulars?"

"They were on a training exercise. DOE requires an ongoing rotation of tests and monitoring, so sometimes we get shifted to another building to cover when a regular crew isn't available. The explosion happened on our last night shift at LB5."

"'We' means you and your supervisor?"

"Yeah. Taylor Christensen."

"You still work with Taylor?"

"Yeah. We're back at our regular station, Research Center 12. With my headaches and cough, I'm only out there half time right now."

"And this Taylor's got no coughs, no radiation-related problems."

Kieran shook his head. "No, but he had his mask on that night."

"And you say they did a whole body count on you after the explosion—for radiation. Which was negative."

Kieran shifted in his seat. "Yes."

"And the blood and urine testing—for chemicals—showed no exposure to chemicals with long-term health effects."

"Well, eight months is pretty long term."

Ryan raised his hands. "I mean carcinogenic chemicals."

Kieran nodded. "That's right."

"And you're convinced you were exposed to damaging radiation because . . . ?"

"Like I said when I described the explosion, the radiation monitors in the hallway were lighting up like pinball machines."

"You saw that while you were falling to the floor."

Kieran nodded defiantly.

"In the middle of an explosion that knocked you out."

"That's right."

"And they've told you your dosimetry badge showed no radiation exposure, either."

Kieran was fidgeting now. From the corner of his eye, Ryan could see the same irritation in his sister.

"No."

"But you don't believe them about that, either."

Kieran's hands were clenched on the table. "If LB5's half as crapped up as the rest of the plutonium processing buildings on the reservation, an explosion like that should've shaken it up like a snow globe. They didn't tell me I got a safe dose; they told me I got *no* dose. It doesn't make any sense."

"Any reason you think they'd lie about these things?"

"I don't know," he said, his eyes cautious.

"Has your lawyer got experts to prove you've been exposed to radiation?"

Hands clasped tightly. "I think so, yes. I think she said the same expert was working on both."

"And your lawyer withdrew because . . . ?"

Kieran's voice dropped a notch, his eyes wavering from Ryan's. "She said it was better if I found a more experienced trial lawyer."

The large air conditioners that cooled the place were the only sounds beyond their table in the nearly empty restaurant. Emily sat as quiet and frozen as the gray scenes in the photos filling the walls. There was still no sign that she was getting it. Ryan's frustration mounted another notch.

"You grew up here, did you?"

Kieran nodded.

"Went to high school in Sherman?"

"Yes."

"Kind of like a small town, isn't it."

"Yes. I suppose."

"Hanford's pretty much the only major business around here, I'd guess?"

Another nod.

"I'd bet most people work out there, is that right?"

"Many."

"Or at businesses that support the place."

"That's right."

"You ever know anybody that's sued Hanford or its contractors?"

"No."

"Ever know anybody win a verdict against Covington?"

Pause. "No."

His daughter's face was taut. Her eyes never left Kieran's face, never acknowledged her father at her elbow or the holes he was boring in her friend's case.

All right. Then how about this.

"Emily told me about your father. I'm sorry for your loss."

"Thanks."

"He worked at Hanford?"

"Yes."

"And what did he die of?"

Kieran stiffened. "Leukemia."

"Do you think Hanford or Covington was responsible for his disease?"

"What are you asking?"

"It's a simple question, Kieran. Do you think Hanford or Covington lied about your father's death? Like they're lying about your injuries? Are they responsible for your injuries like they were for your dad?"

"You don't have to answer that," Emily said quietly.

The sound of Emily's voice startled Ryan after her long silence.

"Yes you do," Ryan shot back.

"No you don't." Emily slid from the booth and headed toward the restroom.

The moment broke the mounting pressure in him. He saw confusion replacing the anger on Kieran's face. The sister looked close to crying.

Ryan stared after his daughter, suddenly aware of how tight the muscles of his back and arms had become. He knew she wasn't coming back. "I guess we're done," he said.

"I don't get it," Kieran answered, bewildered. "Look, I'll answer the question if you want." His façade of indifference was replaced with desperation.

Ryan shook his head. "It doesn't matter. We'll be staying in Sherman tonight. Emily and I need to talk. You can go—we'll get back to you as soon as we can."

The siblings reluctantly slid from the booth and made their way to the exit, looking lost. Ryan waited until they were gone, then paid the bill and returned to the car. Once there, he started the engine and turned on the radio while he waited for his daughter to emerge.

So maybe he'd gotten hard on the boy. But it was Emily's fault. She'd made him hammer Kieran about what should have been obvious to any lawyer who'd ever been in a courtroom. His interrogation had made it obvious that the boy's story about the radiation monitors was flawed. Kieran had no reasonable basis to believe he was exposed to radiation or seriously harmful chemicals. They'd be in enemy territory trying a case against Hanford or its contractors in Sherman. And it was obvious that Kieran probably had another agenda related to his father.

Covington Nuclear's lawyer would be merciless in pursuing these questions.

And the boy's explanation that his lawyer withdrew so he

could find a better lawyer sounded as plausible as the breakup excuse that "it's about me, not you." This kid's lawyer withdrew because she finally had the sense to recognize it was a lousy case.

He felt faintly nauseous. Why had he taken this meeting? He should have been honest with Emily before they came all the way to Sherman. He'd only made it worse.

It was fifteen minutes before Emily finally left the restaurant. He caught her mood in her strides as she approached the car. When Emily got angry—very angry—her every movement became fluid and calm, as though her rage was a caged beast she was quietly pondering when to release. And pity the nearest person when she set it free.

Emily stayed quiet for the entire drive to the Winchester Bed and Breakfast. She left the car in complete silence, taking the stairs to the second floor with soundless footfalls, and closing her room door gently behind her before Ryan could suggest they talk.

He stood alone in the hall shaking his head. This wasn't new. But he hadn't been close enough to her to witness this phenomena for many years.

But for the final click of her door latch, Emily had faded completely away from her father, melting softly and furiously into the dry desert air.

CHAPTER 7

COVINGTON NUCLEAR HEADQUARTERS

It was nearing seven in the evening, but Adam Worth knew from experience that common notions of time ended at the door to the office of the Vice-President of Environmental Operations. He straightened his bow tie and went in.

And nearly collided with another man coming out. The man looked to be an engineer, with a navy sport coat and an iPad in one hand. Mostly he looked stomped on: head down, shirt partly untucked. The man brushed past Adam and hurried into the hallway without looking up.

Cameron Foote's secretary nodded curtly as Adam approached her desk guarding the vice-president's inner office. Despite the late hour, her back was as rigid as an honor guard. They said people and their dogs came to resemble one another through the years. That adage passed through Adam's mind now regarding the vice-president and his secretary, loyal as a collie to the man.

"Mr. Foote is expecting you," she said, gesturing toward the interior office door. Adam thanked her and went in.

Foote's office matched the man: sparely furnished, but every item intentional—from framed pictures of the VP with two senators to the pen set with *Semper Fi* engraved on its base.

"Hello, Adam," Cameron Foote's voice boomed before he was past the threshold.

"Hello, sir."

Even seated, Foote cut an impressive figure: every inch the ex-Marine and Wharton MBA man he was. Tough and straight-backed. Unrelenting eyes. Perhaps he could have completed the image if he'd surrendered to the vanity of shaving his balding head. As lean and disciplined as he already appeared, it was probably unnecessary.

Foote gestured toward the single chair in front of his dark mahogany desk.

"Okay, Adam. Give me the status on Project Wolffia."

Foote always knifed to the core of things. It was an American attribute perfected in the vice-president, but one that Adam, a naturalized citizen, still found disconcerting.

"The cleanup of the lower levels of LB5 since the explosion is complete, sir. And the new testing equipment is installed."

"Good. Good. Have you found all the necessary replacement personnel?"

"Almost. We still require a new team leader, but I'm in dialogue with the likely candidate now."

"Very important. Leadership always is. Then we should have Project Wolffia up and running again shortly."

It was a question. It was also a command. The image of the wounded engineer retreating from Foote's office crossed Adam's mind. He brushed his bow tie, bracing himself.

"Well, you'll recall, sir," Adam said, "the legal case brought by the young stabilizing engineer relating to the LB5 explosion?"

"Yes. Kieran Mullaney."

One vanity to which Foote *had* surrendered was taking every opportunity to display his grasp and memory of details. "Yes, sir. Mr. Mullaney. His case is approaching trial. His lawyer has withdrawn but he's searching for replacement counsel."

Foote grunted his acknowledgment. "So what's the issue?"

"Well, if the matter does proceed to trial, there remain several . . . dangling ends. Specifically, sir, you remember Mr. Patrick Martin—the security guard. The one who submitted a statement that night on the shooting incident? So long as the case is active, there remains the possibility of that evidence . . . coming out."

Again, the grunt. But the face remained impassive to the obvious point Adam was trying to make.

"In addition, sir, you know that if the case goes to trial, the Department of Energy inspectors' office might take notice of any new evidence regarding the LB5 explosion that wasn't in our report."

Silence. *He's making me walk all the way onto the scaffold unassisted*, Adam thought. *Then* he'll hang me.

"I believe, sir, under the circumstances, that we should consider steps to insure that we retain maximum control over any information about the project coming out in the court action."

Cameron Foote was not a tall man—perhaps five foot eight. Despite his display of studied calm, Adam knew he was like piano wire underneath—so stretched that Adam once wondered whether the VP had always been this size or simply shrank over time from being so tightly wound.

Now Foote's face remained a carving of composure and control as the quiet in the room took on the character of nails on a blackboard to Adam. From experience, Adam knew that he liked it that way: the vice-president enjoyed creating an artificial calm before unleashing a storm.

"If you're waiting for me to say we can delay restart of the project in light of this mall cop's report and the coming trial," Foote said at last, straightening his already rigid back, "the answer is no. You'll just have to keep things well managed."

"Sir," Adam protested, "the Wolffia team is nearly assembled and ready to go. I'm just wondering if we should delay the restart for a few months."

Foote considered Adam for a moment. "Have you read the paper today?"

Adam was caught off guard by the turn of conversation.

"No, sir."

Foote reached behind him to the credenza and gathered a folded copy of the *Wall Street Journal*. Unfolding it, he spread the sheet on his desk facing Adam.

"Page one, above the fold: Iran continues to operate its centrifuges to develop its nuclear arsenal. Lower corner, right: North Korea tested another weapon. Last week there was a report on the number of warheads China has accumulated."

The VP's finger stayed rooted on the paper as he looked Adam in the eye.

"The people I report to—the very few written into the project—will tell you it's about a potential four hundred billion dollar profit. Let them crunch the numbers. I'm telling you it's about a tool that this country and the West will need sooner rather than later. Now, you were brought onboard because, in the four years before your tenure, your predecessor couldn't get the job done. How many people do you have working for you on this project altogether? Including the LB5 personnel, the core science team, the special security team, and those guys out of Los Alamos. How many?"

"Counting the temporary medical personnel, forty-seven, sir."

"Forty-seven, and more money at your fingertips than God. If those resources are still inadequate, you tell me how. Otherwise, justify my faith in hiring you for this project. Do what you have to and get it done. We've already been delayed eight months by that explosion. I want Wolffia operational again at LB5. Immediately."

The dismissal in Foote's voice was unmistakable. Adam acknowledged his orders with a final "Yes, sir," then stood and left the room.

As he passed through the space to the outer door, Adam

wondered if the secretary took pleasure in the parade of the fallen leaving Cameron Foote's office each day. Did she derive some satisfaction—maybe smile behind their backs—as they dragged themselves back into the halls of the Covington Nuclear headquarters?

He shut the door behind him. The hall was empty this late. Adam turned toward the elevators leading to his own office on the second floor.

That could have gone better. But at least his options were clear: there were none. Not only did he have to get the project back on track, he had to do what was necessary to protect the project from the potential vagaries of this American lawsuit that refused to die.

He arrived at his quiet office in the corner of the empty Personnel Department. Gathering his briefcase, he locked up and headed toward the exit for home.

One thing was quite certain. As busy as the past two years had been since he assumed his false title and rank in the Personnel Office, things were about to become much busier. Several tasks he'd been putting off had suddenly become the highest of priorities.

CHAPTER 8

Emily must've gotten it by now, Ryan thought as he woke to sunlight piercing the window blinds of his room at the B&B. She'd been practicing law for two years—three if you counted her clerkship with Judge Freyling. After she got away from Kieran last night and had time to mull it over, she'd have seen the light. It was time to clear the air and head for home. Buoyed, he hustled out of bed, showered quickly, and stepped next door.

Several knocks at Emily's room went unanswered. He glanced at his watch. It was still early. She was probably still asleep. He'd circle back after breakfast—or catch her when she came down.

The dining room was half full, with a single man shuffling from table to table. Ryan didn't mind, he was in no hurry today. He took a seat by a window, setting his laptop on the chair beside him.

A copy of the local *Sherman Courier* was folded on the table, and he paged through it as he waited for the attendant to reach him. The Sherman high school summer baseball league was going well. There was a belated memorial service for three Hanford researchers killed in an auto accident on the reservation grounds the previous year. A welcome rain was expected sometime later this coming week.

Still no Emily. The rushed but cheerful attendant approached in an apron.

"Good morning, Mr. Hart," the man said, smiling.

Ryan nodded absently.

"I checked you in last night. I'm the owner: Pavia Nikovic. We're serving eggs Benedict this morning with Canadian bacon and toast with some local preserves. Sound alright?"

"Coffee first," Ryan said. "Black."

The man nodded understandingly.

Ryan felt his cell phone vibrate. He pulled it from his pocket and saw that he had a text from Emily.

"Dad—I'm with Pauline Strand," the message read.

Ryan texted back, frustrated at how slow the process always was for him. *"Who's she?"*

The reply was instantaneous: *"Kieran's last attorney."*

Ryan cursed under his breath. Now he remembered the name.

"We met at a cafe. It's not far." Another text flashed onto Ryan's screen. *"I think you should join us."*

Not exactly capitulation. He cursed again, knowing he couldn't decline.

"Send the address," he responded just as Pavia was arriving with the coffee. "I'll take this to go," he muttered, grabbing his laptop to leave.

Ryan drove the fifteen blocks from the Winchester Inn to the Daily Grind. A bell rang as he came through the door into the thick smell of roasting coffee beans. Ryan quickly scanned the place.

Pauline Strand was seated inside, across from Emily in a booth by the window. The Sherman lawyer's bar entry had made her out to be in her late sixties—but with a fashionable dress and light makeup, she could've passed for ten years younger.

She was very slender, her eyes framed by dark-rimmed glasses. A ponytail of gray hair fell to her shoulder blades, pulled back tightly from her forehead and bound in a double-wrapped band.

A computer was open at her side and a tall stack of papers lay at her elbow inside an open briefcase. Three large cups of something steaming were on the table between Pauline and Emily.

Ryan tossed his empty Styrofoam cup from the inn into a wastebasket near the entrance and approached. The woman looked up and smiled, extending a thin hand.

"Pauline Strand. You've got a nice daughter here, Ryan."

Ryan was still simmering at being dragged here this morning, and had no interest in small talk. "I know," he said, taking a seat. "You were Kieran's counsel?"

"Well, there was nobody else in this town fool enough to represent the boy—so yes." The woman slid one of the cups of coffee across the table. "It's hot. Black."

Ryan noticed that Emily still wasn't looking at him. He looked at the offered cup for a moment, then grasped it, deciding he'd take the extra caffeine today.

"I did a few minutes' research before coming over here," Pauline said. "You've got a little experience. I got the right Ryan L. Hart, didn't I? *Friedman versus Totten Gear? Ingebretson versus Spirit Motors?*"

"Yes," Ryan answered, then added, "the Spirit Motors case I handled with my wife."

Pauline nodded. "Well, that's the kind of trial experience Kieran needs. Though Emily tells me you're a little concerned about the case."

He shuddered at the description his daughter probably gave of the dinner the night before. "Some," he responded noncommittally.

The smile again. "So ask me."

It felt like round two in a fight Ryan thought he'd won last night, with Emily again sitting stiffly at his side. So be it.

"All right. Who's your judge in the case?"

"This is in federal court, as you probably know. There are only two judges sitting at the Sherman Federal Courthouse:

Judge Richard Renway and a newcomer appointed last fall, Celeste Johnston. Renway's got Kieran's case. Fact is, he gets all the Hanford cases."

"Is he smart?"

The shrug. "He thinks so. Got some quirks. But, yes, he's smart enough."

"Is he fair?"

Pauline shook her head. "Depends on the context. The man was born on orchard land out near the reservation, land that's still in the family. He went to Washington State undergrad and Gonzaga law school. He's been on the bench since the 1980s. My point is, he's a local boy and he's always been a solid friend of Hanford and its contractors."

Emily had grown as still as on the ride back from the Atomic Café.

"Kieran said Covington denies they're responsible for the LB5 explosion," Ryan pressed on. "How's that possible when they had the contract to maintain safety in the buildings?"

"I've wondered the same thing," the gray-haired lawyer smiled. "I don't see how they avoid responsibility based on the evidence to date. But I think they have something up their sleeve."

"Why do you say that?"

"Because in their last interrogatory answers, Covington's lawyer revealed that Kieran got into an argument with a techie before his shift. A supply tech named Red Whalen who worked up front at LB5. I don't see the relevance of that new tidbit of information unless they're building up to some new defense in the case."

The lady was sharper than he'd assumed. "Have you got experts to explain the cause of the explosion?" Ryan asked.

"Yes."

The hesitation was so minute Ryan wondered if he'd imagined it. "How good."

78

She shrugged. "There's just one: Dr. Nadine out of Princeton University. He says the explosion happened because water evaporation concentrated the remaining chemicals in the tank, making them reactive."

"Does your Princeton guy say how that happened? Weren't they monitoring the tanks?"

The hesitation lengthened. "Well, he mentioned that. In fact, based on Covington's internal inspection records, it's iffy whether the chemicals should have been so concentrated that they would explode. But they *did* explode, so he says that's the most plausible scientific explanation."

A little wobbly, but he liked the Princeton connection. "Is it true that Covington did a whole body count of Kieran that came up negative? And the same on the dosimetry badge?"

"Yes. And before you ask, I haven't got an explanation for that."

"So you have no experts to support Kieran's claim that he was exposed to radiation."

Pauline smiled. "Dr. Nadine's supposed to be working on that for me, too. The only choice he's given me so far is blood testing—which is beyond my wallet size. I'm hoping he'll eventually support an argument of radiation exposure based upon Kieran's immune system weakness."

Ryan recalled Kieran's statement about suffering coughing and headaches for months now.

"But you don't have any real expert proof to support Kieran's contention that he was exposed to radiation at this point."

"No. Truth is I don't."

"But do you believe him?" Emily jumped in quickly.

Pauline gave Emily a grim smile. "I've been working with the boy since November. And yes, I believe he's telling the truth about what he saw and experienced. I believe him when he says he was exposed to radiation."

Ryan thought about running through his cross-examination of Kieran again about radiation exposure. He rejected it as unnecessary—and likely dangerous with his daughter at his side.

"But you've got no proof, Pauline. Right?"

The older lawyer looked to Ryan. "That's right, Counselor."

"And we'd face a hometown jury in the case, wouldn't we." It was more a statement than a question, and Ryan did nothing to dampen the negative tone in his voice.

For the first time, Pauline Strand looked at Ryan with eyes of dawning awareness of his resolve to not take Kieran's case. "Well, that's not a simple question, Ryan. If you can spare another hour or two, I was planning on giving you a tour of the Hanford works—what you can see from outside the grounds. Sherman too. I'd rather answer your last question after that."

More wasted time. But maybe this wasn't all bad—Ryan almost had Emily convinced. If he still knew anything about his daughter, he could sense it in her face. If this could bring about a surrender instead of the alternative, it was worth indulging her with a little more time. "All right."

Pauline pointed out the window at Ryan's car. "Good. Then let's take the fine machine you arrived in."

They loaded into Ryan's Avalon, with Strand taking the back seat alongside her computer and stuffed briefcase. After passing a few turns, Pauline directed them onto Sherman's main street.

"In 1940, this was the only paved road in Sherman," Pauline began. "Back then, the place was a little farming community that serviced some of the orchards around here. The population was fifty. By 1948, that number had grown to thirty-five thousand."

Emily shook her head. "All workers for Hanford?" she asked.

"Yep," Pauline answered.

They were moving north through light traffic, past storefronts, banks, and the occasional office building. "They had fifty thousand workers build Hanford during the war," Pauline went on. "Once it was done and they'd started enriching uranium and producing plutonium out on the reservation, they still needed an army of workers to run the plant and someplace to house them—away from the factory buildings for safety and security. That's when the housing shifted to Sherman, and the homes starting going up. It was an instant boomtown—except still so secret, they even had the workers' mail delivered to a drop in Seattle and trucked over the mountains."

"Who ran Hanford?" Emily asked.

"Contractors under the Atomic Energy Commission. Later—much later—the AEC was replaced by the Department of Energy. But the day-to-day work was still handled by contractors. Companies like Dupont, General Electric, Fluor Daniels, to name a few. Covington Nuclear just got the contract about six years ago."

They were passing through the heart of downtown now. Pauline pointed out a newer library to the right, then a good-sized hospital a few blocks down on the left. There was a community pool on each side of town, she said, and several riverside parks. Both state and federal courthouses.

"You oughta see the high school," she said with a hint of pride. "Looks like a college campus. We've got a minor league baseball team. All that and elbow room too. It's like Seattle without all the traffic."

"Government built?" Ryan asked.

"Some. But a lot of it's been donated by contractors. Every company that's ever worked at Hanford has known that part of the price for billions of dollars in government contracts out here is pumping money into the community. That's been true since Hanford opened."

Ryan shook his head darkly. This was even more of a company town than he'd suspected when he'd grilled Kieran.

They passed under the freeway, leaving town and continuing

north for several miles until the road came to a T intersection. Pauline directed him to turn left.

"I'm going to take you parallel to the fence line of the Hanford Reservation. You can't see it for a long ways: it's beyond some hills to the east. But after a drive, we'll get to an overlook within sight of the main production works."

The road angled northwest. The terrain here was little different than what Ryan had seen from the highway further south the day before: dry and barren flats overlooked by buttes and rounded hills.

Forty minutes after they'd turned, the ground rose until they reached an overlook offering a vista across the reservation. They parked and got out of the car.

From there, the Hanford security fence was fully visible, like an iron stream flowing across the desert. Far away, against the backdrop of the Columbia River, several domes glinted in the late morning sun, like distant mosques. Other structures were visible as well—including the cooling towers of two nuclear reactors and smaller buildings scattered across the landscape.

"All told, they built over six hundred buildings out there," Pauline said, leaning against the car. "Production labs, storage facilities, nuclear reactors for power and for production. They're spread out over the northeast half of the reservation mostly, where we're looking now. LB5's a little further east and south. It's not visible here."

"How bad is the contamination out there?" Emily asked.

Pauline whistled. "Millions of tons of radioactive wastewater and solid waste still out there. A pool of contaminated groundwater two hundred miles or more, seeping toward the Columbia. Estimates are they've lost enough plutonium on the grounds to fuel eighty hydrogen bombs. Nobody knows where it's all at. Give you an example: they used to ship the plutonium from here to Rocky Flats and Los Alamos on special trains that were painted white, usually at night. I've had workers tell me the white trains got so contaminated that they just dug caves out on the reservation, laid tracks, drove 'em in, and sealed them— locomotives and all. Same with some trucks they used out there: filled them with irradiated tools and buried the whole thing."

Ryan caught Pauline's eye. "And most of the people you know in Sherman are associated with Hanford," he said matter-of-factly.

Emily glanced at him. Pauline smiled knowingly. "In some way or another."

"Dad," Emily said, the first she'd spoken to him since dinner the night before, "Kieran's case is in federal court, not state district court. The jury could be drawn from anywhere in eastern Washington—not just the town of Sherman."

Pauline held up a hand. "Yeah, honey, but your dad's right— the final jury pool will be heavily weighted with folks with a Hanford connection."

The lawyer crossed her arms and examined Ryan. "Before you draw too many conclusions, though, let me tell you: the Hanford workers that make up Sherman and this area worked for decades producing plutonium for the government and its contractors—and now on the cleanup. So it's true these people are very loyal to the reservation and its contractors. But that loyalty's always come with a big asterisk. Working with plutonium and all of the poisons involved in that process, a fat paycheck wasn't ever enough to convince them to risk their lives out in this desert. The government and its contractors told these folks that they were keeping America safe, building the bombs that kept Russia at bay through the Cold War—working for a higher calling. And they believed in the mission; some still do. Some think that one day America will wake up and need plutonium or some other bomb again to protect America—and Hanford will answer that call."

Ryan could see that Emily looked angry and crestfallen, like she was hearing the last nail being pounded into the coffin of Kieran's case.

"But even the mission couldn't seal the deal, if it weren't for the promise," Pauline went on. "These folks aren't robots. A condition of their loyalty has always been an unspoken agreement that the government and its contractors wouldn't lie to them. Not with all the hazards they put up with. They'd always be honest about the risks. You prove that promise has been broken by Covington at LB5, I believe you can beat 'em with a Sherman jury."

They'd been in the sun long enough that Ryan felt the heat building under his shirt, adding to his fatigue at this game. He wanted to go back to the B&B, gather his bags, and head for home. If Emily didn't get it by now, then he'd never convince her.

"If Kieran's case is so tough," Emily asked Pauline in a strained voice, "then why'd you take it?"

A light breeze blew wisps of gray hair across the lawyer's face. "Because nobody else would," she said, reaching up and nestling the strands behind her ear. "And I believed in him. I knew I was out of my league, but I believed in him."

"Then why'd you quit," Ryan snapped.

She looked at him and smiled. "Because of my sure-as-the-sun-comes-up certainty that I was going to lose. I don't have enough of the right courtroom experience; I don't have enough money. And I don't know what Covington's got up its sleeve, but something's coming. When it hits, Kieran deserves a lawyer like you."

"Two months until trial?" Emily asked after another interval of silence.

"Two months to trial," Pauline repeated. "Unless you can get an extension. But final expert reports are due in a few weeks."

The thin lawyer turned away from Emily toward Ryan. "Now I've got a question for you. Kieran's mostly focused on knowing what he might've been exposed to. But if you could prove serious radiation exposure, how much do you think his case is worth?"

"Two million," Ryan said, the words out of his mouth automatically. "Give or take half a million. That's with a decent, unbiased jury. It also assumes serious evidence to support exposure and likely long-term health effects."

Their drive back to town was as quiet as the preceding night. When they reached Pauline's small office building, she stepped out of the sidewalk with her computer and case, then leaned back into the open passenger-side window.

"There's something else you ought to know," she said, staring across Emily to Ryan. "The day I withdrew from the case, as I was leaving the courtroom, Covington's lawyer made an offer to settle."

Startled, Ryan matched her gaze. "*After* you withdrew?"

"Yep," she nodded. "Fifty thousand dollars. Kieran turned them down, by the way. Since you hadn't asked about it, I assumed Kieran didn't mention it. That's why I hesitated to tell you."

This made no sense. "Why would they offer a settlement when he's on the ropes?"

The lawyer smiled. "I thought you'd find that interesting."

The slender lawyer turned up the sidewalk carrying her computer and files. As they drove away, Ryan was left with the impression that each hand was full of a burden big enough to overwhelm her.

Poppy opened his eyes as he felt the bed creak and heard Suzy's footsteps padding into the bathroom. He glanced at the clock: eleven a.m.

Working the late shift, it wasn't often he and Suzy shared the bed for so many hours together. He hoped his rough sleeping these past months hadn't kept her awake again last night.

He hadn't had this much trouble sleeping since his first extended operation in the Navy aboard the USS *New Jersey*. He hadn't expected discomfort on the ship—it wasn't like he was in a submarine. But after growing up in the open country of eastern Washington, even a battleship seemed confining.

He'd brought back three things from his tour with the navy: satisfaction at his service, complete disinterest in ever sailing the ocean's surface again, and his nickname—a shortening of "Popeye" that a midshipman slapped on him after he'd gone up three weight classes to win a boxing competition for the ship. The name followed him home when another local boy returned from the *New Jersey* to Hanford a year after Poppy.

No one but Poppy recalled the name's origins, but Poppy didn't mind. He remembered its source with pride. Besides, he'd never been that crazy about "Pat" anyway.

Poppy rolled to his feet and headed toward the living room. The headache was mercifully absent this morning. Even his chest felt clearer than it usually did when he awoke.

He picked up the paper from the front stoop and ambled back to the dining room table. His computer was there and Poppy opened it to check his emails.

Amidst the junk mail was an email from Covington headquarters. Poppy opened it.

He had sent a total of five emails to Covington HQ the past eight months. The first had been a respectful note about more testing to see if he'd picked up radiation in the LB5 explosion. That one had gone completely unanswered. Poppy's second went further, also asking whether he was going to be interviewed about what he'd seen and heard that night. When that one and a couple others were ignored, he'd dropped the courtesy a month before, reminding "to whom it might concern" of the gunshot his partner had fired that appeared nowhere in the newspaper reports about Covington's investigation report.

This was the first reply. Oddly, it appeared to have come from the Covington Personnel Office.

Dear Mr. Martin—

Thank you for the information you have shared in your emails these past months. Please be assured that your perspectives and experiences that night have been fully considered. . . .

He skipped to the bottom.

Regarding further radiation testing, the study completed by top nuclear experts has confirmed the absence of a radiation release at LB5 . . .

Nothing about interviewing him about that night. No mention of his repeated questions about Lew's gunshot. No offer of examinations. Just more bureau-blather.

He looked at the bottom of the email. There was no name assigned the message—just "Covington Nuclear Human Resources."

So who was even dealing with this mess?

Poppy spent the next fifteen minutes preparing a reply. If they thought he was going to stop bugging them based on an email like that, they'd know better soon. He finished the note, read it quickly, then pushed Send.

"Hon, get dressed," Suzy said as she came into the dining room. He looked up at her from the computer.

Prettier than ever, he thought—even with worrying about him. "And wipe that scowl from your face," she finished, smiling. "You're taking me to lunch."

With an effort, Poppy smiled back. She deserved it, he thought. She needed a respite from this as much as he did.

For a moment, he wondered if he should've sent the email so quickly, whether he should have thought about it for awhile. But no. He'd been pussyfooting with these guys long enough. Now they'd know for sure he wasn't going away. Not without some answers. Besides, the email was gone; he couldn't bring it back.

"I'm fine with that, long as you're buying," he said, standing and walking toward the bedroom to change—and swatting her gently as he passed by.

CHAPTER 9

Ryan sat in his room for half an hour after they returned from the drive around Hanford, leaving Emily alone. At last, he rose, grabbed his bags, and headed downstairs to load them into the Avalon—before returning to her door and knocking.

"Come in," her voice called through the door.

Emily was seated on the window seat. Her face looked drawn. Her bag, he saw, was still unpacked at the end of the bed.

Ryan worried at the sight of it. "Why isn't your bag in your car, Emily? We've got to check out."

"Go ahead," she returned.

"You're coming, right?"

"No."

His stomach lurched. "Come on, Emily. You can't be serious. This is a killer of a case. We'd just be prolonging this kid's agony by taking it on."

He saw now that his daughter's eyes wore the placidity of a decision. "His name's Kieran, Dad. And I already extended my stay at the B&B. I'm calling Frank tomorrow to take my vacation, plus a leave of absence. I understand what you're saying about Kieran's case. You don't have to represent him. But I will."

"Don't be idiotic," he shot back. "You can't represent him in this, of all cases."

"Take a look at my diploma," she said. "And I've been in a courtroom before."

"For two years. In criminal cases."

She sat silent.

"Why? Why do you have to do this?"

The defiance in Emily's eyes became something harder. "Because he was there for me when Mom was sick," she said softly. "When nobody else was. Nobody. And by the way, Mom thought a lot of Kieran."

"Carolyn met Kieran?" Ryan asked, startled.

Emily shook her head. "No. But we talked about him a lot. When she was in the hospital."

The room emptied of oxygen. Ryan felt an agony of anger and sadness flowing into his chest and face; he knew that Emily could see it too.

What did she know about that time?

"Good luck," he said.

He slammed the door shut behind him and took the stairs to the first floor in a haze. Pavia was there, behind the counter. The proprietor looked disturbed; he'd heard the door slam, Ryan thought distantly.

Ryan sat for half an hour in his Avalon, the engine running, while the hot sun's reflection glinted in the chrome rimming the dusty hood. His mood tilted back and forth on a sharp edge between anger and guilt. Emily didn't understand what those last two years had been like. He'd barely had enough emotional strength for Carolyn. He'd used every drop on the woman he loved. There was none left over for Emily. Now he wouldn't be shamed into taking this miserable case to appease her—or to honor what Emily claimed Carolyn thought of Kieran.

When he finally looked at the car clock it was after two. He reached to put the car into gear.

Instead, he turned off the engine. Grabbing his bags, he climbed the front stairs to the B&B, returning to Pavia, who looked up at Ryan with anxious eyes.

"I want to keep my room for another day. That okay?"

The hotel owner nodded.

Ryan headed back upstairs to his room. He was going for a run.

He weaved through the hot air and the busy foot traffic on the path through River Park. Blurred flashes of color from joggers and runners passed by as he pushed his pace faster and faster, the sweat burning his eyes, each breath coming more quickly after the last.

A side path approached on his right, heading up a steep hill. Ryan took it, ignoring the resistance of his burning thighs. He pumped his arms, driving up the slope, gasping out a cadence, until just as his legs were wavering, the path flattened onto an open hilltop with a thick copse of trees visible on the far side.

His hands dropped to his knees as he staggered to a halt, gasping deep breaths until his shoulders eased back and he could stand up again.

The hilltop was empty except for two people near the ridgeline to his left. On a bench, a woman sat with a stroller at her side, looking away from Ryan. The other was a red-haired man with a runner's build in white running shorts and a T-shirt gazing off at the vista of the southern horizon.

It was the woman who kept his attention. Her sundress was crimson. Blond hair fell to just beneath the line of her jaw, ending in a light curl—like Carolyn used to wear it. From behind, she might have been a young Carolyn, arriving at their Seattle law office on a warm summer day.

The sight of it jolted Ryan so soon after his argument with Emily. His thoughts went to the years right after graduating from law school. He'd never really planned to have a law partner, he recalled, unable to imagine tying himself to someone with a say on how he practiced. He'd get a job with a good firm, learn the ropes, start his own solo practice.

But Carolyn had arrived, and she'd spoiled it all. From their first days together out of law school, they made career decisions together he never would have made on his own. Even taking on tough, messy cases because Carolyn insisted it was the right thing to do. Like Emily was trying to force him to take Kieran's case right now.

Emily could tell him all day long to go back to Seattle. But then she'd take Kieran's case and Covington and its lawyers would bury her alive. Then it would be his fault. She'd already made it clear it was his fault for not being there when Carolyn was sick. And he knew she was really charging him with much more than that.

This mess and his guilt were tangled lines and he couldn't find the ends to unravel them.

Standing on the hill, the conditional surrender eased over him like a whisper. Alright, he told himself: he wouldn't go home the way things were. He wouldn't be dragged into this case—not this way. But he'd help. He'd protect her from the worst of it. Advise her. Write the checks to sustain the case.

But that was all.

He looked again at Carolyn's ghost on the bench. It was Carolyn who'd spoiled it all. She'd become his partner in law, his partner in life. Terrified at the prospect of losing her, he'd made a mess of her final time with him, ignoring her pleas that he hold something back for Emily and for himself. And now that she was gone, he couldn't remember how to practice law without her. Do most anything without her, really.

He turned away from the woman and began a slow jog back down the hill toward the Winchester Inn.

❖❖❖

His wet running shirt still clung to his chest and back as Ryan knocked at his daughter's room. Hearing no footsteps, he raised his hand to knock again—when the door opened suddenly.

92

Emily looked at him with blank eyes. "I thought you'd left," she said flatly.

"Can I come in?" he asked.

She walked away, leaving the door open.

"If you're intent on taking this boy's case," Ryan said, following her in, "I'll write the checks. There'll be a lot of them, believe me. But it'll be on a 50 percent contingency fee."

It was a punishment: Emily saw that. It was a price tag that captured Ryan's disdain for their chances of seeing a dime of return, let alone two million dollars.

"That's too high," she said. "And this is a friend. Forty percent."

"The case is a mess. And he's not a friend; he's a client. Forty-five. That's final."

Emily's eyes narrowed in capitulation. "All right."

"And I'll help—but you want this, so you're counsel of record. You make all the court appearances. I'll be in the background. Plus, you agree this stays business."

He detected a positive glimmer at his offer of help, but it was quickly controlled. "Agreed."

He turned to leave.

"What changed your mind?" she called out.

He thought about telling her of the image of Carolyn on the hill. But he wasn't inclined to share anything just now, let alone that. And if he confessed it was partly because of his failures as a father, he feared it would only unleash a torrent of agreement.

"First lesson, Counselor," he replied, "when you get a ruling in your favor, don't ask too many questions. Just take it and run."

CHAPTER 10

From the back benches of courtroom 3, Ryan looked at the counsel table where Emily sat with Kieran at her side. The courtroom was vacant except for the three of them. Emily was chewing on her lip, staring uneasily up at the empty judge's bench.

Ryan understood her nerves. This was new territory for Emily—a civil case, not a criminal one. A products liability lawsuit was nothing like a felony defense.

And even if all that weren't true, federal courtrooms were always more imposing than the state ones where Emily's experience lay. The rooms were big: there was no economy of space as in the state courts. The ceilings were higher, the judge's dais more elevated. Even the dark, lush woods that wrapped the interior were finer. If he were only three years out of law school, Ryan conceded, he might be intimidated, too.

But Emily wasn't looking to him for support today. He was a tolerated presence. His limited offer to help had garnered an equally limited thaw in the tension between them. So far, on the legal side, she'd only asked him to help gather and begin reviewing pleadings and documents from Pauline Strand's office. He'd also taken it on himself to lease a partially remodeled annex from Pavia next door to the Winchester Inn: a cheaper alternative to staying at the B&B. The annex remodeling had apparently stalled, leaving the building empty, and Pavia had jumped at the chance to rent it for a few months. The proprietor had even thrown in two foldout beds and spare furniture for the duration.

Still, Emily had accepted Ryan's first piece of cautious advice: to seek an emergency extension of the trial date, deadlines to collect evidence, and the date for exchange of final expert reports. The need for the extensions was self-evident, but Emily had seemed overwhelmed the day she'd begun the case in earnest— and the suggestion had given her an anchor to begin case prep. She hadn't, he noticed, run the motion pleadings by him before filing them with the court.

He glanced around the empty cavern of a courtroom. For all his resolve about Emily handling this case as the lead, sitting as a spectator while his daughter prepared for oral argument against a big, well-funded opponent was surreal and unnerving. Like watching a race he ought to be running.

She was digging in her briefcase again; likely her nerves about the argument. But Ryan was growing troubled by something else. The motion should have begun twenty minutes ago. He looked to the empty chairs behind the bench and at the other counsel table. A judge being late was common. An opposing attorney being late at the same time was cause for alarm.

There was a creak from the door behind the bench leading to the judge's chambers. It swung open wide and a man in a rumpled sport coat came through, bellowing, "All rise."

They stood as the court reporter entered the courtroom, transcription machine in hand, followed by the dark-haired judge with a narrow face that looked as though it had been pressed tight between bookends. He was cloaked in a choirboy blue rather than black robe—a first in Ryan's experience—and carried a file under his arm. The judge was talking over his shoulder to a man in his fifties with a leather briefcase in one hand, dressed in a brown suit with matching suspenders. They parted and the man with the briefcase strode to the empty counsel's table.

Ryan felt his stomach grinding. This had to be Eric King, Covington's attorney, he thought. The lawyer didn't bother to look at Ryan or Emily as he sat down.

The grind deepened. This was as bad as he'd feared: Covington's lawyer meeting alone with the judge, before the hearing. Neither one was even trying to hide it.

Judge Renway reached the bench and sat, dropping his file on the desk and looking up at Emily for the first time. He motioned with his hand for everyone to sit.

"Ms. Hart?" Judge Renway said toward counsel table.

Emily rose, looking more calm than Ryan felt. "Yes, Your Honor."

The judge conferred a professional smile. "Ms. Hart, I've read your moving papers. Let's cut to the chase. You're asking for more time for trial and the discovery and expert report deadlines. But you must have known before you appeared in this case a few days ago that I already gave an extension of those deadlines when I allowed Ms. Strand to withdraw as counsel."

"Yes, Your Honor," Emily said, "but we had no chance to take advantage of that earlier extension, since we only just joined the case."

The judge's brow furrowed over his thin face. "I suppose that's true, but at some point, defendant Covington Nuclear is entitled to have your client's claims against it resolved once and for all. And Ms. Strand had ample time to prepare experts. In fact, she named her expert over three months ago. I don't see the need for a lot of leeway to finalize expert opinions. No, I'm inclined to deny your request. Unless you've got new arguments that aren't in your moving papers."

How about a demand for equal time in judge's chambers, Ryan wanted to shout out.

"No, Your Honor," she answered, clutching her brief in both hands. "Except to repeat that we're joining this case with only two months to trial and only three weeks to finalize expert reports. Mr. Mullaney has significantly less resources than Covington. We just ask for a chance to get our arms around the case."

Emily spoke with confidence, Ryan noted with respect, not wavering as she looked at this judge dressed in his uncharacteristic blue robe. Judge Renway rubbed a hand across his forehead, then shook his head and turned to Covington's counsel. "What do you say, Mr. King?"

The attorney to Emily's right stood up, leaning on his fists on the table.

"Your Honor, we agreed to Pauline Strand's request to withdraw; we didn't even object to the extra time she requested for Mr. Mullaney to find new counsel. But enough is enough. The dilemma facing Ms. Strand and now Ms. Hart is that the evidence for their client's case isn't going to get any better with an extra month or an extra year. We stand on our objection to further delays."

The judge turned back to Emily's table. "I'm denying your request for additional time for discovery and until trial, Ms. Hart," he said. "As for additional time to finalize expert reports, once again your predecessor had plenty of time to prepare. But I'll agree to push that deadline to a week before trial, unless opposing counsel has a serious objection."

King stood and smiled magnanimously. "No, Your Honor. That would be fine."

"Good," the judge replied. "Then I'll see you all at the pretrial hearing, a week before commencement of trial."

Ryan's anger overflowed at the nonchalance of the judge's ruling. His last restraint collapsed at the memory of the judge emerging with the Covington lawyer from chambers—and the realization that Emily had failed to make a record of the galling event. He was on his feet before the judge could stand.

"Perhaps," he called out, "if Ms. Hart had the same opportunity as Mr. King to meet privately with Your Honor in chambers before the motion . . ."

Like butter on a hot plate, the cool smile melted from the judge's flushed face. *"And just who are you,"* he boomed.

"Ryan Hart, sir. I'm . . . assisting Ms. Hart in this matter."

Emily's eyes were performing surgery on him, while Kieran simply looked perplexed. Eric King was watching him over his shoulder with cold interest.

But Ryan focused only on the judge. The man looked ready to gather his blue robe and come over the bench at him.

"Are you a lawyer?" he spat.

"Yes, sir."

"You're not listed as counsel of record in this case."

"That's correct. I'm not."

The anger was welling in his voice, not subsiding, as the judge spoke again. "Well, Mr. Hart, I don't know how you practice law wherever you're from, but statements like that come with consequences in my courtroom."

So do actions like yours, Ryan thought. *So sanction me; give us that platform to appeal your ruling. Because by denying the extension, you're already putting a torpedo into a sinking ship.*

"Your Honor." Emily was back on her feet now, facing the bench, her voice pleading. "Mr. Hart is . . . my father. As he said, he's . . . trying to assist me with this lawsuit."

The judge's eyes still flickered with hostility, but his hand loosened on the gavel clutched in one fist. Whether because of his daughter's appeal or in acknowledgment of the appearance of his meeting with King before the hearing, the judge shook his head a final time. "Ms. Hart, I suggest you get your *father* under control before any further proceedings in this matter."

The judge pounded his desk with a loud blow of the gavel, then shot to his feet and marched from the room, the billow of his blue robe nearly enveloping the court reporter following on his heels.

The other court personnel shuffled from the room as well, until the door closed behind the final clerk. But the Covington lawyer was already on his feet the instant the judge left the courtroom, headed toward the exit like he was race walking. Ryan launched himself in the same direction.

Eric King was halfway down the hall at the elevator bank by the time Ryan caught him. His eyes flinched as Ryan came at him in a charge.

"What do you want," King asked as Ryan stopped six inches from his chest and glared down at the shorter man.

"Catching up on old times in chambers?" Ryan asked.

The lawyer's eyes measured the inches between the two of them. With each passing second, Ryan could see King relax a little more, as it grew clearer that Ryan had enough control not to start a brawl right there in the corridor.

The lawyer's silence only made Ryan angrier. "This how you do things in Sherman?" Ryan asked tightly.

"I don't know what you mean," the Covington lawyer responded. "If you're asking if we do things efficiently here, yes. It's a habit we acquired when my parents were keeping our country safe, while yours, living on the Sound, were probably deciding between a drive up the coast or skiing in the pass."

The lawyer took a step back away from Ryan and scorn filled his face. "Judge Renway's been on the bench for more than thirty years. You're reading too much into this. Did I stop by to say hello to the judge before the hearing? Yes. This is a small town. But if you think you can gain any advantage by impugning this judge's reputation, you're sadly mistaken."

Ryan didn't buy it for a moment, but his anger was fading into a sickening sense of the futility of this confrontation.

King shook his head. "Well, *Dad*," he said, reaching into his briefcase and producing a three-ring binder, "maybe you could give this to your daughter for me."

He handed it to Ryan, who glanced at its cover. It was titled "Covington Nuclear Report on the October 2013 Event at LB5—Amended."

"After we got notice that Kieran Mullaney had retained new counsel," King went on, "Covington elected to revise its investigation report to clarify a few points. Like adding the conclusion that Vat 17 exploded because a valve appears to have been turned at its base, allowing fluid to escape. That's what caused the concentration in the vat, and therefore the explosion. And since your hot-headed client was the last one in room 365 before the explosion, you can draw your own conclusions. We're confident the jury will."

King shook his head at Ryan's stunned silence. "Show that to your Princeton expert and see how long he stays on board with your case. The fact is, your daughter's client should've taken the settlement offer. The last one's off the table. I may be able to scrape together some authority for a nuisance settlement. But your client's dead in this town because this *amended* report," he said, tapping it in Ryan's hands, "is now written in stone."

The elevator door opened and the Covington lawyer disappeared inside. Ryan turned and walked slowly up the hall in an angry haze, nearly bumping into Emily as she emerged from the courtroom.

Her face was crimson. "I don't know what you think you were doing in there, but you made it clear this is my case, so stay out of it. And what did you do just now—punch King out?"

"No," Ryan said. "I should have."

"Don't you *ever* do that again," she repeated through tight lips. Ryan saw Kieran place a restraining hand on her shoulder.

Ryan didn't reply. Emily's eyes wavered as she glanced at the binder in his hand. "What's that?"

"We've got to talk, Emily," Ryan said quietly.

His daughter recognized the tone in his voice. She reached for the binder as the red drained from her face.

CHAPTER 11

Ryan finished reviewing Covington's amended investigation report for the third time. Then he set it beside him on the living room love seat—next to the report he'd just reread from their expert, Dr. Philip Nadine of Princeton University.

Dr. Nadine's report was scrap paper now. The new "amended" Covington report made Dr. Nadine's expert opinions about the explosion irrelevant.

Ryan looked to Emily, seated across the room at the kitchen table. She was staring back at him with a lost gaze of rising anxiety.

"So what's this 'amended' investigation report from Covington mean?" Kieran broke the silence from his chair by the front window.

Weary of playing the bad cop, Ryan was relieved as Emily turned to Kieran to respond. "The report implies you caused the explosion," she said softly.

Kieran looked like she'd slapped him across the face. "What do you mean?"

Emily didn't go on. *Great*, Ryan thought.

"Their experts," he stepped in, "say that that natural concentration of fluids in Vat 17 from water evaporation wasn't the only cause of the explosion," he said. "Evaporation contributed, but the explosion was finally triggered when somebody opened a valve below the vat, draining more fluid. Since you were the last person in the room, they're obviously going to argue you did it."

Kieran's eyes grew defiant. "Okay. But I didn't."

"Did you fight with one of the techs before going on duty?"

Kieran looked perplexed at Ryan's change of subject. "No," he said. "I gave the supply tech a hard time because he'd been a jerk to Taylor and me the whole two weeks we'd been working out there. I told him I wanted my boots back that'd been confiscated my first night at LB5. It wasn't a fight."

Emily was watching Kieran carefully, but still lying back from joining the fray.

"Did you come into contact with Vat 17 before the explosion?" Ryan asked.

The boy closed his eyes, exhaling slowly. "No. Absolutely not. Other than to touch the side to see how hot it was."

"No contact," Ryan pressed harder. "That's what you're telling us. None . . . at . . . all."

At the edge of his vision, Emily's eyes sharpened—angry, Ryan thought, at the inquisitor's tone in his voice. Her mouth opened, then shut as they both saw Kieran's face go blank.

"I . . . my T-shirt did get caught on something under the vat," Kieran said. "It might have been a valve."

Emily closed her eyes. "That's contact," she muttered.

"But I didn't touch it."

"Kieran," Emily said roughly, "I don't think you're getting it here. The report doesn't say you were 'giving the tech a hard time.' It says you were so angry that your supervisor, Taylor, had to intervene. That implies you opened the valve on Vat 17 deliberately—to make trouble your last night on LB5."

Kieran leaned over, his face flushed so deep Ryan thought he was going to be sick. When he sat up again, Kieran's angry tone matched Emily's.

"That vat was getting ready to explode before I got near it," Kieran insisted. "I didn't do anything to set it off."

"How do you know?" Emily responded before Ryan could. "You just admitted your T-shirt caught on the valve."

"Because my T-shirt just hooked the valve for a moment," Kieran shot back. He stood and started to pace.

How long does it take to turn a valve, Ryan thought. "When you were deposed five months ago," he said instead, pointing across the living room to the partially emptied boxes of records and depo transcripts from Pauline Strand, "you didn't mention your T-shirt getting caught on the valve at all."

"I didn't remember it until now," Kieran answered defensively.

"Well, Covington's investigators apparently figured it out," Ryan said. "They say the valve was turned by someone or something and you were the last one in there. Now that you recall the business of the T-shirt, they'll say you used your T-shirt to help turn a sticky old valve—and did it deliberately. Even if the jury accepts the valve turning as unintentional, they'll still conclude you're responsible for the explosion—especially after not mentioning it at your deposition."

Kieran threw a fierce glance at Ryan. "So are you representing Covington now?"

"My dad's right," Emily jumped in, surprising Ryan at her defense.

The young man fell silent.

In stone. Eric King's words at the elevators came back to Ryan now. He raised a hand to get Kieran's attention. "Covington's lawyer told me at the courthouse that this amended report is now 'written in stone.' Do you know what he meant?"

Kieran shook his head. "Sounds like a figure of speech."

In stone. In stone. "When King offered the settlement," Ryan pressed, "did he threaten you that Covington might change their investigation report unless you agreed to settle?"

"What do I care if they change the lies in their report," Kieran muttered, resuming his pacing.

Emily looked like she was sinking into her chair. "Kieran, just answer my dad's question," she said impatiently. "Did Covington threaten to change their investigation report if you didn't settle?"

Kieran met Emily with a cold stare. "Yes. Pauline told me something about that. They didn't explain what they meant. But Pauline said that when King offered the settlement, he suggested that if I turned them down and insisted on keeping the case going with new attorneys, I wouldn't like how the final report read."

Emily shook her head. "And you didn't think that was important to tell us?"

It was strange for Ryan to hear Emily's anger directed at someone other than himself. When Kieran didn't reply, he spoke up again.

"Let me tell you why you should care. If they can convince a jury that you acted deliberately to cause the explosion, two things are going to happen. First, when word gets out, you will become a *very* unpopular man in a town like Sherman. Second, you'll likely get charged criminally for sabotaging a secure federal facility."

Emily watched Kieran resume his seat and cover his face with his hands.

"King implied he'd still be willing to settle," Ryan continued, gentling his tone. "He said that a settlement wouldn't change this final report, but that might be bluster. Maybe Emily could still negotiate for Covington to back off on this amended report as part of a settlement."

They watched Kieran in strained silence.

"What about exposure?" Kieran said at last through his fingers.

"What do you mean?" Emily asked.

"Exposure. Pauline told me their original report claimed I wasn't exposed to radiation."

"That's correct," Ryan answered. "This report repeats that there was no measurable radiation released by the blast because the mixing room was clean. They said the most you or anyone else experienced was chemical exposure causing temporary symptoms."

"Pauline told me they don't even mention the radiation monitors going off in the hallway."

"You're right," Ryan said. "The report says the monitors showed no radiation detected in the hall."

"So if I take their settlement, I'm never going to know what radiation I was exposed to. I could go three years, five, ten—and I'll never know how much I absorbed until I get diagnosed with cancer. Like my father."

Ryan nodded. "You settle and there'll be no more investigation."

Kieran released his fingers and looked from Emily to her father and back again. "That's why I wouldn't take their money. Fifty thousand. Five million. It doesn't matter. I've got to know what I was exposed to."

In the silence that settled again over the room, Ryan looked at Emily—imploring her with his eyes to abandon this. She had to see how necessary it now was to withdraw. She had to convince Kieran to take a settlement. The logic of that decision was unassailable.

Staring at Emily facing Kieran, doubt arose in Ryan's mind. Why did Covington threaten to amend their investigation report with this new information as part of their settlement offer? Because that meant they already had the information before they made the offer, and were willing, in effect, to hide evidence that Kieran had caused the explosion. If they thought Kieran intentionally caused a near disaster out there, why would they ever agree to do that?

Ryan refused to dwell on it. Except more questions followed, like trickles through a cracking dam.

Why did Covington offer a settlement *at all*—then *renew* the offer amidst the threats at the elevator this morning? Especially right after Covington scored another blow with this blue-robed judge's ruling.

Say the words, Emily. Tell Kieran to settle.

And why was there no raw data on the radiation monitors in the report's appendix? If that data was so conclusive, why wasn't it included in a formal investigation report?

Finish this now.

Except she wasn't going to finish this. He watched as Emily reached out a hand to Kieran, resting it on the young man's downturned head.

Ryan's hope collapsed. A minute passed, maybe less, but to Ryan it felt like awakening from a long dream. He realized he was absently scanning the room, surveying the tornado of boxes from Pauline Strand's office, the rented photocopier, the office supplies that Melissa had assembled and they'd retrieved last week from his Seattle office, and the piles of case documents and transcripts they'd already begun to review. It felt like he was searching for something he'd lost.

Fifty days until trial—a little less to get experts to respond to this new amended report. His eyes came back to rest on Covington's investigation report and their own expert report from Dr. Nadine. Scrap paper now. A final urge gripped him: despite his promise to help, he would pack up and head to the car.

But there sat Kieran across the living room, believing so completely that he'd been exposed that he was willing to put his freedom on the line rather than take easy money to walk. Compared with Covington, claiming its exposure evidence was so strong, yet still offering fifty thousand dollars for this boy to go away.

Ryan reached for the Nadine report and headed upstairs. He'd taken it this far, he'd take it a little further. And they had a lot of work to do between now and the pretrial hearing.

CHAPTER 12

FORTY-SEVEN DAYS UNTIL TRIAL

Adam came running back down the Riverside Park hillside in the sweltering afternoon sun at a fast pace. He had to hurry. He shouldn't have gone for a run this afternoon at all; he really didn't have time for it. But if he hadn't, this evening his legs would be twitching, torturing him for his neglect like phantom limbs.

He was halfway down the slope when a runner passed him going up—a runner Adam had started noticing in the area the last couple of weeks. Slender and in his midforties, the man's running style was average—but he ran with a ferocity that resonated with Adam: the pumping arms, high driving knees, and unwavering, fiery eyes. They glowed with a focus that connected to the core of Adam—the unrelenting focus that Adam *always felt*, even when he longed to escape. With those eyes, the other runner could have been kin.

Then the man was past, heading uphill. Adam lengthened his stride as he reached the trail at the base of the hill, heading uptown toward Covington headquarters.

Twenty minutes later, in the basement locker room of the headquarters building, Adam shed his white running shorts and T-shirt, dropping them into a nylon bag. From the locker bearing his initials, he withdrew a fresh towel and strode toward the shower.

He'd received a phone report about the case hearing from King just before his run. As the Covington lawyer described it, they'd largely won the motion and retained their trial date. That was encouraging. Unfortunately, neither the Mullaney plaintiff nor the new attorneys struck King as ready to settle the case. At least not yet—not without more bruising.

Well, they'd have to consider how to land some fresh blows.

The lukewarm shower water coursed over Adam, so refreshing after the intensity of the hot, fast run. If there was any moment when the heated pace in his brain relented—when his thoughts briefly grew more placid and philosophic—it was now, after the catharsis of violently paced exercise.

This was an important time for him, Adam thought, a critical time even. "*When kings arise and walls fall and worlds are set afire,*" his father would say. More than eight months ago, they'd suffered the explosion and Adam had believed his world was going to crumble. He'd even begun to make plans for exit strategies, expecting Cameron Foote to fire him. All the dreams of the bonus attached to Project Wolffia had evaporated.

But Foote had surprised him, leaving him on as manager of the Project. And now the new replacement team was nearly assembled and singing optimistic appraisals from their predecessors' records that the Project was poised for success.

Adam rubbed the towel across his back as he left the shower. Inside his locker hung eight crisply starched white shirts, each still surrounded by plastic from the cleaners. He tore the sheeting off one and put it on. Then he raised his chin in the mirror hung from the locker door, carefully retying his green Brooks Brothers bow tie.

It was good that things were looking up once more. Still, deep fatigue lingered in the eyes that looked back at him. So many things had been necessary to fight for the project. Especially since the explosions. Adam asked himself again if he would have taken it on knowing all of the cost and risks involved.

Of course he would have, he answered the image. Because he'd *always* known the risks of the Project, known them before he was fully read into it. He'd known them that moment in Cameron Foote's recruitment interview when the VP had hinted to Adam of the bonus attached to the Project's success. After all, risk and reward were precisely correlated at Covington—and the bonus attached to Project Wolffia was staggering.

At that moment of truth in his interview, Adam had known better than to respond to Cameron Foote's words by reacting to the money. The potential number rang in his head like pealing church bells—but Adam was astute enough to know his audience. Foote wasn't looking for a man driven by avarice; he was searching for a common soul who shared his belief about what the Project could mean—for America and "the West." So Adam had silenced the bells and pressed Foote with questions about the political and social impact of Project Wolffia, never mentioning the money again. It had been an important test and he had passed.

But the risks for Adam in this project were very real—and Foote's refusal to delay its restart during the pendency of the lawsuit only made them greater still. That made this a "soul check time," another phrase his father would use, describing any pivotal moment where the choice was to back away from risk or to go all in.

Soul check time. The last time he'd heard the phrase, his father was imparting wisdom to Adam at his stock brokerage office on Manchester Street in Christchurch, giving a final speech to his youngest boy before packing him into a cab for the ride to the airport and America. Though surrounded by the warm, rich hues of teak furniture and framed prints of fox hunts and mallards taking flight, Adam had felt only the chill of the air-conditioned room and a readiness to be gone.

College in America. Under other circumstances, he might have been excited. But Adam knew he was headed into exile, not reward. His parents were shipping Adam off with a palpable sense of relief—relief that his father's smile and insider voice that last day couldn't conceal. The message was obvious: there would be no career for Adam in his father's brokerage office, alongside his two older brothers. He'd be denied that career because he didn't "fit in"—words he'd overheard his father say in the face of his mother's protests only the week before. He was a "strange boy," his father had said—to Adam's discerning ear, with perhaps the slightest hint of fear. America would "do him good," he had then declared with finality.

Soul check time. Standing in the shadows of the masculine office that final day, his father had grasped Adam's shoulder in a last imitation of fatherly affection. "In life, as in investing," he'd said, "there are times when you must decide whether to retreat or charge ahead. In those moments, be confident, be strong; but most of all, trust your soul." Then he'd smiled. "You'll do fine, son. Because when all else fails, you've got the unfailing compass of the Worth family heart."

Except, of course, he hadn't. Like his father's other pat phrases, Adam had heard the "Worth family heart" phrase used often at the dining room table. It seemed that Adam was expected to understand its meaning instinctively, because he never recalled a discussion defining its characteristics. And though he'd often tried, Adam had never conjured a definition that made sense to him.

Still, his observations of his family had rendered one conclusion with certainty—whatever the Worth family heart was, he didn't have it. And now he wasn't even sure he ever wanted it.

Adam slid on his suit jacket, affirming his appearance once more in the locker mirror. Except for a few uncomfortable holidays, he'd never been back for an extended period to New Zealand, nor had family members visited, and all communication had been listless and scarce. He wondered what his father thought of him now, this family outcast who lacked their commonly admired attributes. Were they surprised at the responsibilities Adam had assumed at Covington Nuclear? The position he'd attained?

Adam shook off the memories. Back to present measures. The best outcome—the safest outcome for the Project—was still a settlement of the Mullaney case. Based on King's assessment, they needed to raise the pressure on Mullaney and his attorneys for that to happen. Very well: he'd have to call his chief of security for the Project for help on that front.

In the meantime, until a settlement was assured, he had two other tasks to complete for the safety of the Project. He'd delayed them too long. Both tasks were distasteful, both carried risks. But both were best done this evening.

Which meant that he still had a long day ahead.

CHAPTER 13

Seated at the desk in the roof shack of PCL 237, Poppy was three hours into the shift, his head now splitting from ear to ear. He looked up from his paper work at young Jake Waters, checking the weapons rack across the room. The image of it reminded Poppy of Lew's obsession with his weapon, Beverly. Except Jake was no Lewis Vandervork. Lew'd been sharp enough to get most of his jokes.

The wall phone jangled. Jake lunged for it before Poppy could move.

"It's for you," the young man said after a moment, holding out the receiver.

Of course it's for me, Poppy thought, taking the phone. *You've been here for all of a month. You think the company president's checking up on how it's going so far?*

They were rotating new kids through here every couple of months since the explosion. Poppy missed Lewis; he was young too, but he'd already broken him in. Lewis was a talker, but he did his job. A fine marksman. And most important, he knew how to play gin. Poppy'd given up trying to teach any of these new ones. They burned out their eyes on screens all day. Anything that didn't glow, like a deck of cards, was something out of a museum. At least Lewis had made the effort to learn the game.

"Security checkpoint three, Poppy speaking," he said into the phone.

"Pops, it's Dave. I need you to come down to my office."

"Dave, we were just going to do our rounds. How about forty-five minutes?"

The voice that responded was uncharacteristically rough. "Now, Pops. Uh, I've got someone from Covington HR here also."

Human Resources? Maybe it was a response to his emails at last. "Okay—on my way."

It had to be about his emails. Maybe it was the interview. But why would Covington HR make a special trip to do this on Poppy's night shift; why wouldn't they just call him in?

He turned to the kid. "You're gonna have to do the rounds yourself."

Jake returned a look that was unsettlingly like Poppy's son the first time he was told he could take out the car alone. "Do it right, Jake," Poppy said sternly. "I'll be back in half an hour or so."

An internal staircase dropped from the roof to the first floor, emptying onto the front side corridor. Poppy took it now to the hallway where all the paper pushers and managers worked. He strode the length of the corridor, noticing again its sterile smell, fueled by the powerful HVAC motors and filters that held the building under negative pressure. He'd go nuts stuck in this place for a whole shift, Poppy thought. Like working in an oversized casket.

He reached the manager's office at the end of the hall, cleared his lungs of the new congestion gathering there, and stuck his head around the corner.

Dave Prior's eyes were furrowed tensely beneath brushy eyebrows set in a pale face. Seated next to him in the cramped office was a man younger than Prior and Poppy by a good thirty years. With a full head of red hair, he wore a green bow tie over a crisp white shirt. Yep, he had the look of Human Resources. Probably a grandkid of one of the folks who actually used to operate these plants.

The manager noticed him and gestured to enter. Poppy took a seat in the narrow space in front of Prior's desk. The HR rep stood and extended a hand, introducing himself as Adam Worth. Before sitting down again, the HR guy rounded Poppy's chair and shut the door behind them. Poppy's discomfort did an immediate uptick.

"Pops," the building manager launched in, "we've got something we've got to clear up. As you know, Covington's the general contractor at Hanford and has final authority over your company, Darter Security, on personnel matters. Well, something's come up. I'll let Adam here explain."

Adam smiled and held up a piece of paper. "Mr. Martin, this is your report from the incident at LB5 last fall."

This was a good start—they were finally going to talk about his statement, Poppy thought with satisfaction. Though he wondered who this kid was, talking with a slight accent. Australian maybe?

He nodded in response. "What about it?"

"It's about that gunshot you claim you heard."

"Heard and saw," Poppy said, caught off guard by the word *claim*. "At least I saw the weapon in Lewis's hand after he fired."

Adam's smile didn't waver as he went on like Poppy hadn't spoken. "Covington Nuclear would like you to withdraw your statement. Resubmit it and take out that reference."

Poppy was stunned. "I don't get it." He glanced at Dave, who was looking down at the desk.

Worth slid the signed statement across the desk. "As you know, we've completed the LB5 incident investigation. We just want to clean up this anomaly, keep the record straight."

Poppy shook his head; this couldn't be what they came here for. "You want to keep the record straight. That's fine. So why do you want me to change my report?"

"With all due respect, Mr. Martin, you didn't hear Lewis fire his weapon."

Poppy struggled to keep the heat out of his voice. "What are you talking about?" *Calm yourself, hon*, he could hear his wife saying. *Remember your blood pressure.*

Adam's face was as placid as a lake at sunset. "It didn't happen. We'd like you to remove the reference to avoid any embarrassment for you in the matter."

Poppy looked around the building manager's cramped office, trying to ignore the thunder in his chest. Maybe this kid just needed some clarification. He took a breath and started in again.

"Look, I heard what I heard," he said as calmly as he could muster. "It was right after I lost the manager at LB5 on the walkie-talkie. Before I fired my own weapon, I heard the shot as plain as on the range, then I looked across the roof and saw Lewis pointing his rifle toward the ground. It was obvious he'd discharged it."

The young man's face didn't produce a ripple. "You were mistaken. Your partner never touched his trigger. We've confirmed that in three separate interviews."

"You mean with Lewis?" Poppy asked.

Adam nodded.

So at least *they* had talked to Lewis. Poppy wanted to ask about his partner, but kept his mind on track. This had to be a mistake. He hesitated, visualizing Lewis in the roof shack in the dark of that evening, his eyes round with fear. But this left him no choice: he'd have to mention it.

"You know, I didn't want to say anything, but Lewis was pretty scared that night—we all were," Poppy said. "Maybe he's just confused. His weapon will tell you I'm right."

Adam shook his head. "We've checked that, of course. It confirms what I'm telling you."

Poppy looked over at Dave, still studying the desk surface.

"Mr. Martin, we're not saying you're lying," Adam went on solicitously, adjusting his bow tie automatically with one hand, like he was scratching an itch. "We're just saying you're mistaken, that's all. After all, you'd inhaled some of that smoke; you were coughing hard. You'd just been through the incident yourself. Your ears were probably ringing."

Smoke? To describe that hellish-looking plume? Like the word *incident* the kid had used twice now to describe the explosion. Poppy saw bureaucratic paint all over this.

He stared over the valley of Dave's desk at the bow-tied figure, feeling his pulse pound in his temples.

"Are you telling me to lie about what I saw?"

Dave shifted uncomfortably in his chair, though the HR rep didn't waiver. "I'm telling you the point is settled," Adam said.

As strong as Poppy'd felt his heart pounding, now it felt like it ought to stop. He stared in disbelief at the stolid HR rep, searching for the slightest hint the man knew this was wrong. Poppy felt like he was shouting into a canyon and waiting for an echo that wouldn't come.

"I won't do it," he said tightly.

Adam scrutinized Poppy for several seconds, no disappointment or anger appearing in his eyes. At last, he set the statement on the desk surface, along with a blank form.

"We'll give you a few days to revise the statement. You can return the amended one here to Mr. Prior."

Poppy's anger and confusion mounted. The gun wasn't the only thing he'd heard and seen that night. There were things he hadn't bothered to put in the statement, not wanting to get someone in trouble for what he'd assumed were screw-ups outside his responsibility.

"If you know everything that happened that night," Poppy muttered, "tell me why'd they shut off the lights."

For the first time, Adam's eyes widened a notch. "What do you mean?"

"I mean when the LB5 lights went out while I was on the roof."

The HR rep shrugged. "Oh that. I believe they've concluded

that they had a short. Things got shaken up during the incident. Took everything off line for a bit."

"Then if everything went off line, how'd they finally blow the take-cover sirens?"

Adam paused. "Separate breakers," he responded at last. "As you know, everything's redundant."

"Yeah, I know," Poppy replied. "Every building in Hanford has backups for every single circuit. So tell me again: why'd the lights go down?"

The HR rep didn't respond.

Poppy's voice grew hard. "You know what alpha radiation from plutonium can do when it's inside you?"

"Of course," Adam said, unflinching.

"You see it in a slide show down at headquarters, did you?"

Silence.

Poppy half rose out of his chair. "*So when are you boys at headquarters going to tell me what was in that cloud that night!*"

At this, Adam clasped Poppy in a long gaze. The rigid mask slid away, replaced by a stony smile—cold as an undertaker's condolence, Poppy thought. The HR rep turned to Dave.

"Mr. Prior, I'm afraid I'll have to ask you to release Mr. Martin for a few days. I don't believe he's been examined on a psychological level for the aftereffects of the incident. I was hoping to clear things up this evening, but his continued fixation on this particular point of the gunshot only highlights the need for in-depth testing. It may go so far as to impact his security clearance."

Dave looked stunned. "When?"

"Starting tonight. Indefinite leave. We'll make arrangements for the examinations."

Poppy didn't like small spaces, but he'd never had real claustrophobia before. It had to be what he was feeling now—like the walls of this box of an office were an arm's length apart and closing. He wanted to shout at this pale-faced man, younger than his eldest boy, who had to know that a psych exam could end what remained of his career here.

He needed to get away and clear his head, let his heart slow down before he came over the desk at this guy and made the psych exam a formality.

Without another word, Poppy stood, took the statement forms from the desk, and made the half step toward the closed door. There, he turned back, stifling the rancor in his voice with an enormous effort. "Know where I can find Lew?" Poppy asked. "He owes me twenty on our gin games."

Adam Worth smiled wanly, a counterfeit of friendliness Poppy'd seen in an IRS agent once. "I'm afraid I couldn't say."

Poppy glanced at Dave, who looked back in pained helplessness.

"Dave, my headache's gotten a whole lot worse," Poppy said. "I'm cutting out early. Besides," he finished, holding up the forms, "I've got some paper work to do."

Without awaiting a reply, Poppy turned and headed down the corridor toward the exit into the parking lot.

CHAPTER 14

Dr. Schutten awoke disoriented. It was very dark. Still, he expected to see *something* through the bedroom window shades—or the faint glow of the nightlight in the master bathroom.

Except now he remembered that this wasn't his bedroom. He felt the firm hospital mattress beneath his hips, the lassitude in his arms and legs that had to be from the painkillers. This was the room that had become a virtual cell, where he'd been sedated for pain for so many months that he'd nearly lost track of time.

What had woken him up?

"Dr. Schutten?"

He turned his head to the left. The outline of a man was just visible, seated across the room.

"Yes," he answered in a voice as dry as crumbling leaves.

"Dr. Schutten, I didn't turn on the light because I didn't want to startle you. Are you feeling well enough to talk?"

"I suppose," he rasped.

"Good. Doctor, I know we've covered this ground many times, but I've been asked to run a few questions by you once again."

"I've told you everything I remember."

"Well, I'm sure you have. But we're restarting Project Wolffia very soon. The new team leader couldn't come to interview you, but asked me to run a few questions by you once more. Is that alright?"

He felt so tired. "Alright," the doctor answered reluctantly. "Who is the new team leader?"

The voice hesitated. "Well, that's secure information just now. Can I proceed?"

"First, please answer me truthfully. I'm not recovering from the gunshot wound, am I."

"The physician assures us you'll be fine. There were . . . complications from the radiation you absorbed."

Liar. The sympathy in his voice was as thin as frost.

"Now may we continue, Doctor?"

Such nonsense. "Yes."

"Good. Dr. Schutten, in the last successful test at LB5 the night before the explosion, did the trigger configuration fully conform to the parameters contained in Dr. Fenton's notes?"

The trigger configuration. The explosion.

The memories of that night were always vivid—particularly when they crept up on him in the dark. Dr. Fenton was with Matthew making final adjustments to the trigger across the lab in the open testing chamber—the furthest point from the emergency exit. Annie was nearer, running monitoring protocols.

Annie had looked up at him with a look of inquiry—sweet, sweet Annie, she was always the most sensitive, in every way. Then he sensed what had inspired her glance, too: a subtle shift in pressure in a room where pressure was controlled with such precision—instantly followed by the sound of liquid rumbling, gurgling, descending from above. Then a deeper pressure change, like a sudden drop in an airplane—and Annie's eyes changing from questioning to stricken, as she called his name in a voice like shattering glass.

This wasn't a glove-box breach like the month before—that had been bad enough, but mostly contained and with enough warning to escape the lab. This drastic and uncontrolled pressure change was catastrophic, coming as it did when the test chamber was *still open*, with the chemical trigger set to respond to just such an event.

He shouted and rushed for the emergency exit door. It *was* him, wasn't it—shouting a warning? Could it have been Annie or Matthew or Dr. Fenton? He was nearly out of the interior door when the first enormous explosion struck; fumbling with the little-used exterior door when the second one knocked him down; and stumbling up the outside stairs when the third muffled roar came through both sets of shut doors, shaking the concrete beneath him. He'd taken two quick steps on the grass beyond the exit well of the staircase before the sledgehammer struck his back, followed by an echo of gunfire and the cold earth against his cheek.

Though he tried to fight it, panic now washed over him like released floodwaters. Dr. Schutten grasped the hospital bed with the hand of his uninjured side, easing his breathing to control it. Easy relaxed breaths—just as the nurse had instructed him. Again. Again.

The memory slowly faded and his mind began to clear.

When he finally opened his eyes once more, he saw that the figure hadn't moved in the darkness. No call for a nurse. No expression of concern.

"Can we proceed?" the man asked.

"I suppose," Dr. Schutten answered harshly.

The questions came now in quick succession, and he answered through a thin haze of lingering anxiety. At last, the voice took on a tone of finality.

"And you're sure the trigger configuration at the last successful test *fully conformed* to the prototype parameters contained in Dr. Fenton's notes?"

"Yes."

"Good." The figure finally stood.

Suddenly, Dr. Schutten didn't want to be alone. "The explosion was so unexpected," he said hurriedly. "The pressure spike could not have occurred at a worse time, especially with the test plutonium in the lab. And Dr. Fenton once warned that a major test failure might overtax the aging HVAC system at LB5—even blow out the smokestack filters. He feared radiation could be released inside and outside of the building. Was he right? Did that happen?"

The figure stopped moving. "Yes. The plutonium near the test chamber was burned. And the filters were blown. Radiation was released."

"Annie was such a sweet girl," Dr. Schutten rushed to continue. "She was married and had two small children. She hated the secrecy of the Project. They had me over to dinner once."

No response.

"I shouted, you know," Dr. Schutten added urgently. "Before I left the room. Could you tell that Annie and the others had been warned? Did they nearly escape?"

Pause. "Yes, Doctor," he said. "They nearly escaped."

The figure began moving once more.

"Wait," Dr. Schutten called out. "It's been so long. Was there a service for Annie and the others?"

"Yes," the man said. "There was a belated special memorial service. Just recently, actually. You weren't well enough to be there, so we didn't tell you about it. But perhaps we can arrange to get you out to their resting place soon."

Adam stopped outside the door to Dr. Schutten's suite and took a deep breath. His first meeting earlier tonight out on the reservation grounds with the security guard, Martin, had been tense enough. But these meetings with Dr. Schutten were far more draining, though in a different sort of way. Mostly it was the man's growing maudlin displays. Adam wondered how he would face his own death. With more dignity, he assured himself.

He picked up Dr. Schutten's medical records folder from

where he'd left it on the floor before entering the room. Yes, he'd read it correctly. The physician's most recent notes confirmed the gunshot wound was still not healing, the necrosis almost certainly due to radiation poisoning. It was obvious the scientist correctly sensed the seriousness of his condition. It was a matter of weeks or even days now.

Adam glanced at the treating physician's final chart note from his last visit, hinting that Dr. Schutten would have stood a greater chance of survival in the Sherman Hospital rather than here, in this jury-rigged suite at the Sherman Retirement Home. Adam shook his head angrily. The specialist wasn't being flown here weekly at a princely sum to render ethical judgments, much less record them: he was here to attempt to treat the man. If they could have taken Schutten to the hospital, they would have—but how was that possible given the secrecy of the Project?

If Adam wasn't already planning on eventually destroying these records, he'd have torn the physician's comments out on the spot.

At least Dr. Schutten was a solitary bachelor, enabling Adam to pay his household expenses without arousing suspicions these past months. Such a lonely life. There hadn't been a single personal inquiry about the man in all that time.

Adam smiled at the most important news of the night. Dr. Schutten's answers today confirmed once again how close they'd been last fall before the explosion. The minor test failure they'd managed to cover up in September had been no more than a stumble compared to the October surprise. The earlier test failure *had* caused the loss of four injured workers, forcing him to bring in the unvetted temporary replacements to keep up pretenses with the DOE. And it was the presence of those replacements during the October explosion that were such a source of headaches for Adam now.

But those headaches were, at last, under control. Adam glanced at his watch.

Three a.m. No wonder his eyelids felt like sandpaper.

He left the private suite, nodding to the security guard posted at the door, then walked down the hall to the lift. The floor numbers over the door tracked his descent as Adam pondered other details—whether to give the retirement home the sixty-day notice to release Covington's lease on Schutten's suite, whether his plan for Schutten's remains was appropriate. He supposed there was no rush on the notice. They were certainly under no budget constraints, and the cover story of a wealthy man seeking seclusion for his illness was standing up. As for Dr. Schutten's resting place, their choices were few.

The elevator reached the ground floor and he left past the front desk of the retirement home, unmanned at this late hour. The skeleton staff must have been making their rounds.

As he stepped through the exit into the cool evening air, Adam decided he'd send a coded report to Vice-President Foote about Dr. Schutten yet tonight. He liked the idea of Foote receiving an email from his project supervisor with a time stamp of four a.m.

And as a topper—as a cherry on the dish—he'd mention what a great day was approaching for America, laced with some veiled excitement. That should make the old man's morning.

CHAPTER 15

Ryan stood in the shadow of Princeton's Firestone Library, searching the adjacent plaza for a campus map. A student in shorts with a messenger bag over one shoulder passed his view.

"Excuse me," Ryan called out. "Can you tell me where Jadwin Hall is located?"

"Other end of campus," the boy said, gesturing past the tall gothic chapel on the far side of the plaza. "Down Washington Street by the football stadium."

Ryan nodded as the boy turned away.

Emily was pulling the fundamental tasks of trial preparation today: interviewing witnesses, preparing witness testimony, outlining a trial strategy. She had grudgingly accepted the notion that she had no time to do all that plus address the critical expert issue, and so had agreed to Ryan taking this meeting with Dr. Nadine.

It was Ryan who decided a face to face with the expert was worth the time and expense. With his greater experience, Ryan saw more clearly than Emily that this case rested on the fulcrum of a scientific explanation for the explosion—and Kieran's innocence in setting it off.

The "other end of campus" was a longer walk than he'd expected—and hotter, too. By the time Ryan reached Jadwin

Hall, the physics building next to the football stadium, he was not only sweating but fifteen minutes late for his appointment.

To his relief, the genial bearded man who greeted him at the door of Dr. Nadine's sixth-floor office looked unperturbed. He simply waved Ryan into a windowless office so tight there was little room for more than a desk and a visitor's chair.

Ryan had barely settled into his seat when the professor volunteered that he'd only just read the Covington amended report faxed days before. "And I'm afraid I haven't got good news. I tried calling before you made the trip, but you'd already left on your flight."

"What do you mean?" Ryan asked, worried.

The professor shrugged. "I mentioned to Pauline when I prepared my first report how extraordinary it was that Mr. Mullaney entered the mixing room in LB5 just as the tank was about to explode. Of course it's possible that your client had the misfortune to arrive at the precise moment the contents of Vat 17 had evaporated down to the point of reactivity. But I'd always been troubled by the coincidental timing of the event."

The professor picked up his copy of the amended report from Covington. "Covington's current explanation—that your client turned a valve below Vat 17 seconds before the explosion, bleeding off fluid and accelerating the explosion—frankly, makes more sense."

"Allegedly turned the valve," Ryan said.

The professor smiled. "Of course. I understood from your email that Mr. Mullaney denies turning the valve. But Covington's description of events makes more scientific sense than the alternative your client posits—with the extraordinary coincidence of timing."

"But," Ryan protested, "what about the fact that the tank was sweating and showing signs of significant pressure before my client even approached it. Doesn't that imply the timing *could* have been accidental?"

The professor's eyes were skeptical even before he spoke. "Well, I suppose it does—assuming, of course, that your client is accurately describing what he observed about Vat 17."

"And there's nothing in the data you reviewed to counter Covington's conclusion?"

The professor shook his head. "Nothing in the documents Pauline shared. If there's something more you have, I'd be glad to look at it."

Given how detached he'd been about this case, Ryan was surprised how much he dreaded calling Emily with this disappointing news.

Ryan turned to his last hope for this visit. "Pauline said you were working on proving radiation exposure as well."

The professor shrugged. "Not precisely. I told her that we could do blood studies to see if he showed exposure to radionuclides. Those have become quite refined these days. But I also told her it would cost tens of thousands of dollars."

"How many tens?"

"Fifty thousand dollars, I'd imagine."

"Can it still be done?" Ryan asked.

He shook his head. "I don't see how in the short time you have before trial."

Ryan quizzed the professor for another hour, trying unsuccessfully to nudge an acknowledgment of some weakness in Covington's position. It was finally clear there was no purpose in prolonging this.

Ryan stood—and Dr. Nadine with him.

"Of course I understand my opinion may not be terribly helpful now," the professor said. "But I'd move quickly for other expert assistance. I'm sure you appreciate that it might not prove so easy to find."

"I know that time is short," Ryan responded.

"Yes. But more than that." He pulled a thin book off a bookcase to his left—the size of a pamphlet. "This is a registry of nuclear scientists in the United States. If you page through it, you'll see that the vast majority of its limited members do plenty of work in the public sector—for projects supervised by the DOE or for the few large nuclear companies like Covington. Over the past thirty years, Covington Nuclear has had research contracts with dozens of universities. I'm aware of three Physics Department chairs endowed by Covington. This is a small research field, Ryan. There aren't a lot of physics departments or professors willing to risk burning bridges with the government or the nuclear industry for a few weeks of work with a plaintiff's lawyer in Sherman, Washington."

Ryan didn't want to hear this. "I've worked in products liability cases for a long time," he pressed back. "I've always been able to find expert help."

The professor shook his head with a look of sympathy. "Well, this is a small club. Let me give you an example from your case. Your predecessor, Pauline, located me by cold calling a dozen universities on the East Coast, starting in Boston and working her way south. She hadn't gotten past New York before emails from colleagues had made me aware of her trip. No one was *spying* on her, Mr. Hart. In fact academics are usually jealous of employment and research opportunities and keep them to themselves. But when Pauline made the rounds, the emails flew like warnings of an approaching plague."

Ryan's disbelief was becoming tinged with anger. "Then why'd you agree to render an opinion in the case?"

He shrugged. "I'm a curmudgeon, Mr. Hart. Ask my wife. And I already have my tenure. Besides, before Covington amended its report, it wasn't a particularly controversial opinion anyway."

Ryan turned to the door.

"There is one thing," Dr. Nadine said, stopping him. "It's more of an absence of information than a worthy argument."

Anything. "What's that?"

"Well, witnesses—including your client—described three

explosions. The original report and this amended one explain that by saying Vat 17's explosion must have triggered explosions of other chemicals residing in other tanks around the room."

"So?"

Dr. Nadine smiled again. "Well, it's a worthy hypothesis, but I've seen no records of the contents of other tanks to support it. I asked Pauline about that at one time, but she was very busy with other matters in the case and didn't get back to me. I didn't press, since the cause of the primary explosion seemed cut and dry, and supported Covington's liability. But, well, it is a curiosity that that loose end wasn't tied up by Covington in this amended report."

CHAPTER 16

"Yeah, Dad," Emily said. "All right . . . okay. I'll see you tomorrow afternoon then."

She hung up her cell, bitter at the news from her father's trip to Princeton. Despite holding him at his word about taking a limited role in Kieran's case—especially after that display in the courtroom—she now realized that part of her still expected him to pull a rabbit out of the hat. She didn't know if that was an expectation of a father or of an experienced trial lawyer. Either way, it was time to move on from the illusion.

Emily picked up her keys and left the Annex into the late afternoon sunlight, headed to her car at the curb. The last two weeks were a blur of preparing for the emergency motion, meetings with those witnesses they could interview without a subpoena, mapping out trial strategy, and completing the review of Pauline's papers. Kieran had helped with the latter task and they'd made progress, though the stacks looked only dented, not beaten.

But the differences between her experience preparing for two- to four-day criminal trials and this several-week monstrosity were growing more obvious by the hour.

Which made her ambivalent about her decision to take a break this evening. But she didn't want to refuse this invitation. Today was Kieran's birthday. His sister, Laura, had called to tell her that somebody had left a voice message for Kieran to fill in at the union softball game and she and her mother had insisted he go, since he'd missed the games all spring. Could Emily make it on short notice to join them for a small surprise party?

She started the car and did a U-turn to head across town. A break tonight was probably a great idea, she admitted. It would be good to think about anything except the case for an evening. And Emily had never really met Kieran's mother, Amanda—or spent much time with Laura these past few weeks.

Her route took her along Bikini Atoll Avenue. It was several blocks from Sherman's main street but still busy this Saturday afternoon. The drive allowed her time to think—and her thoughts turned to Kieran.

Working together with him the past two weeks had started to raze some of the barriers between them again. Especially after his acknowledgment last night that his silence since college was rooted in disappointment at how his life had stagnated while classmates went on to good jobs, travel, graduate school. It was an admission he'd delivered offhandedly, over a stack of documents. But she'd read the apology in his words.

She also admired his refusal to drop the case—even after she and her father made their doubts so clear. It reminded her of the boy she'd thought her closest friend in college: anchored in principle. He'd changed—his underlying seriousness was deeper than even during those tough times at the university. But he'd lost none of his kindness or empathy—illustrated by his devotion to moving his family away from Hanford.

Emily wondered how he saw her now. Did he see something in her that reminded him of who she was in college? Did he see anything worth renewing a friendship that neither of them chose to end in the first place?

Halfway across town, Emily slowed behind a Jeep at a stoplight. She glanced to her right. There, on the sidewalk, she recognized the solitary man walking with a calm, purposeful stride. It was Ted Pollock, appearing as he had at the ranch, with casual work clothes and his twin braids falling out from beneath the wide-brimmed hat. He was looking straight ahead, and didn't appear to have noticed her. A few steps more and he turned to enter the door of a single story, windowless Chinese restaurant.

Emily stared after him, immediately reminded of her discomfort at the man's unrelenting gaze the afternoon of the ride.

A horn sounded. Startled, Emily saw that the Jeep had disappeared and the light had changed. She slowly accelerated, looking each direction as she entered the intersection.

It was halfway down the block to her right, and far enough away that she couldn't be sure. But it looked like Kieran's Corolla, parked under the spreading leaves of a linden tree opposite the rear of the Chinese restaurant. She had only the briefest of views before she was past the intersection altogether.

Corollas weren't rare in Sherman any more than in Seattle. Besides, Kieran was at the softball game. But it was curious.

She set the thought aside and drove on.

Sitting on the couch in the living room, Poppy caught Suzy's glances from the kitchen. Forty-two years of marriage had given Poppy an advanced degree in knowing when his wife was worrying—and why. Right now, Suzy was wondering why he'd called in sick again last night, after swearing he was done staying home. She was also wondering why he'd stomped around the last thirty-six hours without saying a whole sentence—and trying to imagine what catastrophe could be so bad that he was hunched on the couch watching a Yankees-Angels game, when he hated both teams.

Poppy knew she'd let him stew as long as he needed, and he'd tell her when he was ready. That was great—except for how much this was bothering her. But he just couldn't bring himself to tell her that Covington was strong-arming him to change his statement about what happened at LB5. Especially since he was considering doing it.

He pushed himself off the couch and ambled into the kitchen. "You know, Suzy," he said, reaching for an apple on the kitchen counter, "I think I'll head over to the union softball game after all. I hear they've lost every weekend I've missed the past month."

She smiled. "I think that's a good idea, honey," she replied.

"You think Michael'd be there today?" he asked. Their oldest boy, Michael, had followed Poppy into the Guards Union and security work at Hanford.

Suzy shook her head. "No, you won't see him at the field. I know for a fact that he and Yvonne took Michael Jr. to the pool today."

He leaned over and kissed her on the neck. Then he went to his bedroom to change.

The drive to the ball field took Poppy down Sherman's main boulevard for a few blocks, then onto Oppenheimer Avenue. That road soon reached the end of town, weaving beneath cliffs leading to the riverfront and the River Park ball fields.

Poppy looked up at the sun-bleached bluffs. He'd lived around these hills his entire life, climbed most of them when he was a boy. Except for his time in the navy, he'd never lived anywhere else. But right now, he could be driving through a crater on Mars: that's how much he felt like a stranger in this place.

Four decades he'd worked at Hanford after the service and not once had he been treated this way. Making him change his statement—after failing to even interview him for the investigation report in the first place. Poppy's stomach knotted.

A twist in the road brought lightning flashes of sunlight reflecting off the Columbia River directly into Poppy's eyes. He winced in pain, pulled the brim of his cap lower, and reached into his breast pocket for his sunglasses.

He'd seen the article in the *Sherman Courier* a few days before that said Covington had released a new investigation report implying a stabilizing engineer on duty that night might have turned a valve and deliberately caused the explosion. That was hard to imagine: why would somebody do something like that? But it didn't change anything. All Poppy knew was that Covington was acting like no contractor before in its handling of this explosion. And somehow he'd gotten right in their cross-hairs as a result.

He couldn't complain to Darter Security—they wouldn't buck Covington and risk their subcontract, even if they thought he was getting treated poorly. He could complain to the union, but they were in wage negotiations with Covington and the subs and weren't likely to back him very aggressively. Besides, the union didn't have the clout it used to back in the day.

The headache was coming on again and Poppy's chest was filling up once more. He was just starting to wonder if softball was a lousy idea when the park came into view.

Poppy stopped the truck next to the field fence, grabbed his glove from the passenger seat, and walked slowly around the dug-out to the dusty third-base line. The Hanford Security Guards team was warming up on the field.

"Hey, Poppy," somebody shouted from the outfield. "Great to see you." The greeting was echoed across the diamond. Poppy felt his enthusiasm rising. He shrugged off the pain in his head and the thickening in his chest, pulled on his glove, and trotted out for warm-ups.

It was fun for a few minutes to be shagging balls again. Still, all the jokes from his teammates about how rusty he was—all the pats on the back as they ran by—didn't erase the worsening headache and growing roughness in his throat. By the time he jogged into the dugout for the game to start, Poppy turned down a chance to take first base. "I'll come in later," he shouted back at the offer.

Three innings passed. Poppy's eyes were strained—even with the sunglasses. He squinted across to the opponents' bench at their mixed team of engineers and radiologic techs, his frustration mounting.

The coughing was unavoidable now. The first was little more than clearing his throat, but a hacking cascade followed that left his chest aching and his eyes teared.

"Poppy. You okay?"

He rubbed his eyes and looked out on the field. Craig Westin, the security guards' union steward and softball team captain, was shouting from the pitcher's mound. Everyone from both teams was watching him.

Poppy waved Craig off. "Fine," he called out, then rubbed his chest at the pain from the effort.

He passed again on an invitation to play the next time the guards took to the field. As play resumed his thoughts meandered until he sensed the field quieting. He looked up.

The game had halted as everyone stared toward the other dugout. Another ballplayer had arrived: a young man, broad in the shoulders, with blond hair fringing his cap. Through his narrowed vision, Poppy watched as he stepped down into the opposing dugout by first base and sat at the end of the bench.

The ballplayers in the other dugout didn't greet their new teammate. Still, every eye on the field and on the other bench was staring at him like he'd been delivered from the sky.

The umpire called, "Play ball," and Craig turned slowly back to face the latest batter. On the third pitch he lined out to the shortstop for the third out.

The guards team filed back into the dugout. Westin sat next to Poppy, manhandling a water bottle and glaring toward the other bench where the newcomer still sat after his teammates took the field.

"What's going on, Craig?" Poppy asked. "Who's the new guy?"

Craig shook his head. "It's that kid—Kieran Mullaney," the shop steward said, his voice sharp-edged and low. "The one suing about the LB5 explosion last fall—and now it turns out he caused the explosion."

Poppy looked back at the far bench. So that was the tech in the Covington report. Several of Poppy's teammates were still looking in Kieran's direction as well.

"The kid was a newbie," Westin went on. "Had a little over a year on site before the explosion. Can't believe it—starting a lawsuit when he made it happen at LB5. Now he's got the guts to show up here."

The other team was still warming up for the inning as Westin set his water bottle down. He took the three steps out of the dugout, striding over to the third baseman, who turned at his approach. Craig spoke with him for several seconds before returning to the dugout.

Poppy watched the exchange with growing worry. As he came back to the dugout, Westin cornered several of his teammates at the other end of the bench for a whispered conference. After a moment, Craig came back and sat down again beside Poppy.

"He's just a kid, Craig," Poppy said. "Let it go."

The steward turned on him. "You were at LB5 that night, you went to the hospital. I can hear you've still got something going on in your lungs. You didn't start a lawsuit, did you? And you sure didn't pull any sabotage out on the grounds."

"No," Poppy said quietly.

Craig looked away. "Of course not."

As the security guards finished their turn at bat and took the field once more, Poppy surveyed the field through the fog of his headache. He watched as Craig shifted Hank Carisella from center field to first base. At six foot four and weighing over two-fifty, the former tackle on the Sherman football team was the biggest man in the guards' union. Craig then walked over to the first-base umpire—Terry Wolner from the machinists local—for a whispered discussion, before stepping back to the mound.

Poppy sank back into the cloud of his headache, closing his eyes and leaning his head back against the wall. He listened to the occasional chatter on the field, the thump of throws hitting leather. Then the field grew quiet again and he opened his eyes. Kieran was striding to the batter's box.

Poppy felt his stomach twist. He looked younger than Michael.

As the young man took practice swings, Poppy watched the guards' outfielders each shift up, as though to get a closer look at the specimen at the plate. In that same moment, Hank Carisella took a step in tight toward first base.

Craig eased a straight, fat pitch across home plate—big as a basketball, Poppy thought—and the boy stepped in and hit it sailing far out over the center fielder's head.

Kieran dropped his bat and sprinted toward first, but the center fielder was just jogging for the ball, more intent on looking across his shoulder toward first than fielding. Poppy watched, mystified, as the umpire turned *away* from the play—but he was the only one, because the rest of the fielders and the whole of the opposing dugout were fixed on the young man gathering speed down the chalked line toward first. As he approached the base, the mountain at first didn't step away, but forward—raising a shoulder and elbow and leaning in as though he were charging a ball carrier racing for a touchdown.

The thud was so loud that Poppy found himself standing as Kieran's feet went up and his body went down, as hard as if he'd hit a telephone pole. Then it was silent again—as quiet, Poppy thought, as that moment before the sirens went off that night on the roof of LB5. He glanced around: twenty other faces, including the umpire's, were joined with him in a silent chorus of stares at the boy writhing in the dirt, his hands cradling his face.

Kieran's moans were audible across the field. The kid was stupid coming out here this afternoon, Poppy told himself over the agony of the sound. Not a single one of the boy's teammates was coming to help him up. The hostility from his fellow workers had to be as thick as oil: how could he miss it? Poppy cursed the stubbornness or stupidity of the boy as he rolled to his knees with blood pouring from between the fingers over his face. He wanted to be angry, but what he really felt was guilt and a welling of shame so powerful it crowded away even the throb of his headache.

The boy was up on his feet now, with Hank Carisella stopped only a yard away and others around the field coming closer. Worse yet, the kid had dropped one bloody hand to his side and was staring at the first baseman, showing no signs of leaving.

Poppy came out of the dugout, jogging across the field as Carisella took another step toward the boy. He pushed past Craig Madsen and the catcher, approaching the kid from behind. The gap between the boy and Carisella was down to a foot when Poppy reached the kid's shoulder and squeezed between them.

"What're you doin', pops," a voice called out. Carisella pulled back half a step and stared down at him, perplexed.

Poppy stared back. "Keepin' a bunch of fools with *security clearance* from losing 'em by starting a brawl," he said, grabbing the boy's arm and pulling him out of the shrinking scrum.

Relief flooded Poppy when the boy let himself be dragged away. All the way to the parking lot, with the kid in tow, the tension from the field felt like a target centered on Poppy's back. He knew they wouldn't touch *him*—but he didn't want to test how far he'd go for this boy if they tried to drag him away.

Only once he'd started the truck and begun to drive, with the boy seated beside him, did Poppy feel himself begin to relax.

CHAPTER 17

They were already two miles away from the field when the boy spoke for the first time.

"I've gotta get my car."

"Get somebody to drive you back later," Poppy said. "It's not such a great idea to go back to the field right now."

He glanced at the boy. The nose was definitely broken, though the bleeding had slowed. "You've gotta get that straightened," Poppy said, nodding toward his face. "I'll take you to the ER."

"Later. I just want to go home," the boy answered.

Poppy shook his head. "Trust me. You want it straightened now. Before it starts to heal—and before you let folks at home get a look at it."

It was nearly an hour and a half at the hospital before they were back in the car, the boy holding an icepack to his face and muttering directions to his house. Poppy had kept his peace until now, but knew he had to ask. He opened his mouth—when Kieran spoke up again.

"Thanks for getting me out of there."

"Sure." He paused. "I'm Patrick Martin."

"Kieran Mullaney."

The ice broken, Poppy couldn't hold it back. "Did you do it?"

The boy looked at him from behind the pack. "You mean LB5? No."

Silence.

"If you thought I might've done it, why'd you get me out of there?" the boy asked.

Poppy thought about his own experiences the past month—how nothing about the explosion was making any sense. Maybe he believed the boy's denial just because Covington clearly didn't. Was that why he'd helped him? Then Poppy pictured his own son facing off against that crowd at the game and realized he didn't have a single answer to share.

"Listen," he said, ignoring the question, "why'd you go to the game? I mean, you must've known there'd be some hostility after what they printed in the paper."

Kieran shook his head. "I got a call from somebody on my team saying they were short. I thought it'd be okay."

Someone inviting him to the game? That made no sense. There wasn't a friendly face on the field from either team when the boy arrived.

They pulled up to a stop sign. Kieran raised his hand to point toward a spacious-looking rambler half a block down to the left. Before driving over to it, Poppy reached in the back of his cab, pulling out a spare work shirt he kept behind his seat and handing it to Kieran. Then he reached back again for a bottle of water.

"You've still got some blood on your neck and hands. Clean yourself up a bit. And the shirt's large, it ought to fit you."

Kieran looked at him cautiously, then moved to comply.

The boy was still sitting in the truck, looking down, pouring water on the edge of his own bloodied shirt to wipe his hands, when a white van pulled across the front of Poppy's truck, drawing to a stop in front of the boy's rambler. The side windows were opaque, denying Poppy a view of the driver as it passed.

Two men appeared from the far side of the van, both wearing jeans, ski masks, and work gloves. One carried a dark bag: he ran up the lawn, disappearing on the side of the boy's house. The other stayed close beside the rear fender of the van.

Poppy watched, stunned. The man at the rear of the van scanned the quiet neighborhood—his eyes coming to rest on Poppy's truck.

Within seconds, the other man came back around the house—the bag now crumpled and empty in his hands. With a final lingering stare at Poppy, the watcher at the rear of the van joined his partner, disappearing around the far side of the van. Poppy heard the thud of a sliding door.

"What the . . ." Kieran muttered, facing up now—then he was out the passenger door. Poppy threw open his own door and tried to chase after as the van screeched away from the curb, turning left at the next block.

Kieran followed the van at a sprint, but it was obvious he wasn't going to get close. Farther back, Poppy slowed his own jog, coughing from the effort. Then he turned back toward the side of the house where the man with the bag had disappeared.

The house was bordered by a long, narrow vegetable garden. Several vines twined around metal trellises, some bearing tiny tomatoes. Poppy glanced around.

A patch of black caught his eye, nestled against the concrete foundation of the house. Poppy leaned closer. It was three dead crows buried head first in the loamy soil, their black feathers splayed around them. Wrapped around one was a medallion attached to a chain.

Poppy was bewildered at the image, but he knew instantly what the medallion was: a standard-issue radiation dosimetry badge. He reached down to turn it over and see the coloration—green for safe and deepening hues of red for radiation.

He stood and stepped back. Even in the shade, the bright red of the badge's surface was as scarlet as a freshly opened wound.

"What is it?"

Poppy looked over his shoulder at Kieran just as the boy's eyes widened with recognition.

"I've got a Geiger counter in my truck," Poppy said. Without waiting for a response, Poppy jogged once more to retrieve the Eberline 530 counter from the tool compartment in the bed of his truck. It was an old model, a gift from his father when he'd retired in the early eighties. But Poppy'd kept it in good shape and always charged.

When Poppy returned, Kieran had been joined by two women: a younger one, maybe sixteen, and a woman nearer Kieran's age. Kieran had them both back up several yards. Not waiting for introductions, Poppy stepped in front with the gray box in one hand and the wand in the other, extending the wand in the direction of the carcasses.

The static was unbroken as he waved it back and forth, carefully moving closer and closer to the red medallion and the birds. At last he stood directly over them. The static still didn't waiver, humming with the low, steady clatter marking an absence of radiation. Poppy felt his shoulders relax.

"What's going on?" the older girl said—then the younger one shouted in alarm, "What happened to your face!"

Before Kieran could answer, Poppy held up a hand. "I've gotta go," he said.

The young man nodded. "Thanks again."

Why was all this happening, Poppy wondered as he walked slowly back to the truck. Especially now—so long after the explosion. Was it the article about the new Covington report in the *Courier*? Could it be because the case was in litigation?

But then in the wake of that article, why'd the kid get a call to attend a game where everybody there wanted to take his head off?

Poppy started the truck and turned left, passing Kieran and the two women talking at the side of the house. Then he took another left at the corner where the van had turned to leave, circling back to head west toward home.

It was sitting around the curve, just far enough up the block to be invisible to the house. For an instant he thought about stopping—or maybe turning around and telling Kieran. Instead, Poppy pressed the pedal to pass by as quickly as he could.

It was the white van, its occupants hidden behind the reflections off its darkened windows. And the reappearance of the van wasn't the only thing that startled Poppy.

As he raced past, he saw that the van had no license plates.

It was past midnight when Emily pulled her Hyundai into the Riverside ball-field parking lot with Kieran seated next to her. The dark shape of Kieran's lonely Corolla was visible across the lot, moonlight glinting off the back window.

The evening had been an emotional roller coaster. She'd been shocked at the vision of the dead crows and dosimetry badge at the side of the house, then seeing Kieran's battered face from the game. At her insistence, they'd taken pictures of the scene before cleaning it up—then all had agreed to tell Kieran's mother that he'd had an accident at the game. Amanda was already struggling with her own health issues; she didn't need this worry about her son. Kieran had also overridden Emily's protests and insisted they not call the police: that would have made it impossible to keep it secret from his mother.

But then, miraculously, the evening had morphed into something . . . better. Maybe it was the enforced silence about the traumatic events or the great desire she and Kieran clearly shared to escape it all for a while. But as time passed through the birthday dinner and opening gifts, there came a point where Emily realized that a whole hour had gone by in which she hadn't thought about the case or the softball game or her disappointment in her father or even the terrible symbols buried at the side of the house. As the night rolled on, she could almost imagine that Kieran and she were back at college, entertaining his visiting mother and sister, secure again in the comfort of their shared secrets and burdens.

They approached the car in the stillness until her lights shone on the driver's door. "Look." Kieran pointed.

It all came crashing back in on Emily again. Visible in the headlights, a front tire was flat. Her eyes rose to the front windshield. A spider web of cracks covered its surface.

Emily was shaking as she helped Kieran get the spare and jack out of the trunk—from the cold or the renewed anger and fear, she didn't know. He handed her a jacket out of the back of the Corolla, and she stood beside him in the chilly evening, surveying the wreckage of the already aging car as he changed the tire.

Mercifully, they'd slashed only the one tire. Twenty minutes later, Kieran finished, then stowed the flat and tools in the trunk.

"Can you see alright to drive home?" she asked as he turned to face her.

He nodded. "Well enough." As he spoke, she could see the weariness in his battered face in the full light of the Hyundai's car lights.

"I should've given you a gift for your birthday," she said, trying to conjure something to lift him. "I . . . I got too caught up in the lawyer-client thing in my head."

He shook his head. "Seriously, Emily, don't worry. I was just glad you came. It felt like old times."

Emily nodded her agreement, smiling to hide the ache at seeing him so discouraged again. Then, without thinking, she leaned in and kissed him on the cheek.

She pulled slowly away, and for an instant thought he might follow. But he didn't. Just fashioned a smile with his lip as big as a thumb and both eyes darkly rimmed. Emily nearly laughed.

She drove back to the Annex replaying the end of the evening in her mind. It was confusing and heady. That was because of the crows, she told herself. And the damaged car.

Except that was a lie. The celebration this evening had taken her back to before her mother died. Back when Emily still clung to hope she would recover and things could be as they had been.

Back when a part of her still secretly idolized her father, before that had faded and their stunted relationship had crystallized into something more distant and edged. Before Emily had defeated loneliness by plowing long hours into law school and career. Defeated it, or kept it at bay.

Her headlights closed in on the Winchester Bed and Breakfast and her father's car parked out front of the Annex. Emily pulled to the curb, turned off her car, and sat quietly in the dark.

She had to keep a handle on what she was starting to feel about Kieran, Emily told herself. He was a client now. This was her first private case; all she needed was for something to start and to get caught in an ethics violation. Then there was the promise to her father.

She got out of the car into the evening stillness. Who was she kidding, she thought, walking up the sidewalk to the Annex. She didn't care about the ethics of it. And she didn't care what her father would think. He hadn't had a voice in her life for a long time now.

For an instant, she recalled standing beside him at her mother's funeral. They'd been shoulder to shoulder, yet his presence hadn't shielded her from the pain. The image was so vivid that for a brief moment her chest ached.

It faded away and she returned to the present: standing on the Annex stoop in the tranquility of the desert night, wondering what had unearthed the memory.

Then she knew. As she opened the Annex door, she realized that the past few weeks working with Kieran were the first time she'd lived without an undercurrent of loss since the day her mother had died.

CHAPTER 18

The planc was descending into SeaTac International with Dr. Minh Trân gripping hard to the arms of his seat in the main cabin. There was another shock of turbulence, dropping the plane and lifting him weightless from his seat for agonizing seconds. Please, he prayed, get this plane to the ground. Soon.

He hated flying. He had ever since his first flight. That day, the helicopter had lurched and bounded as it skimmed treetops, his mother gripping him to her chest so tightly that he labored to breathe, while tracers weaved a pattern in the dusky sky and spent rounds pinged off the thin metal skin of the craft. He was four years old, escaping from his native home on one of the last helicopters out of Danang in 1975. The images and memories remained crystal fresh after all this time, though some he'd only understood years later. But one legacy of that flight required no interpretation—Minh had hated flying and would do so until the day he died.

The American Airlines Boeing 787 from Dallas mercifully thudded to a hard landing at SeaTac International Airport. Thankful to be down, Minh shouldered his carry-on and exited the plane toward the middle of the shuffling crowd of passengers moving from the aircraft and up the gangway.

He stepped into the concourse and immediately glanced at

the wall clock: 1:45 p.m. Good. There was a flight display a short walk away. He went there and scanned the digital array. There it was: flight 1209 from Philadelphia. On time; arriving at gate S1. Then he checked the connecting flights to Sherman Airport. Gate C5.

Dr. Trân resettled his shoulder bag and took the train to the S concourse. From there, he walked to gate S1 and found a chair in a food court nearby to await the arrival of the Philadelphia flight. He had plenty of time—over an hour—but he never left issues of timing to chance. He laid his bag on the ground, checked his watch one more time, and settled in to wait.

As he got off the plane from Philadelphia, Ryan wished he had time to head up to Seattle and check in with Melissa. Though they'd stayed in touch every few days by phone, and the office was largely dead anyway, he ought to at least glance at the mail. But there'd be no time for that today, with his connection to Sherman in less than an hour.

As he made his way to the trains to the C concourse, Ryan couldn't shake the countdown in his head: now five weeks until their expert reports were due. And with Dr. Nadine softening on his support for Kieran's case, he had to at least try to find somebody with more zeal as a potential replacement for the Princeton professor.

The fact was that the day was approaching when a good attorney—an objective attorney—would have "the talk" with Kieran, discussing the prospect of a humbling approach to Eric King to see if they could get a settlement back on the table—one that hopefully included Covington's agreement not to pursue Kieran as the perpetrator of the explosion.

Kieran might not want a settlement in *any* form, but it was better than a simple dismissal of his claims and possible criminal charges down the road.

This was why lawyers shouldn't represent friends, Ryan thought as he quickened his pace down the concourse. Because sometimes good attorneys had to stand back and punch their own clients in the nose with the bad news about what was best for them.

Ryan was bumped hard, throwing him off his stride.

"Oh, please forgive me. I'm very sorry."

"That's all right," Ryan said, turning. Behind him stood a man a head smaller than himself, wearing jeans and a wind-breaker. Prescription glasses were slung up to the line of his short-cropped hair. He was Asian—Vietnamese, he guessed.

"I'm just hurrying to my connection," the man said. "I'm worried I'll be late. And I confess, I'm a little nervous. I hate flying puddle jumpers."

"Me too," Ryan agreed.

"Where are you headed?" the man asked, matching Ryan's pace.

"Sherman."

The man shook his head. "Well, if we go down, at least I'll know someone on the flight."

"You're on the flight to Sherman?"

The man nodded without missing a stride. "Yes. Actually, I have a consulting job in Spokane. I just need to pick up a few things in Sherman before driving there."

"What kind of consulting do you do?" Ryan asked distractedly.

"Nuclear physics. Actually, my specialty is nuclear chemistry, but this particular job is a little more generic."

They stopped in front of a sliding door to await the train to Concourse C. "Nuclear chemistry?" Ryan repeated.

"Yes," the Vietnamese man responded, before glancing nervously at his watch again.

"Really. Nuclear chemistry."

"Yes."

The train came rolling in fast, then settled to a stop. A moment

149

later, the doors opened and Ryan followed the diminutive man into the car. The train lurched forward, then settled into a steady pace.

"I'm Ryan Hart," he said, extending a hand.

The man smiled. "Dr. Minh Trân."

"Do you have a card, Dr. Trân?"

The man looked surprised. "Yes." He reached into his coat pocket and pulled one out, handing it to Ryan.

"Do you do any legal consulting work, Doctor?"

"On occasion," the doctor said. The train was slowing now. "Concourse C," a female voice called over the intercom.

"But I've been terribly busy lately," the doctor finished.

They exited the car together. Ryan glanced around—until the doctor pointed to the arrow directing them to an escalator heading to gates C1 through 5. They were nearing gate 5 when the doctor reached into his hip pocket, pulling out a cell phone. He stared at the screen for a moment, then put it to his ear.

They parted there in the concourse. The plane to Sherman was small, but he didn't see where the doctor was seated—nor did he see him exit the plane. But Ryan was still thinking about the man as he retrieved his car in the lot and started the short drive to the Annex.

CHAPTER 19

THIRTY-EIGHT DAYS UNTIL TRIAL

"Pat, are you ever going to pass the potatoes?"

Poppy stirred, looking up at his wife's anxious eyes and the looks of everyone else around the dining room table. "Sorry, Suzy," he said, handing the heaped dish across to her.

Michael, to his right, was throwing his father worried glances. His son's wife, Yvonne, at the far end of the table, was working on her food, trying to ignore the awkwardness, while Megan, their youngest, seated next to Suzy, wasn't even trying to hide her concern.

Only five-year-old Michael Jr. paid no attention as he piled his own serving of potatoes into a shape like a mountain.

Poppy hated what he was doing to everybody. His worry and fretting had everyone tied in knots. "Hey," he started in with a forced grin, "that new guy I'm working with told me a story the other day. . . ." He only half understood the joke about Twitter, but it worked for now. Michael and Yvonne smiled and went back to their own food. Suzy nodded. Only Megan refused to be mollified.

Thirty years and more out at Hanford, and Poppy'd never seen them as worried about their dad as now. Megan was working in accounting at one of the Hanford subcontractors; Michael was three years into his own career as a Hanford guard

151

while taking night classes and talking about law school. They all understood Hanford and the risks associated with it. But they had no clue why their dad was moping and muttering like a homeless man, because he wasn't telling anybody what was bothering him, leaving them to guess and assume the worst. He couldn't keep this up.

The remainder of the meal, Poppy worked to stay engaged. It wasn't easy, and he wasn't completely successful. Later, as they finished stacking the dishes beside the kitchen sink full of steaming water, Megan came up behind him and gave him a hug. He grabbed her hands and squeezed.

"Say, Suzy," he said to his wife at the refrigerator. "It's still early enough. I think I'd like to go over and see dad at the home."

"Want company?" Megan asked, releasing him.

"Oh, you know, that's great," Poppy answered a little too quickly, "but maybe just this once I could use a few minutes alone with your grandpa."

He ached at the look of surprise in Megan's eyes. "That's fine, Dad," she answered.

He'd never turned down one of his kids wanting to visit their grandfather before, and it bothered him to do it now. "Next time," Poppy said with a smile.

"Go ahead," Suzy said to Poppy, eyeing him like a stranger in her kitchen. "They'll close soon."

Poppy was barely aware of the drive until he pulled into the Sherman Retirement Home parking lot. Endowed by Hanford contractors back in the seventies, it was cheap, well run, and the best alternative this side of Yakima or Spokane. So many Hanford veterans eventually settled into this place that the aging residents had nicknamed it the "fourth shift."

Poppy asked at the nurses' desk if they could bring Rodney Martin down to the lawn. Then he made his way through the community hall and past the double glass doors to the outside patio.

The evening was warm. That was good. So long as it was comfortable outside, his father preferred getting together here, where the sun glinted off the Columbia River at the end of a lawn mowed as close as a putting green. "Beats staring at the pill bottles in my room," his father would grunt.

It was a joke, not a complaint. Poppy marveled that a man once so powerful had kept his sense of humor, reduced at eighty-nine to a wheelchair rigged for oxygen. Still setting examples, he thought.

He found a porch chair facing the Columbia to watch the shifting shades of gray on its surface, trying to lose himself in the dusky comfort of its steady flow. Whatever it took to release the worry pains in his stomach and the blanket of exhaustion in his head.

What should he do about his statement about LB5?

All the years he'd worked there, and his father before him. His grandparents had witnessed the day in 1943 when engineers, bulldozers, and construction workers had gathered like ants along the banks of the river to start building the city of structures that would become the Hanford Nuclear Reservation. Poppy recalled, at age twelve, the day Rodney got permission from his bosses to drive his son onto the grounds to the ruins of the town of Hanford. It had been a sleepy place, his father said, a small farming community, before the residents were cleared out almost overnight to make way for the plutonium factory. They'd left behind as their lives' monuments only the empty shells of houses, stores, and a single school.

His father and he strode down the rutted road of Hanford's silent main street together, its abandoned buildings charred and darkened from years of DOE-sanctioned fire practice by outside communities. Stopping before the burned-out hulk of a house, Rodney stretched out his hand to touch blackened paint on the remains of its clapboard walls.

"This is the house where I was raised," Rodney explained

quietly, speaking as much to the home's remains as to Poppy at his side. "I left to fight in a war where I saw bombed-out villages from Normandy to the Ruhr. I was so grateful America was spared. Then I got back to Hanford and my own hometown was emptied forever. My parents hadn't even been allowed to tell your uncle and me before we got back. 'Security,' they said."

Everything his family had given to Hanford. Now this was what Hanford was giving back.

"Patrick?"

The voice was weak and breathy. Poppy planted a smile on his face before turning to the wheelchair and giving his father a hug.

"Hey, Dad."

"We're closing for visitors in forty-five minutes," the nurse behind the wheelchair said before leaving. Poppy thanked her, then pulled his chair closer to his dad.

Rodney's gaze was strong, but his eyes were at war with crooked fingers on spotted hands laced with dark veins. Thin gray strands of hair were combed across his head, and the skin of his face and neck was stretched and mottled. Poppy saw past it, picturing the man who'd once amazed co-workers by lifting 150-pound barrels fully overhead.

For ten minutes, a cooling breeze rolled up the slope from the river as he answered his father's questions about grandchildren and great grandchildren. It was a blessing that his father still remembered them all. Their talk turned briefly to Sherman: the winning streak for the local minor league baseball team, the new ballpark on the east side of town.

The conversation waned.

"So aren't you going to tell me what's troubling you, son?" his father broke into his thoughts.

"It's nothing," Poppy said. He'd come planning to ask for advice. But now, sitting in the reflection of an orange sunset floating over the Columbia, he saw only a frail man who'd earned his rest. "I think I should go."

His father shook his head slowly. "Don't lie to your old man. You've got no talent for it. You never did. Besides, you're wasting my time—and it's the thing I've got the least of."

Poppy smiled. He knew if he left now his dad would worry. "I've just been having some problems on the reservation. Getting some pressure from management I've never had before."

"I already know you were in that explosion last fall," his father said, his voice fading into a wheeze. After a moment, he went on. "Suzy told me right after and made me promise not to tell you I knew. Pretty silly, don't you think? Us both keeping the same secret from one another?"

Poppy smiled. "Yeah, Dad. But who's gonna argue with Suzy."

"She also tells me you've still got some health issues, son," his father said, after a long breath. "That right?"

"Some coughs. Headaches," Poppy answered, then added, "but I'm getting better."

His dad shook his head. "I told you, Patrick, you've always been a terrible liar. No sense trying to acquire the habit now. What's management trying to do to you?"

Poppy opened up, beginning with the explosion and ending with the confrontation with the HR rep and the demand that he change his statement. His father nodded as he spoke, gazing past Poppy's shoulder toward the river.

"I've never heard anyone complain about something like this on the res," Poppy finished.

His dad nodded. "Yeah, well, you might not hear about it even if it happened," he said. "You know there's not much tolerance for complaining. From workers or management. But for what it's worth, I've never heard anything like it either."

Poppy nodded, thinking about the incident at the ball field

with Kieran Mullaney and the dead crows that followed. He'd come this far. Poppy told the rest of the story.

He thought he'd be shocked. Instead, Rodney just shook his head. "Didn't think they did that kind of thing anymore."

"What kind of thing, Dad?"

His father adjusted himself in his seat a little. "Back in my day, the dead crows were a warning."

"It's happened before?" Poppy asked, stunned.

His father nodded. "Yes."

In all of his Hanford stories, his father had never mentioned this before. "Well, I guess it's a warning now, too," Poppy said. "They're trying to intimidate—"

"No," his father objected, shaking his head. "Not intimidate. Past that. Warn. In the sixties, some of the guys got into the anti-war movement. Then some went beyond and got anti-nuclear. The stupidest ones got real loud about it. Finally, somebody in the union told them to tone it down. When that didn't work, a core group sent the protestors the black crows. Head down in the earth meant they were silenced. It was supposed to be the final warning. Before the workers dealt with their own. You can figure what that meant—working in a plutonium factory."

The evening breeze was growing cooler as night approached, and Poppy contemplated what that meant for Kieran Mullaney. "So what happened in the end," he asked.

His father shook his head. "Most got quiet. A few quit. There was a rumor about one guy who didn't listen and found out they were serious. I heard he got dosed—but people get dosed out there without anybody doing it to them. I never knew if it was really connected to the crows."

His father looked bone weary now. Poppy was uncertain again whether he should have had this conversation tonight.

The last sunlight had faded from the western sky, and stars had not yet filled the void. Thinking about his father's words,

Poppy traced the trajectory of a shooting star that blazed across the sky before disappearing just above the horizon.

The nurse arrived. "It's time to go, Mr. Hart."

Both Poppy and his father answered with an okay, making Rodney smile weakly a final time.

"Look, son," his father said to Poppy before she could take him away. "When you reach my age, you sit here waiting for the Lord to take you, and you look back on your life. It's all you've still got—and you count yourself lucky if you can do *that*. Well, you've had a good run at Hanford. It's supported your family, and you've stayed safe until now. They've treated you right and you've been the good soldier. But don't let this new company— this Covington Nuclear—change the view you'll have from my chair someday. Don't let 'em make you do something you'll sit here and regret."

As she wheeled him away, Poppy could already see his father's head resting on his chest.

CHAPTER 20

Emily sipped her coffee, looking across the table at Taylor Christensen, holding his second bottle of Summit Ale. The bulky man nestled the bottle under his moustache and took another long drink.

Taylor had suggested meeting here at the Lightning Ale House after his shift. She didn't mind. It was just that she'd expected a breakfast meeting, not a talk over beers at nine in the morning.

Taylor's eyes were red—though, in fairness, he was coming off an overnight shift. More surprising was that he wasn't anything like Emily had expected. Both too young and too nervous, he didn't seem like the stolid, steady Hanford veteran who'd been Kieran's supervisor for nearly two years.

"I appreciate the meeting," Emily said cautiously.

"Sure," Taylor answered. She noticed his eyes do another sweep of the room from their corner table.

"I saw that Pauline Strand deposed you early on about LB5," Emily went on. "I'm meeting with witnesses who we'll need to testify at Kieran's trial to see if they remember anything they didn't say in their depositions."

Emily felt a wave of discomfort as Taylor's eyes looked her over like he was wondering if she was wearing a wire. "What kind of things?" he asked.

"Well, anything about the explosion that night. What you saw. What you know that might give a clue on how it started."

Most of the men and women Emily represented at the Seattle Public Defender's office were guilty. What distinguished them was how they covered that guilt—denials; occasional remorse; an acknowledgment of guilt, but with an explanation.

Taylor looked like the last of these. Either that or he was scared. Neither possibility made sense to Emily.

"You represent Kieran," Taylor said—though she'd told him that in the phone call when she set up this meeting, and again only moments before.

"Yes."

"So anything I say or show you, you'll keep a secret," Taylor said.

Emily shook her head carefully. "No. You're not a client. I'll have to reveal anything you share with me with the other side."

Taylor's eyes grew more veiled as he took another drink.

"But, depending on what it is," Emily hastened to add, "I may be able to keep your identity to myself—if it's evidence I can confirm from another source."

That seemed more satisfying to Taylor. She could see him thinking. "Kieran's a pretty good kid," Taylor finally said. Emily thought there was a slight slur in his speech now. Two beers in a man of his size made that seem unlikely—but maybe he'd had more before she arrived.

The big man reached into his pocket and pulled out a double-folded piece of paper, handing it to Emily.

The document was a photocopy, slightly askew, with the title cropped. Made in haste, she thought. The left side of the page listed years stretching from 1990 to 2012, while the top was headed with columns numbered one to eighteen. The boxes created by this matrix each contained chemical symbols, alongside percentages.

The eighteen columns matched the number of vats in the

LB5 mixing room, Emily thought. It looked like testing data for containers—identifying their chemical contents and the percentages of each chemical over time. She asked if that was what the paper showed. He nodded.

"Yeah. For room 365 in LB5."

Emily's eyes widened. "Where'd you get it?"

"From Covington headquarters. As a stabilizing tech, I had access to the sampling archives. I went right there from the hospital the morning after the explosion, before Covington's inspectors came in. I wanted to see if could find anything about what caused the explosion."

"Do they know you took it?"

He shook his head. "Don't think so. My security clearance got me through the door into the archives, but I didn't sign the log-in sheet. I was in a hurry, hadn't even been home yet."

Emily's mind was racing, recalling Dr. Nadine's comments to her father about this data.

"I don't know if it's helpful," Taylor added. "But you can have it. Just keep my name out of it."

"You didn't mention this in your deposition," she said.

"Yeah. I didn't tell the investigators or Covington's attorney about it either when they grilled me. I thought it might land me in trouble given the way Covington was circling the wagons about the explosion."

"Why now?"

Taylor finished the bottle with a long final drink, his eyes growing hot. "Because I saw what they did to Kieran at the softball game."

Emily saw Taylor turn and try to flag the waitress, who was hustling to deliver breakfast meals to the few patrons in the place. She wondered how long Taylor's breakfasts had looked like this one.

"What do you mean, 'circling the wagons'?" she asked.

He shrugged, looking unconcerned in an unconvincing way.

"Things are touchy out there. Covington's lawyer interviewed me three times in the last nine months. He told me not to talk about LB5—but after the third time, did he think I'd need him to say that out loud? And then I got a call from some guy in the HR Department a little while ago reminding me of the same thing. He had the guts to hint that my hours might get cut in the future because of a slowdown out there. Who'd he think he was kidding? I got the warning."

The waitress arrived with the third bottle. Anxious to call her father, Emily reached into her purse and put a twenty-dollar bill on the table.

"I'll get breakf— this," she said.

Taylor raised the new bottle in a salute as she stood to leave.

Ryan was seated on the couch, his cell phone in one hand, a legal pad in the other. Between calls, he was thinking of how weary he'd grown of his daily armistice with Emily. As she'd left this morning, he'd suggested she could have doubled for Taylor Swift in a *Law and Order* episode. The smile he'd hoped for had the half-life of a puff of smoke.

His respect for Emily's capacity for work was growing: she was throwing herself into trial preparation like a gladiator. He might have admired her intensity more if he didn't fear her zeal was proportionate to her growing feelings for Kieran. Emily spent most of her time with Kieran now. Ate most of her meals with him. It also hadn't escaped Ryan's attention that she took more care about clothes and makeup when Kieran was coming to help at the Annex.

Ryan returned to his task. Since the Princeton trip, Emily had left him to keep working on lining up expert testimony. The list on his legal pad was phone numbers culled from a copy of the nuclear registry Dr. Nadine had shown him. He'd started with forty-seven potential nuclear scientists—then shortened that list to twelve who lacked any obvious affiliations with the DOE, Covington, or other nuclear industry companies. Eight of those had already declined to help, based on the short notice. That left two men and one woman who'd promised to think it over and check their schedules—though only one had shown real interest. Dr. Virgil Strong of USC. The guy's credentials were top notch; Ryan was keeping his fingers crossed.

He reached into his shirt pocket and pulled out the card nested there. And then there was Dr. Trân. Ryan had checked him on the Internet. Also great credentials. No known affiliations with industry. If anything, he was even more perfect than Strong.

Way too perfect. Even at Sherman Airport, what were the chances of literally running into a nuclear chemist. A man versed in the perfect discipline for their needs arriving just as they were desperate for a replacement scientist. It would be a serious stunt for King or Covington to thrust a decoy expert into their path. But after what he'd seen in Judge Renway's courtroom, Ryan wasn't sure what limits King or his masters would respect.

No. If there was any chance that Dr. Trân could be a plant, Ryan wasn't desperate enough yet to take a chance that the man might drain his bank account and then produce a useless opinion—or worse, produce a great opinion, only to recant or collapse on the stand.

He glanced at the other notepad sitting on the coffee table, recording his Internet research on labs able to perform blood testing to detect radiation exposure. Ryan was waiting on half a dozen callbacks from that list with prices and availability. There had to be some alternative to Professor Nadine's quote of fifty thousand dollars.

His cell phone buzzed in his hand. It was Emily.

"Yes."

"Dad," Emily said, her voice keyed up. "Remember you told me that Dr. Nadine said he hadn't seen any backup data from the other mixing room vats? Data that would show if they could have caused the second and third explosions?"

"Yes."

"I think I've got something." In a fast tempo, Emily described her meeting with Taylor Christensen. "I'm bringing the sheet home right now."

Hard work made breaks, Ryan thought—and Emily was working like two lawyers now. "That's great," he said.

As soon as they ended the call, Ryan started to punch in Dr. Nadine's number. He needed to get this to their expert immediately and schedule a conference call to discuss it.

"Hello?" a voice answered after several rings.

"Dr. Nadine? It's Ryan Hart."

"Oh. Mr. Hart." The professor sounded surprised.

"Listen, I'm calling because we found a new document that might shed light on the contents of the other vats in the mixing room. You remember raising that issue in your office when I was there?"

"I haven't heard from you since our meeting, Mr. Hart."

"I know," Ryan answered. "We've been very busy getting up to speed in the case. But about the other vats . . ."

"After our conversation, I assumed that you'd decided to get other assistance."

Ryan squeezed the phone. "I never said that."

"Well, I'm sorry, but I thought you did. I'm afraid I've taken on a new engagement. I'm leaving for Berlin this evening and I'll be gone for the rest of the summer. Perhaps I should have confirmed my impression from our meeting, but I was convinced you'd made up your mind to hire someone else."

Ryan hadn't let Nadine go yet to avoid this very possibility: getting caught without a new person to take this man's place. "Professor, you can't do that. We've got no replacement for you, and this new information could be helpful."

Silence. "I'm very sorry."

Ryan's tone tightened. "We've got a contract. You've been paid for your—"

"Actually, Mr. Hart, if you'll check with Ms. Strand, you'll find that I *haven't* been paid for my services, beyond an initial thousand dollar retainer last fall. Ms. Strand repeatedly pled poverty. Under the circumstances, I'll have my department return the retainer. Good luck."

The line went dead.

Emily was going to be sick about this, he thought. As sick as Ryan was feeling already.

He raised the phone again and pressed another number. Moments later he reached a voicemail. As he waited for the signal to leave his message, his eyes fell once again on Dr. Trân's card. He picked it up just as the line beeped.

"Hello. Dr. Strong? Ryan Hart. I spoke with you earlier in the week about expert help in a case in Sherman, Washington. It's become urgent that I get an immediate response. . . ."

CHAPTER 21

THIRTY-FIVE DAYS UNTIL TRIAL

"That doesn't make any sense." Kieran shook his head. "That's not the Taylor Christensen I know."

The swelling was nearly gone from Kieran's nose and eyes, Emily saw. "No signs of nerves? That he's been drinking too much?"

"You know I'm only working half time now," Kieran said, shaking his head. "Maybe he's a little short with me. More tense. But given how everybody else treats me, I assumed his silence was support."

Emily held up the paper Taylor had given her. "Well, this would suggest it is."

Kieran nodded. "Any hopeful word on the experts from your dad?"

"Nope," Emily said. Kieran was watching her closely. When she didn't say more, he leaned closer.

"You planning on giving your hotshot lawyer dad a break any time soon?" he asked.

"I am giving him a break," she responded, looking away. "I'm giving him his wish. A little back-up work on your case and nothing more."

Kieran nudged her gently. "He's also writing a boatload of checks."

"He's got plenty," she answered tersely.

"Yeah, but he's still parting with them," Kieran responded quickly.

"He didn't want to take your case, remember?"

Kieran shrugged. "But he did. Look, Emily, you know how much I appreciate what you're doing—and how much it means to me. But I also appreciate what he's doing."

Emily didn't respond.

"How bad was he when your mother was sick?" Kieran pressed.

Emily stared at Kieran for a moment, as the question stirred coals of old fires in her. "Near the end of my first semester of law school," she began, "the night before my first final, I was freaking out. I wanted to call my mother to talk, but with everything she was going through, I couldn't trouble her with it. So I called my dad—something I never did. I reached him on his cell in Mexico. He'd taken Mom there. Hadn't said a word to me; just wisked her off over the weekend.

"I asked him what he was doing. He was chasing after a miracle cure in Guadalupe or someplace like that. I don't remember what. My dad, the sophisticated lawyer. Mom didn't have the strength or heart to tell him that it was over. She was content and at peace. These trips he put her through, they weren't about Mom. They were about what Dad couldn't accept, what he wanted. Like always. I never did tell him why I'd called and he didn't ask."

Kieran lowered his voice, speaking softly. "Can you really blame him, Ems?" he said at last.

She looked away and picked up a stack of papers. "It's not about blame," she said. "It's about choices. He always chose what he needed. And he chose not to be around."

Until now, a voice inside her corrected. He's here now. He hadn't completely disappeared on her this time. Not yet.

It wasn't a point she was willing to concede at the moment.

She silenced the voice and looked back at Kieran. "Let's get back to the case," she said.

Poppy was up early, especially for a morning after a night shift. By noon he was dressed and ready to head out the door.

Three hours should be enough time for Michael and him to get down to their favorite hunting grounds south of Sherman for a short hike. The mule deer season wasn't for months, but Michael had called the night before asking if he wanted to hike the area.

Poppy had jumped at the invitation. Not only did he need this kind of break, but it had been years since Michael'd had the time to hike or hunt with his old man. Poppy would do the hike, then truck over for a quick visit with his dad at the retirement home before tonight's late shift. He went to his dresser and grabbed his keys and a bag of clothes he'd assembled for work.

As he lifted the bag, papers slid off the dresser from underneath, floating to the floor.

Poppy knelt and picked them up. They were his original statement and the replacement form from the HR guy—Adam Worth. Poppy stood for a moment looking at them in the late morning light coming through the bedroom window.

He'd told himself he'd take care of this, one way or the other. Still, here the papers sat. Weeks had passed, and he hadn't even told Suzy yet about the whole mess.

He stared at the papers for a long moment. Then he folded the pages and slid them into his pocket.

Twenty minutes later, he was driving with Michael beside him, pulling onto Highway 16 heading south out of town. It was ten miles to the milestone of the Yellow River, then another twenty miles through dry country until the highway rose into hills covered with a patchwork of pine and larch.

All of this area was familiar to Poppy. He'd hiked and hunted it with his father, then with his own children. As they gained elevation, Poppy could see for miles to the south and east. The afternoon sun highlighted the stark contrasts in the surrounding landscape—green trees and brown hills; further east, the orange outcroppings of the desert.

They pulled over to park at the wayside rest that served as the trailhead and soon were hiking, with Poppy leading at a brisk pace. "See if you can keep up, Mike," he called over his shoulder.

Michael had no trouble at all. Within twenty minutes, Poppy felt his chest growing thick and his pace slowing. Michael came up near his shoulder.

"You okay, Dad?"

Poppy nodded, hating the question. "Fine."

The trail rose for a few miles until they reached a rock outcropping, like a finger pointed west toward the horizon. It was Poppy's favorite place on the hike—and a welcome stop for a rest. Leaning against a pine, he surveyed the view in each direction, listening to a silence so deep his ears strained for a challenging sound.

A singular conviction passed through him: he loved this land. He would never leave it.

Poppy glanced to Michael, kneeling a few yards in front of him and taking in the same view. His son was starting a career at Hanford. Maybe he'd go to law school. Even if he did, there was a good chance that Sherman would be his eventual home. Last summer, Poppy was content and even proud that his boy's upbringing might lead him to spend his own life here, raising his family where he'd been raised.

But now Poppy wondered if that was what he wanted for his only son—or his daughter. And Michael Junior. Everything had changed so quickly in the past nine months. Did he really want them to spend their lives in Sherman?

He thought about the papers back in the truck. Poppy hadn't told his wife or the rest of the family what was going on because he had a good idea how they'd react. Suzy'd tell him to tell Covington to shove it. Michael would echo that, then insist his dad go to the guards' union. Megan, his firebrand, would just threaten to torch the place herself.

Except it wasn't as simple as any of those notions. Filing a grievance or telling the bow-tied HR guy at Covington that he wouldn't change his statement could be satisfying for a day or two. Then it might cost Poppy his job, with the firepower Covington could bring to bear—just when they were helping Michael with some of his son's medical issues and trying to save for retirement.

Still, keeping this secret from his family any longer wasn't fair to anyone. It was clear that his silence was already affecting them: Suzy and Megan were openly worried and it was obvious Michael had suggested this hike today out of worry about his old man.

Besides, didn't they deserve to know how Hanford was changing?

He took a deep breath and started telling Michael the story. It was all new to his son. He'd heard about the softball game and his dad's role in it, of course: it had been all around the union the next day. But Michael had chalked up his dad's intervention as a simple act of kindness. Now, hearing the context, Michael's eyes grew glassy with anger.

As Poppy'd predicted, Michael pressed him hard to go to the union. He let him make his case, then shook his head.

"Son, I can't do that. Covington will challenge my story and yank my clearance. I don't know if I can win that fight."

"Then *I'll* go to the union."

Poppy shook his head more vehemently. "This is my battle. Covington might already be keeping an eye on you as my son. The last thing I want is to get you and your family dragged into this—especially if I refuse to change my statement."

He'd couched his decision as still unmade. Poppy looked

into his boy's eyes and knew that there was nothing left to decide. Now that he'd told Michael the truth, there was no way he could face his boy if he backed down from Covington and altered the statement.

"Mike," Poppy said, "you've got to promise no matter what happens the next few months—no matter how much you want to help out—you'll stay out of this."

"I can't do that, Dad."

"Then you make this harder, not easier."

The whole hike back to the truck and drive to Sherman, Poppy worked to exact the promise he needed. He received it as he dropped Michael off at his house.

Poppy pulled away and drove a few blocks more before pulling over. There he closed his eyes and whispered a simple prayer.

He opened his eyes again, hoping for confirmation about his decision to act. Nothing came to him. No flash or prophetic whisper. All he felt was twisted and spun around—and a little scared. Like he had for weeks.

But then it'd never worked that way, Poppy told himself. He knew what he had to do.

On the road again, Poppy drove directly to the Covington Nuclear building, just a block from the federal and state courthouses. Poppy parked on the street and made his way to the front entrance.

It was near closing time, but the guard directed him to the Human Resources Department on the second floor. Poppy walked the crowded halls, asking for more directions until he found the right door.

The HR Department was about what he expected: a large open room with offices surrounding it, stuffed with cubicles. A pretty young woman passing by stopped and asked if she could help. Poppy held out the report in his hand.

"Could you give this to Adam Worth, please?"

"Of course," she said with a smile.

Poppy wondered, as he joined the flow of Covington employees working their way to the building exit, what Worth would do when he saw the unchanged copy of his original statement with *The Truth* written across the bottom.

He ran some errands after that, moving from store to store half aware before heading to the retirement home. As he walked the aisles, Poppy had a feeling of discomfort that he couldn't place, something different than the fear of retaliation or the worry about what he'd been exposed to at LB5.

It was nearing dark when he finally pulled the truck into the retirement home parking lot. As he turned the key and the engine grew quiet, he finally realized the source of his discomfort.

For the first time since he'd begun his career at Hanford decades ago, here in the heart of his hometown of Sherman, he felt utterly alone.

CHAPTER 22

"Explain that to me again," Adam Worth said, standing in the empty lobby of the Sherman Retirement Home, where he'd stopped when his phone buzzed.

Eric King's sigh came over the cell phone. "All right. Kieran Mullaney's attorneys don't have to get us their final expert reports for a few more weeks. But under the rules, they *do* have to update us on the identity of any new experts they intend to use. This afternoon we received the names of two new experts that Emily Hart and her father are substituting for Dr. Nadine, their Princeton expert."

"Give me the names."

"Dr. Virgil Strong out of USC and a Dr. Minh Trân. Looks like Trân's a consultant type, unaffiliated with any university."

"So they're using two experts now, to replace their Princeton man?"

"Yes, or they could be identifying both but only planning on using one. Hedging their bets until they see their reports."

Only one of these new names was familiar to Adam. The prospect of being in the dark about a potential expert in the case disturbed him.

"Keep me apprised if you hear anything more," Adam said, and turned off the call.

This news from King came on the heels of Patrick Martin's

melodramatic delivery that afternoon of his unaltered original statement. Sixty-three years old, with no chance of finding other employment approaching Hanford's pay scale, and Martin was risking his job over this. It was a gesture Adam hadn't expected. But if this security guard thought he was bluffing, he'd know better soon.

He wondered if his father would claim to admire such a man.

Adam pulled up his iPhone contact list and punched the name.

"This is Dr. Janniston," he heard the line answered.

"Doctor, this is Adam Worth. Do you recall me alerting you that we might need an exhaustive psych exam of one of the victims of the October sixteenth explosion?"

"Yes."

"Well, we'll need to move forward on it. As soon as possible."

"That will be difficult. Such an exam could take days—weeks, possibly."

"This is imperative, Doctor. And I'd like a face-to-face with you about this man before you meet with him."

There was a grunt of shock. "I'd have to move things around. I might be able to get up there in a week and a half—though there would be a *significant* cost. . . ."

"That's not an issue, Dr. Janniston. We need a *very* complete evaluation, and quickly. Very thorough. Frankly, we're concerned about the man's mental stability in view of paranoid statements he's been making."

"Alright. What is the man's name?"

"Patrick Martin."

"I'll email you my travel arrangements."

Adam ended the call. Good. That was now in the works.

He pocketed his phone and continued on his way to the elevator. At the end of the fourth-floor hallway, the security guard at Dr. Schutten's suite acknowledged him as Adam approached.

"They're all inside," the man said.

Adam nodded and entered, closing the door behind him.

He had never been in a closed room so soon after someone had died. The sense of death was palpable here—more than just the somber mien of the treating doctor and his nurse as they packed their equipment and monitors, greater than the silence of the three other guards in the room awaiting Adam's arrival. There was a personality to death, Adam mused. This had substance.

Schutten's body was already enclosed in a lead-lined body bag. Adam took the treating physician into a corner and spoke quietly with him for a few moments. The doctor reacted with awe—just as Adam had hoped—when he handed him a check for twice the doctor's charges. Good, Adam thought. He knew now he'd have no debate about retaining the medical records or the importance of the confidentiality agreement the doctor and nurse had already signed.

With a final nod, Adam signaled the security crew. The three men quickly converged on the bag and heaved it from the bed onto a gurney. Adam followed as they pushed the gurney from the room.

It was fully dark outside when they left the retirement home entrance and pushed the gurney up to the two Land Rovers parked at the entrance curb. Adam glanced quickly around while the men transferred the bag into the back of the nearest vehicle. He hated the risk of being seen here. If the treating doctor hadn't insisted on delivery of his check before leaving for the airport, Adam wouldn't have come. But now that he was here, he might as well accompany the body to the disposal site; he'd wanted to inspect the place again for some time now.

It was very quiet at this late hour. The only sound, beyond the guard's grunts and the creaking shocks of the Land Rover as the body landed on the floor, was the hurried footsteps of someone approaching from the parking lot. It was a man, moving rapidly through the splash of light from the overhead lamps at the door before entering the home.

"Ready, sir," one of the guards called out, pushing shut the rear hatch.

Adam nodded and walked toward the Land Rover that held Dr. Schutten's remains.

Adam gripped the strap above the passenger door of the black Land Rover as it followed the rutted path running along the eastern base of Rattlesnake Ridge. They were far enough inside the reservation and sufficiently sheltered from the nearest highway by the ridge to permit headlights if they wished. He told the driver so, and the lights came on.

Adam adjusted the HEPA mask strapped across his nose and mouth. He never traveled through the back country of the Hanford Reservation without one. The chief of security for the project behind the wheel didn't wear one, nor did the two other security staffers in the first Land Rover, just ahead. In fact, he'd caught the Chief's sideways glance of humor when Adam donned his own mask.

He didn't care. They could risk inhaling stray radiation particles out here on the reservation—where the DOE and its contractors had misplaced over a ton and a half of plutonium over the years. Adam was twenty-eight and planned for a long and prosperous life.

The lead security vehicle ahead of them rounded a rugged outcropping in the base of the ridge and slowed. Then it turned off the narrow path, making room for Adam's, which pulled alongside.

He stepped out of the SUV and looked around the dark and silent landscape beyond the play of the headlights. In two years at Hanford, Adam had not once felt appreciation for the arid lands of the Hanford Reservation. He'd seen it often in daylight, when blue camas, black-eyed susan, and prickly pear sprinkled the brown and gray desert with color. But it wasn't enough compensation for miles upon miles of hot, dusty flats—with only gullies and round-topped ridges to break up the monotony of the place. This was the perfect locale to dump radioactive waste, he thought: this place and radiation were made for each other.

But then he was in a foul mood. Though he'd elected to come here tonight, he never liked driving out onto the reservation to the "pit."

The Chief had parked so that the car lamps lit up the terrain for fifty feet at the base of the gradual slope they faced. The other SUV's lights were on high, broadening the illumination another ninety feet up the slope of the hill.

Even after decades and in the near darkness at his feet, Adam could make out the faint dips in the ground where the temporary rail ties had once lead up to the illuminated hillside. Behind them, Adam knew, the marks grew fainter the further east one walked, as the ground grew harder—until their traces disappeared completely half a mile from this spot.

The Chief and other security man were already donning Demron hazmat suits. He joined them, pulling on the dark, lightweight radiation gear and crowning it with the mask that covered his head with its own filtration system extending from the faceplate like a boar's snout.

Adam was still adjusting his mask when he was startled to see, in the dim starlight to the west, the movement of large creatures across the horizon. Through his feet, Adam felt the ground vibrate faintly from their passing.

"It's wild horses, sir," the Chief said calmly. "Mustangs. We must've startled them. They come through this draw on their way west. They get through the fence lines occasionally and muck up the motion sensors. They'll stop west of here where there's grass and water, and they get rounded up in the daylight."

Relieved, Adam finished settling his suit around him. The Chief checked to see that all of them were fully sealed in their protective suits. Then, from a canvas bag inside the Rover, he produced flashlights, which he passed to each of them. Adam took his and then reached back into the vehicle for an electronic pad the shape of a small notebook.

"Let's get the good doctor underground," Adam said, his voice magnified through the filter.

The Chief led the way. He reached into the open SUV and grasped a handle on the end of the lead bag, pulling it out with a grunt. A second man grabbed the far end just before it slid from the vehicle onto the ground. Together they trudged up the face of the slope.

Nearly thirty yards up the hill, they stopped, dropping the bag onto the ground. The Chief pulled out his flashlight and searched for a moment before bending down and feeling along the sloping soil at his feet with both hands. After a moment his fingers stopped, then tightened around something under the ground's surface. He stood with a grunt at the effort, lifting a heavy camouflage fascia from the slope, then pulling it back and away. Inches of accumulated dirt and rocks scattered from its surface.

The Chief moved aside, allowing the car lights to illuminate an eight-foot square of dark gray iron underneath, its shape smooth except for a raised plate along one edge. Adam stooped and pressed the flat pad in his hand against the mating metal plate on the slab, then used his free hand to type a code into the keypad that topped the instrument. It required some effort through the Demron gloves, but after three tries he heard a clang of sliding metal from beneath the plate.

As Adam stepped to one side, the Chief and his men grasped inset handles and pulled the slab up and over, resting the hinged iron door atop the fascia. Then, flashlights in hand, the Chief and one man hoisted the bag and stepped into the opening revealed in the face of the slope.

Their feet clanged on the metal staircase within as they disappeared. Adam waited. He heard the muffled footsteps halt, then the echoes of a faint thud of the heavy bag striking a metal surface. Scraping sounds followed, like something was being moved. Then the flashlights reappeared, ascending out of the hole as the team reemerged into the cool air.

The chief was about to close the metal door when Adam stopped him. He pulled his own flashlight from his pocket, flicked it on, and stepped into the opening.

With slow, careful steps, Adam descended into the darkness, splaying the light from side to side. At the bottom of the metal stairs, he turned the flashlight's glare from the ground to the structures directly ahead of him.

He'd only been there once before in the night, in the hours when there was no sunlight from the open door overhead and the only illumination was the spot of a flashlight. That solitary circle of light played now against the white surface of the two metal boxcars, reflecting a ghostly hue around the entirety of the small cavern.

The rear boxcar was closed, its door locked shut. Behind that door, Adam knew, lay debris and scrap from the Project—material from the LB5 accident that preceded the big one last October.

He shone the flashlight on the other boxcar directly ahead. Its cargo door was fully open.

Dr. Schutten's body bag lay on the floor of this boxcar. It rested next to dozens of neat piles of debris retrieved and carted here from the October LB5 explosion. Adam knew what each pile represented: he'd catalogued them himself.

On the furthest side of the boxcar, beyond the debris, the flashlight caught the bulky form of the other three bags placed there nine months before. The families of the other three researchers had long since said their good-byes to sealed caskets, empty except for ballast. Given the cover story that they'd died in a fiery car crash, no one had questioned the need for closed caskets. They couldn't possibly have returned the first three bodies to the families, not with the radiation levels they'd absorbed in the explosion.

It'd been easier dealing with Dr. Schutten. He had no close friends or relatives. No one awaited his final remains. And placing Dr. Schutten's body here until they'd decided the final disposal site for all of them was as logical as it was convenient.

Adam directed the flashlight further to his right, illuminating the locomotive coupled to the boxcars. Only the rear half of the engine had been excavated for Project Wolffia. Half in and half out of the surrounding soil, it looked as though it had been driven headlong into the wall of the cavern. He took a step closer.

The rear access door to the locomotive still bore the heavy chain and padlock that Adam had placed there himself. Good.

Satisfied, Adam took the steps back up the metal staircase. As soon as he emerged, the Chief and his men closed the iron door, covering it with the heavily weighted fascia. The Chief's crew used a spade he'd retrieved from his Land Rover and scattered shovelfuls of dirt evenly across its surface. Then they all retreated to the SUVs, where one of the guards produced a canister and sprayed the surfaces of their suits for decontamination.

Ten minutes later, Adam was feeling the jolts and bumps of the dirt path leading back to the highway.

He'd be pleased when they reclosed the pit for good. His predecessor on the project had overseen the disinterment of the "white train" as a storage site for the waste and byproducts of Project Wolffia. But it was his problem now. His unease was less about radiation exposure than the stark consequences if the contents of the train were ever discovered. There was enough illegal about the Project itself without the DOE or someone else discovering the human remains interred here in the buried white train.

He looked out at the passing shadows of terrain. Foote never expressed concern about accidental discovery of the pit. The vice-president had always been more concerned about an intentional betrayal by Project workers, like these security guards. Adam wasn't troubled by that prospect. Those in the know had been selected with great care: their psychological profiles examined by Dr. Janniston, subjected to repeated interviews—even their financial status and stability vetted. The chief of security was from Los Alamos, a third-generation nuclear defense worker himself. Most of the remaining Project security team was from Hanford—but the one commonality they shared was an unshakable belief in America's need for nuclear protection as deep as Cameron Foote's. It was a belief that diminished concern about the precise nature of Project Wolffia—so long as they were assured it served the mission.

"My father worked at Hanford," the Chief said, breaking his characteristic silence. "He once told me he remembered when this train was buried."

"Really," Adam answered, only mildly interested.

"Yep. He saw it loaded once, too. He said the white trains would pull into the loading area around ten o'clock at night and they'd bring out the lead containers with the plutonium, easing it into the cars like it was made of glass. It was loud during loading, he said, because the filtered air coolers were rolling all the time on the cars, running cool air through them to keep the plutonium from overheating. It was a new moon and the night was so dark it was like watching some kind of spirit fly off when that bright white train pulled out. He said the route took it along the north shore of the Columbia to down near Celilo, then south and east to Rocky Flats."

"Mmm. That must've been a sight," Adam said distractedly.

The chief went silent as he maneuvered the rough road. "You mentioned earlier that we might need to put some pressure on Patrick Martin," he said at last.

"Yes."

"So do we go ahead with that?"

He thought about the skill of Dr. Janniston. Should he wait to allow Janniston to induce Martin to change his statement? Or should he couple Janniston's efforts with more aggressive measures by the security team?

There were risks involved in overplaying things. Besides, Dr. Janniston would get Martin to change his report; Adam had seen the psychologist at work when they'd screened the workers, and he was convinced of it. If that failed, then he'd have the security team apply additional outside pressure. And if all that was unsuccessful, in the last extremity they'd crush Martin's credibility with Janniston's psychological report.

"Be prepared to put some pressure on Martin, but wait until I give the word," Adam said.

The Chief nodded. "I'm told Mr. Martin's family goes way back to the town of Hanford itself."

"Then he should be cooperating," Adam responded.

"A good family man, too," the Chief said, almost under his breath.

Was that a tone of reluctance? Adam felt the weariness of his pace the past few weeks weighing him down. He set his head back against the headrest and closed his eyes.

"Then if it comes to it, I suggest that's where you start," Adam said as he drifted asleep. "With his family."

Poppy couldn't understand what he was witnessing. Parked here in a depression along the highway, slumped down in his seat and half frozen in the dark truck cab, he couldn't figure out what was going on just seventy yards away.

Three hours ago, he'd recognized Adam Worth in the entryway to the retirement home. He probably would have known it was him regardless, with his lean body and that uncreased face—but the bow tie was the clincher. There he stood while three other guys put a body bag in the back of an SUV.

Poppy couldn't help himself. It was all too strange. As soon as they pulled away, he'd trotted back to the truck and followed.

It wasn't hard to follow without looking suspicious—anybody on this highway had to go a long ways to turn off, since the road followed the reservation fence line until you reached the exit for Terrence Heights and Yakima. Still, he'd nearly given himself away by slowing when the SUVs took an unexpected turn off the highway toward the fence line. Poppy'd only just managed to give it gas and pass by, turning around at the next dip in the highway and coming back to the scene slowly with his headlights off. Then he'd pulled into this depression—deep enough and far enough off the side of the road so that no southbound cars would illuminate the truck.

He'd settled into place in time to see a man relocking a gate in the fence line just yards from a concrete guard station, as the SUVs rumbled across the desert and disappeared into the interior of the reservation.

Now, hours later, Poppy was watching the two Land Rovers return, their headlights off. They pulled up to the concrete bunker as the man reappeared and opened the gate once more. Then the Land Rovers pulled through the gate and onto the highway, their lights flicking on as they hit the pavement moving away from Poppy. Moments later, the man joined them—driving past the gate, relocking it behind his car, then driving off in the direction of the SUVs.

Poppy sat back up in the dark cab trying to figure out what he'd just seen.

He'd lived here all his life, worked in security at Hanford for decades. He knew with certainty that this guard station and entry onto the reservation grounds had been unmanned for years.

So what were they doing taking a body onto the Hanford grounds? And why use an entrance to the grounds that went off line two decades ago?

Did this have something to do with LB5 and what was happening to him? It seemed a strange notion, one that took the unreality of all he was experiencing to a new place. He'd always thought that they'd cross a line someday and everything would go back to the way it was. But this crossed into territory so bizarre that things might never be the same again.

Poppy reached to restart his truck. Then he stopped dead, recalling again the image of those cars conveying a corpse out onto the reservation grounds.

It had just occurred to him that he still had no idea where Lewis Vandervork had gone.

CHAPTER 23

THIRD DAYS UNTIL TRIAL

Ryan looked at the Vietnamese scientist seated across from him in Jackie's Diner in Spokane. The doctor was wearing the same casual style of clothes Ryan recalled in the airport: a sweater, khakis, and button-down shirt. Dr. Trân's glasses were again perched precariously on his forehead just below the hairline. The diminutive man was scrutinizing the document which Taylor Christensen had given his daughter only a few days before: the one that Ryan and Emily had already dubbed "the mixing room matrix." At Trân's elbow was a copy of the Covington amended report, as well as Dr. Nadine's expert opinion.

Dr. Trân looked up with a solemn face. "Ordinarily, it would be impossible given the short timelines involved. But I have a few weeks between jobs to spare with my work finishing here in Spokane. Perhaps I could arrange more if I needed to testify. So yes. I would be happy to assist with expert opinions in your case."

"That's great," Ryan responded, hiding his skepticism about the man before him. "Tell me your impressions about the amended Covington report."

Dr. Trân nodded. "Very well. This Covington material is really only half a report. There are few appendices or backup data. There are also apparent gaps, though I would need access to your documents to see what may have been missed."

Ryan leaned over to his leather briefcase at his side. He pulled out a twenty-page single-spaced document and slid it across the table to Dr. Trân.

"This is a summary of every document that Covington has provided us in this case. We can PDF you anything on that list. But these documents will have to do. Discovery in the case is closed."

The doctor nodded.

"What about radiation exposure?" Ryan asked. He'd already mentioned the blood studies that Pauline Strand had been unable to afford. "Is there any way to get radiation blood studies done in time?"

"How long again, exactly?"

"Twenty-three days until our reports are due."

The doctor grew thoughtful. "These types of studies are mostly performed at universities under contract to the Department of Energy or the nuclear industry. But I believe I can prevail upon an independent lab to perform the work."

"So quickly?"

Minh nodded, smiling. "It would take a call to be certain, but it is possible."

"How much?"

"Umm. That would require some calls as well. But I believe I could convince some colleagues to do a blood study quickly and at a discount—say, ten thousand dollars."

Again, Ryan suppressed his natural reaction.

Dr. Virgil Strong had finally committed to Kieran's case this morning by phone. Ryan had nearly fallen on his knees with relief. "I'll need every day from now until trial to prepare," the USC professor had cautioned. "It will be very close." Ryan had assured him that was acceptable—then sent the sizeable retainer check by FedEx within the hour.

Because it had to be acceptable. All of Ryan's research indicated Strong had the potential to give Kieran's case instant credibility. If the professor concluded that Vat 17 would have exploded whether or not their client touched the valve, then a jury would give that great weight. With a PhD in nuclear engineering and eighteen years as a tenured faculty member at the University of Southern California, he would dominate the courtroom. It was, Ryan thought, an extraordinary stroke of good fortune that he was available and willing to step in.

Which brought Ryan back to the man seated in front of him. With Strong committed, he ordinarily would have canceled this scheduled meeting with Dr. Trân—especially given his doubt about the man. But despite everything, Trân's credentials were as unassailable as Strong's. A refugee from Vietnam as a child, Trân had been one of the youngest doctoral students in physics to ever graduate from Princeton University. He'd written stacks of articles in the area of health physics, several of which Ryan had reviewed. More importantly, Ryan could find few direct connections between the man and the American nuclear industry—mostly he'd worked as an independent consultant for special interest groups and foreign and tribal governments. If anything, he had much less connection with the nuclear industry and DOE than Strong.

So Ryan had taken the meeting—setting aside, for the moment, the strange circumstances of their introduction at the airport. And it had gone fairly well, until this bombshell: Trân claiming to be able to perform the blood testing for ten thousand dollars. After Dr. Nadine had quoted fifty thousand, and Dr. Strong the same. Considering it, Ryan's skepticism soared again.

Still Ryan couldn't shake a nagging worry about relying solely on Strong so close to trial. Especially when Dr. Trân was making it relatively inexpensive to try him out. Perhaps Covington was pulling his strings, especially given his offer of a Walmart-priced blood study. But in view of the man's credentials and Ryan's desperation to insure the expert report they needed, maybe he should pay the price for a backup.

"All right, Dr. Trân," he finally said. "You're hired."

The scientist nodded. "Excellent."

Ryan reached for the tab. "Let me know which documents you'll want from the list, and I'll have Emily email them to you."

"Good." Dr. Trân smiled. "I will be in touch about arranging for your client's blood to be taken and shipped to the lab I mentioned."

Then he leaned across the table with a questioning look. "You mentioned earlier that you have a difficult judge in the case. Judge Renway, you said?"

Ryan nodded. "Yes. Nothing we can do about that."

Trân nodded solemnly. "I see. Do you suppose he'd permit me to tour the site of the explosion?"

Ryan pondered the request for a moment. Pauline had toured room 365 when she was still counsel. Ryan had seen the pictures. It looked like a terrorist hit. The room was leveled and Vat 17 had disintegrated, though part of the steel tube and all of the valve had survived. There wasn't much to see—plus, at this late date, Renway would have to approve another inspection. That was about as likely as a winning lottery ticket.

"I'll see," Ryan answered.

Dr. Trân smiled once again, then plucked the check from Ryan's hand.

"Allow me, Mr. Hart."

The Vietnamese man gathered his papers and left the table to pay at the register. Ryan watched him go, shaking his head.

So what did this mean, he wondered. What did it mean when his consultant picked up the tab—and the man hadn't even asked for a retainer?

CHAPTER 24

Poppy dropped the list of names he'd been calling the last few days as another explosion of coughs built in his chest. Before he could stand, they erupted, bending him over and wracking his lungs until he was gasping for air. His stomach muscles ached by the time he finally straightened, stood, and stumbled to the bathroom for the prescription his wife had filled before heading to her sister's house for the afternoon.

Pills in one hand, he cupped a mouthful of water with the other beneath the tap and gulped them down. After a moment, he eased straight, confronting his bloodshot eyes in the bathroom mirror.

Poppy walked unsteadily back into the living room. He dropped onto the couch, where he picked up his cell phone as well as the list once again.

Poppy skimmed the scribbled names. Fourteen were struck off. None had been helpful. Most had echoed Poppy's surprise about Lew's disappearance. That left half a dozen to go.

After ruminating for a day about what he'd witnessed that night outside the reservation, Poppy had turned to searching for Lewis. But first, he'd told Suzy everything—including HR's effort to make him change his statement. Over several days, she'd cycled through stages of emotion from relief at learning the source of Poppy's strange behavior to volcanic anger from concern about where this all would lead. In the end, she'd offered to help him with his search for Lewis.

Poppy had gently but firmly turned her down. She had a job of her own. More importantly, he knew Suzy. If he let her, she'd throw herself into it and tear herself down with worry and anxiety in the process. It'd be better if one of them stayed on the sidelines for now. He'd thanked her with a smile and a kiss.

But his search these past few days hadn't paid any dividends. He'd confirmed that Lewis didn't have close family in town. Lew's parents lived in Missouri, though Poppy was having trouble running them down. Lew had worked at Hanford for three years, yet Poppy couldn't locate anyone Lewis had reached out to on his way out the door—or anytime in the months since the explosion.

Poppy ran his finger down the dwindling list. The next in line was a man identified by someone at work as Lew's former roommate. He punched in the number.

"Hello?" a man answered. He sounded young.

Poppy identified himself and explained why he was calling.

"No, sorry, man," the voice said. "Not a word. Nada. I was out of town when that explosion happened. I come back and he's checked out. Left cash for the last couple months on the lease. And he hasn't answered a text or posted on Facebook since he went ghost."

"Thanks," Poppy said. He was about to punch out of the call when the voice came back.

"Tried Bev?"

"Who?"

"Beverly Cortez. She was an on-again, off-again girlfriend of Lew's. They had the mother of all fights last summer. Has *she* got a temper. Lew called her his 'exploding piñata.' Smart as a whip, but . . ."

Bev, Poppy thought as the man rambled on. Beverly. The name Lew had assigned to his weapon.

"What's the number," Poppy interrupted.

"Uh, I don't have it. But I know the number where she used to work. Lew had it up on our bulletin board forever."

Poppy wrote down the number. As soon as he was off the line, he tried it. A young woman answered and told him she couldn't give out a home number for Beverly, but would try to reach her with a message.

"Okay," Poppy said. "Please tell her that I'm trying to reach Lewis Vandervork. Tell her it's very, very important."

He set down the phone. Almost the instant it hit the table, it started vibrating from an incoming call. Poppy picked it up, hoping it was the girl. It wasn't and he didn't recognize the area code.

The voice over his phone was tight and high pitched. "Mr. Martin?"

Poppy answered cautiously. "Yes."

"Mr. Martin, my name is Dr. Zachary Janniston."

The name rang no bells with Poppy. Maybe it was someone new at his clinic. "Yes," he said again.

"Mr. Martin, I've been retained by Covington Nuclear to administer some psychological tests."

Poppy felt a fist tighten in his stomach. "I don't understand," he said uncertainly.

"We can discuss the parameters of the testing when we get together, but I must ask you to meet me at a local hotel where I've rented some space for us to talk."

"I don't understand," Poppy repeated, trying to collect himself.

"If you have any questions, you can call Adam Worth at the Human Resources Department, Mr. Martin."

"When," Poppy asked, his throat constricting. "When do you want to meet?"

"Tomorrow morning. Eight o'clock." The voice rattled off the name of the hotel. "I'm informed that you need not report for your shift tonight. They've already been informed you will be on medical leave. I'll see you in the morning then, Mr. Martin."

The line went dead.

CHAPTER 25

Ryan reached the summit of the River Park hill less winded today, a combination of a slower pace and a cooler afternoon.

A slight breeze wicked the sweat from his face as he jogged over to the bench he'd seen on his first run in the park. It was empty now. He took a seat and settled back to bring down his heart rate and take in the view.

He'd left Emily at the Annex comparing the witnesses identified in Covington's Amended Investigation Report and those Pauline Strand had interviewed or deposed. With only a few gaps, their predecessor had done a fairly good job; she'd taken depositions from most of the people Ryan would have. Pauline had taken only short depositions or passed on workers who'd never made it into the "dark side" of LB5 that night—probably assuming they'd have no knowledge of the cause of the explosion. That included the two HVAC men warned to get indoors by the roof security guard—and the guard himself, identified only by job title in Covington's report. With deposition costs as high as a thousand dollars apiece, Strand had to make strategic calls, Ryan conceded, and distinguishing between indoor and outdoor employees was a reasonable place to draw a line.

Ryan had offered to help with contacting witnesses, but Emily

192

had declined. "Concentrate on the experts," she'd said, though that was mostly a waiting game since he'd hired Strong and Trân to complete their reports and blood studies.

Emily's insistence on keeping the lion's share of pretrial preparation was the obvious source of the fatigue mounting in his daughter's face. Now with trial less than three weeks away, they'd have to broach their respective roles at trial.

The elephant in the room on that front was Ryan's obvious experience advantage over Emily, who was untested in a major trial. But the way things were going, she was unlikely to permit him any more of a role at trial than he had in the prep.

He probably had it coming, given how clearly he'd limited his initial offer to help. And he'd been impressed with her performance in court and the work she'd performed these past weeks. Still, he couldn't shake his worry at the near certainty that Emily would be hopelessly outgunned against the more experienced Covington lawyer—regardless of her zeal and preparation, and regardless of what expert opinions they generated to support her.

Another runner broke the plane of Ryan's vision, looking familiar with his red hair, white shorts, and a yellow shirt. The man slowed then halted as though he was taking a break as well, before slowly turning toward Ryan.

"I've seen you up here before," the man said.

Ryan looked in his direction and nodded. "Same here."

He was young—maybe in his late twenties or early thirties. His face was slim, with hair cut close but not buzzed. Ryan recalled that he had always seen him wearing the same white shorts.

"Beautiful," Ryan said, gesturing toward the horizon.

The man nodded. "Always."

"You live in Sherman?"

The man nodded again. "Yes. For a couple of years. You?"

"Just here for a trial. I'm a lawyer."

A flicker of interest flashed in the man's eyes. "What trial?"

Ryan was curious how the man would react. "An injury case," he said. "An incident out at Hanford."

A look of amusement came over the runner's face. "Don't you love that word, *incident*," he said.

Ryan smiled. "Yeah, you've got me; that's pretty vague. It was the explosion last fall."

The comment brought on a full smile. "I knew what you were probably talking about. That was a big deal around here. I'm told they don't get many explosions at Hanford anymore. Last fall's *incident* gave everybody something to talk about for awhile."

"What do they say about it?"

The runner looked off again toward the view. "Oh, I don't know. I heard one of the workers might've done it intentionally. I suppose that's what most people believe. The whole thing got some blood up."

That was what he feared. "What do you do for a living?" Ryan asked.

The man paused as though catching his breath for an instant. "I'm in insurance. Life insurance. I'm Larry Mann, by the way."

"Ryan Hart," he responded, taking the extended hand.

"So what do you think. Got a good shot at winning?"

Ryan shook his head. "You never know. Juries usually get it right if you give them the right evidence."

"That so?"

"Yes. That's so."

"Well," Larry said, beginning to jog in place, "I've got to be off. Maybe I'll see you around here again. And good luck with your case."

Ryan waited until the man had gone over the slope of the hill toward town. Then he stood to follow, wondering if Mann's comments reflected what most Sherman residents thought about the case. He'd taken too little time to get out and talk to people to find out for himself.

Which brought Ryan back again to the approaching trial and his role in it. He supposed that if Emily didn't raise the issue, he shouldn't either. Still, he dreaded what he might have to witness from the sidelines.

The slope began to fall more steeply and Ryan lengthened his strides. Ahead he could still see Larry Mann, though the runner was moving away. Then he passed out of view around a curve in the trail ahead—and his disappearance triggered in Ryan a final thought about the runner.

Was that an Australian or an English accent he'd detected in Larry Mann's voice?

"Mr. Martin, whom do you believe is lying to you—and what do you believe motivates them to lie to you?"

Poppy sat on a rust-colored couch in suite 142 of the Treadway Inn. To his right was a dark wood table, next to an antiqued armoire. On the wall to the left were two prints of old wood-burning locomotives—one winding through a valley of firs and birch, the other crossing a river on a tall wooden bridge.

In the middle of his field of vision, his fingers flicking over the keyboard of a computer balanced on his lap, sat Dr. Zachary Janniston.

Poppy knew his limits in hotel rooms—even ones as spacious and upscale as this. In the navy he'd discovered how crazy he could get if he was cooped up for too long. It had never gone to full-blown claustrophobia like Poppy had felt down in his super's office that night with Adam Worth—that was a first. It had always been more like pressure building in a steam boiler, like what ran those locomotives in the prints on the wall.

He was feeling it now, heating up his chest and head, making him hunger for moving air on his hands and face or the sight of an open sky. It'd been seven hours so far today in this hotel room where everything was in its place and the air didn't seem to circulate. Eight hours yesterday. Four hours the first day before that. Bringing in lunch. Not letting him go until four thirty or five thirty—like he was punching off a shift.

Seated at the wooden table, he'd done MMPIs; Borderline Personality Disorder tests; tests for ADD and ADHD; mood disorder questionnaires; and other tests he couldn't even remember. They hadn't even bothered to hide the test titles—like they wanted him to know what labels they were thinking of sticking to him and his record. And between the tests, Janniston's high-pitched monotone had droned on for hour after tortured hour.

He couldn't leave. Janniston told him he was there for the duration, and he'd confirmed it with a call to the union shop. Under the collective bargaining agreement, they could yank his security clearance if he didn't fully cooperate.

But if he kept taking tests and answering questions much longer, there was a chance that this pale-faced psychologist with ferret eyes and ears as big as his fist would find Poppy's limit—and if Poppy came at him, Janniston could declare him psychologically unfit in a heartbeat. He couldn't give them that.

Janniston was waiting patiently for an answer with a thin-lipped stare.

"What was the question again?" Poppy asked.

"Who do you believe is lying to you—and what do you believe motivates them to lie to you?"

He'd done it again. Poppy could wait ten minutes then ask for a repeat of the question, and every time, without even looking at his open laptop, this Janniston would come back with the *identical wording*. It was like Chinese water torture.

"I heard a gunshot on the roof of LB5 that night," Poppy replied. "I don't know why and I don't know who's behind it, but I'm being asked to change my statement about it. I won't."

There. It was the same answer Poppy'd given to dozens of questions over the past three days. Security guards could memorize too.

"Do you understand that your fellow security guard on the roof that evening denied firing any shot?"

"They tell me so."

"You don't believe that?"

"I haven't spoken with Lew since that night."

"So you believe you're being lied to about that as well."

"Yes."

"And do you understand that there is no evidence of a rifle, other than yours, being fired on the roof that night?"

"That's what they've said."

"Also something you do not believe?"

Poppy nodded.

"Mr. Martin, do you believe people are trying to persecute you?"

Poppy contemplated the question as he thought back three days. It was his first afternoon with Janniston, and the psychologist had released him after a short day. Poppy'd driven to the southwest end of town. A buddy of Poppy's at the union hall had tipped him off that the lawyers representing Kieran Mullaney had rented a place over near the Winchester Inn.

He'd heard nothing back from Bev Cortez or any of his other contacts about Lewis. But maybe, Poppy had considered, the lawyers representing the Mullaney boy had learned where Lew was through the lawsuit. With that hope in mind, Poppy had driven his truck to the old River Knoll neighborhood, with its colonial houses and double-sized lawns. He'd driven past the inn and the building next door that the union hall buddy had identified—a building that looked like it was under renovation. Then he'd stopped his truck around the far corner and walked to a shady spot beneath a tree within sight of the place.

197

He'd just about gotten up the courage to cross the street and go knock on the door when the white van came into sight, approaching from the direction that Poppy had come not twenty minutes before. It pulled onto a different side street a block away from Poppy's resting place.

Poppy carefully crossed the lawns in the direction that the van had disappeared, staying close to the front of each house. At the last house on the block, he cut around to the back. There he pressed against the vinyl siding and carefully looked around its edge.

The van was parked a third of the way up the side street, its back hatch facing the Winchester Inn and the adjacent building into which Kieran and his attorneys were located. No one had gotten out. No one was visible in the front passenger seat. Beyond that, he couldn't see the driver's side, and the back glass was too opaque for Poppy to see inside.

He could see, though, that the van still had no plates.

Poppy knew he couldn't go see Kieran and his lawyers now even if he wanted to—or even risk telephoning. If the place was being watched, who was to say they didn't have the inside of the place bugged too? If they caught Poppy talking to the lawyers, they'd fire him for sure.

He wasn't ready for that. So he crept back up the street, staying out of view of the van, and drove away.

"Mr. Martin?"

Poppy became aware of the psychologist again, sitting motionless beside the paintings on the wall, still waiting for his answer.

"Sorry. What was the question?"

"Do you believe people are trying to persecute you?"

Poppy sighed. He looked to the left, toward the dark locomotive amidst the woodland, set against the white bark of the birch trees it was rolling past. It took him away from the stale air of this place and the eyes of his tormentor. He began to count the birch trees, as he mouthed the words that required no attention to repeat once again.

"Yes. Because I heard a gunshot on the roof of LB5 that night," he said slowly. "I don't know why and I don't know who's behind it, but I'm being asked to change my statement about it. I won't."

CHAPTER 26

The bustle of activity by the new Wolffia team in the bowels of LB5 was heartening tonight. Adam surveyed the scientists and techs making final testing preparations approvingly, listening to the snippets of discussions audible to him here at the primary monitoring station.

Most of the talk was unintelligible to him. Adam was a manager. He was not a nuclear scientist. Nor did he aspire to be one. He'd studied enough physics and been in his job long enough to follow a conversation between two of this breed. But he couldn't begin to contribute, any more than a beginning Spanish student listening to the banter of two native speakers.

But then again, he didn't need to. If the talk grew too complicated, he had a Project staff person who could translate. What Adam *did* need to understand was whether Project Wolffia was achieving its goal. And tonight, he was standing in the LB5 laboratory with high expectations.

It was his boss, Cameron Foote, who defined success for this Project. Project Wolffia, he'd say, would be worth its seven years and nine figures in research costs the day it produced a high-energy chemical trigger—the device that made the radioactive heart of a nuclear bomb detonate with its enormous capacity for destruction. Only in this case, the dramatically smaller trigger could make possible smaller bombs with proportionately more plutonium—capable of delivering a neutron pulse of radiation ten times that of current nuclear weapons. Bombs would become far cheaper, far more lightweight, and far more capable of being transported to a battlefield to irradiate men and material, rendering both permanently useless. Smaller, more potent radiation weapons would change everything, bypassing the stalemate of heavy thermonuclear bombs. *The West,* Vice-President Foote would say, *would instantly capture the high ground.*

That was it, pure and simple.

Adam always permitted his enthusiasm to show when Foote spoke on the subject. But underneath, he was keenly interested in a more tangible result: billions of dollars more in profits flowing to Covington Nuclear. Which meant an extraordinary bonus trickling to Adam.

Adam looked around the lab at the scientists settling in, preparing to begin the test. Development of this trigger was not, he reminded himself, necessarily illegal under international treaties. But the United States had been denying any effort to produce such components since the late 1990s. Which was why this team was working for a private company seeking to achieve the trigger on its own, working secretly in the lower levels of a defunct plutonium facility. Totally bypassing the cumbersome oversight, bureaucratic roadblocks, and political barriers of a congressionally approved program.

"Moving through channels," Foote had told Adam when he'd brought him on board, "the Project would require triple the time, tenfold the cost, and more political guts than the whole of Washington could muster in a thousand years. That's not an option for America."

Foote had concluded his lecture, saying, "And what better use of resources than setting up the lab in this moribund plutonium facility, already under Covington's supervision and control—a place already contaminated and slated for demolition. A location where Covington need only complete experimentation before LB5 is torn down—a convenient fact since Covington is in charge of the cleanup and destruction schedule for the entirety of Hanford, including this building."

Adam had often wondered, given the secrecy of the Project, how many others even within Covington knew of it. Less than half a dozen key executives and managers, he'd guess: people capable of keeping the flow of research dollars coming to Sherman and LB5. And how many, he'd wondered, were driven by the patriotic principles that motivated Cameron Foote—as opposed to the enormous expectation of profit to be garnered from the sale of the new chemical triggers to the United States military?

And most curious of all, of those "in the know" about Project Wolffia, how many had ever heard Adam's name? Except for Cameron Foote, he would bet not a single one.

"We're ready to proceed," Dr. John Wilson said. As the replacement head of the Wolffia team, Adam had insisted he be at his side during the test. Adam nodded in response, instinctively checking his protective eyewear.

The gear should have been unnecessary. They were outside of the specially constructed (and since the October explosion, reconstructed) concrete-and-steel-reinforced chamber where the red mercury trigger was about to be tested. All contingencies had been evaluated and controlled to avoid pressure changes—such as those caused by the errant Vat 17 that had spelled failure for the previous experiment. Besides, their observation of the event would be indirect: through the video feed from within the chamber.

A tech began a countdown. Adam's cynical side wanted to dismiss it as melodramatic—but after the effort of the past two years, he couldn't stay removed from the excitement of it all.

It reached zero.

Viewed through the video feed, the flash was like a miniature sun going nova, spreading across the length of the chamber at terrific speed—like a ball of fire shot from a cannon. Then, as quickly as it had happened, it was over.

The half a dozen scientists and analysts spread across the room were transfixed by their monitors. Adam turned to Dr. Wilson, who was looking over the shoulder of a team member's monitor to his left.

"Was it successful?" Adam asked.

Dr. Wilson demurred for a moment. Then he stood up. "We have to examine the data, the heat production, whether it properly detonated the assays of plutonium in the chamber. And we'll have to reproduce this a few more times at different heat gradients to ensure reliability."

Adam wanted to shake the man for a simple response. "Is the trigger a success or not?"

The dour scientist couldn't even bring himself to smile. "Well, if you must have an immediate answer, I'd say yes. A qualified yes."

Adam wanted to shout out loud at these words. He grinned for the both of them. "Congratulations, Doctor," he said. Across the room a ripple of muted high fives and smiles were visible.

Did physicists ever party, Adam wondered through his own exultation.

He savored the moment. And there was another positive from this event as well. For the first time in months, he could look forward to his call to Cameron Foote later this evening.

CHAPTER 27

Ten Days Until Trial

Seated near the window, Ryan examined the latest email from Dr. Strong on his laptop. More reassurances that the report would be done on time—which meant within the next two days. Still missing were any details about his conclusions.

Maybe Ryan should have insisted on a face to face with Strong before moving forward—like he had with Dr. Nadine. He'd decided not to make the trip to California based upon his hard-earned experience that the more exalted an expert's pedigree, the more their capacity to punish pushy lawyers by demonstrating their "intellectual independence." More than once that had resulted in aloof, scholarly opinions rather than ones that advocated a client's case. Ryan didn't want that to happen in Kieran's case—especially with no time for revisions to the expert's product.

Still, in their numerous phone conferences, Dr. Strong had made no noise about an inability to support Kieran's claims. He'd just stayed maddeningly vague.

The knock at the front door startled Ryan from his thoughts. It was likely Dr. Trân, twenty minutes early.

Neither Kieran nor Emily had stirred from their seats on the couch to answer the door. Kieran was staring across the room while Emily looked near to taking his hand.

The young man was understandably nervous today: Trân was coming to share his opinions—including those about Kieran's radiation exposure. It hadn't helped that the doctor insisted on explaining them in person. Ryan hadn't seen Kieran this withdrawn since their first meeting at the Atomic Café nearly two months ago.

Ryan opened the door to face the smiling figure of Dr. Trân. He stepped aside and waved him in.

Dr. Trân looked as though he hadn't stopped smiling since their last meeting in Spokane. Still dressed casually, his reading glasses remained balanced so close to the edge of his forehead that Ryan felt the urge to nudge them back.

He introduced the doctor, who took a seat in a spare chair. Without any fanfare, the man opened a leather valise and produced multiple copies of two binders—the first titled "Cause of the Explosion at LB5"; the second, "Blood Study Results— Kieran Mullaney." The instant everyone had received a set, he settled back and began addressing them in the objective tone of a lecturing professor.

"The explosions that injured Kieran Mullaney were not caused solely, or even principally, by detonation of the contents of Vat 17," he said.

Ryan couldn't have heard that correctly. He asked the doctor to repeat his statement. He did so—word for word.

"How do you reach *that* opinion," Ryan burst out.

The doctor's smile did not waiver. "Vat 17's contents lacked the explosive potential to breach the safety doors between the mixing room and the third-floor corridor to LB5. Yet those doors were destroyed after Mr. Mullaney left the room. So while the Vat 17 chemicals were involved, they could not have been the primary fuel for the October sixteenth explosions."

Ryan had hoped for an expert who would contest Covington's contention that Kieran caused the explosion by turning the Vat 17 valve, but this was a giant leap beyond even that. How could

Vat 17 not have had a significant role in the explosion? His paranoia about the man kicked in once more. Was Trân creating a theory so absurd that no jury could accept it?

Ryan had never told Emily or Kieran about his skepticism regarding Dr. Trân—nor his reasons for it. He hadn't wanted to undermine their confidence in the man until he was sure he had Dr. Strong's report. Now he wished he hadn't kept silent on the topic.

"Explain," Ryan demanded firmly.

Dr. Trân nodded, then directed them each to a diagram in the center of his cause report. It showed a vat, with a description of its contents and chemical formulae beneath it.

"Vat 17 contained tributyl phosphate, hydrochloric acid, and other chemicals capable of detonating if sufficiently concentrated. The Vat 17 sampling data for the year before the explosion, coupled with Mr. Mullaney's description of the container that night, supports a conclusion that the active chemicals in the vat were reaching a concentration of reactivity after years of water evaporation. Assuming Mr. Mullaney opened the valve under the vat, that action likely released a stream of fluid out of the steel tube beneath the tank, further concentrating the chemicals and accelerating a likely explosion."

"Then you agree with the Covington experts," Emily said.

"Only to this point," Trân responded. "The Covington experts go on to conclude that the Vat 17 chemicals then exploded immediately, followed by chemicals in containers elsewhere in the room. I don't agree. The accelerated concentration of the Vat 17 chemicals may have resulted in an explosion minutes or an hour later, but not likely within seconds. And more importantly, Covington's conclusion fails to account for the fact that the chemicals in Vat 17 lacked sufficient explosive potential to blow through the mixing room blast doors after Mr. Mullaney escaped the room. I've evaluated the tolerances for those doors, and the Vat 17 chemicals were insufficient to achieve that end."

"Couldn't Vat 17 *plus* the chemicals of other vats have been enough?" Kieran asked.

Dr. Trân shook his head, directing them to a bar graph identifying the eighteen vats in room 365 and their contents.

"My examination of the mixing-room matrix document that you recently obtained demonstrates that there were no chemicals elsewhere in 365, even combined with the Vat 17 materials, capable of opening the blast doors."

This was starting to sound like blather on blather. Ryan held his tongue as Dr. Trân flipped to yet another diagram.

"I've examined seismographic data from Spokane, Boise, and Portland which detected the October sixteenth explosions. Covington postulates that the later explosions resulted from chemicals in vats elsewhere in the room, ignited by the Vat 17 explosion. But the seismographic data confirms that the second and third explosions were nearly as powerful as the first. That would only be possible if chemicals elsewhere in the room had the same explosive potential as those of Vat 17. They did not. In fact, they were considerably less explosive."

"If the Vat 17 chemicals couldn't have ruptured the doors," Emily said, "and the other vats in the room weren't powerful enough to cause the later explosions, what powered the three explosions that night?"

Dr. Trân shrugged. "I can only conclude other explosive substances unaccounted for."

"What substances?" Kieran asked, agitated. "From where?"

Dr. Trân set the Cause binder down. "Building diagrams show that the steel tube below Vat 17—the one you came into contact with, Mr. Mullaney—was once used to convey its contents to glove boxes and production rooms in the lower levels of LB5. By opening the valve on that pipe, you not only sped the occurrence of an explosion of the Vat 17 chemicals, you also opened a conduit for the pressure and heat developing in that vat to the lower production areas in the building. I believe that heat and pressure caused an explosion of materials in the lower levels."

"I'd like to hear an answer to Kieran's question," Ryan demanded. "What materials are we talking about?"

Dr. Trân leaned back and folded his arms across his chest. "I can't say. But given the magnitude of the three explosions, substances of high explosive potential. Very powerful materials, based upon the seismic data alone."

"Hanford was where they made atomic bombs," Emily said. "There must have been plenty of things in LB5 that could cause a big blast."

Dr. Trân shook his head vigorously. "No, no, no. Your first statement is mistaken. Hanford manufactured plutonium, the fissile fuel for nuclear weapons, but not the bombs themselves. Plutonium can only cause a nuclear explosion if triggered by a detonation mechanism." He proceeded to describe what a nuclear trigger was.

"You're saying plutonium can never detonate by itself," Ryan said, "but only with one of these triggers."

"That's not entirely true," Dr. Trân responded. "Plutonium, if left in proximity to another radioactive substance, can generate a natural critical reaction without the aid of a detonator. Such critical reactions generate dangerous localized heat and radiation. But a natural critical reaction, by itself, could not have caused explosions of the magnitude experienced at LB5 last October. Those explosions were more consistent with the powerful *detonating materials* that operate as triggers for nuclear weapons."

"So maybe they left a nuclear trigger in the LB5 basement that caused the explosion," Emily said.

Dr. Trân shrugged once more. "Those devices aren't treated like office supplies. They would not have been *left* in the LB5 lower levels. And explosive triggers were never manufactured or stored at Hanford—for obvious reasons. Hanford's plutonium was shipped elsewhere for assembly into bombs. Nevertheless, I must agree that, based upon the magnitude and method of the LB5 explosion, such a trigger or its components may have been in the lower levels of LB5 that night, and served as the source of the explosion."

"They would have detected residue of a nuclear trigger after the explosion if one was involved," Ryan argued.

"Yes," Dr. Trân said. "If they chose to look for it."

Now the whole thing was a conspiracy, Ryan thought dismissively. "So that's really your theory," Ryan said impatiently. "That something that had no place in Hanford was somehow in LB5 that night, and Vat 17 just happened to make it explode."

Dr. Trân didn't meet Ryan's gaze when he answered. "Yes. And for that reason, Kieran was not responsible for his own injuries that night."

This guy expects Emily to take that theory into the courtroom with no other proof than Trân's calculations of the limited explosive potential of the mixing-room contents, Ryan fumed. When was Emily going to jump down the doctor's throat on this thin excuse for a theory?

Without waiting for more objections, Dr. Trân turned to the other report binder. "I believe this conclusion is also supported by the radiation data. According to the pre-explosion sampling records you obtained, room 365 was 'clean'—showing little radionuclide residue through the years. Yet Mr. Mullaney saw the hallway monitors signaling radiation moving down the corridor, past him, as he was fleeing room 365."

Dr. Trân directed them to the final section of the Cause report, to a diagram of the corridor with a series of calculations below it.

"If room 365 was clear of radionuclides, the radiation tripping the corridor monitors must have come from another location. And since it took five to ten seconds for the hall monitors to be triggered—the time between the first blast until Mr. Mullaney saw the monitors register radiation—I conclude the first explosion created a clear pathway between room 365 and the lower levels, while the second and third spread radiation from those levels back into 365 and beyond into the corridor. Which means there was radioactive material in significant quantities in the lower levels."

"So you're saying the source of the *explosion* in the lower levels of LB5 was also the source of the *radiation*," Emily said.

"In all likelihood."

"Well, if that were true," Ryan said, skepticism flooding his tone, "then Kieran would definitely have been exposed to radiation."

It was out before Ryan realized what he'd just said. Instantly, the room grew quiet.

"Well, yes," Dr. Trân said gently. "And I've confirmed that in the blood tests."

He turned to Kieran, and for the first time his smile was gone. "I am sorry to report, Mr. Mullaney, that our blood tests show damage to your chromosomes resulting from exposure to moderate-level radiation—radiation beyond what your prior dosimetry history can account for."

Kieran's expression of interest was gone. Emily took his hand.

"How bad?" the young man asked.

The scientist shook his head. "If we knew the quantity of radioactive material involved, we could make a better dispersion analysis. Based solely on the blood tests, we can only confirm the obvious: that the levels were not sufficiently acute to be life-threatening. Because radionuclides can affect your immune system, they may have contributed to the slow pace of your bronchial recovery. Combined with your occupational exposure, there is a greater likelihood of cancers later in life. In the best case, the levels may have been low enough to cause no major impact during a normal life span."

Kieran began to fade, sliding into an expression of disorientation. Ryan recognized the look. He'd seen it on Carolyn's face the day they'd received the news from her physician about her cancer. And Emily looked as stricken as Kieran—like Ryan probably did that day years ago.

Ryan felt the boy's concern, but he was also suddenly swept with another reaction: a suddenly shocking conclusion. It swept over him that this Trân could be right. Everything up until now had seemed mere speculation than science. But blood tests confirming radiation injury changed everything.

"What about the whole-body counts at the hospital that said Kieran wasn't exposed?" Ryan asked.

Dr. Trân shook his head. "Whole-body counters measure radiation released from the body. Those counts are only useful if the machinery has been properly calibrated. Covington has produced no evidence of its calibration for Mr. Mullaney that night."

And Pauline Strand, who hadn't gone far down the road of proving exposure before she withdrew, almost certainly didn't ask for that data when discovery was still allowed, Ryan thought.

Emily looked up from Kieran. "And Covington's claim about the hall monitor and dosimetry badge data?"

"I have no explanation for that," Dr. Trân explained. "But Covington's people also collected all that data."

Dr. Trân turned to Ryan now. "Mr. Hart, I informed you in Spokane that I would like to tour room 365. Now I believe my time is better spent visiting the lower levels of LB5—examining blast patterns evident in damaged rooms and hallways, perhaps finding samples of chemical and radioactive residues."

Ryan hadn't taken Dr. Trân's prior request very seriously. He simply nodded now, still watching Emily and Kieran.

"You're really ready to testify to each of these conclusions at trial," Ryan said.

Dr. Trân nodded with a return of his smile. "Of course."

Ryan nodded, stood, and showed Dr. Trân to the door. Then he turned again to the couple on the couch. Emily had an arm around Kieran, who was quietly holding himself together.

Ryan was torn between offering encouragement and absorbing everything Trân had related. Coming from him, encouragement would likely sound trite, he concluded.

"I'm going for a walk" was all Ryan said. Emily nodded.

He went out the back today, cutting across a small patch of yard and onto the next street. He walked, lost in thought, for what must have been miles, seeing sprinklers ladling water onto summer-parched lawns, smoke from barbecues rising into the blue sky from a few backyards.

It was a typical Saturday in America. Except in this town, as recently as twenty-five years ago, they'd celebrated weekends downwind from the world's largest plutonium factory. Those days weren't completely in the past: they still celebrated in the shadow of contamination that would terrify most Americans.

How had they done it? How did they still do it? Take their kids to the park, sit through football games outside in the fall, share beers around those barbecues in the open air. All with such danger so close.

The same way then as now, he supposed. With trust and faith—including an abiding trust in the people they worked for. Which meant, in the present day, the managers at Covington Nuclear.

He couldn't have done it, Ryan concluded. He couldn't even bring himself to fully trust Dr. Trân, whose opinions, while helpful to their case and logical, rested upon so many unprovable assumptions and too little proof. Chief among them was explosives in LB5 they had no evidence existed—other than by deductive elimination of other causes for the explosion. Then there were the blood test results, which seemed to confirm everything Dr. Trân was saying. What if, Ryan asked himself, Dr. Trân was a plant? What if he was setting them up with a plan to either recant on the stand or draw them into relying on opinions that could be riddled with holes?

Of course, a voice in his head responded, *the pitfalls in Trân's report were only relevant if Emily was forced to use him. If Dr. Strong came through, Dr. Trân would become an expensive footnote to the case.*

But what kind of a case was it when they didn't even know if they could trust their own expert? The same one, he thought with disgust, where their opponent already held a serious advantage with the judge and potentially the jury, and where his daughter was going up against King, a man who had years of civil trial experience representing Covington Nuclear in court.

Ryan halted at a street corner, coming out of his reverie long enough to realize that he'd paid no attention to where the walk had now led him. He looked around until he recognized the street he was on. Then he pivoted and began walking in the direction leading back to the Annex.

So what did he do now? Here he was, bankrolling a potentially two-million-dollar case—a fact that had hardly registered with him these past weeks, because he hadn't really believed in its likely success. He'd written the checks and put in the hours, based not on an expectation of a payday, but to avoid a final parting with Emily. Ryan could never recall a case he'd handled where he didn't have a strong belief in the client and the cause—and the potential to win.

But then, his faith in his cases until now was Carolyn's doing, wasn't it. His thoughts drifted to breakfast the morning after a night of celebrating graduation from law school, seated with Carolyn in the grandeur of the old Olympic Hotel. It was there that she'd made a toast over orange juice. "We'll never represent an insurance company," she'd said. "And we'll never sue a teacher. Or a farmer. And we'll only take on the fights truly worth fighting."

He'd accepted the toast without comment, just a clinking of

glass. But he'd looked into those gorgeous eyes that were his to enjoy forever and thought, *And we'll never lose. Because I'll knock down our opponents while you capture jurors' hearts. Like you captured the hearts of those judges at the mock trial. Like you captured mine.*

He'd marveled over the years at how she'd made the bone-bruising reality of litigation tolerable. Harsh tactics and sharp practices never seemed to reach her, and her optimism, in turn, curbed the cynicism that might otherwise have overtaken Ryan. That had now overtaken him.

And yet, with the success they'd enjoyed and her obvious love of the practice, she still hadn't hesitated to leave it all for Emily. Seven years later, sitting together on the patio of Pasco's Tex-Mex Grill overlooking Lake Union, Carolyn had nodded toward their young daughter, watching the boats on the water below. Then she'd smiled at him with those same eyes he'd seen at Starbucks years before.

"I'm leaving law for awhile," she'd said simply. "I can't take another week separated from my only daughter. She needs me."

Then she'd taken Ryan's hands. "I'll come back to practice with you again after she's older. You'll do fine without me for awhile."

He'd looked past her shoulder toward a passing catamaran on the lake, its jib sail puffed with wind like a sack stuffed with possibility. It *would* be fine, he'd thought. Just never the same.

She filled in the space with Emily that his absences created—that both their absences had been creating. And she continued to partner with him in law as his mentor of the heart—advising on cases to take or leave, listening at home in the evenings, even helping him strategize and prepare closing arguments. And he kept winning. Maybe with more sweat and less grace. But he won. And he never stopped planning for the day she'd return to the practice with him. Until the cancer arrived that made a mockery of all planning.

He was within sight of the Annex now, just another half a block away. This street was quieter than most. There were no children in the yards or traffic passing. Only a lone white van parked at the curb between Ryan and the Annex's front door.

Emily was leaving the house, arm in arm with Kieran. They stopped beside Kieran's battered car. Ryan watched as they turned and spoke a moment before she took his face in her hands and kissed him.

He wanted to be shocked and angry, but he was neither. Her feelings for Kieran had been no secret for weeks now, only their depth. He wanted to warn her about falling in love with someone you might lose too soon, but watching her looking at Kieran as he'd once looked at Carolyn, Ryan knew that was a waste of time.

Could he believe in Kieran's case now? Perhaps not as much as Emily. But yes, he guessed he did, though mostly by the same deductive logic Dr. Trân had applied today. He believed that Kieran did not deliberately turn the Vat 17 valve. He believed that the boy wasn't capable of that kind of deceit—or of keeping it a secret this long from Emily and himself. He believed that Kieran was genuinely harmed that night—perhaps quite seriously. He believed that Covington was covering up what happened that night. Though he wasn't sure he bought the depths of conspiracy implied by Dr. Trân, any cover-up still implied guilt and secrets. And maybe—just maybe—he could accept the possibility of Dr. Trân's logic about the cause of the explosion.

So yes, he believed enough in Kieran's case, and all that was very relevant and very important. But where did that leave him? Should he offer to do more? Shoulder a major role in the approaching trial? Emily still hadn't asked—and perhaps she'd never ask. But after what he'd just seen confirmed about Emily's feelings for Kieran on the Annex lawn, maybe that couldn't matter anymore. Not if it was in his power to make a difference in the life of someone Emily cared about the way he'd cared for Carolyn.

Kieran and Emily were gone by the time Ryan entered the Annex front door. Emily was nowhere downstairs. He took the staircase to her bedroom door, which was ajar.

"Emily?" he called, pushing it gently open.

She was seated on the bed, facing away. She turned as he entered, her eyes shot through with hopelessness.

"I can't help Kieran. I can't win his case, Dad. I can't beat them. I keep telling myself that I can, but I can't."

Ryan sat down on the bed beside her and put his arm around her shoulder.

"Yeah," he said quietly. "Let's talk about that."

CHAPTER 28

Adam leaned back in his desk chair as he finished his review of the summary of Dr. Virgil Strong's expert report.

This was satisfactory, he thought. He picked up the phone and called the contact number Cameron Foote had provided.

"Sharon? Yes. I'm just checking to see if the award letter has been released to the USC Health Sciences Department yet. The one confirming the final decision to fund the new chair. No? Well, could you please see that it goes out today? Fax and mail. Thank you."

Adam knew Dr. Virgil Strong. He'd looked into hiring him for the Project at one time. The man was a top expert in nuclear physics, though his personality had not been judged suitable for their purposes in Project Wolffia. So when the scientist's name came up as a potential expert for the Mullaney lawyers, Adam had been seriously troubled.

He'd considered bribery, but Virgil Strong was almost certainly above a direct solicitation, which was, in any event, extremely tricky business. No, a better course was to take advantage of the fact that the man was no less ambitious than any professor in line for department head at a major university.

The offer of a newly funded chair honoring Dr. Strong's work in health physics had not even been conveyed by Covington Nuclear, but through a foundation openly funded by Covington's parent company. Adam hadn't asked Cameron Foote what channels he'd used to convey the information to Dr. Strong that the chair was under "immediate" consideration by the foundation.

They hadn't wished to buy the man. They'd only needed to influence him. This summary of Strong's report to Mullaney's attorneys, obtained by a graduate student of Strong's on a highly paid summer internship with Covington Nuclear at Los Alamos, proved they had been successful.

If this summary was correct, Strong's expert report in the Mullaney case took no risks, plumbed no depths. It was entirely satisfactory.

And the Health Sciences Department at the University of Southern California would get its new chair.

Ryan slowed his pace as he reached the Annex. He wasn't a morning runner; he preferred exercise as catharsis after a full day of work. But today it felt good to get out early, with the pretrial status conference in the afternoon. Especially given his anxiety about receiving Dr. Strong's reports: the professor's secretary had left a message on Friday that they would be delivered before noon this morning.

He'd spoken with Dr. Strong several more times at the end of last week, sending more documents and answering questions about Kieran's recollections. He'd considered conveying Dr. Trân's reports to the USC professor. In the end he hadn't, uncertain what effect they would have.

But this was unprecedented for Ryan, to be hours from exchanging final expert reports with an opposing attorney without even having seen them himself.

A FedEx truck approached from down the street. Ryan stood on the lawn and watched it slow beside him.

A uniformed man appeared from the driver's side. "Are you Ryan Hart?" he asked.

At Ryan's nod, the man handed him a thick envelope, which Ryan signed for. He was tearing open the package as the man said, "Have a good one," and stepped away.

There was a single bound document inside: Cause of LB5 Explosion and Related Health Effects. Under the title was stamped "Dr. Virgil Strong, Member, Faculty of University of Southern California Health Physics Department."

Ryan flipped straight to the back to read the "Summary of Opinions" just as Emily came out of the Annex to join him.

"How's it look?" she asked tentatively.

Ryan didn't glance up, but began to read out loud.

"In sum, based upon the chemical data, blast force, time parameters . . ."

He skipped ahead.

". . . it is my expert opinion that the October 16, 2013, explosions in Lab Building 5 of the Hanford Reservation were most likely caused by an autocatalytic event, triggered by the opening of a valve on the bottom of Vat 17 by person or persons unknown. . . . It is also my opinion that there is insufficient evidence from the blood samples to conclude that Kieran Mullaney was exposed to ionizing radiation as a result of the explosions."

Ryan felt the blood drain from his face. "Strong's sided with Covington Nuclear," he muttered.

His cell phone pressed hard against his ear. Ryan paced the hall outside Judge Renway's courtroom in the Sherman Federal Courthouse.

"I'm sorry, Mr. Hart, but Professor Strong isn't available just now," the secretary said calmly. "I'm glad to take a message."

Ryan struggled to keep his voice down. "I've left four messages today already."

"I am *so* sorry, Mr. Hart," the solicitous woman responded. "I've forwarded your earlier messages to Dr. Strong's office, but I don't believe he's even been in yet today. I'll be sure to alert him to the urgency of your calls just as soon as I see him."

"Add this message to the last, please," Ryan spat. "Tell him to collect the rest of his fee from Covington Nuclear."

He nearly tossed the phone across the hall.

Strong's report, with a few quibbles, had validated Covington's position in this case—even to the point of downplaying the significance of the blood results. In twenty years of practice, Ryan had never had an expert so clearly turned. And they'd done it with such impeccable timing.

Fifty thousand dollars for Strong's version of the blood study, plus the prepaid portion of Strong's fees. All fodder for the shredder.

Ryan took a deep breath to get his heart rate under control. Covington had gotten to Strong—or maybe they'd always had him. His paranoia meter soared. Could he really trust Dr. Trân—or was *his* betrayal just being delayed until trial?

His hands had stopped shaking enough that Ryan pushed through the doors into Judge Renway's courtroom.

"Your Honor," Emily protested from counsel table, "we need this inspection of the lower levels of LB5 because our expert concludes that the explosion likely *started* in those lower glove boxes."

The judge, resplendent in his blue robe, was peering over the bench at Emily. "Ms. Hart, discovery closed in this case months ago. Now you want Covington to prepare the building for an inspection—including sampling—only seven days before trial?"

"Yes, Your Honor," Emily pressed. She was on her feet, with

Kieran at her side looking down at the table. "Final expert reports were only due today; months ago, we couldn't have known what other evidence might be relevant in light of our expert's conclusions."

The judge shook his head with a look Ryan interpreted as self-righteous solemnity. "The expert reports were only due so late at *your* request. And your expert could have alerted you to additional evidence he desired when still in the process of preparing his report."

King, occupying the counsel table to Emily's left, looked smug and satisfied. Why not, Ryan thought. He didn't even need to open his mouth. The judge was making every argument for him.

"If I can remind the court," Emily said, leaning into her own table, "we have only been attorneys in this case for less than sixty days. We have been working day and night to meet this Court's schedule—"

The judge's expression grew darker as he interrupted. "And I will remind *Counsel* that you knew the deadlines when you took the case."

Through the veil of his disappointment today, Ryan felt proud of Emily. She wasn't giving an inch. There was no need for him to resume his seat at counsel table next to Kieran: Emily was holding her own, even if this judge wasn't budging.

Emily launched several more tacks, none of which made the slightest dent in the judge's position. At last, Renway brought down the gavel.

"For the last time, your request is denied, Counsel. And since that was the last matter to cover today, we're adjourned until trial commences next Monday afternoon, a week from today."

King gathered his papers and left the courtroom at his usual rocket pace—as though fearing Ryan would follow again. The clerks followed the judge out. Kieran stood and thanked Emily dispiritedly. "I've gotta make a quick call," he said, then left the room.

Emily and Ryan were alone in the cavernous courtroom. "Nothing from Strong?" she asked quietly.

Ryan shook his head. "Nope. He's ducking my calls. We're done with him."

"Then I guess it's Dr. Trân."

Ryan smiled with more optimism than he felt. "I guess so."

He gestured toward the door. "You think Kieran's doing okay?"

Emily shook her head. "No. But he's putting on a good face. Especially with Renway slapping us down again."

Ryan nodded. "This was a foregone conclusion. But you did well today, Counselor."

They pulled together their papers—including Covington's final expert reports that they'd received that morning from Eric King. Ryan had already reviewed them quickly: there was little new. But then, Covington didn't need anything new at this stage. Most of the arrows in this case were already in their quiver—including the judge who'd just left the courtroom.

They did have a small element of surprise for the first day of trial: Ryan's participation. The last three days, he and Emily had hammered out a new split of responsibility. This was still Emily's case. But Ryan had the opening statement, Kieran's testimony, and other key parts of their case in chief—parts where his experience would count the most. Emily had closing arguments, most of the workers—including Taylor Christensen—and, at Ryan's suggestion, Dr. Trân.

Emily's unspoken relief had been immediate and powerful. Her role was still primary, but she no longer stood alone on the front line of a complex, difficult trial.

"Come on," Ryan said. "The lawyer who sits in the gallery buys lunch."

Emily smiled weakly. "That a tradition?"

Ryan patted her back. "It is now."

CHAPTER 29

"Poppy. *Poppy Martin*."

He looked up from the handful of washers he held in his open hand. The lighting in aisle four of the Sherman Ace Hardware was a little dim—or maybe his eyes were just tired—but he didn't recognize the barrel-chested man striding toward him.

The man drew close and Poppy realized there was a reason he didn't recognize the grinning thick-armed man who was acting like Poppy was a lost cousin: he'd never seen him before in his life.

"Poppy," the man began, still grinning, "my name's Mel Emerson. I transferred to Hanford a few years ago from Los Alamos. I heard you were in that explosion last October, out at LB5. I wanted to say I'm really sorry you got caught up in that mess. See, I was one of the regular guards you replaced that night."

Poppy looked him over, wondering why he'd never met a guard who'd been at Hanford that long—and why, in that case, this Emerson had recognized him. He wasn't sure how to respond. "You're welcome," he said, awkwardly.

Emerson just stood there, as though waiting for Poppy to say something more. His discomfort growing, Poppy muttered a "See you around" and dropped all but two of the washers back into the open bin before starting in the opposite direction, toward the checkout counter.

Poppy's tension rose as Emerson matched his steps down the aisle. *What's he following me for,* he thought. *And why's he walking so close?*

"Hey, listen, Poppy," Emerson said as they reached the cashier. "I heard about that business at the softball game a few weeks back. You showed real guts stepping in for that kid. Real guts. Some of the guys at LB5, when they heard about that, weren't too happy. But I told them, that Poppy's a man of principle."

Poppy's stomach knotted. "Thanks, Mel," he muttered again, trying to look disinterested as he reached into his hip pocket for his wallet.

Now he was *really* too close, leaning in like he was Poppy's best friend about to give him a secret stock tip.

"Yep, that really took guts, Poppy," Emerson went on. "Especially since you've got to be as mad as anybody about this lawsuit by Kieran Mullaney, am I right?"

Poppy ignored the last comment, accepting his change with a nod at the cashier who was trying to look away from the conversation, then striding toward the exit with Emerson on his heels. Out on the street, he sensed Emerson's presence the instant before he felt a grip on his arm, bringing him to a stop.

He turned hard on the man. "*What do you want.*"

Emerson's eyes narrowed. "You sound angry, Poppy. You don't have any reason to be mad at me. I didn't cause the explosion. The Mullaney kid did. He's the one you should be mad at."

Poppy sized the man up. Though he'd been looking from a distance, this guy wasn't too far off from the height and shape of the man who'd gone up to Kieran's house with the crows that day. Maybe even one of the guys in the shadows of the retirement home that night, loading the body into the SUV under the lamplight.

"The kid's a gold digger, Poppy," Emerson went on. "We all know the risks of working at a nuclear defense facility. If he doesn't like it, he can quit and move to Seattle or Portland. He shouldn't mess with the mission. There's plenty of others who would kill for his job."

Kill for his job. An image arose of the crows in Mullaney's garden.

"Just what mission are we talking about, Emerson," Poppy said.

The man leaned in close again. "We all know the mission, Poppy. It's never changed. And there's no sidelines here. In this industry, nobody's ever had that luxury. You've gotta pick sides."

He's talking about my refusal to change my statement, Poppy thought, a fire lighting in his chest.

"So whose side are *you* on?" Poppy muttered, stepping back enough to throw a punch.

He wondered if he could take this guy, who had three inches and fifteen years on him. He could or he couldn't, but Poppy was past caring. Everything that was happening to him was suddenly centered on this man standing three feet away in the hardware store parking lot. He *wanted* this to happen now.

Emerson scrutinized Poppy's face without any doubt about what was coming. He shook his head and stepped away. "This isn't about me and you, Poppy. It's not personal. It's about decisions that have consequences. For us. For the people we care about."

Emerson turned and strode quickly away. He was out of reach before Poppy was sure that it was over, sure that he'd *let* it be over. The man was getting into his car when Poppy finally unclenched his fists, feeling the blood flow back into his fingers. His chest was still pounding and his ears buzzing with adrenaline as he looked around to get reoriented and remember where the truck was.

He'd just gotten into the cab when his phone went off. The sudden sound annoyed him; he didn't want to talk to anybody just now. He had to think. Plus, the caller ID read *unknown.* Still, he punched the button to answer.

"Yeah," he said.

"Is this Poppy Martin?"

"Yeah," he answered uncertainly. The voice was faint. "Who's this?"

"Beverly Cortez," the voice came back. "You've been trying to call me. But I won't talk to you on your phone."

Lew's girlfriend. His heart raced again. Before he could speak, the woman continued. "Maybe we can talk out at the Atomic Café."

The line went dead. Poppy fumbled with his keys for a moment before getting them into the ignition and throwing the shift lever into gear.

On the drive to the Atomic Café, Poppy checked his mirrors so often he felt a kink growing in his neck. He saw nothing. But the renewed pounding in his chest still hadn't stopped by the time he pulled into the café parking lot.

The lot was almost empty. Poppy parked near the door and went into the restaurant.

Only two elderly couples occupied tables this afternoon. Poppy checked his watch. Two forty-five. He found a bench and took a seat facing the door, next to a window overlooking the lot.

The waitress refilled his coffee twenty minutes later. In all that time, no one had even pulled into the parking lot. He was wondering how long he was supposed to wait when he heard, in the background, a telephone ringing. Not a cell ringtone. A real, old-fashioned phone.

The sound was coming from the small lobby area near the front door. Poppy glanced in that direction. No one was there. But a phone kept ringing.

He stood and walked to the entryway. A battered pay phone hung on the wall. Poppy'd hardly noticed this museum piece before; he'd walked right by it like most everyone probably did, with their cells resting in their pockets. He picked up the receiver.

"Yeah," he answered.

"Mr. Martin? Is that you?"

"Yeah. Beverly?"

"Um-hmm."

"How'd you get this number?"

"I called the café and they gave it to me. I knew the phone was there. Lew and I used to go. I've only got a few minutes. I wanted to tell you that you've got to stop calling me."

"Beverly, I'm just trying to find Lew. I was his partner. I haven't heard from him for eight months."

"I know who you are. Lew used to talk about you."

"Do you know where he is?"

The line went silent. "I was told," Poppy continued, "that Covington asked Darter Security to transfer him out to Covington's operations in Savannah River out east. Is that true?"

"That's what they told me, too. Please stop trying to reach me."

He feared she was about to hang up. "Wait, wait. I have to find Lew. Covington's trying to get me to change my statement about what happened that night, especially about Lew firing his rifle."

Silence. "I don't know anything about that."

She didn't sound convincing. Poppy's mind raced. "Have you spoken with Lew since the explosion?"

"Just once."

"When."

Silence. "That night. From the hospital. They'd taken his cell, but he called from a nurse's desk."

"What did he tell you."

More silence. "I can't tell you."

Now the tentacles of fear reached over the line and into Poppy. "Have you tried to reach him in Savannah River?"

"No."

"Why not?"

"There've been messages, texts from his phone. He says I'll hear from him when he's ready and I shouldn't try to reach him until then."

That tone. "You don't believe it, do you, Beverly."

She didn't respond for a moment, then answered, "No."

"Please, Beverly. I've got to know. What did Lewis tell you that last time you talked?"

But for the soft breathing over the line, this time Poppy would have been sure the girl had hung up.

"He said he was okay," she finally said in a near whisper. "He was worried about you at the hospital that night. But he told me they'd warned him not to say anything about the explosion, so I couldn't repeat anything he told me. Lew never could keep a secret. I'm afraid . . . I'm afraid Lew could get in trouble for my telling you this."

Poppy wracked his memory for something to keep her on the line.

"How long did you date, Beverly?" he asked.

There was a pause. "A year."

"Did you know he named his rifle for you? Did you know that?"

It sounded stupid—but nothing else came to mind. "No," she answered after a moment.

"He did. He must have thought a lot about you."

A sob came across the line.

"Beverly," Poppy kept on softly, "did Lew say whether he fired a shot that night?"

Quiet. "Yes."

"Did he say what he was shooting at?"

"A man. A man in a white coat."

"Did he hit him?"

Silence. "He thought so."

"What else did he say?"

Her voice grew more strained with each breath. "The guy was

228

coming out of an emergency exit where no one ought to have been. That's all. He told me to keep it to myself, that maybe he could talk more after."

"After what?"

"After his meeting."

Poppy's stomach tightened. "Meeting with who?"

"He didn't say. Somebody from the Human Resources office."

"And you haven't heard from Lew since?"

There was a clicking sound over the line.

"*It's them*," Beverly moaned.

"How can I reach you again?" Poppy pleaded. "I couldn't find an address for you. You've got to tell me how I can reach you again."

The clicks fluttered in rapid succession.

"*You can't.*"

"Be careful," Poppy said. The line went dead.

Poppy dropped the phone back on the cradle. He looked out the door into the parking lot. No new cars had arrived at the restaurant. He looked around the corner into the dining room. The old folks were still the only occupants, nursing drinks while the waitress cleared the tables.

This was an old pay phone. He could hardly remember what it was like to use one. Maybe the clicks were a bad line, or because they'd run out of time on the call.

Poppy went back and handed the waitress a few dollars for his coffee, then he returned to his truck.

Suzy'd be at work now. He had to make sure she was safe and talk this through with her. It all was getting too crazy.

CHAPTER 30

It began while Emily was resting in her room: the faint *thwat-a-thwat-a-thwat* of her dad's speed bag in the basement. She'd heard it every day since the pretrial hearing. When they'd gotten back from the courthouse that day, her father had gone to the sporting goods store and bought the bag, installing it in the Annex basement.

Emily rolled to a sitting position and reached for her shoes. She wondered how she'd feel if her father hadn't stepped up for the trial. A part of her regretted making him take Kieran's case—especially hearing the bag day after day.

But then she hadn't made her father this way; he'd always lived a life of intensity. She recalled her mother softly chiding him at times, soothing him when it got to be too much, when the grind of his pace was reflected in an icy mood or exhausted face. Her mother's special touch almost certainly made his life better—and a gentler father when he was around. Did it make him a better lawyer?

Her experience these past weeks now made Emily aware that her father must have reciprocated her mother's love in his own way. Though too young at the time to remember, she wondered if he had shouldered the worst of the litigation for her mother—taking on the Dr. Strongs and the Judge Renways of their world, just as he was beginning to do in this case. Perhaps in that way, he'd helped to preserve the best parts of her mother—the empathy and compassion she showered back on Emily and her father. Three months ago she would have rejected the notion. She couldn't any longer. Because he was striving to do it for Emily right now.

The image of her father as that kind of protector had never occurred to her before this summer. She'd only begun to consider the possibility that his absence growing up might have been the price for her mother's presence in Emily's life.

The pounding of the speed bag continued unrelenting as Emily forced herself to her feet and headed downstairs to pick up the trial work once more.

Dr. Minh Trân had spent the afternoon and early evening of this Friday before trial completing errands in Sherman. Though Ryan Hart had told him which day of trial he'd likely testify, the lawyer had also asked him to be available to help with cross-examination of Covington's experts. So he'd extended his reservation at the Holiday Inn Suites for two full weeks.

He pulled his rental car into the hotel parking lot and turned out the headlights. It was far past suppertime, and he felt a deep weariness. The report had been exhausting to prepare in such a short time frame, and he was still recovering from sleep deprivation. Tonight he prayed that room service was still available, and that he could get an early bedtime.

His cell phone rang. "Yes?" he answered.

"Dr. Trân, the package we told you about has finally arrived. It's waiting at the front desk."

The call was not unexpected, but the timing was miserable.

"Are you still alright with delivering it?" the voice asked when he failed to answer immediately.

"Yes. It's fine."

"Good. Please just leave it at the door. We'll be in touch." The line went dead.

Minh let out a sigh at another hour of tasks before supper and bed. He got out of the car and trudged into the hotel lobby.

The desk receptionist smiled when he asked if there was anything left for him. She crouched behind the counter and stood a moment later with a full-sized manila envelope. Minh took it and headed back out to the car.

Once more behind the wheel, Minh set the envelope on the passenger seat. He considered driving straightaway to deliver it, without looking at its contents. But he couldn't do that. It wasn't in his nature—as a scientist or a man—and despite his implicit trust in his sponsors, he would not deliver a package ignorant of its contents.

He smiled to see that the envelope was unsealed. Apparently his patrons knew him well. He opened it and withdrew a set of folded papers.

They looked official. He turned on the interior light and held them up.

All of the pages were photocopies. *Promissory Note*, the top document read. *Loan Agreement* was the title on the next clipped bunch of pages.

Minh contemplated why it was better that *he* take the risk of discovery for a task like this rather than his sponsors. He was a scientist, not a delivery boy. But he'd do it, of course. After all his years working with his sponsors, neither pride nor petulance would prevent him from this simple task.

He began to put the papers back in the envelope—then stopped. Out of an abundance of caution, he removed a handkerchief from his hip pocket and carefully wiped the pages wherever he had touched them. He did the same with the envelope.

Minh started the car and then pulled his smartphone from

his pocket. He pressed the GPS app and activated the voice command. When the mechanical beep signaled the phone's readiness, Minh held it close.

"Directions," he began, "to Judge Howard Renway, 1965 Alvarado Boulevard . . ."

CHAPTER 31

FIRST DAY OF TRIAL

Emily looked up from the intensity of her work on the laptop, glancing around the kitchen to clear her head. She'd thought the preparation in the month and a half following their arrival at Sherman had been serious. The past ten days had proved her wrong. Never had she worked so hard. Not even for the bar exam.

Dressed in his suit, her father was perched at his usual spot on the couch, organizing his examination, cross-examination, and rebuttal testimony questions for witnesses on his own laptop. All prepared in just seven days.

Emily had slipped away for a quick breakfast with Kieran this morning. Going out the door, she'd heard the sound of her father pounding away again at the speed bag in the basement. This evening, she knew he'd likely go for a run after court—just as he did every evening.

She'd finally asked her father this weekend if the workouts were to relieve the pressure. He'd answered yes, but also for training. Trial was physically demanding, he'd said. "And better than the Atkins diet. I lose a pound a day usually."

Then he'd changed the subject, for the first time offering her direct advice on trial preparation. He knew that she'd taken

234

plenty of testimony before, but it was different in a complex trial where witnesses could be on the stand for hours or days.

"Remember, Emily, that when you're taking a witness's testimony, you've got to elicit the story with enough detail to explain and illustrate, but you can never risk putting a jury to sleep. Once they're gone in a case of this length, they're hard to wake up again." And in the process, he'd cautioned, "Be prepared that some witnesses you thought would be helpful could turn hostile—resisting questions, changing stories from earlier deposition testimony. Think of it like conversing with someone with multiple personalities; be prepared for whoever emerges once the questioning starts."

She'd tried not to chafe at advice she thought unnecessary after her time trying cases—forcing herself to acknowledge that the cases she'd tried at the Public Defender's office the past two years were one to three day trials, with only a handful of witnesses and few scientific issues.

Emily glanced at her watch. Two hours until they left for the courthouse, where Kieran would meet them.

This past weekend she'd hardly seen Kieran; every minute was crammed with trial preparation. At her father's suggestion, he was taking Kieran's testimony. He'd hinted it was just a casual preference, but Emily knew that he had grown aware of her feelings for Kieran. She could guess what he was thinking: that all they needed was for the jury to suspect her personal attachment to the client. Who knew how they'd treat that revelation.

There was a metal clank of the mailbox hung by the front door. The only mail they were receiving here were court notices or letters from Covington's counsel. Her father got up and walked to the door. He returned a moment later with only a slim envelope in his hands.

"It's a hand delivery from the court," Ryan said curiously. He tore it open and held it up to read.

"What is it, Dad?" Emily asked absently as her gaze stayed

fixed on her laptop. When he didn't respond, she glanced up. His face had a look of pure astonishment.

"Judge Renway just removed himself from the case," he said.

❖❖❖

Adam was stopped on the side of the road where he'd pulled over when King called, clutching his phone like he was strangling it.

"Explain to me again how this happened," he demanded bitterly.

"I . . . I'm not sure," Eric King was stammering now, his patented bravado gone. "I got a message from Judge Renway Sunday afternoon, asking me to stop by his chambers this morning. I got there early. He ushered me in and told me he had to recuse himself from the case."

"Why?"

"He said he owned orchards downwind from Hanford that had been in his family for generations. Apparently he refinanced a loan on that land a couple of years ago. One of the terms of the loan was that it could be accelerated if there was a 'sudden release' of radiation from Hanford. Since this Mullaney case is trying to prove a radiation release at LB5, and his orchards are near the building, the judge has a stake in the outcome of the case. It creates a hopeless conflict."

Adam's fingers were cramping around the cell. *And why did he just figure this out now.*

King was equal parts defensive and nervous. "He told me he hadn't paid much attention to the acceleration clause before, with Hanford closed down. But somebody dropped a copy of his loan documents at his door Friday night with that clause circled. He thought about turning it over to the FBI—treat it as some kind of extortion. Except there's no demand attached, of any kind. All it does is point out his ethical conflict. He decided he had to drop out before it got public."

"Who dropped off the loan papers at Renway's house," Adam demanded.

"He doesn't know. They were left at his door."

It had to be Hart. Where had he come up with those papers?

"Can the judge be paid to stay on the case?" Adam asked.

"You mean a *bribe*?" King blurted out. "Bribe a federal judge? Renway isn't *that* kind of asset. He's just a judge with a soft spot for Hanford."

Adam's anger compounded at the lecturing tone. "So who replaces him?"

"It's a new judge: Celeste Johnston. She started as a federal judge a year ago. Used to be a state court judge in Seattle, so she's on the bench in King County. She's African-American. Moderate. Smart."

Adam's head was swimming as the lawyer continued. "Listen, Adam, this doesn't have to be that big of a setback. I contacted the calendar clerk's office. Judge Johnston's calendar is mostly free, so they have no intention of pushing back trial. That means we'll still start in a couple of hours. With no time to prepare, it'll be all Judge Johnston can do to get up to speed. I'd be amazed if she revisited any of Judge Renway's decisions in the case. Given the evidence, we've still got this locked up."

King always had as much optimism as money could buy. Adam didn't believe in uncertainties, and this was the second source of uncertainty in two weeks. Despite King's failed attempt to mollify him, these setbacks were adding up.

"Keep me alerted," he snapped.

As he dropped the phone onto the passenger seat, Adam considered calling Foote to apprise him. But that wasn't such a good idea. If he called Foote about this turn of events, it would sound like a major setback. If he told Foote in the course of their next conversation about the successful Wolffia test, he could paint Renway's departure as no serious problem.

He pulled back onto the road. Adam wished he could sit in

on trial. But he couldn't, and he had to let the idea go. Besides, he had lots yet to do. The successful Project test ended the first phase of seven long years of research, but there were more tests to run—then the necessity to begin production planning and reach out to the DOE and defense departments about the new technology. And while Foote would be leading that effort, Adam knew he was expected to be very close by.

The next few months were going to be busy enough without sitting in a courtroom. Despite his dwindling confidence in King, he had to rely on the lawyer to see this through.

Still, Adam told himself, he'd have to keep more careful tabs on the events at the courthouse than he'd ever planned or hoped for.

CHAPTER 32

Judge Johnston was presiding over her courtroom gingerly on this first afternoon of the trial. Not unexpected, Ryan thought, with only hours to step in. Now Ryan and Emily sat waiting in the moments after jury selection while the judge finished conferring with her clerk.

Just before noon, Ryan had reached Judge Freyling in Seattle by phone for his impressions of their new judge, based on their time together on the King County bench. Freyling had not hesitated to respond. "Decisive," he'd said. "Prepares well. Don't push her, though. She's got a slow fuse, but you don't want to be the one at the podium when she goes off."

They might have to ignore that last advice, Ryan thought—if they had to take this chance to alter Renway's rulings to date.

Emily passed him a note: *What do you think of the jury?*

They hadn't had a chance to talk since the last juror was selected. He glanced at the final panel of three men and five women in the box—six regulars and two alternates. They were the product of nearly three hours of dueling questions, or "voir dire," of the candidates, with King pitted against Emily and Ryan, taking turns. Two of the jurors now looked resentful, probably convinced the government had just unfairly stolen two weeks of their lives. In contrast, several wore expressions of excitement.

Ryan scribbled back a quick note: *Fine. Good to have more women, who'll be more sympathetic. Wish there was less "Hanford" in the box.*

It was an accurate summary of his feelings. As Pauline had warned, avoiding Hanford's influence in the jury box had been impossible. Ryan and Emily had taken turns asking everything from family histories to favorite magazines to travel preferences in an effort to tease out the jury candidates' perspectives on Hanford. These eight jurors—ages twenty-two to sixty-four—included a high school teacher, a doctor, a saleswoman, two office workers, two homemakers, and a mechanic. They had been the ones who displayed the least slavish affinity to Hanford, in Emily's and Ryan's estimation. Still, only the teacher and the pharmaceuticals saleswoman lacked any apparent Hanford ties whatsoever.

But then, each side had only three "preemptory" challenges, the strongest card a lawyer had to play in voir dire—the ability to eliminate prospective jurors without proving prejudice. Ryan had insisted they use two of theirs to take out hard-edged male candidates who would have eviscerated Kieran's case. The third was a more subtle choice, but Emily had prevailed, convincing Ryan that a woman chiropractor was casting bad vibrations about the case. Ryan would have paid a large amount of money for two more preemptories, but absent that choice, this was probably as good as they could hope for.

He glanced at defense counsel's table. Eric King had a young female associate with him today—along with an unknown company rep from Covington HQ to serve as the company's symbol at trial. Ryan thought his principal qualifications for being there appeared to be his youth, a cleft chin, and a suit that fit well.

King wore multicolored suspenders peeking from a navy blue suit and sported a fine shine on his shoes. His associate was equally well dressed—overdressed, actually, for somebody who'd likely spend her days shepherding papers for King. She'd best not expect to take any witnesses of her own, Ryan thought. King wasn't the kind to yield the spotlight to a subordinate. Ryan had him pegged as incapable of imagining anyone else taking a turn at the podium for the defense.

Emily seemed cooler today than at the lead-up motions. He knew that her energy, commitment, and obvious belief in her client would be attractive assets to a jury. Plus her style would make for a good contrast with his own, and a father-daughter team would generate jury interest.

All these were helpful. And they'd need all the help they could summon in the coming weeks.

Butterflies roiled Ryan's stomach, driving a soft tapping of his shoe. He was curious why these signs of adrenaline seemed odd to him today. Didn't he always react this way the first day of trial? Then he thought of the half a dozen cases he'd tried since Carolyn's death and realized that he hadn't experienced pretrial nerves before any of them.

Ryan allowed himself a final glance at Emily, organizing her notes for the start of trial. Her hair was pulled back like he'd seen it the last time in the King County Courthouse. She also wore the same no-nonsense suit, which hid none of her beauty.

What would his wife have thought if she could've seen their daughter at counsel table at his side?

"All right," Judge Johnston announced, raising her eyes from her bench papers. "I have a few procedural matters to attend to with counsel, ladies and gentlemen of the jury. So you will be dismissed until tomorrow morning."

The bailiff directed the jurors out of the box and into the jury room. As the door closed behind the last of them, Judge Johnston turned her gaze back to the attorneys.

"Mr. Hart," she began, "you mentioned a motion you wanted to raise before we do opening arguments tomorrow?"

Ryan stood. "Yes, Your Honor. We wish to renew our motion to inspect the lower levels of LB5 building."

The judge nodded with an expression of skepticism. "Judge Renway's prior ruling was very clear on this matter, Mr. Hart. I hope you don't expect me to revisit every one of my predecessor's pretrial rulings."

"No, Your Honor," Ryan responded, though he planned to do just that if necessary, "but we were only aware of the need for this inspection when our expert, Dr. Trân, presented us with his conclusion that the cause of the explosions harming Mr. Mullaney originated in the lower levels of LB5 and not in room 365."

Ryan went on to cover the ground Emily had already struggled over with Judge Renway—was it only a week ago? He focused especially on the unfairness of being denied access to evidence so critical to a fair jury decision.

As he finished, the judge shook her head gently. "I understand the plight of new counsel on a case," she said. "But I'm also sympathetic to a defendant faced with new evidence on the first day of trial." She cocked her head toward opposing counsel. "Mr. King, I imagine you have an opinion on this matter."

Eric King stood at counsel table, unbuttoning his suit coat as he reached his feet.

"Judge, of course you're right," the Covington lawyer began collegially. "Their expert's wild speculation about explosive materials elsewhere in LB5 is imaginative, but pure conjecture. As for arranging a tour of LB5, Counsel seems to forget that the building is a former plutonium manufacturing facility. It would take *considerable effort* to make that facility safe for tourists such as Mr. Hart's expert. Not a single argument made by Mr. Hart is any different from those presented earlier to Judge Renway. This motion is an irresponsible fishing expedition—and too late."

Ryan was on his feet before King could sit down. "Your Honor, Mr. King's argument that LB5 is unsafe for an inspection is interesting, given that his experts' investigation report concludes that no serious radiation was detected inside the building *even after three explosions shook it up last fall*. Unless Mr. King wishes to amend his expert report and acknowledge hazardous radionuclides in LB5 since the explosion, an inspection should require no special precautions at all."

He had her attention. It was a mistake, Ryan thought, for King to adhere to a style that had worked with Renway. Johnston wasn't King's dancing partner like Renway had been.

But though Judge Johnston studied Ryan and Emily for a few long minutes, she finally shook her head.

"I'm sorry, Counsel, but your motion is denied," the judge called out. "You make . . . good points. But it is simply too late."

As the judge left the courtroom for the noon recess, Ryan deliberately glanced away from his opponent, refusing to give King the satisfaction of seeing disappointment. This wasn't over—they'd revisit the motion after Dr. Trân testified.

As he packed his papers, Ryan glanced at Emily, whose face displayed her own dismay at the judge's ruling. The sight of it took him back to his first trial against Lester Schmidt.

"Mr. Hart, you did well," Judge Freyling had said the day that trial ended, reemerging from chambers into the courtroom where only Ryan remained, gathering his papers. "I just have three suggestions about your courtroom demeanor: never let discouragement show in the courtroom; never signal to a jury that you've lost a round; and never gave an ounce of satisfaction to an opponent."

It was advice he'd have to pass on to Emily before the next day of the trial.

"No, Mr. Martin. This is a big complex, and I'm just the records manager. I see that a Mr. Lewis Vandervork rented an apartment in building 3 for several months last fall and winter. But he gave up the space in February and moved out."

Poppy thanked the landlord and ended the call. He set his phone on the kitchen counter.

For a week since his conversation with Beverly Cortez, Poppy had used every spare moment to try to track Lewis down in Savannah River, South Carolina—all by long distance. First, he'd called the Personnel Office at the Savannah River facility. They'd told him they could only confirm from records that Lew had been working out there for four months before quitting. Then he'd reached Lew's parents in Missouri, who said he'd texted them about his move to Savannah River, then kept in touch by text sporadically. His last one had said he was leaving his job and would be traveling and out of touch through the summer. Now this conversation with Lew's former landlord.

Everything pointed to Lew moving to South Carolina from Sherman, working four months, then falling off the face of the earth. So far as Poppy could learn, the only person who'd actually spoken with Lew since the explosion was Beverly Cortez—that very night. And since her call at the Atomic Café, he couldn't find her, either.

He shook his head in frustration. Wherever Beverly was, it wasn't in Sherman—it wasn't that big of a town. She also didn't have a Facebook page, didn't advertise her address or phone number online, and didn't want to be found—by anyone.

But Poppy was uncertain if it was right to keep trying to find her anyway, given how frightened she seemed. The last thing he wanted to do was drag her deeper into this mess than she was willing to go, especially if it did put her at risk.

Whatever he was going to do, he had to act soon. Janniston was almost through with him: they were down to "a few more sessions," the shrink had said. So his medical leave was running out, and with it his spare time to try to find Lew.

He heard the door from the garage open. "Patrick, I'm home from the store," Suzy called out.

Poppy forced himself to shed the malaise he was feeling. "I'm in the kitchen, Suzy," he answered as cheerfully as he could muster. Then he stood and headed to the door to help her with the groceries.

CHAPTER 33

Early morning sunlight streamed through courtroom windows as tall as a cathedral's. Ryan grasped the podium and faced the jurors for the opening statement of Kieran's case.

It had been a quick preparation. Usually Ryan spent days on an opening statement, but with everything else to prepare, he'd had only hours for this one. Still, he felt ready.

As usual, Ryan picked the most sympathetic juror for his focus, watering the plant most likely to thrive. It was the smiling schoolteacher in her forties, with auburn hair and a look of quickness and intelligence. She had two children under the age of twenty, and a father who'd recently passed away from cancer.

"Ladies and gentlemen of the jury," he began, gazing across the box before returning to the teacher. "No one should be sentenced to the purgatory of the unknown. Not when their health is endangered."

The schoolteacher's eyes flickered understanding. *Good*. He pressed on.

Ryan's opening went nearly an hour, touching all the themes of their case: Covington's failed duty to keep LB5 safe, its failure to adequately test Kieran for radiation, the fear of future cancer with which Kieran had to live. By the end, the recognition and understanding in the teacher's eyes appeared in a few of the other jurors' as well.

"The defendant, Covington Nuclear," Ryan said, nearing the
end, "was operating under a *two-billion-dollar contract* with
the Department of Energy . . ."

"*Objection*, Your Honor," King called out, rising to his feet.
"Irrelevant and highly prejudicial."

"Objection sustained," the judge called back immediately.

Ryan's gaze never left the jury box. He didn't care that King
had won the objection; he'd expected as much. The nine-figure
contract was out there now. He'd never have to remind them
again.

He moved on, closing with a promise that Emily and he would
prove that the explosion resulted from explosive materials left in
the lower levels of LB5—Dr. Trân's hypothesis. It was, he hoped
silently, a promise he could keep. Then he sat down.

Emily slid a note across the table. *"Nice job, Dad."*

King followed, standing to move to center stage. As he did,
Ryan eased down in his chair, folding his arms across his chest
and examining each of the light fixtures in the ceiling in turn.
Boring stuff, he hoped to signal, not worth a juror's attention. He held the pose, even as low voltage flowed through
every muscle in his body at King's recitation of dosimetry
and whole-body-count evidence that Ryan knew they couldn't
directly counter.

It was nearly an hour later when King ended with a flourish and took his seat. The judge glanced at the wall clock and
declared a recess. "We'll pick up again this afternoon," she
instructed the jury. "Be sure you don't discuss the case among
yourselves—until the case is closed and all of the evidence is in."

Ryan stood, smiling confidently as the jury left the room. It
was more posturing. Optimistically, he knew only two jurors
had begun the case sympathetic to Kieran: the teacher and the
mechanic. It was too meager a beginning.

❖❖❖

"Mr. Mullaney," Ryan said to Kieran from the podium as the afternoon session began. "Describe what you saw when you entered the vat room."

Kieran was dressed in dark slacks, a white shirt, and a muted tie. It was a statement of respect for the process, but one that avoided portraying him as someone he wasn't. The young man was clearly nervous, but that was all right. The jury would expect that. At least he was following instructions: answering the questions slowly, looking at the jury, thinking before he responded.

Kieran was not an eager witness. Ryan could see he was uncomfortable talking to the strangers in the box about the past year. But he made up for it with a strong sense of unvarnished truth.

Kieran's testimony reached his arrival at room 365 that night. Ryan could see from the corner of his eyes that the jury was riveted on this—the droplets clinging to the side of the tank, the puddle beneath, the rumbling of Vat 17 as it prepared to erupt.

"And did you touch the valve under Vat 17?" Ryan asked.

"Yes," Kieran responded immediately. "I didn't touch it, but my T-shirt caught it. I had to disentangle it."

Good, no hesitation. It should take some sting out of King's cross on Kieran's failure to mention it in his deposition.

Ryan coaxed the full story from Kieran—including the months of hacking coughs and headaches, the fears of absorbed radiation, even how those fears were compounded by his father's death.

The jury had gauged Kieran's credibility for nearly two hours before Ryan circled back to the valve.

"Now, Mr. Mullaney," Ryan asked, "Covington has alleged in this case that you deliberately turned the valve on Vat 17 out of anger at a fellow employee. Did you?"

"No, sir," Kieran replied with emphasis.

"You didn't turn that valve because you were angry at another worker at LB5—a Mr. Steven Whalen?"

"No," Kieran said, shaking his head.

"Do you know Mr. Whalen?"

"Yes."

"Did you argue with him the evening shift before the explosion?"

"No."

"Did you *speak* with him before that shift?"

"Yes. I joked about my boots. You see, they check our clothes and shoes when we come off shift to see if we picked up any rads . . . uh, radioactive dust or debris on the dark side. My first night at LB5, the Geiger counter showed that my boots were hot, so Mr. Whalen took them away. He told me I'd have them back in a day or two, but they were still gone after a couple of weeks. So I was giving him a hard time that last night at LB5. I also joked that my HEPA filter mask didn't fit well. But I wasn't mad—it wasn't an argument."

Ryan left the podium, bracing himself. Listening helplessly to a client on cross was worse than torture, because at least torture offered physical pain as a distraction.

King walked at a deliberate pace from counsel table to the podium. Like a stalker, Ryan thought.

"So you say that you did *not* argue with Steven Whalen before the explosion," he began slowly.

"No, sir, I did not."

"Didn't raise your voice?"

Kieran shook his head adamantly. "No."

"Didn't make a threatening move toward the man."

Kieran looked shocked. "Not at all."

"So," King said, quickening the pace, "if Steve Whalen testifies that you had such an argument—that you were physically threatening him—you're telling this jury that Mr. Madsen is lying?"

"I'd say he was . . . wrong."

King nodded with a light smile.

So that was what the Madsen witness was going to tell this

jury: that there was a physical threat involved. Ryan scribbled a note to Emily. *"Taylor Christensen's essential to counter this."* Christensen was Emily's witness. She read the note and nodded.

King ambled his way toward the explosion, arriving at last at Kieran's escape down the third floor corridor.

"Mr. Mullaney," he said, his voice rising for the coming point, "when you described the explosion in the third floor corridor, you spoke of the radiation monitors 'activating' as you fell."

"That's right."

"In fact, that was moments from when you became *unconscious* from that explosion, isn't that true?"

Don't fight this, Ryan prayed. You can't contest the truth; even if it hurts, just lie down and get it over with.

Kieran's eyes glowed with anger. "Yes," he muttered.

"Think you might have *imagined* the monitors going off?"

"No."

"Well, the hallway was a tornado of flying debris and dust, wouldn't you agree?"

"I don't know if I'd say that."

"Chaotic?"

Kieran resisted for a moment. "Yes."

"And this was after you'd run from the room containing the vat, injured your foot and ribs, and were, as you have admitted—" King made a show of running a finger down his notes— "*terrified*. That was your word: terrified."

Flushed, Kieran let the word escape through tight lips, "Yes."

"Did you have an opportunity to see your dosimetry badge after the explosion?"

"No. They took it from me while I was still unconscious."

"Um-hmm. Well, Covington has. But we'll get to that later in this case. Let's focus on your contact with the vat in the *seconds* before it exploded. Your attorney, Mr. Hart, elicited testimony that your T-shirt got caught in that valve. Did I state that correctly?"

"Yes."

"Yet in your deposition"—King held the transcript in the air—"you didn't mention coming in contact with the valve *at all*, isn't that true?"

"I'd forgotten," Kieran said a little too softly.

He was losing it; Ryan could see it in Kieran's face.

"You'd forgotten it. That's your testimony today, Mr. Mullaney?"

The anger flared. "Yes. I forgot it," he snapped.

"It's a pretty important thing to forget, isn't it?" King said.

Kieran shot a glance at Emily. Ryan saw her take an exaggerated breath. Kieran did the same. His eyes softened slightly.

"I was so focused on the vat," he said more slowly to King, "and on getting out of that room, I guess it didn't seem so important to me at the time."

King smiled. "Well, you didn't forget some of the other little details that night, did you. Like your shoes getting wet, slipping as you ran?"

"No."

"Didn't forget getting your foot caught in the door."

"No."

"Seeing your supervisor holding your HEPA mask?"

"That's right."

"The hall monitors; you say you remember them very well, don't you."

"Yes."

"Turning that valve, that was a pretty convenient memory lapse, wouldn't you agree, Mr. Mullaney?"

"Objection," Ryan called out. "Argumentative."

"Sustained," the judge responded.

"I didn't turn it," Kieran blurted out. "My T-shirt caught it."

King only smiled. He paused, looking as though he was considering circling the point again. Then, with a final look of satisfaction, he moved on.

Another hour of questioning passed before King finally relinquished the podium and Ryan completed his redirect. By then, King had scored too many blows on Kieran. The young man had done his best, but he was coming off the stand scarred.

Ryan passed him a note when he returned to sit at counsel table. *Good job.* Kieran crumpled it in his hand.

The judge's clerk approached the bench, whispering in her ear.

"I've been informed I have some matters to attend to," Judge Johnston said as the clerk stepped away. "We will recess until tomorrow morning."

As the jury filed out, Ryan turned to the gallery. Dr. Trân sat in the rear of the courtroom, the ever-present smile on his face. The expert nodded his understanding that he would definitely testify the next morning.

Ryan also saw another man in the gallery he didn't recognize. He had a sport coat and tie and a note pad in hand. He wondered if the man was a reporter from the *Sherman Courier.*

"You ready for your expert tomorrow?" Ryan whispered to Emily as his daughter finished packing.

She couldn't mask the disquiet in her eyes. "Hope so," she answered.

"Just be yourself," Ryan reassured her.

It was trite, but he'd been peppering her with advice about Trân's testimony for the whole week. If he said any more at this point, she'd think he had no confidence in her. Worse, he'd reveal how much weight was resting on her examination of the expert.

"Yep. Just be yourself," Ryan repeated as he gathered his papers with a final smile in his daughter's direction. "You'll do fine."

She smiled back confidently. It was, Ryan thought, an unconvincing display.

CHAPTER 34

"I'm shot," Kieran said, shaking his head. "I'd love to get something to eat with you, Ems, but I think I'd better get some rest. Maybe I can stop over at the Annex later."

Emily smiled her understanding. Kieran had just spent four hours on the stand. His eyes were lined and weary. "That's fine," she said.

Emily walked him out to the parking lot, where they parted. She slid into her car for the drive to the Annex.

Maybe she'd still eat out, Emily thought as she turned the key. Her dad had driven separately today to run some errands and wouldn't be back until later tonight. She really preferred not to be alone with her trial prep all evening.

Then it struck her. She could pick up some Chinese and take it to eat with Kieran and his family before starting to work. It would be a treat—and save her a lonely meal. She glanced up and down the parking lot. Kieran's car was nowhere in sight.

No matter. She'd hurry, pick up the food, and catch him at home.

She was only a few blocks from the courthouse when she saw his Corolla, the sun scattering reflections off the broken front windshield half a block ahead. Two more blocks and he'd be turning again toward home.

Except he didn't turn. He drove straight on. A quarter mile farther and he took the highway ramp north out of town.

Mystified, Emily hesitated a moment then followed up the ramp.

The traffic was light on the highway, but Emily hung far back, her discomfort rising the farther they traveled from town. Twenty-five minutes later, the Corolla turned off the highway onto a dirt road, passing over a hill and leaving a cloud of dust hanging in its wake.

The road was familiar. It led to Ted Pollock's ranch.

Emily pulled the Hyundai over on the shoulder and stopped. Why would he be going to the ranch? And why would he lie about it? Suddenly the memory returned of seeing Pollock at the Chinese restaurant—with a car like Kieran's Corolla parked just behind it.

She'd never asked Kieran about that day. After seeing him injured the same afternoon, the sight of the rancher and the Corolla at the Chinese restaurant had been completely forgotten.

Traffic cleared and Emily made a U-turn, anger and confusion descending over her. She'd never be able to focus on her final preparation for Dr. Trân's testimony until she had this sorted out.

She picked up the phone to call Kieran, but then she set it back down. Maybe there was an innocent explanation. If so, she didn't want to confess she'd followed him for half an hour like a jealous schoolgirl.

What about his sister? Laura might know what was going on. But even if she could reach her, Emily didn't want to pry out a confidence about her brother. Kieran's ailing mother was out of the question.

Pauline Strand. She'd handled the case for eight months and might have an explanation for why Kieran would be meeting with Pollock—twice in a matter of weeks, and this time smack in the middle of the trial. Since they'd adjourned trial early today, the lawyer might even still be in her office.

Emily reached the exit for Sherman and pulled off the highway headed back into town.

The gray-haired attorney sat behind her desk with a cup of coffee cradled between her fingers. "It's a nice surprise, you showing up, Emily," she smiled. "I've wanted to get over and watch the trial, but part of me can't stand the thought of it. Too stressful."

Emily nodded agreeably. "It's going well enough for now. My father's helping with the trial."

Pauline's smile widened. "I heard that. I was very pleased. So what can I do for you?"

Emily stared for a moment over the menagerie of case files crowding the desk that separated them.

"I'm wondering if you could tell me whether Ted Pollock has anything to do with Kieran's case."

Pauline's eyes vacillated. That answered one question, Emily thought immediately. Clearly she knew who Pollock was.

"Have you asked Kieran?" Pauline responded.

"No. I wanted to ask you first."

More hesitation.

"Pauline," Emily pressed, "you almost begged me to take this case two months ago. I've got a right to all the information you've got."

She could see the lawyer beginning to relent. "All right," Pauline said at last. "Yes. Ted introduced Kieran to me. He asked me to take Kieran's case."

Emily shook her head, perplexed. "Why? Did you know Pollock?"

"Yes."

The questions tumbled into her mind faster than Emily could assemble any order.

"So why would Pollock be taking Kieran to lawyers? Does he have an interest in the case?"

"Maybe."

"What's that mean?"

"He's a Yakama, Emily. And the case has to do with Hanford."

Emily shook her head. "I still don't get it."

Pauline set down her coffee cup. "The Yakama Reservation is smack in the middle of this state, downwind from Hanford. Hanford's also sitting right on the Yakama's traditional hunting, fishing, and gathering ground; they've still got treaty rights out there if the place is ever cleaned up enough to use again."

Why would that implicate Pollock personally in Kieran's trial? "So how did you know Ted Pollock?" she asked.

"I grew up on the Columbia River myself," Pauline said. "Down near the Dalles dam. When I was young, my father took me to visit the Yakama summer camps on the river to buy salmon and eels. Ted was just a few years older than me. We met then."

"And you're still friends?"

She settled deeper into her chair. "We don't see each other much these days, but yes, we've kept in touch."

Pauline reached behind her and took a framed photograph off the wall, handing it to Emily. It showed fragile wooden platforms built out over fast-flowing water, with fishermen spearing and casting nets into the rapids below. "That's Ted," she said, pointing to a child behind one of the men on the platform, "about the time we met."

"You're still not telling me what Ted Pollock's real connection is to the case."

Pauline looked solemnly back at Emily. "That's because I don't really know. You'd have to ask Kieran. Or Ted himself. All I know is that one day last November, Ted came in here with Kieran. I hadn't seen him for years at that point. He set Kieran down to tell his story, and when the boy was done, he asked if I'd represent him—at least until Kieran could get other counsel. I said yes."

Emily surveyed the elderly lawyer. Pauline had to know more than that.

Reading her thoughts, Pauline leaned into the desk toward Emily. "I'm telling you the truth, Emily: I don't know how those two connected up. Maybe I should've asked, but I didn't—because I respected Ted. I also believed in Kieran, and wanted to help. But if Ted had an interest in Kieran bringing his lawsuit, I'd guess that there's something about the LB5 explosion that has significance to the Yakama people, too."

CHAPTER 35

Dr. Trân appeared relaxed and confident seated in the witness box. Emily wished she felt the same at the podium.

For the first five minutes of eliciting testimony, Emily was sure she could feel the eight pairs of jurors' eyes riddling her with holes. Three more sets were hitting her back, from the hostile group at defense counsel's table. That didn't include the judge or her staff. Then there were Kieran and her dad.

Kieran. She hadn't even tried to reach him again last night or this morning, not until she'd thought through the conversation with Strand. Nor did she want to jeopardize her dad's recent commitment to the case by raising it with him.

She had to focus. Standing alone here, Emily couldn't help worrying about their joint decision to have her first witness in the case be Dr. Trân. This was such new territory for her: a key scientific witness. And her nerves weren't helped by her father's uncharacteristic comment to the judge, before the jury was called in, that this was Emily's first expert witness in a civil trial.

Emily worked through Dr. Trân's qualifications for the judge and jury. It seemed to go smoothly; his background on chemistry related to nuclear technologies was very strong. There was no way that King could challenge his basis to express an expert opinion today.

"Based on your education and experience," Emily finally said as she concluded eliciting his credentials, "do you have an opinion as to the cause of the explosions in LB5?"

Dr. Trân nodded. "I do."

"What is your opinion?"

"It is my opinion that pressure or heat from the reacting chemicals in Vat 17 detonated explosive substances in the lower levels of LB5. Those substances, in turn, hastened and combined with detonation of the contents of Vat 17 and other vats in room 365—resulted in three explosions in all. I believe that Covington was negligent for the presence of the reactive chemicals in Vat 17 and for the other substances in the lower levels of LB5. And finally, I believe that the three explosions that evening exposed Mr. Mullaney to radiation."

"Objection," King called as Trân wrapped up his summary. "Lack of foundation. Request to *voir dire* the witness."

Startled, Emily looked around at her father, who gazed placidly back.

Voir dire, challenging an expert's credentials to express an opinion, was permitted by the court rules, but the tactic was rare enough that Emily had never experienced it in her short trial career. So how did King think he could succeed here with somebody as credentialed as Dr. Trân?

"You may question the witness, Mr. King," the judge instantly replied.

Emily stepped uncertainly away from the podium as King came forward, a tight-lipped smile on his face.

"Dr. Trân," he said, establishing himself at the podium, "your opinion is that there were other substances in LB5 capable of detonating—substances outside of room 365?"

"Of course."

"And those substances were detonated as a result of Vat 17's explosion."

"Not precisely. Those substances detonated from heat and

pressure in Vat 17, transferred through a tube to the lower levels of LB5."

"Fine. And exactly what evidence do you have for these explosive materials in the lower levels of LB5?"

"The strength of the explosions—which was sufficient to breach the blast doors to room 365. That fact, combined with the absence of such materials in room 365, of course," Dr. Trân said with a smile.

"Well, let's take that first point. What is your evidence regarding the 'strength of the three explosions'?"

Dr. Trân explained about the seismographic data.

"Mm-hmm. So you have no *direct evidence* of the existence or strength of other explosive substances in LB5 the night of the explosion."

"No. Because I have not had the opportunity to inspect LB5."

"I see. And upon what do you base your conclusion that there were no other chemicals in room 365 capable of causing the second and third explosions?"

"I have reviewed the sampling data in room 365 going back two decades. That data is on a sheet provided to me by Mr. Mullaney's attorneys, and is attached to my report. None of the vats held chemicals in sufficient volume to fuel such powerful explosions."

"We'll discuss that 'data sheet' at a later time. But even considering that data sheet, Dr. Trân, you would agree that sampling data is a poor way to predict an explosion, wouldn't you?"

"I don't understand."

"Well, years of sampling didn't lead anyone to predict that Vat 17 would be heading toward its own explosion that night, did they."

For the first time Dr. Trân hesitated. "Well, that's true, but—"

"So isn't it plausible that historic sampling on other vats in room 365 failed to give a true picture of the explosive potential in those other vats as well?"

Dr. Trân's smile faltered. "I disagree. Vat 17's potential to explode is now discernible from the data. It's just that no one had analyzed that data properly."

"But Dr. Trân," King said with a grin, shaking his head, "isn't my suggestion—that the explosive potential for the other vat contents in room 365 was underestimated—more plausible than phantom explosive substances outside of room 365, for which you have not a scintilla of real proof?"

"Well," Dr. Trân said, "it's true that my argument is circumstantial because I have had no—"

"And there is one unassailable fact we all agree upon: that Kieran Mullaney's turning of the valve on Vat 17 that evening was an essential piece to triggering an explosion."

"Well, stated that way, yes, but—"

"Isn't it also true that you've never worked for or on behalf of the Department of Energy, Mr. Trân?"

"No, I haven't."

"Nor have you ever worked for any university."

"Only as a consultant."

"But you've never joined a faculty."

"Correct."

"Yet you've testified in—" King pulled a document from the bottom of the pile of papers he'd brought to the podium—"in twelve other cases, all against companies like Covington Nuclear in the nuclear industry. Isn't that correct?"

Dr. Trân's hesitation was longer this time. "Yes."

"Not once *in favor of* the nuclear industry."

"I've never been asked."

"Is that a *yes*, Dr. Trân?"

"Yes."

King turned to the judge. "Your Honor, this witness lacks critical evidentiary support for his opinions about the cause of the LB5 explosions. His opinion rests on rank speculation. Even this 'material data' sheet for the vats in room 365 has not yet been introduced into evidence. I move that his prior testimony be stricken, and that he be prohibited from offering an opinion."

Emily looked toward counsel table. Kieran appeared to be in shock. She looked to her father over the alarm thundering in her chest. This was all on her. They were about to lose this witness—and with it the case. And it was her fault.

Did he realize that? Because her father was looking away—at neither her, the judge, nor the jury. Off toward a suddenly interesting corner of the room. Calm as he'd been when she'd started with Dr. Trân.

She looked to the bench and Judge Johnston and saw that she was . . . hesitating. In fact, her gaze had moved from King and was focused on Emily. The instant ruling Emily had half expected had not arrived. And was that sympathy in her eyes?

"Ms. Hart," Judge Johnston asked gently, "do you have anything to say?"

Emily fought to rise above the panic clouding her mind. The argument King was making was flawed. She knew it, but her mind was a blur. King had deliberately muddied the proceedings. The questions about who the scientist had testified for were irrelevant to his qualifications to testify today, just intended to pump up the judge against Dr. Trân. The data sheet from Taylor Christensen wasn't yet in evidence, but the expert could still rely upon it until it was introduced. And King's arguments in support of kicking Dr. Trân out of the trial were fundamentally flawed because . . .

"Judge," she blurted out, "everything Mr. King has said is nothing more than *cross-examination*."

Emily took a breath and slowed her cadence. "The points Mr. King has raised may impact the weight the jury gives the evidence, but it can't prevent Dr. Trân from expressing his opinions to the jury. As for the data sheets, Dr. Trân can rely upon them—and if they're not introduced later, Mr. King can point to their absence in closing arguments or move that his testimony be stricken at that time. But Dr. Trân is a highly qualified expert and whatever Covington's attorney *thinks* of his opinions, the doctor is qualified to express them."

The judge was listening.

"Also, Your Honor," Emily continued with more confidence, "we are operating with the disadvantage of not having been in the lower levels of LB5, based upon Judge Renway's earlier ruling."

Judge Johnston nodded, then looked to the opposing attorney.

"Mr. King," Judge Johnston began slowly, "I am inclined to permit Ms. Hart to continue her examination of this witness." The judge turned to the jury. "Ladies and gentlemen, I am going to permit this evidence at this time. It is possible that I will rule some or all of this evidence inadmissible at a future point in the trial—and if so, I will instruct you to disregard it. But for now, you are to treat this evidence as you would any other."

The judge looked back and nodded to Emily with a slight smile. "Counsel, you may continue."

Through a haze, Emily did.

Standing in the empty hall with her dad, Emily was just beginning to relax from the day's ordeal. Dr. Trân had already left to make a "business call." Kieran had also dashed. The jury and judge were gone.

Emily's legs twitched with exhaustion.

"You did great," Ryan said, smiling. "You got in everything Trân had to offer, from the cause of the explosion to the blood evidence."

"I don't know, Dad," she said. "That was too close. I didn't see that coming."

"Um-hmm. Well, you handled it like a pro."

Emily looked at her father's face, expecting him to agree that King's objection had been a surprise. "Dad, you didn't know that was going to happen, did you?"

Her father didn't respond.

"Dad, if you thought this might happen, why didn't you tell me?"

His eyes softened. "I wasn't certain. But if King did object, I knew you'd handle it just fine."

Emily was too exhausted to express the anger she was feeling. "No, Dad, I didn't. I was scared out of my mind. I've only used expert evidence a few times at the PD's office—and nothing like this. You were the one who first suggested I take Trân."

"Until a week ago, you had every witness in this case," Ryan said softly. "I just suggested you *keep* Dr. Trân."

She wasn't listening as she recalled her father's comments to the judge before the day's evidence.

"And you told the judge that it was my first expert witness. You did that on purpose, didn't you. To make the judge sympathetic."

Ryan's face grew serious. "Listen, Ems, we've got to face up to something here. As much as I hate this smug lawyer we're facing, King's right—Trân's theory of substances outside of room 365 is logical, but the evidence for it is nonexistent. Without proof, maybe from an inspection of LB5, King's going to take another run at having Dr. Trân's testimony stricken. And he may succeed next time. And then we lose."

His voice grew more gentle. "But it occurred to me that when it came to letting in the evidence in the first place, Judge Johnston might give you more leeway than me. Because every trial lawyer remembers their first expert witness."

"Oh, Dad," Emily said, closing her eyes. "How could you do that to me. Let me go up to that podium unprepared."

She felt his hands on her shoulders and opened her eyes again. The smile on his face lacked even a trace of an apology.

"You weren't unprepared. You've been preparing for a week. And if you'd had a stock answer to King's objection all set, Judge Johnston would've seen through that in a heartbeat. She needed to see King attacking the underdog, a lawyer fighting to defend her first expert. She needed the urge to reward your passion. Besides, you want to be a trial lawyer, remember? Thinking on your feet: *that* is being a trial lawyer."

He shouldn't have left her naked like that. Emily was too exhausted to argue it any further, but she knew he was wrong to do it. She wasn't a beginner; he didn't have to manipulate her to win the fight. She'd never put another lawyer through something like this, regardless of the strategic advantage.

They began walking down the hall. And yet, she thought, her dad was right about one thing: the strategy had worked. She'd have found another way, but it had worked.

That realization birthed another: that even if he'd tricked her, it was her at the podium. She'd done it. And her father had seen her do it. The man who was the master of courtroom tactics had just watched her succeed.

"Is there somebody in the back yard?" Suzy called toward the living room from the kitchen. "Checking the meter maybe?"

Poppy was focused on his laptop, doing his thousandth search for any mention of Lew on the Internet and Facebook, LinkedIn, anything. "Don't know," he called back.

"Well, could you check?"

He grunted an assent and reluctantly got up from the computer. Putting on his shoes at the door, Poppy went out the side exit, through the garage, to the back yard.

There was no one in the back. He walked around to the side yard.

A white van was pulling away from the curb.

Poppy started to run after it—but it was no use. His heart pounding, he turned around and jogged to the back yard.

They were lined up in a row against the side of the house next to the rosebushes: five crows, buried hurriedly, head first in the soil. A white medallion was draped across their carcasses.

Poppy started to approach—then stopped. Going back into the garage, he grabbed the Eberline counter from his truck and returned. From ten feet away, he began to wave the wand in the direction of the black carcasses.

At six feet, the counter began to rise. At four, it was wailing.

He had to call Security, Poppy thought over his accelerating fear.

Except . . . who would they send? Who could he trust?

"What's that sound, Poppy?" his wife called through the kitchen window.

"Suzy, go pack a bag," he said, trying hard to sound calm. "I'd like you to stay at your sister's tonight."

CHAPTER 36

"I got your text to call," Eric King's voice said over the phone. "I've only got a minute before noon recess is over. But don't worry. Things are going great."

Adam was seated at his desk, behind the closed door of his office in the HR Department. Now he had to put up with more puffing from his overconfident barrister. "I would appreciate details, Eric."

"Okay. Today, they're going through a bunch of workers from LB5. They're getting nothing from them."

"And yesterday?"

Hesitation. "Yesterday, it was Dr. Trân. Their expert."

"I know who Dr. Trân is. Did he testify?"

Pause. "Yes."

"I thought you told me you could keep him from testifying. You said there was too little evidence to support his opinions."

"Yes, well, I thought that would be true. I was . . . a little surprised that the judge overruled my objection. But," the lawyer hastened, "the judge reserved the possibility of excluding the testimony later."

What good would that do after the jury had already heard it?

"Anyway," King went on, "we'll cut up his testimony with our own experts."

"What did Trân say?"

King outlined the scientist's testimony.

Adam was staggered. "He testified there were other explosives in the building?"

"Yes."

"Did he say what kind?"

"Powerful ones, he claimed. Like were used in nuclear triggers. The judge didn't let him go too far down that speculative road. But hey, his testimony shouldn't be such a surprise: I sent over his expert opinions three days ago."

King had. And with preparation for the run-up to the big test at LB5, combined with King's assurance that Trân would never get to testify, Adam had failed to review them.

"But he's got no real proof," the lawyer went on. "Like I said, we'll cut him up with our own experts."

He couldn't trust what he might say next, so Adam moved to end the conversation. "Keep me apprised," he said.

Where had Trân come up with this opinion? Did he know any more than the threads of proof King just described over the phone?

Adam went to his corner closet mirror to check his bow tie. The face that looked back was shaken.

This wasn't the only bad news. The chief of security for Wolffia had reported that Patrick Martin was contacting people in Savannah River trying to locate Lewis Vandervork. That meant not only that Dr. Janniston had failed after weeks of exams to force Martin's cooperation, but also that Martin was actively pursuing information he *could not have access to*.

Adam had already told the Chief to raise the pressure on Martin. Now he was wondering if increased pressure was enough.

Adam returned to his desk. All right, he told himself, put it in perspective. What was most critical here was that Martin not testify. If he didn't take the stand, Martin's knowledge or suspicion was irrelevant.

That was why they'd kept the man's name out of the investigation report in the first place. And it had worked so far. The first lawyer hadn't bothered to take Martin's deposition and Martin hadn't made the trial witness list. Once they were through this trial, the man's suspicions would have no platform—especially after they ruined him with a negative psych evaluation.

Still, Adam railed silently again at Foote's insistence on going forward with Wolffia this summer. Only two months' wait and they could have run the final Project tests without the balancing act of this trial. Then it wouldn't have been necessary to take the precaution of confronting Patrick Martin on his statement, which clearly set the man off, or worry about a court-ordered inspection of LB5.

Plus, a few more months and Lewis Vandervork's trail would have been that much colder.

Adam opened his desk drawer and pulled out the coin purse that contained the dexamphctamine tablets Schutten's treating physician had sent him. Though he hadn't planned for it at the time, it was another thing besides the physician's silence that the generous check had bought Adam.

Four hours of sleep a night were taking their toll. The stimulants he'd begun using the past week should only be necessary a little while longer, he told himself, just while they wrapped the follow-up testing and prepared to move the lab south.

He took a pill with a glass of water from the desk. For a moment, he thought of all the work still to complete today. Then he took another.

Ryan stood at the podium glancing quickly through his notes. With Kieran and Dr. Trân done, the rest of their case was becoming more of a fishing expedition. They were working through witnesses from LB5, seining for any evidence to support

Dr. Trân's theories. These included technicians at LB5 who'd sampled the vats in room 365 over the years, other stabilizing engineers who'd worked at LB5, at least one data technician, and anyone who might confirm evidence of the "detonation substances."

Frank Schroeder, the HVAC worker now on the stand, was dressed in dungarees and a sweatshirt. The message was clear: he had no need to impress anybody. And he was also making it perfectly clear he didn't want to be there.

Like all of these "outside" witnesses who predated Dr. Trân's theories, Schroeder hadn't been asked in his deposition key questions that might reveal the existence of other explosives. The past ten minutes had already established that Frank Schroeder had never, in his life, graced the dark side of LB5. That eliminated any chance he might have seen explosives in the LB5 lower levels. Ryan's only decision now was whether to take the time to go through the events of October sixteenth, since he already had the tech on the stand.

He would, Ryan decided. It should only take a few questions.

"I was in a cafeteria building—at the corner of LB5," Schroeder replied to Ryan's questioning. "Johnny Rose and I, we were having our midshift dinner. Then we started down the hill toward the front side to get back to work. That's when it happened."

"What happened?"

"The big explosion. Only it was muffled, since we were outside."

"What did you do?"

"Well, there was no siren. If there's an emergency, they'll blow the 'take-cover' siren, and then you're supposed to get inside—anywhere inside. Except there was no siren. So me and Johnny, we stopped and talked for a sec about what to do. Then we kept walking."

"Which way?"

"Toward the front side, along the side of the building."

"Did you keep going all the way to the front side?"

"Nope. Because then this guy fired a weapon. Up on the roof."

"Did you know this man?"

The HVAC guy shrugged. "I guess he was a security guard. I'd never met him before, but I know they have guards up on the roof."

Guards. Plural. The investigation report had only mentioned the one. "What did you do when you heard the gunshot?"

"Well, this guy on the roof was trying to get our attention, I guess. Because we looked up and he was waving us back to the cafeteria. And we saw why—because there was a big cloud of smoke rolling off the roof."

Ryan stopped for a moment. This was news too. Nothing in the investigation report told of a cloud of smoke coming off the roof.

"So what did you do?"

"Well, we ran like a couple of rabbits." The jurors laughed.

"Ran where?" Ryan continued as soon as the laughter tapered off.

"Back to the cafeteria. And then, just as were getting there, the sirens finally went off."

"They went off?"

"Yes. Just as we were going inside. And it's a good thing we'd gotten back there—because then the *lights* went out."

More news. "What lights?"

"The perimeter lights. All of them. Went out for about ten minutes, then came back on again. It was really strange."

"Do you know why that happened?"

"Nope. Never saw anything like it."

"Do you know the security guard's name? The one that fired his rifle?"

"Yeah. I went to the hospital afterwards with everybody who might've gotten exposed. I was asking around about the guy on the roof, the guy who'd warned us. I wanted to thank him. Then

I ran into the other guard. His name was Lewis something. His last name started with a V, but it was tough to pronounce, and I don't remember it. But he told me his partner had warned us. I remember his name because it was a lot easier. That guy was Poppy Martin. I think his real name was Patrick."

Knight passed on any cross-examination of this witness. Ryan took his seat as Emily started with the next witness—Schubert's fellow worker, Johnny Rose.

Ryan listened only vaguely to the testimony, running Schroeder's description through his mind. He'd read it so often that Ryan had almost memorized the investigation report. There was nothing in there about lights going out, late sirens, smoke. And there was nothing in there about two security guards on the roof.

The absence of the witnesses was especially curious. It was hard to imagine what difference it could make to their evidence since the guards were outside the building that night. But it was strange so many details relating to the events outside the building were completely left out of the report.

Ryan felt a tug on his coat and looked up. It was Kieran, leaning across Emily's empty chair.

"Mr. Hart," he whispered. *"This Patrick Martin that the last witness talked about? I know the man."*

Ryan looked at Kieran sitting across the table with Emily at his side. The Atomic Café was growing busy as the dinner hour neared. Ryan paid no notice as he fixed Kieran in his stare.

"You lied to us," Ryan said angrily.

Kieran leaned back, his eyes guarded. "That's not true. I just . . . I didn't know this Patrick Martin was involved at LB5. He was just a guy who helped me out at the softball game."

"You lied about what really happened at the softball game, too. You said it was an accident. You lied about how your car got damaged. You didn't tell me about the crows in your yard."

"Dad, he didn't lie to *me*," Emily jumped in tiredly. "I knew about all of it. Martin didn't say anything about being at LB5 that night, so Kieran couldn't know. But Kieran told me the truth about the game and the rest of it."

Ryan turned his anger on Emily. "Then why didn't *you* say anything."

"Because you weren't in the case back then."

"I was writing the checks and doing half the work."

Emily shrugged dispiritedly—in keeping with the foul mood she'd displayed most of the day. "It was still my case then," she said. "I was going to try it. Besides, I thought you'd overreact. Like you're doing now."

She turned to Kieran. "Is there anything else you're holding back?" The question was sharp edged, harsher than Ryan expected after she'd just defended the boy.

"No," Kieran answered carefully.

Ryan shook his head. There should be a special torture for clients who held back information from their lawyers. Maybe for guilty daughters, too.

He'd let it go, Ryan thought, forcing himself to cool down. But now that they knew about the smoke and the sirens, they should certainly call this Martin as a witness and see if there was any reason he and his fellow guard weren't identified in the investigation report.

"And you're sure it's your fellow workers who're doing this— the crows and the beating?" Ryan asked.

"I don't know. I mean, my nose was broken at a union softball game, so it must have been the Hanford crew. The crows and the white van . . . I only saw those guys for a minute, and they had masks. But who else could it be?"

Ryan thought about the next day. Around midday tomorrow, Taylor Christensen was testifying. They should slip Patrick Martin in after Christensen.

Ryan pulled out his cell phone and called directory assistance.

"Patrick Martin," he said when the operator came on. "And could you confirm his address?"

The operator came back and Ryan scribbled the address on his napkin. "All right. Thanks."

He handed it to Emily, then checked his watch.

"It's six o'clock. Let's get back to the Annex and drum up a subpoena for this Martin to testify tomorrow. Since he wasn't on our witness list, King may complain to the judge—but given that their investigation report didn't mention the sirens and lights going out, we can probably parlay those omissions into permission to slip him onto the stand."

From his living room chair before the front window, Poppy watched the van pull up and stop at the curve in the darkness. With the nearest street light half a block away, Poppy couldn't make out the make or model. But it sure wasn't white.

Thank God Suzy was still at her sister's place, until he was sure it was safe to return. Whenever that would be.

Poppy turned out the floor lamp at his shoulder, settling the room into darkness. Placing his book on the floor, he picked up the shotgun lying there, easing it across his lap.

A man emerged from the driver's side of the van. He stood for a moment on the lawn. Then he slowly trod up the slope toward the front door until he went out of Poppy's view. Before he did, Poppy saw that his right hand was holding an object.

The doorbell clanged. Poppy got up, holding the shotgun in his right hand, barrel down. With his shoulder and the weapon against the wall, he undid the door latch and opened it with his free hand.

Through the narrow slot, Poppy looked out at a young man—who stared uncertainly back.

"What do you want," Poppy demanded.

"Are you Patrick Martin?"

Poppy nodded.

The man's right hand appeared suddenly from behind his back, thrusting toward the door gap. Poppy took a startled step back, as he heard the sound of papers sliding to the floor at his feet.

"Mr. Martin, you've been served."

CHAPTER 37

Adam Worth's phone was ringing. It looked like the attorney again. He rolled over to squint at the alarm clock. Seven a.m. Three hours sleep this night.

"Yes," he slurred into the cell.

"Adam, I know you don't like me calling on your cell," Eric King began defensively, "but I tried calling you at the office yesterday afternoon and you didn't get back. I wanted to let you know that we had a little surprise yesterday. Two HVAC workers testified. They both mentioned the smoke coming off the roof of the building that night."

Adam's mind, foggy with sleep a moment ago, started to rouse.

"You still there?" King asked.

"Yes."

"Well, I thought I ought to call because you remember that the smoke business never came out in depositions, and wasn't in the investigation report. But Hart's getting desperate and is calling everybody at LB5 that night. And one of the HVAC guys also gave the name of the security guard on the roof of LB5 that night, the one you told me not to bother interviewing. Plus he said there was a second guard on the roof that evening. Now Hart's subpoenaed the first guard to testify later this morning."

Adam stiffened. "Isn't it too late to add new witnesses?"

"Yes. But the judge will probably cut them some slack since the man's name wasn't given in the investigation report."

"Fight it," Adam spat.

"Fight it?"

"Fight to keep Martin off the stand."

Adam heard a rustling of papers through the phone. "Uh, how did you know that witness's name?"

"Just keep the man from testifying," Adam's voice stabbed over the line.

The lawyer's response was subdued. "I can try. But I've got to have a reason."

"What if the man's incompetent to testify?"

"What do you mean?"

"I mean sick. Mentally."

Pause. "That could work."

"All right. I'll get back to you."

Adam cut off the call, then searched his contacts for the psychologist's number.

"Dr. Janniston?"

"Yes," the psychologist's sleepy voice came over the phone. "What time is it? I was asleep."

"Yes," Adam said. "I'm sorry to wake you. I have to know: have you finished your evaluation of Patrick Martin?"

"You mean my report? Why no. I was going to finish it today."

"I need it immediately. You have to finish your report and get it over to our lawyer, Eric King, before eight thirty."

"That's impossible. I couldn't possibly have it done by then. Perhaps by eleven if I rushed."

Adam cursed—then realized he'd done it aloud. He didn't bother to apologize.

"Then get your report done as quickly as possible and over to the courthouse. *You have to do this now.* And I want every one of those conclusions we discussed. Do you understand? No equivocating."

"I understand," the psychologist said huffily.

Adam hung up and immediately called back the lawyer. "Eric. I'm sending you an expert report with a complete psychological profile on Martin. It will declare that the man is unable to discern truth from fantasy. But you won't have it for a few hours. The psychologist is bringing it to the courthouse."

"That's . . . good," the puzzled lawyer fumbled. "Uh, okay. I can try to keep Martin off the stand before then, but until I have this report you're telling me about for the first time, it won't be easy."

Adam ignored the tone of the final comment. "It's on its way," he said, then punched off the call.

For an instant, Adam again considered heading to the courthouse himself. He instantly realized once more how ridiculous that notion was. He'd made up that stupid name, Larry Mann, at the park. Plus the guard would recognize him. The last thing he needed was to become associated with the case. He might even get called as a witness then.

The next few hours were going to be painful. But he'd just have to wait for a call back from King.

"Thank you, Mr. Stiles. No further questions."

Ryan returned to counsel table as King called out, "No questions for this witness." Ryan sat, looking over at Emily, who would be handling the next witness this morning: Taylor Christensen.

The courtroom door opened and a large man walked through. Kieran, who'd met his supervisor downstairs when he arrived, was a step behind. Taylor was dressed in relaxed clothes. A thick moustache flowed over his upper lip.

Taylor walked to the far side of the courtroom and sat in the gallery there. The judge nodded to Emily, who called out, "Plaintiff calls Taylor Christensen."

Taylor stood and walked through the swinging doors in the bar toward the witness box as Kieran returned to counsel table. As the supervisor sat down, Ryan noticed that he wasn't returning Kieran's gaze.

Ryan's warning barometer began to rise. As the court reporter swore Christensen in, Ryan hastily scribbled a note and slid it to Emily. *Ems—Be careful.*

She looked at him quizzically, then nodded and walked up to the podium.

"Mr. Christensen," Emily asked, "what is your job at Hanford?"

"Stabilizing engineer."

"What do you do?"

"Measurements and samples. We sample in our assigned buildings to track for the presence of radiation or harmful chemicals, while the buildings are waiting to be finally decommissioned and torn down."

Ryan detected the slightest tremor in the big man's voice. And his gaze still dodged Kieran's.

"Have you always been a stabilizing engineer at Hanford?"

"Yes."

The answers were clipped.

Emily worked through Taylor's background, arriving at last to the night of the explosion.

"And you and Mr. Mullaney were on temporary duty at LB5 that night."

"That's right. Two weeks."

"You went into the 'dark side' through the door next to the supply manager's station?"

"Yes."

"Was there any discussion between the plaintiff, Mr. Mullaney, and the supply manager that night?"

Pause. "Yes."

Ryan felt his heart rate rising.

"Is it fair to say that it was just a discussion?"

Christensen paused, then his voice betrayed the tremor again as he answered, "It was more than that."

They'd just gone through the ice. Emily had to get out of this water fast. Ryan fought the urge to come to her side and take over the cross.

"Uh . . . what do you mean?"

No, Emily. Taylor Christensen had just made himself hostile to Kieran's case. Back away.

"I mean," Taylor launched in slowly, "Kieran was ticked off and he let Red Whalen know it. First he lit into him about his boots. Then he started in about his HEPA mask."

Get out the deposition, Emily. Use the deposition.

As though reading his thoughts, Emily pulled the deposition transcript from beneath her notes. "Mr. Christensen, when asked at your deposition about any talk between Mr. Mullaney and Mr. Whalen that night, isn't it true that you said, and I quote: 'Kieran complained *a little*.'"

"Yes."

Good, Emily. Now drop it.

"But now you're saying Kieran Mullaney argued with the tech."

The big man on the stand shook his head. "Well, I've thought about it more. And I talked about it with Whalen, too."

"Steve Whalen?"

"Yeah. I met with him night before last. We had a beer together."

Covington got to Taylor through Whalen. Why else would the man be having a beer with the supply tech just days before Taylor testified?

Ryan couldn't see Emily's eyes, but he could sense, in her stiffening demeanor, that her concern matched his own. Mercifully, she finally abandoned this topic and turned to the even more important ground they had to cover with Christensen.

Ryan leaned forward in his seat as she pulled the room 365 vat document from a file folder—the "mixing-room matrix" Taylor had given Emily weeks ago. Ryan held his breath as Emily approached and presented it to the witness.

"Do you recognize this document, Mr. Christensen?"

Taylor smoothed his moustache with his spare hand as he stared at the page for a few long seconds. Then he looked up at Emily with glassy eyes.

"No, ma'am. I've never seen this paper before."

"Why's he lying?" Kieran was almost shouting. "I still work with Taylor out there. I can't believe he'd lie like this."

"Keep it down," Ryan commanded. After Taylor Christensen's testimony, all they needed now was for a juror to hear Kieran proving he had the temper Taylor painted him with on the stand.

Emily looked stricken. "I'm sorry, Dad. I should've stopped asking about the confrontation with Whalen, but every word from Taylor got worse and I kept thinking I could make it better."

"It's okay," Ryan said. "Covington got to him. You said he was under stress when you saw him."

Taylor's turn on the argument issue was bad enough. But his failure to identify the key vat room document was far worse. Without Taylor's identification, that paper would not make it into evidence.

This was a body blow. He'd seen it in the eyes of the jurors—even those in Kieran's corner. Now they saw Kieran as a potential hot head with an attitude and an agenda. And a cornerstone of Trân's testimony was gone.

Down the hall and around the corner, Ryan could hear the court clerk calling everyone back into the courtroom.

"It's not your fault, Emily. They got to the man," Ryan said with as much assurance as he could manage. "We'll sort it out tonight. Now let's get back and see what this Patrick Martin has to say."

Poppy shifted in his seat in the witness box. This place looked as big as a paneled basketball court, he thought, with every player and spectator staring at him. That included the judge, sitting in her seat in the skybox to his left.

The lawyer at the podium had introduced himself as Ryan Hart, Kieran Mullaney's attorney. The boy was seated at the attorney table, beside the girl he'd seen that day at the boy's house. He could tell Kieran remembered him. Now Hart was launching into questions while the girl at the table beside the Mullaney kid took notes.

The Covington lawyer at the other table made an immediate objection to him testifying. Something about not being on a witness list. The judge brushed it off quickly and they rolled on.

The first twenty minutes were all background questions. Poppy felt so nervous he almost forgot his home address. Then Hart asked about his education. His stint in the navy. His work history at Hanford.

A bird came to rest on the courtroom window ledge directly in Poppy's sight. It was a thrush, with spots and orange coloring on its wings. It perched there only for a moment, its head twitching about, then flew away.

It was going to start now, Poppy thought. The real questions were coming. Poppy had the overpowering urge to follow the bird off the ledge.

"Were you on the roof of LB5 the night of the explosion last fall?"

"Yes, sir."

"Do you recall that night?"

"Yes, sir."

"Mr. Martin," Kieran's attorney was asking, "why don't you just describe what you saw on the roof that night?"

Pause. "What do you mean?"

The lawyer smiled slightly. "Okay, let's break it down. What's the first thing you noticed about the explosion?"

"It knocked me down."

"Where were you?"

"I was in the guard shack on the roof."

"What did you do after you were knocked down?"

"After the roof stopped shaking, I got up and went outside."

"How many explosions do you recall?"

Pause. "Three."

"Which one was the most powerful?"

He paused. "I think the last one. Or the last two."

"What did you see on the roof?"

"I saw . . . smoke."

The lawyer seemed to grow more interested. "What kind of smoke?"

Poppy described it briefly. Hart followed up, making Poppy describe the plume—it's color and movement and source. Then a description of what he remembered about the HVAC workers on the path west of LB5. The lights going out. His own exposure to the plume.

Still, no question forced him to reveal Lewis—or the shot he'd fired. Or the man Lew said came out of the building that night.

The lawyer asked if Poppy had ever been to the vat room where the first explosion originated. Poppy told him no. The lower levels of LB5? No. Did he know what caused the explosion? No.

Maybe it was the tension, or maybe it was just because he'd had a reprieve from the cough for several hours, but Poppy could feel the congestion growing in his lungs.

Hart seemed to be losing interest. Poppy watched as the girl walked up to the podium and handed him a note. Hart looked at it, then back to Poppy.

The lawyer asked Poppy if he was alone on the roof that night. No, he answered. That seemed to interest Hart, and he made some notes. Who was the other guard? Lewis Vandervork, Poppy replied. Did he still work with Mr. Vandervork? No. Did he know where he was? No, Poppy answered truthfully. He'd been told Lewis had transferred to Savannah River.

The lawyer was shuffling his notes as though he was about to go to another subject.

"Mr. Martin, before we move on," he said, "other than what you've already testified to, did you observe anything else on the roof that evening that was in any way related to the explosion?"

He'd been holding it back, but now Poppy felt his lungs spasming. A sudden coughing fit doubled him over in his chair. Through watered eyes, he saw the other lawyer—the Covington one—push back like he was contagious. The girl with Kieran ran around the table and handed Ryan Hart a glass of water that he brought up to Poppy.

The fits eased. Poppy took the glass with a gasped "Thanks" and swallowed. He ran a sleeve across his eyes, then sat up once again.

"Are you okay?" Hart asked.

"Yeah."

"Do you want a break?"

Poppy hesitated, clearing his throat once more. "No," he said softly.

"Alright. Court reporter, please read back the last question."

"'Mr. Martin,'" she read in a monotone, "'other than what you've already testified to, did you observe anything else on the roof that evening that was in any way related to the explosion?'"

Silence. The bird came back onto the ledge.

"Mr. Martin," the lawyer said. "Would you like me to repeat the question once more?"

"No. I heard you." An image of the buried crows filled Poppy's head; then the hotel room where the psychologist had cornered him the past weeks. Suzy's hug as he went out the door each day—including the long one he'd gotten this morning.

"Lewis shot a man that night from the roof," Poppy said to the lawyer at the podium, "a man who shouldn't have been there. Then Lewis disappeared. They made him disappear. Now I think they're coming for me."

Poppy'd never been in a courtroom before today, but he knew he must have crossed some line here. He could see it in the blank faces around him, the sudden rustle of the people in the jury box across the room. And in the wide eyes of the lawyer at the Covington table, who was rising to his feet about to shout.

And then, as if it all weren't unreal enough, there was Janniston, the psychologist, coming through the courtroom doors like he was on fire, rushing something in his hand up to the lawyers at the Covington table.

Everything was foreign to Poppy now, and he suddenly didn't care a lick what the rules might be in this place. So he said it—the next words coming out of his mouth intended just for Ryan Hart, the lawyer at the podium. Except as he said it, he knew that Hart couldn't possibly hear him over the shouts from the other guy—the Covington lawyer who was now on his feet waving the papers he'd just got from Janniston, waving them toward the judge on Poppy's left.

"I want a lawyer," Poppy tried to say to Hart. "Will you represent me?"

Ryan saw the place exploding. Still standing at the podium, he couldn't believe what he'd just heard from this graying, worried-looking security guard on the witness stand.

Eric King was shouting an objection and waving some papers at the judge that a skinny, tired-looking man had just pushed into his hands. King was shouting an objection about Patrick

Martin lacking foundation for the testimony he'd just given, or was about to give, and lacking capacity to testify.

Judge Johnston was banging her gavel so hard it hurt Ryan's ears. Then Johnston was calling for the bailiff to get the jury out of the room.

Through the chaos, Ryan looked to this sixty-three-year-old Patrick Martin on the witness stand who'd just given Kieran Mullaney's case a sliver of light.

As he looked, the security guard mouthed some words. He could only make out the last four. They were, *Will you represent me?* And now the man was staring back at Ryan, waiting for an answer.

Through the chaos that was only starting to settle down, Ryan gave the man a nod.

CHAPTER 38

"This witness is *incompetent* to testify," King was bellowing, pointing in the direction of Patrick Martin, still on the witness stand.

The jury was out of the room at last, the sudden silence still charged with the chaos it replaced.

King approached the judge and handed her a document.

"This is a report from Dr. Zachary Janniston, who has been treating this witness— "

"Treating me?" the witness shouted, his face red.

The judge whirled on the man, her usual smile replaced with cold fury. "Mr. Martin, you will be quiet or you *will* be escorted from my courtroom."

"Your Honor," King continued, "as this report reflects, Mr. Martin here is a very sick man. Ever since Mr. Hart belatedly informed us he would be calling this witness today, we've hurried to gather what information we could about Mr. Martin—and, frankly, to determine why Mr. Martin was not interviewed for purposes of the official investigation report."

King held up his own set of the documents. "What I've provided this court and counsel just now is a psychological evaluation of Mr. Martin. For the past several weeks, he has been examined and treated by Dr. Janniston . . ."

Ryan was paging through the documents as King went on.

"Covington commissioned an evaluation of Mr. Martin to determine his competency to retain his security status at Hanford. As you can see, Mr. Martin is suffering from posttraumatic stress disorder as a result of the explosion, manifested in delusions and paranoia."

Ryan could see the witness barely restraining himself.

"Judge, this man can't testify to what he witnessed on the roof of LB5 that night," King went on, "because he can't distinguish truth from fiction about that night. Allowing him to testify given the medical proof of his incompetence would taint this jury and bog this trial down with days or more of medical testimony."

The judge leaned back with a heavy sigh. "Mr. Hart, what do you say?"

"Judge," Ryan launched in, "I'd say we have to hear from Mr. Martin. First, these psych exams apparently only occurred as we were approaching trial. If Mr. Martin was so delusional, why wasn't he in treatment the past ten months since the explosion? And second, when there's such critical evidence involved, we should at least have a chance for our own evaluation of the witness. At this late date, a last-minute psychologist report is no basis to muzzle this man."

The judge looked like a woman unaccustomed to chaos in her courtroom. Ryan knew her concerns: Should she adjourn for a week for exams and counter exams—putting the jury on ice? Should she send Martin home—and risk a serious appeal issue?

She turned to the witness.

"What do you say, Mr. Martin? About these exams."

The witness began shaking his head and talking rapidly. "They forced me to take these exams because I wouldn't change my report about that night and say Lewis didn't take a shot. Then they locked me in a hotel with this Janniston and gave me tests all day for weeks. Now I've been threatened. They've buried contaminated crows in my garden, Judge."

Ryan listened to Patrick Martin's rants and thought, *This*

man isn't helping himself. He could see the judge watching skeptically his rapid, almost unintelligible explanation.

The judge raised her hands, interrupting Martin. "I'm going to look these records over tonight and through the weekend," she said, holding up the reports King had just given her. "I'll take oral argument on the issue on Monday. We'll be in recess until Monday morning."

Kieran and Emily gathered anxiously with Ryan at counsel table as the judge and staff left the courtroom. When the Covington group had also left, Kieran finally burst out, "Isn't she going to let Martin testify?" Emily's face had the same question.

Ryan shook his head. "I don't know," he whispered. "But get the witness, *now*. Bring him to the Annex. We'll talk there."

Ryan stared at Patrick Martin sitting on the Annex couch, surrounded by Kieran, Emily, and himself. Remnants of delivered pizza sat on plates scattered around the room. It had to be closing in on ten o'clock.

Patrick Martin—Poppy, he'd asked to be called—had gone on for nearly four hours. The story he'd related was so far beyond anything Ryan had imagined that he struggled to give it credence.

A second guard on the roof not mentioned in the investigation report. That man, Poppy's partner, Lewis Vandervork, firing a gun at a third, unseen figure—and supposedly hitting him. Rank intimidation of Poppy by Covington. Efforts to get Martin to change his statement (he had a copy of the original, Patrick had said). Threats and dead crows—matching the crows buried at Kieran's home. Except these were radioactive.

Then an unidentified body, moved from the Sherman retirement home at night, out onto the reservation through a closed security station. And the second guard, Lewis Vandervork, missing.

If Poppy hadn't settled down this evening, telling his story with such careful rhythm and detail and confidence, even Ryan wouldn't have believed him. It was all too fantastic. But this man wasn't delusional. It was no accident that Poppy Martin's name and the very existence of his partner were left out of the Covington investigation reports. It was no wonder that a Covington psychologist had spent three weeks trying to bury this man.

"Can the judge really keep him from testifying?" Kieran asked as Poppy wound down.

Ryan nodded. "She's a federal judge; she can do what she wants. She could do it because she thinks he'll bust open the whole case, adding a week to trial. She could do it because we hadn't revealed Mr. Martin before today. Or she could do it because she buys King's line that Mr. Martin is delusional."

Ryan turned to Poppy, now looking exhausted. "Tell us more about Vandervork's disappearance."

Poppy nodded, proceeding to tell his story, beginning with the last memories he had of Vandervork on the way to the hospital and ending with his conversation with Vandervork's girlfriend.

"Are you saying he could have been the body you saw taken out onto the reservation?" Ryan asked, hardly believing they were discussing this possibility.

Poppy shook his head. "I don't know. I've thought about it a lot. If they'd done away with Lew, I don't see why they'd wait nine months to move him onto the reservation. And I don't have a clue where they'd take his body—or why they'd need two cars and four guys to do it."

The man looked like he was going to keel over. They'd have to let him get some rest. "Do you want to stay here tonight?" Ryan asked.

The guard shook his head. "Nope. I'll stay at home—or at my sister-in-law's place, where my wife's at."

"If you're going home, how about if Kieran stays with you," Ryan said. "Given what you've been through. That okay with you, Kieran?"

Ryan was concerned for the man, but equally concerned with not letting him out of their sight. Kieran nodded. "Things have been quiet at my place since after the softball game, so I suppose that's fine."

Poppy considered the offer for a moment. "No. I'm okay." He smiled sheepishly. "I almost took out your process server with my shotgun."

Then he looked Ryan in the eye. "I've gotta know something for sure, though. Are you my lawyer now?"

"It's too late to get you into this case, Poppy."

"I don't care. I just want a lawyer. I can't do this alone anymore."

Ryan glanced at Emily, whose eyes registered her assent—then looked once more at Poppy.

Ryan nodded again, as he had in the courtroom. "Then yes. You've got yourself two lawyers now."

CHAPTER 39

Sitting in a booth at the Lightning House Brewery amidst a Saturday night crowd, Adam sipped his ale. It was too hoppy, he thought; overdone, like everything in this worthless town.

He looked across the table at their excuse for an attorney who'd just put his self-protective spin on the day's news about Poppy Martin's testimony.

"I did what I could," King said again. "As soon as Janniston's report arrived, I was able to cut the guy off." Then he added, defensively, "You know, we would've interviewed Martin before if you hadn't instructed us to leave the roof guard alone. And whoever this other guard was, we could have interviewed him, too."

Adam had no time to make up a story for this lawyer. He seethed, but said nothing. *I told you to stay away from Martin to avoid a moment like this. Do I have to make a diagram for you?*

The room was off; he shouldn't have had the beer with the three pills he'd taken earlier to get through this awful day. Now all he wanted was to strangle this man. No, that wasn't it: what he really wanted was to strangle Janniston for continually reassuring Adam that the guard was near to "coming around." And while he was at it, throttle his chief of security, who'd failed to frighten the security guard enough to keep him off the stand or at least keep his mouth shut. And especially Cameron Foote, for insisting they drive the Project ahead in the face of Adam's advice. Putting Adam's seven-figure bonus at risk.

They were all incompetent. He should've done it all himself.

Adam rubbed his eyes to stop the tilt the room was taking. "And the judge said she'd decide by Monday whether to let Martin testify?"

King nodded. "And even if she lets him testify, that business about what the other security guard supposedly did still shouldn't get in. It's all hearsay coming from Martin. All Martin can talk about is what he saw on the roof himself."

That and the grilling Janniston had been giving him, Adam wanted to add. *And the crows buried in his yard and who knew what else he may have witnessed.*

King was going on. "And I really do think this judge isn't going to let Martin testify at all, based on the psychologist's report."

Adam clenched his glass tightly with one hand while he fondled his bow tie with the other. Had King forgotten they had a new judge in this case? Renway had been in their corner, but King had already proven clueless about how Johnston would rule.

"But listen, Adam," the attorney went on—except now, even through the layers clouding his vision, Adam saw King straightening in his chair as a tone of command crept into his voice. "You need to tell me if there's anything to what Martin's saying—about somebody else in LB5 when the explosion happened. And about this second guard and the shooting. Martin's implying that something was going on in that building—like their Dr. Trân testified. I really can't do my job with half the facts, Adam. Is there anything to what they're saying?"

Adam felt a fuse taking fire. His heart quickened and his head flooded with sudden rage, the kind he'd kept from surfacing publicly for so many years.

He slammed an open hand on the table, sending beer sloshing from each of their glasses, then rose, gripping the table until his knuckles ached. King shoved back from the table, his eyes wide.

"Listen," Adam hissed, leaning into the shrinking lawyer. "Do you know why Covington hired you? You think for a nanosecond they heard about your overwhelming barrister skills all the way from their world headquarters in New York? Covington goes for firms with offices in DC, New York, LA, maybe Chicago—the ones that *consume* law firms with names like McNary and King from Sherman, Washington. You're the compromise, Eric," Adam slurred, "because maybe, *just maybe*, you can bring some leverage and insight to this damp spot in the middle of a desert. You're a *geographic convenience*. So let me know if this case is making you uncomfortable, Eric King. Otherwise, you do what you're told with the information you're given—and *never* . . . *question me . . . again.*"

Adam settled back down, his fury momentarily spent, glaring blearily at King as he cooled down. Then, it slowly occurred to Adam to wonder how loud he'd actually been. He glanced around the bar. It was crowded and noisy tonight; no one seemed to be looking their way. At least not anymore.

Good. Even through the haze, he knew he had to get out of there. People didn't seem to forget when this side of him came out. And it could happen again, the way he was feeling sitting here with this empty suit. He stood again, carefully.

King had collected himself now and was trying to project a facsimile of his usual bravado. "Adam, you're overreacting," he said, his voice still rattled. "We've got this. We've got the evidence of the whole-body count and the dosimetry badge. And this is still a Hanford jury. We can handle this. We're going to win it."

Adam eased forward, picking up the check.

"So you're going to win this case, are you?" he said, hearing his voice as through a tunnel. "Well, I'll take that as more than a promise, Eric. I'll take that as an *oath*."

CHAPTER 40

Judge Johnston was a torn person this Monday morning—it was broadcast on her face. This hearing wasn't a formality. The judge was still looking for answers.

"Counsel," she began, "we're here this morning, out of the jury's presence, for a hearing to decide whether Mr. Patrick Martin will be permitted to testify—and the extent of that testimony. Mr. Hart, I'm going to let you go first."

Ryan stood at counsel table, Emily seated at his side. Kieran was in the gallery, beside Poppy Martin. The psychologist was in the gallery, too, seated not far from another man: the one with the sport coat who Ryan had occasionally seen in the gallery during the trial.

"Your Honor, Covington's counsel has presented a psychologist's evaluation concluding that Mr. Martin is incompetent to testify because he can't understand the difference between truth and fiction."

Ryan paused. "Trials are about juries sorting truth tellers from liars. We vest that power in jurors because we think humans are endowed, naturally and by life experience, with some skill in that department."

Ryan pointed to Dr. Janniston in the gallery. "Covington is offering the court a tool that it says is superior to that skill. It is a man who claims that the science of psychology has got this one figured out, that there's no need to trouble the jury with

Mr. Martin's ravings. Take this psychologist's word for it, Covington says: Mr. Martin is a liar—or at best, unequipped to tell the truth. They would have you believe that dozens of tests are better suited to judge Mr. Martin's lucidity than your average man or woman in the jury box."

He leaned into the table. "It's a fair question, when we're being asked to put such faith in this psychologist and his tests, to ask where they found this man. Who hired him for the examination of Mr. Martin? Why now? Why not eight months ago?"

He stood straight once more. "Those are important questions. But we don't have to answer them to recognize one overriding and fundamental truth: that even if this psychologist's role has been strictly professional and proper, Covington's argument that this court should rely upon him to exclude Mr. Martin is contrary to our core belief in the jury system. The fact is, weeks of psych exams aren't necessary to *test* Mr. Martin's truthfulness or his sanity. That's the jury's role. And it's also Mr. King's job. Because Mr. King has the right to cross-examine the witness. If Patrick Martin spins a fantasy, Mr. King has the opportunity and the skill to point out the fallacies in his testimony. He can lay it all bare for the jury.

"Judge," he finished, "my personal experience is not evidence. But I will represent to this court that I spent hours this weekend speaking with this witness—a man who saw and heard things Covington saw fit to leave out of its investigation report. This is a man who Covington has been persecuting for weeks before trial in an effort to silence him. During all the hours with our team this weekend, Mr. Martin did not rant, he did not foam at the mouth. If he appeared agitated in this courtroom on Friday, it is only because he has seen and experienced extraordinary things, things that this court and jury need to hear. The court and jury can judge for themselves Mr. Martin's competence through his own words. Two hundred years of American jurisprudence proves they're very good at it."

The judge cocked her head. "All right, Mr. Hart. Then tell me just what Mr. Martin will say."

He'd hoped for this opportunity, and was prepared to take it. For nearly an hour, Ryan described Poppy's story from the weekend, slowly and carefully, replete with details. And as he'd expected, he had the judge's attention the entire time.

When he finally sat down, Emily passed him a note. *"Lucky it isn't Renway on the bench right now."* Ryan nodded his weary agreement.

Judge Johnston turned to Covington's counsel. "Mr. King?"

"Judge," King began, standing, "Dr. Janniston is a preeminent psychologist. Neither you, nor I, nor Mr. Hart—and certainly not the jury—can judge the depths of Mr. Martin's mental disorders. The government relies on people like Dr. Janniston to establish whether workers should receive a security clearance. They're called upon, in effect, to determine who can safely guard our defense establishments. Why should we give any less credit to Dr. Janniston's judgment as to whether Mr. Martin is competent to testify? Or whether a reasonable juror could discern Mr. Martin's delusions?"

King pointed into the gallery toward Poppy. "Mr. Martin suffers from PTSD and related paranoia. That should be self-evident in the fantastic stories this man has already told of persecution, harassment, and missing guards. If he's allowed to spin those tales for the jury, we'll turn this trial into a drawn-out circus. Covington will be forced to call Dr. Janniston to demonstrate Mr. Martin's incapacity—adding days or more to this trial. Then we'll need to bring in half a dozen witnesses to establish that he's not telling the truth. None of this should be necessary, Your Honor. We *implore* the court to avoid delay, and evidence misleading to the jury, by prohibiting Mr. Martin from testifying."

Judge Johnston put a finger to her lips and gazed into the gallery—first at Poppy and then at Dr. Janniston. At last she shook her head skeptically.

"Mr. King, Dr. Janniston may be one heck of a psychologist, but I'm not prepared to surrender my own judgment or the jury's to the opinion of an expert. Unless I see obvious signs of delusional behavior, I'm going to allow Mr. Martin to speak his peace."

She turned to Ryan. "So I will allow Mr. Martin to testify. He can describe what he saw on the roof that night—including the other guard appearing to fire a shot. He can testify about the health impacts he's suffered, since that's germane to Mr. Mullaney's fears of injury. Finally, he can tell the jury about Covington's pressure that he change his original statement, and the psychological testing that followed. But I see no relevance to Mr. Martin's claims of persecution in the form of the buried crows and vans—absent proof linking those actions to Covington Nuclear. Nor will I allow the hearsay Mr. Martin claims he was told over the telephone by this Beverly Cortez about what his partner allegedly saw. Are we clear?"

"Yes, Your Honor," he said, rising.

Ryan's satisfaction was tempered by the limits of the judge's order. Poppy would testify he heard Vandervork fire his weapon; Covington would counter that he was too far away to have heard the weapon and mentally impaired. Poppy would say he was being strong-armed by the psychologist to change his report. Covington would put Janniston on to say that was part of his paranoia.

It was far from a knockout punch. That would only be possible with more support for Dr. Trân's opinions. Still, it was something, and he savored this rare victory in the case.

"One more matter, though," Ryan went on, still on his feet. "While the jury is still in recess, we wish to renew our motion for an inspection of LB5."

The judge shook her head in frustration. "We've had this discussion, Mr. Hart."

"Yes, Your Honor, but Mr. Martin's description to this court of activity in LB5 supports the possibility of other detonation materials in the building. Without a chance to explore the lower levels, we can't establish possible evidence supporting Dr. Trân's opinions and—"

"Hold it right there, Mr. Hart," the judge interrupted, holding up a hand. "This is strike three. You brought this up once with Judge Renway and now twice with me. We have a trial to complete. If you bring me other more compelling evidence of stored explosives in the LB5 building than I've seen to date, maybe I'll consider it. But otherwise, this discussion is *over*."

Ryan nodded woodenly back at the judge. "Yes, Your Honor."

The judge turned to the bailiff. "Bring in the jury."

The jury shuffled into the room again as Emily replaced him at the podium. She'd do a better job with Poppy Martin than he could on this, Ryan thought. Poppy's story was one needing empathy, not confrontation. She'd do a good job, and the guard's testimony should pump some interest in Kieran's case back into the jury—even if it fell short of convincing them of Dr. Trân's theories.

Tired but momentarily content, Ryan settled back into counsel's chair as Poppy Martin took the stand.

CHAPTER 41

Her father had gone for a run as soon as they returned from the adjournment that followed Poppy Martin's testimony. Now Emily sat tensely in the living room, waiting for Kieran to return from the bathroom.

She was going to get some answers tonight.

Kieran came around the corner. "I probably should run a couple of errands for the house," he said, reaching into his pockets. "Got time for dinner later?"

"We've got to talk first," Emily answered tersely. "About Ted Pollock."

Kieran had come away from the courthouse more upbeat than she'd seen him in days. Now she saw him wilt again.

"I've already told you about Ted," he responded hollowly.

Emily shook her head. With her exhaustion after the Trân testimony, then the craziness surrounding Martin leading to his testimony today, she'd thrust her conversation with Pauline Strand into the background. Even so, it was taking a toll on her feelings for Kieran. Weighing it all, Emily had finally decided on today's drive back from the courthouse that she couldn't wait any longer—either to force Kieran to divulge his relationship with Pollock or to reveal what she knew to her father.

"Don't do this," Emily answered wearily, almost sickened by Kieran's continued evasiveness. "I've spent two months out here. I've put my career on hold. I dragged my father and his

300

bank account into supporting you." She stopped herself before going any further.

Kieran surveyed her unyielding eyes painfully. "Emily, I haven't lied to you."

"I'll judge that. Just tell me about Ted Pollock. And if you value our relationship, you'll do it now."

If it wasn't obviously personal before, she'd clearly made it so with these words. To her relief, Kieran's face fell with final resignation. He made his way to the couch and dropped down.

"He approached me first, Emily. Long before I came to you."

Ryan took the hill like he was storming a castle today. This Martin's testimony, even with its limitations, had put his energy levels on fire tonight. He felt like he was flying. There were still big hurdles to overcome, but in Ryan's experience breaks tended to generate more breaks. It was a potential new landscape in the courtroom tomorrow.

Ryan came over the crest onto the ridgetop. There, by the bench, stood Larry Mann. The insurance agent saw him and waved as he approached.

He looked more tired than usual today, Ryan thought. Rings surrounded eyes glazed with fatigue. Mann stood as though weighted to the ground.

"Hello, Ryan," Mann said as he neared. "You're looking fast today."

"Feeling fast today."

Larry smiled. Ryan expected to be asked why. The question never came.

Ryan walked in a circle, keeping loose. "How about dinner tonight?" Mann asked suddenly.

That was a surprise. They'd only talked maybe three times to date, when their paths had crossed on this hill. Mann had never once suggested getting together.

Ryan shook his head. "Not tonight, sorry. Too busy."

"Trial prep?" Larry asked.

"Yes."

"Going well?"

Ryan hesitated. "Better, anyway."

He could see that Mann wanted to ask him more. But he didn't.

Instead he flashed a weak smile. "Well, that's great. Maybe dinner another time?"

"Sure," Ryan answered.

Ryan turned to begin his jog away. "I'll get in touch," Mann called.

"Sure," Ryan answered again over his shoulder.

That was a strange encounter, he thought as he left the bench and Mann behind. It was as though he'd been waiting for him. Then that invitation out of the blue. Ryan wondered what triggered the sudden desire to spend more time together.

As Ryan dropped onto the downward slope back toward town, one other thought occurred to him as well. How could Mann get in touch when he'd never told the man his phone number or where he was staying?

Ryan pulled the Annex door shut behind him then turned to see Kieran seated on the couch. In that instant, Emily emerged from the kitchen.

Both wore expressions of dour seriousness that hadn't been there when Ryan had left for his run.

"What's up?" he asked.

"Dad," Emily immediately launched in, "Kieran has filled me in on a few things. You need to hear this."

"Can I shower first?"

To his surprise, Emily shook her head. "I think we should talk first."

Ryan draped a towel he'd left by the front door across the easy chair, then sat. "All right, what's the news?"

Emily crossed the room to another chair by the window—bypassing, Ryan noted, her usual spot on the couch beside Kieran. "Dad," she began, "Dr. Trân didn't just run into you in the airport like you told me. That happened on purpose."

Ever since his relief that Dr. Trân had testified so forcefully in support of his expert opinions, Ryan had almost convinced himself—despite all his instincts—that their meeting *had* been fortuitous after all. "Go on," he said.

Emily looked at Kieran, who kept staring at the floor. "Kieran?" she called.

The young man looked up reluctantly. "Dr. Trân was hired by Ted Pollock to help you in my case," Kieran said. "He arranged for the doctor to come to Sherman and cross paths with you. He even paid most of Trân's fees."

"I don't understand," Ryan said instantly, in a bewildered understatement.

Kieran's embarrassment or shame muted his response. "Last November, Ted approached me. I was trying to bring the lawsuit, but was having trouble finding a lawyer. I was ready to give up when he came and encouraged me to go ahead with the lawsuit. He said he'd help. Then he hooked me up with Pauline."

Ryan looked to Emily. "And you didn't know any of this?" he asked.

His daughter returned a flash of her own anger. "No, Dad. Of course not."

Ryan returned his stare to Kieran. "Why would he do that?"

Kieran looked to Emily, who stared back, unmoving, from her seat across the room.

"Because Ted has a stake in this case," Kieran said. "He thinks something's going on out at LB5, and he needs my case to help prove it."

CHAPTER 42

Ryan drove his Avalon carefully over the rough dirt road. Even moving slowly, the potholes kept pitching the car into the air, and with it all three of the occupants of his car.

They rounded a final curve. Directly ahead was a single-story ranch-style house with a long, roofed front porch. Two outbuildings bracketed the place. Even through the Avalon's closed windows, Ryan could hear the whinnying of horses as he turned off the car.

Kieran got out and walked alone to the front door of the house, disappearing inside. Ryan followed. He noticed that Emily stayed close to him rather than joining Kieran.

The entryway opened into a large room with a rock-faced fireplace along one wall. Opposite the fireplace, dozens of framed photographs rose nearly to the ceiling. Most depicted Native Americans, some on fishing platforms extended over a river, others holding catches. Many were family photos taken on the open plain or with this house as a backdrop.

One showed a fast-flowing reach, framed together with a photo of a dam.

"Celilo Falls," Ryan heard a voice say, "before and after the government built its dam."

Startled, Ryan turned. A tall man in his late sixties stood at his shoulder, with thick shoulders, sun-weathered skin, and long hair bound in twin braids.

"My name's Ted Pollock," he said.

"Ryan Hart. And this is my daughter, Emily."

"Yes," Ted said, looking at Emily. "I've seen your daughter before."

Ted looked them each over silently for a moment. "Kieran's in the back with my wife. I've got things to do in the barn. Walk with me."

Without another word, the rancher left the house. Ryan and Emily followed him back into the calm air, still warm in the early evening. They matched the man's slow gait toward the nearest outbuilding, where they stepped through a door into cooler darkness and the sudden musk of horses.

Ted walked to one of the dozens of stalls, this one occupied by a tall quarter horse. Stepping over a waist-high rope, he entered the stall and picked up a brush. "You want to know about Dr. Trân," he said from inside the stall.

"No," Ryan responded. "I want to know everything."

Ted didn't acknowledge the statement at first, but began to pull the brush rhythmically across the horse's flank. It was several minutes before he finally asked, "Where do you want me to start?"

"Did you send Dr. Trân to me?" Ryan asked.

Ted nodded. "Yes."

"Did you pay part of his costs?"

"Yes."

"Why?"

"It seemed fair. Dr. Trân had worked for the Yakama tribe on projects through the years. You needed him to save your case. I wanted your case to be saved."

"Kieran told you we were having trouble getting an expert?"

"He said that, yes."

"Who do you work for?"

Ted hesitated. "Ask me again later," he said.

Ryan thought about insisting otherwise, but after a moment

305

went on. "All right. Why didn't you send Dr. Trân to Pauline Strand?"

Ted was reaching beneath the horse's belly now, drawing the brush across it in swift, practiced strokes.

"Pauline Strand is an old friend and a fine woman. She did good work for Kieran. But she never had a chance to win the lawsuit. With or without Dr. Trân's help."

"And you thought we could."

Ted set the brush aside and pulled a hoof pick from his pocket. He ran a hand along a rear leg until the horse obediently responded, raising its hoof for cleaning.

"Well, we hoped so. But Kieran's been telling me you think otherwise."

"That's right," Ryan answered. "Dr. Trân's theory about the three explosions at LB5 and other detonation materials in the building is logical, but falls far short on proof."

"What kind of proof."

"The kind that Trân says we might get in a tour of the lower levels of LB5." Ryan paused. "Or any kind that would convince Judge Johnston to allow us to take that tour."

Ted glanced up in the dim light of the stall. "If you had that kind of proof, could you win the lawsuit?"

Ryan looked the man over. "Show me the evidence and I'll tell you."

They were circling here. But if Pollock had evidence that could generate an LB5 tour, Ryan wanted it. "I *can* promise," he quickly finished, "that without the proof we'll lose."

Ted worked his way around the horse, cleaning each hoof in turn as he listened. "Well, let me think about that, too. Tell me what else you want to know."

Emily spoke up this time. "Why didn't you come to us directly if you wanted to help with Kieran's lawsuit. Instead of making Kieran lie to us."

Ted shook his head. "I'm not interested in the spotlight."

"Why not?" Emily shot back. "And what do you think is going on in LB5?"

Ted patted the horse once more, then slipped past Ryan and Emily out of the stall, moving to the next one.

"Kieran places a lot of faith in you two," he said as he began to tend the colt in the new stall. "He didn't want us to keep anything a secret. I told him that was the price for our help."

"That help is going to be wasted the way things are going," Ryan pressed.

Ted looked back at Ryan for a long interval. Finally he shook his head.

"Okay." He set his brush on a ledge and stepped back out of the stall. "Come with me."

Ryan and Emily followed Ted to the end of the stable and into an empty stall.

On the shavings covering the stall floor sat a dark gray metallic box. Ted took from the wall a glove resembling an oversized oven mitt and some tongs. Opening the box, he put the tongs inside, pulling out a small, ragged shard of metal about the size of his hand. Ryan approached.

"Stay back," Ted said. "It's not very radioactive, but there's no point in coming closer. There are no features you'd recognize on it anyway."

Both Emily and Ryan looked at the shrapnel-like metal from across the stall until Ted set it back in the box again.

"That's a piece of metal Dr. Trân tells us is part of what's going on at LB5," he said.

"What is it?" Emily asked. "Where'd you get it?"

"It's a piece of a casing for an experimental chemical nuclear trigger," Ted answered as he put the glove away. "We got it out on the Hanford Reservation grounds. We're certain it came from LB5."

Ryan's mind was sprinting to piece all this together. So this was why Trân had been so confident in his theories. He wasn't relying on deductive reasoning; he had physical proof in the form of trigger-related detonation material. But then why hadn't they come forward with it? And why did they still hesitate to give them this evidence?

He put the questions to Ted, who stared silently back for a moment. "I think that would be easier to explain if you'd take a little trip with us tonight."

"Where?" Emily asked.

Ted looked at her, then back at Ryan. "Out onto the Hanford grounds. If your father here can ride, I'll take you both there tonight on horseback."

CHAPTER 43

The truck and horse trailer were headed southwest under the midnight sky darkened with a new moon. Out here on the desert, far beyond any lights of town or farms, only the ten-foot swath of their headlights pierced the surrounding black.

They'd left the Pollock ranch and driven a dozen miles or more southwest before turning onto a two-lane highway that angled back to the northwest, parallel to the Hanford Reservation grounds. In the front cab, Ted Pollock sat with a tasseled hat pulled low on his forehead. Ryan sat next to him. Ted's twenty-five-year-old granddaughter, Heather, was in the back seat with Emily along with a slender, quiet man that Ted had introduced only as Ray.

Though he was still awaiting the promised explanation from Pollock, Ryan was content for the moment to sit silently, contemplating why he'd agreed to an incursion onto the Hanford grounds. It was obviously a breach of federal law, and so an act that could end his legal career—as well as his daughter's, who'd insisted on coming along. The only limit Ryan had ultimately placed on the night was an insistence that Kieran remain at the Pollock ranch. He would not agree to their client risking not only the case but his already endangered job and security clearance as well.

So why *had* he taken such an uncharacteristic risk? At first, he'd told himself it was because of the strange turn the case had taken since Taylor Christensen took the stand, and the stark evidence of the trigger casing Ted had shared tonight. But over the past hour of travel he'd concluded these were only part of the reason. The larger truth was that sometime the past few days—hearing Patrick Martin's story and seeing Covington's machinations—Ryan's last hesitation about the case had slid away, replaced by his familiar drive to win. It felt as though he'd stepped into a comfortable pair of shoes he'd once thought lost.

After a quick supper at the ranch, Ted had driven this truck and trailer out to a paddock beyond the hills that surrounded the house. There in the growing dusk, Ryan made out half a dozen shaggy horses pawing at the dusty ground. They were soon joined by Heather, her black hair pulled back in a single braid. Ray had arrived shortly after. Together and without a word to Ryan and Emily, Pollock, Heather, and Ray had loaded four of the horses onto the trailer for this journey. As they worked, Ryan had tried to get more details about the trip—but each time Ted Pollock had put him off. "You'll understand everything soon," he'd said in a tone that made clear they'd learn nothing more just yet.

Ted was slowing the truck now, leaning into the windshield. Ryan couldn't see what he might be looking for in the dark, as nothing about the shadowy road or its borders looked any different than what he'd seen for the past hour. But Ted recognized something, because he eased the truck over onto the shoulder at a spot where the ditch had flattened nearly to ground level. There wasn't another headlight visible on the highway in either direction as Ted drove carefully across the nearly level ditch, out toward the desert to the north.

Once they were fully off the highway, Ted let out a sigh of relief before glancing at Ryan.

"You wanted to know what's going on in LB5?" he asked.

"Yes."

310

"Alright. Dr. Trân believes that the casing I showed you is part of a project to develop a chemical trigger for a nuclear weapon."

"Develop one?" Ryan shook his head in surprise. "Trân said there might be trigger materials in the LB5 lower levels. I thought he meant they were being stored there."

"No," Ted said. "We think it's a lot more ambitious than that."

"Why make a trigger in a decommissioned lab building?" Emily asked. "Doesn't the government have plenty of labs to work on nuclear defense projects?"

"Not the government," Ted answered, his eyes again focused on a trail only he could see in their low headlights. "Covington Nuclear."

"You're saying Covington's working without government sanction," Ryan said.

Ted nodded.

"Why?"

"Because it would mean a lot of money to Covington if they succeeded. The government would pay a great deal for a chemical trigger able to detonate a nuclear reaction in a small bomb; things a large one can't on a battlefield."

"And no one has done it before?" Ryan asked.

Ted shook his head. "Not according to Trân. Not one nearly as small as that casing shard implies. And we believe Covington's very close, if they haven't already succeeded."

"Why wouldn't the government just hire Covington to make the trigger?" Ryan asked.

They hit a small bump and Ted braked gently, glancing over his shoulder worriedly toward the horse trailer and slowing their pace to a near glacial speed. "Because they've officially told the world they haven't, and won't. Though that doesn't mean the government would turn down the technology if it was presented to them complete."

"Then what happened last October?" Emily asked.

Ted glanced at Emily in the rearview mirror. "We believe Covington did its work on the trigger project at LB5 at night so that project personnel could come and go with little visibility. Using these grounds was illegal: we figure it violated at least a dozen federal laws and maybe a couple of international treaties. The explosion happened because no one had predicted the Vat 17 problem. Nobody expected pressure or heat from the chemicals in that tank to occur in the first place, let alone reach the basement through the connecting tubes. Very bad timing."

"And the radiation?" Emily asked. "Where'd that come from?"

"That's why Dr. Trân thinks they're close," Ted said. "He says that at late stages of testing, they'd have small quantities of plutonium present to test the trigger mechanism's success in producing a micro reaction. Dr. Trân believes the plutonium was too close to the trigger when Vat 17 accidentally detonated it. The explosions spread the radiation to the third-floor corridor."

Ryan's initial surprise at this explanation was fading, replaced by a sullen realization of how long he and Emily had been kept in the dark by Ted Pollock and Dr. Trân, and manipulated to serve this man's ends.

"So tell us why you're doing whatever you're doing," Ryan demanded. "Why are you getting involved in Kieran's lawsuit? What's LB5 to you?"

They were easing forward at no more than five to ten miles per hour, as Ted appeared to search for a landmark.

"I'll tell you after I've shown you what we've come to see," he answered distractedly

Ryan had opened his mouth to say no when he felt a hand on his shoulder. He glanced into the back seat. It was Emily, clearly anticipating what he was about to do. In the near darkness of the cab, he saw her shake her head gently with an imploring look.

Ted slowed the truck further, then braked. "We'll walk from here," he said, shutting off the ignition. The headlights he left on.

Ray was out of the truck immediately, heading to the rear of the trailer, while Heather walked out past the pooled light of the headlamps and into the blackness ahead. "I'll go prepare the fence," she said softly to Ted as she went by him.

Ted turned back to Ryan and Emily as he led them to join Ray at the trailer. "We convinced Hanford to give us a contract," Ted said. "A contract to pick up stray horses that wander onto the Hanford Reservation grounds and trip their security motion detectors. The fact is, there aren't that many mustangs left in this area to be a real problem. But the Hanford engineers and security don't know that. And Hanford doesn't have the budget to keep up the fence lines like they did back when production was on. It wasn't too hard to make it look like horses broke onto the grounds every few months. For two years, we've released horses onto the reservation land and forced Hanford security to catch and release them outside the fence line.

"Finally, we approached them and got the contract to pick the horses up west of here, where they run naturally to a water hole. We tell them we sell the horses out east. In fact, we trailer the horses off the reservation grounds, but keep them in the paddock at our ranch. Two years of that and it's gotten to be routine: Hanford expects horses to get onto the grounds every few months. Once they were used to it, we started going in with the mustangs we released."

Ray was leading the first of the four horses off of the trailer, a rope slung around its neck. Ted took the rope from Ray, handed it to Emily, then joined the man in getting the rest of the horses off of the trailer. When all four horses were on the ground, Ted handed one of the ropes to Ryan, then gestured into the darkness where Heather had disappeared. "The fence is about a hundred yards that way," he said.

Emily was the rider in the family, but Ryan wasn't a complete novice when it came to horses. At a glance he saw that these animals were well fed and cared for, but bore the ragged coats and manes of wild horses. "Where are the saddles and bridles?"

he called ahead to Ted. Ted didn't answer as he guided the four of them with their horses over a low ridge. On the other side they walked down a short slope, at the base of which stood Heather. She turned as they neared.

Here beyond the reach of the truck headlights, the desert appeared darker still. Only as Ryan came closer did he see that Heather was standing next to a fence line. At her side, the strands of the fence were broken where they intersected with a metal pole.

"This fence is old," Ted said, pointing to the gap. "Early on we scouted out places where we could breach it and make it look like animals discovered the breaches or knocked the fence down themselves. It helps that this outer fence is not a security priority anymore—and they're years behind in repairs. We identified a couple dozen of these spots, but we're down to four or five unused ones."

Ryan felt his stomach growing edgier at the prospect of actually moving onto the reservation grounds. He watched as Heather walked back and handed a tool to Ray, taking the rope of his horse in exchange.

"Ted, before we step onto these grounds I've got to know where we're going," Ryan finally said, resolved.

The rancher turned to face Ryan as though gauging his seriousness. He glanced at his watch, then back to Ryan. At last, he looked at each of the horses in turn before lifting his hat and running a palm across his braided hair.

"Since the 1940s," Ted began, his voice now falling to a near whisper in the hushed night air, "the radioactive contamination on the Hanford Reservation has created a phenomena of glowing wildlife—rabbits, bucks, sagebrush. Hunters have reported it for decades. Scientific studies confirm it. It's caused by radiation in the soil and water taken up by the plants, the plants consumed by animals. There are patterns for it, linked to where there's buried waste and contaminated water."

"Six years ago, we began to see a new pattern: irradiated animals and plants on the southern and southwestern borders of the reservation where they hadn't been reported before. Heather, my wife, and I began to catalog it with nighttime observations on horseback. The patterns pointed to a large new disposal site in an area near Priest and Rattlesnake Ridges on the Hanford grounds. We triangulated a general location and then, in the last nine months, found the site. We're going there tonight."

Ryan's anxiety wasn't relieved by this new information. Questions crowded his mind. "How many times have you done this already?" he asked.

Ted shook his head, holding up his wrist with the watch. "Ryan, it's eleven forty. The ride from here is about two hours; another two hours from the place we're headed to the draw where Ray will pick us up. So we either leave now or Ray here will take you back to the ranch while we get this done."

Ryan looked at Emily. He could see at a glance that if he left now he'd leave without her. Besides, he couldn't back away now. "Okay," he said. "Let's go."

Ted turned and grabbed his horse's mane in both fists. "Wait," Ryan suddenly called. "Are we going bareback?"

Ted pulled himself up, throwing a leg over his mount's back with a speed and strength Ryan wouldn't have thought possible for a man of his age. Once he'd centered himself, he tied the rope loosely around his waist then looked over his shoulder at Ryan, still on the ground.

"Yep," he answered.

"Why bareback?" Ryan asked plaintively.

"We can't take saddles in case we have to leave the horses and go to cover," Ted answered, straightening his hat. "Then, if the horses are found, there'll be no sign of the riders. You can keep your rope and use it to steady yourself. But if security comes, you've got to get off the horse and take it with you. Let the horse go on alone from there. Find a low spot and stay there. Then we'll send someone in to retrieve you the next evening. It's risky, having two fence breaks on consecutive nights, but we've done it once before. And another thing, as we're riding, hunch low and close to the horse's withers. They still have a few heat sensors scattered around the grounds. If they pick up a heat signal, we want it to look as much like a riderless horse as possible."

The talk about security filled Ryan with a sudden certainty that every word they were speaking must be amplified across the desert right to the nearest guard station. For a brief moment, that thought even drove away his fear of making this ride bareback.

"And what's the contingency if we get caught?" Emily spoke up. Ryan was relieved that her voice was tinged with the same nervousness that he felt.

Sitting atop the tall horse, Ted only shrugged. "In that case, we'll just have to find a good lawyer."

To Ryan, balancing on the horse's back in the dark felt like drifting in an oarless dinghy in the open ocean. Still, his horse knew its way and was deceptively well trained; he could have been on a trail ride for all the ease of guiding it. And the terrain was fairly flat, with only a few hills and gullies to cross.

All he had to do was hang on. Tight.

Clinging to the mare's mane, the only sounds Ryan could hear were the snorts of the horses and the wind shaking brush or kicking up sand. The only sights were variations of shadow. In the lead was Heather's horse, followed by Emily's. Ryan was behind his daughter, with Ted presumably in the rear—though Ryan didn't turn to check, convinced that he'd fall.

Then he felt Ted's presence as his horse came abreast. "About a month or so before the October explosion, we had a breakthrough trying to tie down this site's exact location," the rancher said. "There was a lot of activity out here when we were making our nighttime observations. Occasional headlights. Frequent engine noises. We think they had a smaller experimental problem about that time, maybe another accident. Trân thinks that was why your client was at LB5 on October sixteenth."

"Why would an earlier test failure have placed Kieran on the site?" Ryan whispered.

Ted leaned closer. "Dr. Trân has analyzed the workforce at LB5 for the past few years, from documents Pauline Strand got in discovery. They're all long-term employees at LB5—most from Hanford, though some are transfers from other defense facilities. They even have their own security personnel at the site. Men who never go anywhere else. We think that most or all of the permanent LB5 workers are aware of the experimentation in the lower levels—though probably not the details. They likely think it's government sanctioned. But our theory is that the small accident caused some injuries on site, leaving Covington unexpectedly short. Since they had to show DOE a full roster of maintenance and security personnel, for a short time in October they were forced to bring some people on site who weren't on their team."

"Including Kieran, and Poppy and the rest?"

"You mean Patrick Martin? We didn't know his name until you learned it at trial, but yes. It's the only explanation we can come up with for the risk of bringing Kieran and the others on-site. Then the October explosion made the place we're headed to a regular visiting site for several weeks."

They came over a small hill, and Ryan saw Heather slow her horse and point low past the horse's withers.

As he came closer, the starlight was enough for Ryan to make out faint car tracks on the ground ten feet below them, directed west. With a kick, Heather got her horse moving again, following the tracks.

A hundred yards ahead they rounded a ridge. Heather brought her horse to a halt again before sliding off its flank to the ground. She untied her rope from her waist and cast it around the horse's neck, handing this lead to her father before ascending the sloping ground a few yards away.

Heather stopped halfway up the slope, scuffing her foot in the dirt and then dropping to her knees on the gentle slope and rustling with her fingers in the loose earth. After a moment, her fingers seemed to get purchase. She looked up at her grandfather.

"C'mon and help," Ted grunted in Ryan's direction as he slid from his horse.

Emily took all four horses' ropes as Ryan walked to where Heather and her grandfather were crouched. Kneeling, he dug his fingers into the ground where Ted motioned.

Immediately he could feel it. There was a lip of heavy, weighted cloth here, under the loose soil. At another signal from Ted, they each rose with a handful of the cloth in hand, scattering dirt as it pulled up and away from the slope.

As they set the cover to the ground, Ryan stepped back from the space revealed.

Beneath the overturned earth was a darker surface, smooth and blacker than the surrounding soil. A light suddenly cut the darkness and Ryan turned to see Ted cupping a flashlight in his hand, pointing toward the dark space.

"It's a door," Ted said. "Cut into the underlying rock face here." Then he pointed to a rectangular impression on one side. "That's a magnetic lock."

"What's underneath the door?" Ryan asked.

"The trash of Project Wolffia," Heather said quietly.

Ryan shook his head. "What's Project Wolffia?"

"Some of our . . . friends in Sherman overheard that phrase used by persons we believe were scientists on the project. We think it's their name for the project. Wolffia is the name of the smallest blossoming flower in the world."

Scientists with a sense of humor, Ryan thought. Or irony.

"So how do you know the trash from the project's under here?" Emily called up the slope.

"Other than the observations I already told you about," Ted said, "we've brought Geiger counters. The radiation levels are safe here on the surface, but they've gone up the past year. A lot. Then, around the October explosion, we found that shard I showed you, plus a couple more smaller ones. We must have just missed crossing paths with a hurried disposal trip, because it was the first and only time we found debris here on the surface. We believe it's from the casing for the chemical trigger—the one that exploded in October when Kieran was in the building. That material sealed it for Dr. Trân's conclusion about what they're doing at LB5."

It was cold out tonight, but Ryan scarcely noticed in his growing excitement. If Pollock and his granddaughter were right—and it was all starting to make sense now—then underneath this door was the proof he needed to win Kieran's case. He was standing over the evidence that would turn this jury on a dime.

"So how do we get inside?"

Heather shook her head. "We have no way to open this."

He couldn't have heard that right. "There's got to be a way," he protested.

It was Ted's turn to shake his head now. "We tried to see if we could get a duplicate magnetic key to open it, but this is a sophisticated, programmed mechanism. There's no way for us to get a duplicate key or break in."

"Then we get the authorities out here and force them to open it up," Emily said.

Ted shook his head again. "If we go to the authorities, we have to admit we've been on the grounds. We're more likely to get arrested than convince DOE to search this place. And even if we're successful, by the time we can convince anyone to take us seriously, Covington will have arranged to close this up for good."

Ryan couldn't believe what he was hearing. What was the point of coming out here, taking all this risk, if there was no way to use the evidence under their feet? "Well, we can use that shard," Ryan pressed. "Have Dr. Trân identify it at trial. It might be enough for Judge Johnston to let us inspect LB5—and eventually gather enough evidence to get into this debris pile. It could make Kieran's case."

"Not so fast," Ted answered firmly, turning fully toward Ryan in the dark. "We wish Kieran the best, but winning his case isn't what this is about. The reason we offered to help Kieran was to create an opportunity to prove the existence of Wolffia. We hoped your case would get us a tour of the LB5 rooms where the experiments have gone on, and give Dr. Trân a chance to develop more proof of the project. The important thing here is to gather enough evidence to get DOE's attention and get Project Wolffia shut down for good, along with any future plans Covington might have for secret research at Hanford."

He pointed to the ground. "But like I said before, if we move too soon, make it clear we know about this place while Covington can still manipulate security on the reservation, they'll just remove the debris and bury this site so there's no sign of it. Not only do we fail to shut down Wolffia, we reveal our presence out here and lose years of work. That doesn't do either of us any good."

Which was why they'd stepped so gingerly into the litigation in the first place, Ryan thought.

They stood silently in the dark for several minutes until Ted said they should be leaving. Together, they replaced the cover over the door and spread dirt back across its surface. Ted took care to kick away the signs of their footsteps as Heather walked to the horses, taking the ropes from Emily's hand and examining each animal in turn. "I think we should give them a little more rest," she called up the slope.

Ted nodded and eased himself down onto the ground.

Ryan settled onto the dirt beside him. "I still need to understand something else, Ted. You still haven't explained why you're all wrapped up in this."

Ted picked up a rock and began tracing in the dirt. "It's a hobby," he said.

Ryan shook his head. "I'm serious. You've got me and my daughter up to our eyeballs in this thing, including breaking federal law to be out here."

Ted nodded without looking at Ryan. "I suppose I owe you that." He gestured toward Heather. "My granddaughter here, she's got a degree in environmental health. My wife—you didn't meet Doreen, she's in Toppenish just now. She's a traditionalist with the tribe, but she's got some paper to hang on her wall, too. I've done a little studying of my own."

"That tells me where you got the skill for this," Ryan pressed. "It doesn't tell me why."

Ted smiled as Emily stepped near to join them. "Pushy, aren't you. You sound like a lawyer." He paused. "Have you heard of the rapids they called Celilo Falls on the Columbia?" he asked.

Emily said that she had.

"Well, growing up," Ted began, "most of my people spent their summers at camps on the river, camps like Celilo Falls. Celilo means 'water on the rocks' in the Yakama language. It was a fast rapids below the joining of the Snake and Yakima rivers with the Columbia. We'd net and spear salmon and sturgeon all summer long. Eels if we could get them. We ate them all summer, and air dried some for winter—and for our feasts. Went there every summer, until the government built a dam that drowned the reaches in the 1950s."

He looked up at Emily. "Commercial fishermen were already becoming common all along the Columbia by then, diminishing our take. But it was that dam that ended it all for me. Took away a piece of our life. Except that wasn't all. This land, all of it, used to be Yakama land, before the 1855 Treaty. Even after the Treaty, the Yakama retained hunting, fishing, and gathering rights out here. Then when Hanford was built in 1944, they put a fence around it. That closed dozens of other Yakama fishing sites on the Columbia. Yakama gathering and hunting sites out here were made off limits. Then they started making their plutonium right here, up wind from the reservation, using the Columbia for cooling water and dumping tons of radioactive effluents into the river. All this land around us and the river became one big unofficial dumping ground."

Ted tossed away the stone. "I remember once at our Celilo camp, before the dam, my dad walking with me back to our tent after a night of listening to elders tell stories. We both smelled of campfire smoke, and I was still wrapped up with their tales of chasing horses and riding these hills. My dad bent down and pointed toward the camp, then leaned close, so close I could feel his lips brush my ear, and whispered, 'Remember this, son. Remember this, because it's passing.'"

He paused. "Well, he was right. It was passing. With the coming of Hanford, building the dams, they were changing everything out here."

The night grew silent. Heather was looking away, across the desert. Ryan wondered what she thought of her grandfather's words. Did she feel the loss of a place she'd never experienced herself? That her children would never experience?

Ted grunted. "Production at Hanford finally stopped for good in the late eighties and they tell us, someday, we may retrieve our fishing and hunting rights out here—if they ever get it cleaned up. Get back a little bit of what they took away. Well, that'll never happen if they start treating this like a nuclear dumping site again, or start using Hanford for nuclear research again, like Covington's been secretly doing these past seven years. You ask me why we're all wrapped up in this? To make sure it really does stop and there's something left for them to return to the Yakama."

"So are you working for the Yakama Nation?" Emily asked.

In the faint starlight, Ryan saw Ted shake his head. "That's a political question now, isn't it," he said. "I don't get into politics. I'm just a rancher."

Ryan's stomach twisted at the futility of it all. "Look, Ted. If we bring out the truth through Kieran's lawsuit, everybody wins. Wolffia gets shut down; there's more scrutiny on the cleanup and no more research at Hanford. But we can't do that unless you give me the shard and let me use it to persuade the judge to allow an immediate inspection of LB5. If you're worried about them emptying this site, I could ask her to send magistrates to protect this place pending the inspection."

"What are the chances of her granting that request?" Ted asked.

Ryan thought for a moment. "Fifty percent."

"You sound like a weatherman," Ted said. "I won't put all our work at risk on that kind of confidence."

The fact was, Ryan had no clue whether the judge would order magistrates out on reservation grounds based on a radioactive hunk of metal. With Judge Renway, the chances had been zero. With Johnston?

"Did you have anything to do with Renway dropping off the case?" Emily suddenly blurted out as though the thought had just occurred to her.

Good question, Ryan thought approvingly. Ted shrugged. "I have a cousin who works at Park National Bank," he said. "He told me about orchard land owned by the judge." Ted went on to explain the reasons for the judge's withdrawal.

Ryan scrutinized Ted as he finished his explanation. "That was risky. Renway could have gone to the FBI and tried to run you and your cousin down for collecting his private documents."

"Judge Renway is old," Ted responded. "Like me. I can remember when he was appointed. If he came after us, his 'conflict' would have come out anyway. Maybe other things he's done for Hanford. Why risk a lifetime legacy as a judge? I thought he'd choose the easy path and just step down from Kieran's case."

Ryan thought longer about how they could use the information about this debris site in their case. "I need time to think if there are other options," Ryan insisted wearily. "I can't give this evidence up. And I still want to convince you to give me that shard you have in the stable."

Ted sighed. "It's getting late," he said, the age in his voice more evident now. "I'm old and I'm tired. You think while we finish the ride home."

CHAPTER 44

Ryan sipped his orange juice, struggling to wake up. He'd gotten only a few hours of sleep last night. Most of the remainder of the short night after returning from the Pollock ranch had been spent studying the ceiling, the case wearily circling in his mind.

He'd come up with no new ideas to move the court to allow the inspection, or to satisfy Ted enough to release the shard. Until he did, they'd have to keep things going like the last week: keep taking testimony from more workers and avoid resting Kieran's case until they had a plan to convince Judge Johnston to allow the LB5 inspection.

They could probably buy two days, maybe three. If he hadn't learned how to delay after twenty years in courtrooms, Ryan thought, he'd be a sorry excuse for a trial attorney.

He headed upstairs to wake Emily and hit the shower. He also needed time to stop at a coffee shop on the way to the courthouse. This was at least a two-cup morning. He'd need that much caffeine to dance in front of the judge, jury, and Covington's counsel for the long day ahead.

His office phone rang as Adam was finishing packing a briefcase before heading for the morning's final debriefing of the

Project team. Adam looked at the caller ID screen. It was Vice-President Foote's office.

"Adam Worth here," he answered.

"Hello, Mr. Worth? This is Mr. Foote's secretary. Mr. Foote requests that you come to his office."

Adam looked at his watch. "Uh, I have a meeting. Is it possible—"

"Mr. Foote requests that you come immediately," she interrupted.

Adam said he would, then hung up.

What could be so urgent? His reports to Foote on the Project had been uniformly positive the past couple of weeks. The information about the trial was more of a problem, but Adam had shared little of his unease about what was happening at the courthouse with Foote, and none of the detail.

Five minutes later, Foote's secretary waved him into the inner sanctum with a gesture of her hand. Adam straightened himself and passed through the door.

"Come in, Adam," the VP said, adding unnecessarily, "and close the door."

"Adam," Foote began before he could even reach his seat. "I just got a disturbing call. It relates to your lawsuit."

Your lawsuit. When had this become Adam's lawsuit?

"The call came from the inspector's office at the regional DOE office, Seth Varney. I don't hear from the man very often. As long as our reports meet muster, they typically let us go about our business. But apparently they've had a rep at the trial every day the past week and a half. Varney said that your opponents' expert and Mr. Martin are creating some concerns about the thoroughness of Covington's inspection reports regarding the October explosion."

Adam restrained the "I told you so" response that came to his lips.

"Adam, Mr. Varney wants his man to conduct an inspection of LB5. In particular, they want to inspect the lower levels of

LB5, which have apparently been the subject of much discussion in your trial."

"We can't do that, sir," Adam shot back. "You know we've finished the last successful test, but we haven't removed the equipment. And we made improvements down there since the October explosion: stronger containment walls, a longer glove box and chamber. We couldn't explain those improvements in a closed facility. And since we claim that place hasn't been used since the eighties, and wasn't touched by the explosion, we couldn't begin to explain why the place was emptied and cleaned up."

This was a disaster, Adam thought. The plan was to complete the testing and then slate LB5 for demolition, taking it down before anyone visited the closed lower level of LB5. But they'd assumed there were still weeks to get that done.

"I am aware of the significance of this request," Foote said, his face unmoving. "Is there time to reconfigure the lower levels of LB5 to a condition approximating how they should have looked before Project Wolffia began?"

Adam knew that was impossible, despite how much Foote despised that word. "No," he said simply. "It would take months."

Foote raised his eyebrows. "Then what do you suggest?"

Adam's mind flew through options: razing, discarding. It was not possible to prepare LB5 for a DOE inspection. If they could do that, they could have caved to Hart's requests for an inspection at trial. Short of another explosion down there, he could think of no way to cover up the changes they'd made to the space.

Another explosion.

"Sir," Adam said. "There is one possibility. It has risks."

He expected Foote to ask for a definition of *risks*. He didn't. Instead, the vice-president took Adam's measure across the desk.

"When I hired you for this project," Foote began, "you were finishing that particle reactor work in Georgia. You recall that?"

Adam nodded, wondering why the VP was gearing up for another lecture.

The vice-president returned the nod. "You'd done a fine job. Hit your targets on budget. But one day while I was reviewing your work and considering you for Project Wolffia, a Covington compliance auditor called to tell me he'd discovered a problem. It was an unusual expenditure, fairly well hidden, which the compliance officer traced to an engineer at another company."

The roller coaster of Adam's mood these past few weeks was launched again with a sickening jolt.

"We both know who I'm talking about, don't we, Adam," Foote went on. "The man you bribed for confidential, proprietary software the other company wouldn't sell or license to us."

This was a lead-up to termination, Adam thought. Maybe extortion. But why now?

"I didn't condone it," Foote said, frowning, "and my first inclination was to have you fired. But you didn't steal money from Covington. You stretched the rules to complete a project important to the company. So I buried it."

Foote straightened an already stiff posture. "I buried it. Because that was what I wanted for Project Wolffia. Somebody *that* dedicated to success. You know as well as I that this project, though critical for America, is not a legal undertaking. I needed someone who believed enough in our cause to accept the gray area we're operating in and see it through—even when lines had to be crossed. You do still believe in what we're doing, don't you, Adam?"

This again. "Yes," Adam answered firmly.

"And we're so close."

"Yes."

The unmistakable crease of a smile appeared on Foote's face, so unusual that Adam doubted it at first.

"Adam, don't tell me about the risks. I don't expect you to be a Boy Scout. Do what you must, within reason. Just keep this DOE inspection from destroying everything when we're so close."

CHAPTER 45

Emily was taking the testimony today, moving slowly and steadily, just as Ryan had asked. Strangely, Eric King was absent this morning for the first time, leaving his associate taking notes and preparing for cross-examination.

Maybe King had figured out that this parade of LB5 workers they were putting on the stand was a waste of time, Ryan thought. Maybe he'd decided to get in some golf.

Ryan looked into the gallery. Poppy hadn't returned from his errand yet, but Dr. Trân was in the back. Now that Ryan was aware of the depth of Dr. Trân's knowledge, he had asked the scientist to be present most days in case he had questions.

Ryan looked next at the jury box. The jurors were bored—never a good sign for a plaintiff. Even the schoolteacher was losing patience. She was smart enough to know that the last two days, since Poppy left the stand, had been filler.

They were losing the panel.

Last night, Ryan had finally come up with a plan. It was a painfully long three-point shot, but it was all he could conjure to move the judge to allow them into LB5. And as soon as this witness was done, Ryan would be giving it a try.

"We're running out of time," Ryan had said to the assembly of Kieran, Emily, and Poppy in the Annex living room the night before. "I can't come up with a single piece of evidence strong enough to convince Judge Johnston to change her mind about the LB5 inspection. So I propose we push the judge a different way—by making a late demand for evidence Pauline *would have* demanded if Covington's inspection reports hadn't hidden a number of facts. Then we use that demand as a bargaining chip to get the inspection."

Emily looked lost. They all did. "All right," Ryan said, "just hear me out."

He turned to Poppy. "You said the HR guy who grilled you about your statement claimed the lights went out that night because of a broken fuse. I've been thinking: if the LB5 building manager knew what was going on in LB5 that night—which is almost a certainty—it's likely he had the lights killed to hide the plume you were witnessing, till they sorted out what to do. So we ask for the repair logs for the phantom, nonexistent 'broken fuse.'"

Ryan lifted his fingers to signal point two, still looking Poppy's way. "Second, you said the HR guy told you they tested Lewis's weapon to confirm it was never fired. Okay, we ask for a copy of the alleged LB5 weapons logs to confirm they logged out the weapon for testing."

Next he turned to Kieran. "Third, we ask for your boots that they never returned, to test for radiation you probably picked up from the operations in the lower levels of LB5."

Ryan looked once more to Poppy. "You're concerned that Covington's got Lewis hidden somewhere—or worse. So we demand the records of Lewis's transfer to Savannah River from Darter Security."

Ryan surveyed the group collectively once more. "The judge isn't going to like all these late evidence requests, but she'll be sensitive to the fact that we might have asked for this information earlier if the inspection report had been complete. King will stand up and counter that it could take weeks to gather it all up. '*Fine,*' we'll tell the judge, '*we'll waive our request for all this new evidence—if you'll just permit the LB5 inspection.*'"

Kieran raised a hand. "But then wouldn't we be giving up a lot to get the LB5 inspection?"

Ryan shook his head. "The boots, the weapons log, the transfer records—they all make Covington out to be lying in their explanations to Poppy and Kieran. But none of it's going to win this case. Only proving the existence of the other detonation materials might do that."

He'd looked around the room at Emily's skepticism, Poppy's thoughtfulness, and Kieran's excitement.

"Even if you don't follow through and get those weapon logs," Poppy offered, "my son Michael's a guard. He could probably get a copy of the LB5 weapons log from the central Hanford security office where they're stored monthly."

Ryan nodded. "That's fine, Poppy. But, Emily, do you agree we try this tactic?"

His daughter shook her head. "I've got nothing better, Dad."

It was less than a vote of confidence, but Ryan had taken it as the best he would get.

And now it was time to give it a try. Emily was finishing her examination at the podium. "No further questions," she said. The Covington lawyer looked up from her notes. "No questions, Your Honor," she echoed.

Ryan grasped his potpourri of demands and approached the podium.

"Your Honor," Ryan began. "Plaintiff asks for a moment to address the Court outside the presence of the jury."

Judge Renway gauged Ryan carefully before signaling the bailiff to send the jury out.

As Ryan went through the list of evidence they now sought, he saw the clouds gathering on the judge's face. She knew this would delay the case. Still, to his relief, she allowed him to go on without interruption.

Nearly fifteen minutes later, Ryan was finishing his pitch. As he made his concluding remarks, he heard the courtroom door open behind him. Moments later, Eric King appeared and sat at counsel table, slightly breathless.

Ryan finished with his offer of compromise: the LB5 inspection in lieu of the evidence. As he sat down, he cast a final glance at the anger glowing in the judge's eyes.

King was immediately on his feet.

"Your Honor," the Covington lawyer said, a light sheen of perspiration still visible on his forehead, "this morning I've been conferring with my client. In the interests of moving this case along, Covington is willing to agree to withdraw its objection to an inspection of LB5—subject to noting its safety concerns on the record."

Disbelief flooded the judge's face, mirroring Ryan's own. "You're offering to permit the inspection, Mr. King?" she asked, incredulous.

"Yes, Your Honor. Subject to making our record."

Judge Johnston turned to Ryan, shaking her head. "Mr. Hart, I assume this is acceptable?"

"Yes," he answered, stunned. The judge looked back at King. "Explain your safety concerns."

King nodded. "Judge, I'm informed that the LB5 lower level beneath the room 365 mixing room is a large, empty production room—untouched since the late 1980s. Even so, it must be remembered that these rooms were once the heart of plutonium production in the building and for the reservation. When production closed down, tools, supplies, and equipment were left where they lay. Over the decades it is possible that these objects have absorbed ambient radiation in the atmosphere. This creates the possibility of a criticality incident."

Ryan could hear the clacking of the court reporter's keys as the judge responded, "What do you mean 'criticality incident.'"

"I'm informed," King went on, "that when two radioactive objects come into proximity with one another, it is possible to have a 'critical reaction'—a sudden release of heat and radiation, which could cause a cascade of other critical reactions or a toxic fire. It's impossible to predict with certainty when that will occur, or its magnitude. The care needed to remove objects in LB5 to avoid this event is one of the reasons that LB5 is among the last two dozen or so nonoperational buildings to be fully shut down and demolished."

The judge looked worried. "Based on what you're sharing, Counsel, I'm concerned that it isn't safe to allow the inspection—even if Covington is now willing to proceed."

"Judge," Ryan began anxiously, rising to his feet, "if three explosions strong enough to obliterate room 365 three stories above the levels we want to inspect could not trigger a spontaneous critical reaction, I strongly doubt a simple walk-through inspection will do so."

Ryan looked back at Dr. Trân, still seated in the gallery. "Your Honor, our expert Dr. Minh Trân is here today. I wonder if he could address this issue."

The judge nodded her assent.

"Your Honor," Dr. Trân began, standing, "I would say the risk is minimal, almost nonexistent. These facilities have remained stable for two decades or more. Any explosion resulting from spontaneous reaction of residual radioactive materials is extremely unlikely. I cannot speak, however, to the possibility of detonation of the other substances that I testified were likely involved in the October sixteenth explosion—if some are still there."

The judge was silent for a long interval. "Gentlemen," she said at last, "I will permit an inspection of LB5 tomorrow afternoon at four o'clock. That gives you over twenty-four hours, Mr. King, to prepare the site to avoid danger. I will permit each of you to bring counsel and an expert of your choice. Covington shall designate a guide from LB5 to lead us through the facility. And I intend to participate."

"Your Honor?" King exclaimed.

"Yes, I am going to participate. The implications of plaintiff's counsels' theories in this case are extraordinary. I intend to be present for the walk-through. Bailiff, please dismiss the jury until the day after the inspection Friday morning."

The gavel fell. Within minutes Ryan was alone with Emily and Kieran in the suddenly empty courtroom.

Ryan lingered as Emily gathered her papers, still marveling at King's unbelievable turnabout. As Emily worked, he watched her talking animatedly with Kieran about the turn of events.

Ryan wanted to feel the same enthusiasm Emily was showing—but excited as he was, now that the moment they'd been fighting for had arrived, the emotion eluded him. Because Covington hadn't been forced to this break in the impasse: they'd *agreed* to allow the inspection. Covington and King wouldn't have agreed to this inspection unless they thought there was no evidence in LB5 to help Kieran's case.

Maybe they'd cleaned it up. Maybe there was never anything to find there at all. Either way, this could all prove to be a worthless exercise.

In the midst of his doubts, Ryan thought again of their scientist, Dr. Trân: so confident in his conclusions and so convinced he'd find further support for them in the bowels of LB5. Ryan reminded himself of his wife's repeated advice in their joint practice: that sometimes all you had was your trust in the people around you. It was a simple sentiment that had never been simple for Ryan.

He'd try to heed that advice again tomorrow. He had no other choice. He'd put his trust in the skill of Dr. Trân. When the hour arrived, Ryan would take a deep breath and hope, as they walked the halls of the lower levels of LB5, that their nuclear scientist was smarter than Covington's.

CHAPTER 46

Emily watched the guide as he called them all together by the entrance to the dark side of LB5: her father, Dr. Trân, Eric King, Judge Johnston, and herself. Each held a HEPA mask in his or her hand. Dr. Trân had a set of sampling tools in the other. With the exception of Dr. Trân, everyone looked a little nervous.

The guide introduced himself as Hank. "You're going to be fine," he said with a smile. "There's nothing to be nervous about. I've been working in this building for seven years and I'm still going strong."

Which meant, Emily thought with a chill, that he had to be in on Project Wolffia.

Hank pointed to the dosimetry badge on his own chest, matching the badges each of them wore as well. "These badges will tell how much radiation, if any, you come in contact with on this trip. We can then calculate any dose you absorbed. But again, this is strictly a precaution. The average Hanford worker goes five shifts a week, 240 to 245 shifts a year—and can endure a long career without radiation harm. Isn't that right, Red?"

The supply technician Red Whalen grunted his approval from across the room behind the supply counter.

Despite joining in the exchange with Hank, Emily thought the supply man looked uncomfortable. Red Whalen had to be a Wolffia team member, too, she thought, given his job at this building, and the way they'd used Whalen to turn Taylor Christensen. It suddenly felt to Emily as though they were in the middle of an enemy camp.

With a final gesture to follow, Hank turned and headed through the door into the dark side.

They walked the solitary hallway, their shoes shuffling on the hard floor like a dance troupe without music. Hank led, with Dr. Trân behind him and Eric King at his side. Ryan followed with Emily at his shoulder. The judge was in the back.

Hank called over his shoulder that the log showed there were crew members on duty today, though none in the lower levels. "We'll be on our own there today," he said.

Midway down the lengthy hall, Hank reached a descending stairwell. He switched on a light at the head of the stairs, then led them down.

"What are we going to see?" Ryan called out.

"We're going into a former production room," Hank called back as he walked, "directly below room 365. These rooms were shut down in mid-production. The space we'll be examining has tables and work stations with tools and equipment that were used for processing. The closed glove boxes will have some plutonium residue—or even fully processed material still in the enclosed production space. There is some chemical storage as well. You'll be able to look through the observation ports if you wish."

At the base of the stairs, the group turned left. Emily ran a finger along the wall of the hallway as they walked. The smooth green walls seemed . . . different, even in the dim light.

She put her full hand against the wall's surface. It was freshly painted. That was it. The first-floor walls hadn't been.

Emily saw that Dr. Trân, only a few steps ahead, was also touching the walls, and sliding his feet on the floor's surface. Emily looked down and saw that the floors were newly painted, too. Trân was clearly seeing the same thing.

"Sir," Dr. Trân called, "it appears these walls have been coated with lead paint recently. Isn't that done to cover over and capture potential radionuclides?"

Hank smiled over his shoulder. "That's true. It was likely just precautionary after the explosion last October."

Then why wasn't the first floor painted? Emily thought.

Near the end of this hall, they halted beside a double door to their right. "Now we'll enter a small space between these exterior safety doors and a second set of safety doors leading to the production room," Hank said, pointing to his right. "This is the entryway into the primary LB5 production facility when it was in use prior to 1989—directly below room 365. Once we pass through the second set of doors, we'll be in the actual production space itself. Don't be surprised at the appearance of the room: remember, this facility was shut down suddenly and with every expectation that it might begin production again any day. It will be messy, and perhaps appear a little chaotic."

Hank pushed open one side of the double doors and passed inside. King followed, then Dr. Trân, with Ryan a step behind—and Emily and the judge further back.

The entryway space was wide but not long, with only eight to ten feet separating the two sets of doors. Hank, the Covington lawyer, and Dr. Trân were crowded inside the space, leaving Ryan still partially in the corridor, holding open the spring-loaded door with one hand so that it wouldn't strike Emily and the judge just behind. Emily crowded close to her father's shoulder, curious to look inside the production room as soon as the interior door was opened.

Hank pushed open the production room door, revealing a black space. "Let me get the light," he said, turning to his right and disappearing into the dark room.

King followed, stepping partway into the dark room behind the guide. Ryan and Dr. Trân began to follow.

Through the doorway, at the furthest visible end of the room,

Emily saw a tiny bluish glow appear, growing in intensity and breadth. Like a light bulb about to flame out, she thought.

In that instant, from somewhere inside the darkened space, Emily heard Hank's voice cry out in a high-pitched yell, *"Back out!"*

Emily's stomach tightened and the acrid taste of bile came into her throat. She half turned as the judge stumbled backwards into the hall. Her father grabbed her from behind, picking Emily up and carrying her bodily through the exterior doors as Hank repeated his cry more loudly, *"GET OUT!"*

Then her father stumbled, carrying Emily down with him. She hit the hallway floor, her breath forced from her, as her father struck the floor beside her. She was dimly aware of Dr. Trân and the others stepping over them, hurriedly exiting the exterior doors into the hallway.

The heavy door panels slammed shut behind the last of the group. Instantly, a tremendous boom shuddered the walls, shaking the floor and driving Trân and King off their feet to the ground beside Emily. Only Hank remained standing, his hands balanced against the wall. Emily saw him lean down to lift Judge Johnston to her feet as another blast shook the corridor.

"Back to the front side!" Hank was shouting now, pointing up the hall in the direction from which they'd come. Emily struggled to check her fear as she rose with her father's help, then began a clumsy retreat up the corridor, her hands against the wall to counter the repeated blasts shaking the concrete around them. She reached the staircase and began to ascend, hearing the clatter of the others' footsteps just behind. Then she raced up the steadier first-floor corridor, reaching the entryway, passing through the doors and out of the dark side.

The shuddering explosions had stopped by the time they had all gathered by the supply desk once more, breathless and shaken. Emily watched Red Whalen turn and lift the receiver of a wall phone. Judge Johnston was trying to remain stoic, though

Emily could see that she was near tears. Her father seemed mostly concerned about Emily, forcing her to keep reassuring him that she was fine—while King checked his own arms, legs, and sides repeatedly, as though searching for wounds. Hank stood slightly apart, silently counting their number until, satisfied, he directed them to put on their HEPA masks. Emily did so, slipping the device over her nose and mouth.

What had just passed seemed impossible, Emily thought, like she was tapping into a specter of someone else's memory. They'd just missed incineration in a criticality explosion. And miraculously, they'd all survived it At least they all looked unharmed. She could see others were processing it, too, the relief beginning to replace fear on each of the faces of her companions.

Then her eyes caught Dr. Trân.

Amidst them all, only Dr. Trân now appeared fully calm. He stood in a corner a little away from the rest. His clothes were dirtied from the fall, his thick dark hair disheveled. But otherwise he appeared unshaken by the nearly disastrous event they'd just survived.

Emily didn't know Trân well. Other than her trial prep, she'd spent little time with the scientist. But she could swear that, in contrast to the rest of them, the only emotion Trân displayed was barely restrained anger.

And his gaze was fixed on the back of their guide, Hank, standing just a few yards away.

CHAPTER 47

"Explain once more," her father said.

From his seat on the couch, Dr. Trân nodded. "Of course. First, it is virtually impossible that our mere entry into that production room would trigger a critical reaction. Second, the bluish glow just before the explosion *is* consistent with reports of criticality events—but the explosive reaction should have followed the appearance of the glow *instantaneously*, not after we all had the opportunity to get out of the room."

"Then you're saying . . . what," Emily said, "that it was staged?"

Dr. Trân shrugged.

"If that was true," Ryan said, "then that would mean our guide Hank would have had to help create the appearance of a criticality event in the dark before we could enter—then herd us away from the room. And also set in motion the explosions we all felt."

"That is more plausible than the explosion Covington asserts occurred," Dr. Trân answered.

It seemed too paranoid, Emily thought. Like a conspiracy on a conspiracy. But then she reminded herself, her father had been equally skeptical of Dr. Trân early on—and he'd been right.

"Even if that's true," she asked, "how would we prove it? How could we convince the judge? I saw her in the front side of LB5 afterwards: she was terrified—and probably sure she'd made a mistake letting us in there."

Dr. Trân shook his head. "I don't know. Since Covington's people were the first responders on the scene, by now they will have ensured that the room will be consistent with a series of spontaneous criticality events triggered by our entry."

Ryan was beginning to look numb with fatigue, so Emily continued in the lead. "Won't the very *unlikelihood* of the event get some scrutiny from DOE?" she asked. "Or other nuclear scientists?"

"Of course," Dr. Trân said. "Many will question how it could have happened. But it doesn't matter: skepticism isn't proof. The only *data* on record will fully support Covington's conclusions."

Emily was nearly as overwhelmed as her father this morning—though more with frustration than fatigue. They'd finally gotten the "inspection" they'd been fighting for and all it did was confirm Covington's safety objections, while destroying any trace of potential evidence relating to the October explosions. Plus, the *Sherman Courier* had published a write-up on the accident yesterday, which meant the jury had likely been exposed to news supporting Covington's contention about an empty LB5 lower level.

"We're dead," Kieran said, sitting at her side. "That's it. Unless the jury buys the proof we've given them so far, we're going to lose."

Emily looked at Kieran sympathetically. Her anger at Kieran had eased since Ted Pollock's assurances that he was coerced into keeping quiet. Still, she didn't have the energy to console him just now.

She glanced next at Poppy, sitting silently at the kitchen table and staring across the room toward the front yard. Was he thinking about his former partner, she wondered. Or thinking that he'd put his family at risk taking sides in a lawsuit that was looking like a losing bet.

341

So now where did they go?

"I'm headed out for a run," her father finally muttered. Emily shared his desire to escape. She smiled her understanding and permission as he headed upstairs to change.

Ryan pushed up the familiar hill again, passing only the slowest of runners today. A cooling breeze washed over him, but it was the only positive about this morning's run. His legs felt like barrels full of sand.

On top of that, the exercise wasn't working. This run was doing little to lift his suffocating malaise.

But there might be no cure for that. Though he hated the sound of it, he agreed with Kieran's assessment. Their case was now officially dead in the water.

Mercifully, the top of the hill arrived, moments before he gave in and slowed to a walk. Here on the crest were other park visitors. A group of teens were playing with a Frisbee. Two couples picnicked on blankets spread on the open lawn. Ryan slowly approached the bench.

Standing to one side of the seat today was Larry Mann, in his usual running gear, facing the southern view. He wasn't sweating, Ryan noticed; he must have been up here awhile. Mann turned toward Ryan and smiled.

"How's the trial going?" Mann asked as soon as Ryan drew near.

It seemed like the insurance agent's favorite topic of conversation. Ryan shook his head. "Not so well."

Mann nodded. "I'll confess, I read about the critical explosion in the paper. Very sorry to hear about it."

Maybe he was sorry, but Larry seemed especially charged up today, a serious contrast from the last time they'd seen one another. "You take the good with the bad," Ryan responded.

"It must be tough. Is it hard to get a fair jury here?"

Ryan shrugged. "Don't know. Haven't gotten a verdict yet."

Mann smiled. "Of course. You married, Ryan?"

The sudden change of subject was disconcerting, especially in Ryan's mood. "No. My wife passed away a few years ago."

"Sorry to hear that," Larry responded immediately—so quickly that Ryan had a brief impression his status as a widower wasn't news to the man. "Are you close to your daughter? The one who's trying the case with you? I saw it in the paper."

Ryan watched an airplane passing distantly overhead, the only break on the aqua blue of the sky. "Yes. I think we are."

"That's good," Mann said. "Fathers are supposed to be close to their daughters, aren't they? Sons to mothers, fathers to daughters, right?"

"I suppose."

"My father was a stockbroker," he offered.

"Has he passed away?" Ryan asked.

"*Is* a stockbroker," Mann corrected.

Ryan wanted to get away from this unexpected conversation with the supercharged insurance agent. Standing there answering rapid-paced questions was the last thing Ryan wanted right then. "I'd better get going," he said. "Got lots left to do."

"Me too," Larry said, though he showed no signs of leaving just yet. "See you next time."

Ryan took the downward slope thinking about the strange, almost manic talk with the insurance salesman. It had left Ryan uneasy. Still, by the time he'd reached the flats, his mind had returned to the case.

Kieran was right: they were dead with the evidence as it stood. Their only hope now was to bust open that underground chamber out on the reservation, and hope it contained evidence of the nuclear trigger and LB5. And their only hope to do that now lay in using that recovered shard—which Ted Pollock wouldn't permit them to do.

It occurred to him to try to subpoena the object. But even

if he wanted to cross swords with the Yakama rancher, Ryan was confident that Pollock would rebury the piece before he'd acknowledge its existence and produce it in court.

In his despair, Ryan wondered if there was a hole in the ground with the secret remains of this trigger project, what else might be buried out there on the reservation grounds. How many charted and forgotten pits might there be with hoards of objects poisonous and benign? Buried secrets of Hanford's past—like an underground museum charting man's hubris in creating a factory to manufacture a substance as terrifying as plutonium.

Where in that museum would they display the body that the HR guy took onto the reservation, Ryan wondered. How would that display card read. And who *was* that person who had become one of the lost artifacts under the surface of the Hanford desert? Could it really be Vandervork?

Ryan's mind stopped wandering at the thought of Poppy's partner. Lewis Vandervork. Patrick Martin. The HR rep.

What were the chances that the same HR guy dealing with Poppy Martin and the LB5 explosion evidence would be tasked with running a body out onto the Hanford grounds? What kind of a rotten job did he have to have to get both of these assignments?

Unless they were part of the same assignment. Unless the body really was linked to the explosion at LB5.

Unless the HR rep was deeply involved with both.

That thought devoured all the others. Ryan felt himself picking up the pace. If the body was related to the LB5 explosion, then its burial on the grounds wouldn't be strange at all. It would be natural. And if the body was related to the LB5 explosion, there was one obvious place to put it. And if the HR rep was in charge, who better to take it there?

Ryan was nearly at a sprint by the time he reached the Annex.

❖❖❖

"That's got to be it," Ryan repeated to the group still assembled in the living room.

No one was paying attention to the fact that Ryan still wore his drenched running clothes. With the theory he'd just related between gasping breaths, Ryan had everyone's attention in the room.

"You really think so?" Poppy asked.

"Yes," Ryan said. "You assumed the body you saw that night coming out of the Sherman Retirement Home could be Lewis—until you rejected the notion because of the time lapse since the explosion. But what if the body was someone else injured in the LB5 explosion who *survived* for nine months? What if it was the guy Vandervork's girlfriend says he claimed to have shot? Or somebody else who picked up a serious radiation dose in the explosion? As you said, anyone immediately *killed* by the explosion would have been put in the ground a long time ago—and there's no way they would have stored a body at the retirement home all this time. But they might have cared for someone there."

Emily raised a hand, struggling with a thought. "But, Dad, why take the body out onto the reservation at all? Why not just bury it in a graveyard?"

"Perhaps," Dr. Trân intervened, "because the body was too contaminated to be disposed of by other means. Like the other debris from the explosion."

"So they could have some kind of mausoleum out there where they're burying people?" Poppy asked softly. He turned his gaze on Ryan. "Does that mean Lewis could be there, too?"

"Maybe," Ryan said, "except he wasn't hurt or irradiated in the explosion. The only reason he'd be there is if he died after."

"You mean 'was killed after,'" Poppy said.

Emily shook her head. "But what about the call Lewis made to his girlfriend the night of the explosion?" she asked. "And the texts later. And his apartment and job out at Savannah River that

Poppy told us about. Doesn't that mean he was okay for weeks or months after the explosion? And why murder him way after the fact, then ship him back here just to put him in that hole?"

"The phone call to his girlfriend proves Lewis was alive that night after the explosion," Ryan said, thinking out loud. "But maybe he was killed later that very first night, to prevent him from telling what he saw. If they did, they could've checked Lewis's cell phone and seen that he'd called Beverly Cortez, then followed up with threats to keep her quiet. Even used his phone to create a text trail out to Savannah River, where they got an apartment and a fake job in his name."

"We're still talking murder here, aren't we," Poppy said quietly. No one responded.

Poppy picked up a folder from the floor beside his feet. "Well, I've got another mystery for you then. You never asked me about it the last few days, but my son got that LB5 weapons log I told you about—from central HQ. Like you thought, there's nothing on here about Lew's rifle being checked out for the supposed inspection. In fact, Lew's gun isn't even listed on the log at all here."

Emily walked over and looked over Poppy's shoulder at the chart. "What do you mean? There are three places on the chart for weapons at the LB5 roof station and three serial numbers listed. Nothing's missing."

"Yeah," Poppy said, exasperated, "but the serial numbers on our weapons were consecutive, because we bought 'em for LB5 especially, and I logged them in myself seventeen years ago. When Lew arrived at LB5, he glommed onto one of them and named it after his girlfriend. There're only two rifles here with consecutive numbers. The third one, Lew's, is gone. I've never seen this other number they've got here."

"Why would Lewis's weapon be missing?" Kieran asked. "And where would they put it?"

"How about with Lewis?" Ryan said.

He looked over at Emily, who was lost in thought, piecing it all together.

Ryan didn't have to. The story was already assembled in his mind and it was starting to make sense—like the critical point in a case when a piece of evidence vanquished the last doubt in his mind about what really happened. Except, he reminded himself, in litigation, he could then use that evidence to convince the jury. Here the essential proof was still beyond his reach, in the dirt of the desert or hidden in Ted's stable.

Since the failed inspection at LB5, they really had only one avenue left to confirm their theories: they had to get to whatever was in the ground beneath that door on the reservation, or face the case collapsing in a matter of days. With it would fall Kieran's hope for final proof of his exposure, for compensation, for a chance to leave Sherman with his family. Along with Ted Pollock's hope of shutting down the project out there, or preventing future projects.

If they could only get access to the key to that door.

Ryan turned to Poppy. "What was the name of that HR guy again?"

The guard's lips curled in disgust. "I'll never forget it. Adam Worth."

"Look," Ryan began slowly, "the only person we know who's likely got a key into that hole on the reservation is this Worth—if we assume that's where he put the body Poppy saw."

"How does that help us?" Emily asked. "We can't subpoena it for trial."

"No," Ryan agreed. "So we've got to give Adam Worth a reason to use it."

CHAPTER 48

Adam had just finished toweling off in the Covington locker room when his phone buzzed. He pulled it out of the locker.

"Yes, Eric," he said cheerfully.

"Adam, I just got personally served with an amended exhibit and witness list for trial by Emily Hart."

The case held no anxiety for Adam anymore. Especially after looking Ryan Hart in the eye on the extra-long run he'd just completed. "What's it say?"

"The new exhibit list claims they'll be introducing 'debris from the October sixteenth explosion, including nuclear trigger casings and related detonation evidence.' You have any idea what they're talking about?"

Adam sat down, a wave of nausea rolling over him.

King went on. "It also says they will be producing a rifle. It's got a serial number here if you want it."

No. No.

"And the witness added to their list," King said carefully, "Adam, it's you. The Hart lawyer also served me with a subpoena to have you at the trial on Monday morning."

How could they have gotten into the white train? How could they possibly have found it—let alone gotten through the magnetic lock to collect the debris? The chamber had to be thirty feet underground, through stone and concrete.

"Adam?"

"I'll call you back," Adam said, ending the call.

He had to know what they'd found. However they'd accessed the pit, they couldn't have transported much material away: that would require multiple vehicles. And they couldn't possibly have gotten so many vehicles onto the reservation without being detected. Adam had to find out what they'd recovered and whether it was enough to really prove the existence of a nuclear trigger.

And now he had to empty the pit. Demolish it if possible.

Oh no. Had they seen the bodies, too? If they got into th pit? Of course they had, how could they miss them?

Adam glanced around. The locker room was empty. He press the speed dial to reach the Chief.

"Yeah," Mel Emerson answered.

"We've got to get out there tonight," Adam said. "You've got to get your whole team together, and we've got to empty the white train *tonight*."

A heavy sigh came over the line. "We hadn't planned for this for another month, sir," Emerson began. "We just got the testing equipment from LB5 on railcars for New Mexico two nights ago. We'd have to drum up more hazard railcars for the debris—not to mention figuring out where to dispose of the bodies. Plus, it'll take some doing to be sure our people are covering the monitors at Hanford Security tonight. And if we start at the usual time, it's going to take every minute of dark to do this in one night. I don't know, Mr. Worth—it's going to take a lot of work."

"Just do it!" Adam shouted over the phone, his voice echoing in the showers and lockers around him. He struggled for a moment to calm his voice. "We'll just have to start earlier. And get as many people as you need to do it quickly. *Tonight*, Chief."

"All right," Emerson grunted in frustration. Then the line went dead.

Adam hesitated a moment before reaching into his locker. The coin purse was there. He'd planned to stop taking the blue tabs now, as matters were winding down. But this wasn't over yet.

Adam unzipped it and pulled two, then a third pill, out. It was going to be a long and difficult night.

CHAPTER 49

Emily had to remind herself that this part of the plan was her idea. Not only that, she had insisted she be the one to carry this out, over her father's and Kieran's strong objections. She had no one else to blame for the chilly night air that breached her jacket, or the fear that gripped her chest.

In the end, they'd relented only when she'd agreed that someone else—Heather, as it turned out—would come with her. She looked over at the young woman now. Even in the darkness Emily could see that Heather didn't look the least concerned.

The horses carrying Emily and Heather bareback were padding softly through a night dimly lit by a young, waxing moon. This evening somehow felt so different than the last to Emily. Even the animals had sensed it early on, backing nervously away from their entry point on the fence line before stepping onto the grounds. Maybe it was because last time they'd come onto the reservation Emily's fear had been leavened by the excitement of what they were doing, and the presence of Ted and her father. Or maybe because then detection was only a risk.

This time, detection wasn't a risk. Detection was their goal. And an idea that made great sense in the Annex with an afternoon sun passing through the windows seemed a frail notion out here in the still isolation of night.

They came around a hillock. A hundred yards away was the

security station. No light shone from the guard window. But there was a car parked behind it, so someone must be there tonight. Emily wasn't sure if she was pleased or disappointed.

When Ryan explained his idea of serving new exhibit and witness lists to induce Worth out to the pit to check for the "missing debris," Kieran and Poppy were certain that it would work. Maybe her father's core of realism was taking root in her, but Emily immediately saw this plan more skeptically. How could they be sure that Worth, even if he came, would come immediately, *this very night*? What if he waited until Sunday night? What if he waited until they were forced to offer their nonexistent "evidence" of debris and the rifle at trial?

Which was why Emily proposed they seed the trap with stronger bait—by making it appear that they were collecting more evidence from the hole this very evening. To do that, someone had to be seen on the grounds tonight, heading in that direction. And since Poppy had learned that this guard station was associated with Worth, they decided to try the tactic here. Once they detected Worth entering the grounds, her father, Poppy, and Kieran would come onto the reservation and catch the HR man with the key in his hands.

A cloud of breath escaped from Heather's mouth as she leaned down and gave her stallion an encouraging pat. "Ready?" she whispered.

How could the girl look so calm? Emily gritted her teeth. "Yes."

Heather kicked her stallion hard in the flanks. The animal gathered itself and launched into a gallop, its hoofs digging into the hard soil.

Emily took a last breath. Then she did the same.

The mare leapt forward underneath her, Emily clinging to its mane. The horses rounded the hill, coming into full view of the guard station.

Huddled low on the horse's back, Emily cast a glance across

her shoulder. The light on the guard station came on. A figure appeared, silhouetted in the light. Then the light disappeared again.

They kept up the gallop until they'd moved out of sight of the guard station once more. Then they slowed the animals to a trot and at last a walk.

Emily, out of breath and still clinging to the mane like a lifeline, nearly laughed out loud at the surge of relief from finishing the task. Now, if the guard called Worth, it should take him at least an hour to get out there from Sherman. That would give Heather and her enough time to leave a trail to the pit and continue on to escape further west.

Emily pulled her cell phone from her jacket pocket. Poppy's son, Michael, was hidden in his car within view of the guard's station, watching for Worth to arrive. Still, to be safe, they'd agreed that Emily would let them know when Heather and she had passed by the station.

"Dad?" she said as her father answered. The line was crackling with poor reception.

"Yes," he responded at last.

"The guard saw us. Be ready to come onto the grounds."

CHAPTER 50

"Yes, Mr. Worth," the guard was saying over the phone. "It was two horses, riding in the direction of the pit. They just passed. They were moving fast, probably surprised the station was manned."

Adam was seated in the passenger seat of the lead SUV, his foot tapping a rhythm on the floor. Well, horses explained how the Harts got onto the grounds before without detection. But this still made no sense. Why would the Harts alert them to their access to the white train by serving the exhibit list—then go back out there again?

Unless they'd decided they had too little evidence to impress the judge.

"Thank you, Stu," Adam said, "We'll be there shortly."

This made tonight's operation more interesting. He glanced at his watch. The caravan of SUVs and vans was already within fifteen minutes of the guard station. At this rate, they should be able to catch the riders on the reservation—maybe even before they reached the white-train pit, if they still were headed there.

He turned to Emerson behind the wheel and quickly told the security chief what the guard had said.

"Sir, you might want to call and let the rest of the guys in the trailing SUVs know so we can hurry up the pace."

Adam agreed and began to make the calls.

❖❖❖

Ryan was pacing the fence line like a caged animal. He didn't like this idea. He didn't like his daughter—or Heather—being out there alone. He shouldn't have let Emily convince him.

"But what are the real risks?" she'd argued. "We should be able to reach the hole and ride on past at least half an hour before Worth can even get to the reservation after he's alerted. Since you'll be coming onto the grounds at a point closer to the hole than where we'll start, by then you three will be approaching in Poppy's truck."

She'd made it seem reasonable. But then, Ryan had already learned that she was a good advocate. Now it just seemed like a stupid and risky idea.

Ted stood with his wife, Ray, and two others waiting to open the fence at the last minute. Making a hole big enough for Poppy's truck, and making it seem like a natural break, was a far different task than creating a breach for horses. They planned to stay there until Ryan and the rest returned from the pit, then do what they could to hide the entrance.

Though concerned about the plan, Ted had finally offered to come along onto the grounds. Ryan had declined. It was enough that Heather had agreed to take this risk with them. Besides, they shouldn't need any more people on this trip. All they had to do was catch Worth out of his vehicle with the keys, then force their way in to get pictures and evidence. Three of them should be enough to accomplish that.

And if something *did* go wrong, the cautious side of Ryan argued, it was a good idea anyway to have somebody on this side of the fence knowing where they'd gone.

Ryan looked at his watch for the tenth time in as many minutes. It was way too early to be concerned. Worth shouldn't be to the grounds from Sherman for another forty-five minutes. Besides, Michael would alert them when Worth reached the guard station. And the last thing they wanted was to get to the hole *before* he arrived and take a chance on him seeing them and turning around. No, they wanted to be near and approach fast, surprising Worth out of his vehicle before he could make an escape.

Poppy's cell phone went off. "Yeah, Michael," Ryan heard him say. The security guard paused. "What do you mean? *How many?*"

Ryan watched in alarm as Poppy pocketed his phone again. "Michael says they're at the guard station already," Poppy said tersely. "And it's more than just Worth. Michael just saw them go past the guard station with five SUVs, half a dozen vans, and at least twenty to thirty guys."

Ryan was rocked. "They're not just checking the place," he heard Ted mutter. "They're emptying the pit. And they're an hour earlier than you had planned."

Ryan pulled out his cell phone again and punched in Emily's number. No answer. He tried again.

"There are blackout spots out there," Ted spoke again. He nodded toward Ray, who walked to Ted's truck. Ryan followed him with his eyes until he returned a moment later, his hands full with two rifles. He handed one to Poppy.

"You know how to use it?" Ted asked, looking only at Ryan.

Ryan scanned the weapon in Poppy's hand. "It's an AR-13 semi-automatic. Yes, I know how to use it. But this is supposed to be about gathering evidence for a civil lawsuit."

"Not for us," Ted said. "If they're emptying the hole, there are no secrets left to keep. Once that pit is empty, so is our chance to shut down Wolffia."

Ryan looked again at the rifle in Poppy's hand. "I don't know," he said. "I don't want a shootout."

"Neither do we," Ted answered. "But you opened this box. Before we let this proof leave the grounds, we'll do what we have to. Which means we're coming with you."

CHAPTER 51

Emily and Heather slowed their horses as they came around the ridge and into sight of the slope bearing the entrance to the hole. Even in the cold of the night, the horses were lathered and tired.

"Let's take a three-minute break," Heather said. "But no more: we don't want the horses cooling off too much. Then we'll head to the rendezvous point."

Emily gratefully agreed. Her mare might be tired, but she was exhausted. They'd entered the reservation grounds several miles further east than the last time. That plus the gallop—on bareback—had left her legs wobbly and weak.

Moments later, Emily stood beside the mare, holding the rope around her neck, watching as Heather led her horse up the slope to the cover. "It's still in place," she called down to Emily. "Doesn't look like it's been disturbed since we were here last."

Emily's horse suddenly threw back its head, trying to turn in the direction from which they'd just come. Emily held the rope tight in both hands, but was nearly tugged off her feet.

Now Emily heard it too: the growl of an engine. No, more than one engine.

Emily looked up at Heather, who was already trotting down the slope with her stallion. Heather drew close to where Emily was struggling to calm the mare, threw her rope across her shoulder, and leaned down to give Emily a leg up. The skittish mare kept backing away. Emily wrapped her fingers tight in its mane, settled her boot onto Heather's clasped fingers, and bounced up and across its moving back.

The vehicles were drawing closer.

Heather twined her fingers in the stallion's mane and jumped, hauling herself up as she threw a leg over its back. She straightened, and the rope slid off her shoulder and to the dusty earth.

Heather glanced to the ground where it lay, then at Emily. Emily shook her head.

Without another word, they both kicked their mounts, turning the animals' heads west and away from the sound of the approaching cars.

The lead car of Adam's caravan rounded the ridge and came to a halt below the door to the pit. The SUVs and vans drew up in a line, backing and maneuvering until they were each parked roughly side by side, half with their headlights on the slope, half with their rear bumpers in that direction. Then the team began piling out, pulling on Demron suits and masks.

Adam had no need for a suit just yet. He was already wearing his HEPA mask, but would not be entering the pit until later. He looked around the empty site. Perhaps they'd beaten the riders there. Or maybe the riders had abandoned coming there after the guard saw them. Either way, he was at least sure they couldn't have gotten into the pit and back out again before Adam arrived.

It didn't matter. The priority now was to determine what debris had been taken by Hart's people, then empty the pit.

One of the suited guards approached. "Sir, I found this." He held out a circle of rope.

Adam took it in his hand. It was probably below forty degrees out here tonight, but the rope was still warm in his hands.

"Emerson," he called to the security chief. The man came

close. Adam thrust the magnetic key into his hand. "Have Greg start setting up the C-4 explosives while the team empties the pit," he said rapidly. "As they remove the debris, be sure they keep it grouped in the vans like it is down below so I can inventory it. And I'll need your car keys. Plus two sets of cuffs from the group."

The chief nodded, then retrieved the cuffs and handed them to Adam, along with the SUV keys.

Moments later, Adam was driving west, his lights on high—moving fast over the rough terrain, but not so fast as to miss the unmistakable tracks of hoofprints on the dry desert soil.

Emily and Heather rode side by side, trying to maintain a good pace without overtaxing the tired animals. They were less than a mile from the hole now, Emily estimated—and based on the map she'd seen earlier, still four or five miles to the egress point.

They'd heard the sound of cars drawing close as they galloped from the site of the hole. Then, to Emily's relief, the engine noises had stopped. At that, she'd followed Heather's lead and pulled back from the dangerous nighttime gallop into a fast walk.

Now Heather tugged on her horse's mane and urged it to stop. Emily did the same as her companion raised a finger to her lips.

It took a second before Emily heard it too. An engine sound again. Only one this time, but coming their way.

They each gave their horses a hard kick, driving them forward again into the blackness. Emily held onto the mane tightly as her horse lunged forward, striving wearily to satisfy its rider and keep pace with Heather's stronger stallion ahead.

Another half mile passed as the engine noise grew gradually closer. Heather was still visible a short distance ahead—though she was slowly pulling away. Even in the diffuse moonlight, Emily could see the young woman's head shifting back and forth;

searching, she guessed, for harder terrain where the hoof marks might be invisible in the soil.

The mare faltered under Emily, pitching suddenly forward and nearly driving her over its head. It righted itself, trying to stumble back into a stride just as a light flashed across the terrain, throwing the mare's dark outline out in front.

The horse cut to the right, alarmed at its sudden shadow. Emily's fingers were yanked from its mane and she rolled off its back into the darkness.

Her shoulder hit the ground, sending flashes of pain through her torso. She rolled twice and lay still, gasping for breath as sounds of the mare's hoofbeats disappeared into the night.

Still catching her breath, Emily tried to sit up, but a shot of pain in her right shoulder drew a cry of agony from her lips. The engine was drawing closer now. Panic filling her head, she rolled away from the injured shoulder, scanning the ground for anywhere to hide. There was a boulder a few yards away. She tried to raise herself with her good arm.

The engine noise was roaring as it drew up within a yard from Emily's body. She tried once more to rise.

The light was all around her as Emily dropped with a final cry of pain back onto the desert floor.

CHAPTER 52

"You've got to hurry," Ryan said. They couldn't be going more than fifteen miles an hour.

Running without lights, Poppy was leaning into the dash, squinting out of the Sierra's front window, trying to follow Ted's truck twenty yards ahead.

"I know you're worried, Ryan," Poppy said. "I am, too. But it won't do us a bit of good to drive into a ditch. Or run smack into twenty guys who are probably armed. Besides, this is about timing, not speed. Don't worry—we'll catch that that little Aussie son of—"

Ted's truck ahead suddenly swerved to the right, its front left hood dipping into an unseen trench with a loud thud.

Poppy barely got his Sierra stopped before they collided with the cantilevered vehicle. The three of them emptied onto the desert and joined Ted and his men at the other truck's front bumper.

"Axle may be bent," Ray said, staring into the gully.

Ted turned to Poppy. "You've got the GPS coordinates for the pit. Keep moving. We'll try to get this free. If we have to, we'll follow on foot. We'll catch up shortly, one way or the other."

Poppy nodded. Ryan and Kieran followed him back to the Sierra.

Minutes later they were moving along the edge of the trench that had caught Ted's truck, looking for a way to continue north.

Adam's hands trembled as he walked around the slope from the west, into view of the SUV and van lights illuminating the surface surrounding the pit entrance. The dexys were at full intensity now, shooting him through with an energy and clarity that could light up the night. Maybe he'd overdone it with three tabs, he thought, clenching and unclenching his fists. His pulse was pumping so loudly it nearly covered the grunts of the men passing debris up the submerged staircase and out onto the slope in a bucket brigade.

But he'd get through it. He just had to keep it contained while they got all this finished.

Adam cast one more glance over his shoulder at Emerson's SUV, parked out of view of the work area. He'd made the right decision to leave the girl handcuffed in the car, out of sight of the team. It would make things simpler and leave him more options.

He approached the entrance to the pit where the Chief stood, his hands on the hips of the black suit and his mask in one hand. He turned as Adam joined him.

"Any luck?" Emerson asked.

Adam shook his head. "No. Doesn't matter, though. How much more?"

"We're just finishing up now. You said to leave the four body bags outside of the railcars, with extra powerful charges to atomize them, right?"

Adam nodded.

"Well, I'll check to be sure that's set. Greg had the rest of the explosives already in place the last time I went inside. You can see we removed the door and left it inside as well."

"Good. Chief, I know we planned for you to set off the charges, but I've decided to do it myself. I want you to go back to the railyard with the others."

Emerson squinted with surprise. "You sure?"

Adam nodded firmly. "Yes. Have Greg rig it for a single trigger."

"Whatever you say, boss," Emerson replied. "Stay at least thirty yards back. When you let it go, the whole ceiling of the chamber should come down. The train will be under thirty feet of rock—it'd take excavators weeks to reach it. With the extra charges on the bodies, those should be mostly dust. Six months and a couple of fall rains and there'll scarcely be any sign the chamber was ever opened in the first place."

"Good," Adam said. "Listen, I'll bring your SUV back myself tonight, alone. Catch a ride with one of the others. And have them leave one Demron suit."

Emerson's eyebrows rose. "Okay. If that's what you want."

Adam watched the men, like black ants in their suits, hauling the last of the accumulated debris down the slope. Emerson began to don his mask as he took a step toward the pit entrance.

Adam grabbed his arm. "One more thing, Chief. I don't anticipate any problems, but I want you to spread the word with the crew here tonight. If there is any trouble down the road—if the government decides any of this was handled improperly— I've made a contingency plan. In the event any of them are arrested for whatever reason, you let them know I've set up a fund that will pay for their attorneys. And if by some off chance anybody's convicted, their family will get five hundred thousand dollars a year for every year they spend . . . away. Guaranteed, payable annually."

Emerson's eyes widened. "You're not kidding?"

Adam shook his head quickly. "I'm not. Don't alarm them. Things will be fine. But if something happens, those are the wages for their loyalty and silence."

The Chief was shaking his head now. "But you're not saying what we're doing here is . . . unsanctioned."

"You're correct, I'm not saying that. I am saying that there's always politics where the defense industry is involved, and we're the tip of the spear on this mission. If there's any misunderstanding, we'll take care of them. Just as I said."

The Chief looked at Adam closely. "Okay. It might spook them a little, but I'll spread the word."

The Chief walked up the slope, still shaking his head.

These men believed they were working for a cause. Emerson and the other security personnel were bright enough to suspect they were crossing lines here and there. But mostly, especially given their psychological profiles, they would believe the government would protect them.

Foote would lecture that the belief was enough, because he placed his faith in the power of loyalty. Adam believed in the power of loyalty, supplemented by lots of money. And since Adam was lower on the food chain, and the person these men could identify, he was going to use his own discretion on this one.

Especially since he controlled the budget.

CHAPTER 53

They'd parked nearly a mile from the pit, according to the Garmin. Now Ryan was leading Kieran, with Poppy lagging, across the desert on a careful trot. Poppy and Kieran were carrying the rifle, while Ryan held the single hazmat suit they'd brought along.

Any closer, Poppy had warned, and Worth and the others might hear the engine the way sound carried over the desert, even driving slowly. Ryan had reluctantly agreed. Still, making their way in the dark, without flashlights, was taking forever. And all the gullies and rocks in their path had made them later getting there than Ryan had ever imagined.

In the near distance, maybe half a mile still, they heard the sound of approaching engines. Without a word, all three dropped to the ground.

They were on a gradual downward slope here. Below them, they saw headlights appear. A caravan of cars and vans emerged from around a hill, their headlights growing brighter as they curved along an invisible road headed east. It took nearly five minutes for them all to pass at their deliberate pace.

Maybe they were too late, Ryan thought frantically, watching the caravan taillights disappearing. Was it possible Emily and Heather were in one of those cars? Or had they gotten away and were now approaching the egress point?

Still grasping the suit, Ryan had just pushed off the ground to stand when a thought that had been playing at the back of his consciousness came front and center. It was a statement Poppy had made earlier on the drive, about an Australian.

"Poppy," he began, "before Ted's truck hit the gully, you said something about getting an Australian."

"Yeah."

"Who were you talking about?"

The guard looked quizzically at Ryan in the dark. "Adam Worth, of course. He's got an accent. I'm pretty sure it's Australian."

Stunned, Ryan asked for a description. Wiry. Intense. Red hair. Maybe late twenties.

The insurance salesman, Ryan thought as a frenzy of anger washed over him. It had to be. Larry Mann was Adam Worth.

The last of the vehicles disappeared around the ridge. Adam turned and walked back to Emerson's SUV around the slope to the west.

The girl was gagged in the rear of the vehicle, her hands cuffed together, with another set of cuffs shackling her to a metal loop directly behind the front seat frame. Adam glanced at her. Her eyes flashed a look that alternated between anger and pain.

He'd gathered that she'd injured her shoulder before he'd found her, probably a fall from her horse. Now he could also see that she was shivering.

He started the SUV and drove around the ridge. They'd placed the explosives trigger on the desert soil nearly fifty yards back from the pit opening, beside a four-foot boulder. A Demron suit was heaped next to the trigger.

Adam parked the SUV. Pivoting in his seat, he unlocked the girl's cuffs from the loop, then got out and walked to the rear hatch.

He probably could have been gentler, but he was too tired and too anxious to finish all this to even make the effort. He grabbed her ankles and pulled her out onto the ground.

She slammed to the earth, letting out a sharp gasp of pain. Adam grabbed the cuffs and dragged her to her feet, eliciting another cry through clenched teeth.

The opening to the pit, now without its door, was like a black gash in the hillside. The handcuffed girl was in too much pain to resist as he pulled her toward it, dropping her at the foot of the yawning hole. There, Adam pulled on his Demron suit, frustrated at the necessity for it. He exchanged the HEPA mask for the Demron one, still sweaty from the man who'd just used it. Then he hauled the girl to her feet once more and forced her down the steps into the darkness ahead of him.

Ryan was well ahead of the others by the time he rounded the ridge and came into view of a single SUV parked a distance back from a slope with its lights on. He turned toward the familiar ground to his left. Several dozen yards uphill, the pit was open wide.

By the time Kieran approached from behind, Ryan had the hazmat suit mostly on. He was just preparing to don the mask when Poppy appeared, puffing hard, the rifle clutched in one hand.

Poppy's phone buzzed. He pulled the cell from his pocket, raising it to his ear.

His eyes widened. "Okay," he whispered at last. Lowering the phone, he looked to Ryan.

"That was Ted," Poppy said softly. "Heather just got out. She hadn't brought her phone, so she couldn't call before. But she says Emily didn't make it. She fell somewhere out on the grounds."

Fear refueled the anger that still smoldered in Ryan's chest.

He turned and trotted to the SUV. It was empty. He returned to where he'd placed his phone when he'd donned the hazmat suit. Silently, he pressed in Emily's number.

The faint sound of Emily's ringtone floated, disembodied, on the night air. The sound of it was distant and small.

It was coming from the opening to the hole.

Ryan dropped his phone. Turning to Poppy, he grabbed the rifle from his hand and ran to the slope, starting up at a sprint.

Kieran caught him a few feet from the mouth of the hole, nearly passing him in an effort to enter. Ryan shifted the mask to his rifle hand and reached for Kieran's shoulder, squeezing hard. The boy looked at him with wild eyes.

No, Ryan mouthed, pointing to the hazmat suit he now wore, the only hazmat suit they'd brought along. Kieran shook his head, looking back toward the hole. Ryan squeezed the shoulder once more, then pushed Kieran back into Poppy's waiting arms.

Ryan glanced at the narrow glass visor on the mask and let it drop to the ground before stepping into the gaping darkness.

CHAPTER 54

In the narrow glare of his flashlight, Adam could see that the Hart girl was terrified, the fear far eclipsing the pain. She was cuffed now to the cargo door of the second boxcar. The four body bags were at her feet, wrapped in a dozen or more cubes of the powerful C4 explosive.

Adam looked at her with a faint glimmer of pity. He wondered why her father had sent her alone tonight. Part of him also wondered why she wasn't trying to talk to him. Perhaps it was the fear. It would have made no difference, but he was curious nonetheless.

He stood for a moment longer, running his conclusions a final time through the racecourse of his mind. After talking with Emerson and before the crew departed, he'd checked the gathered debris in each of the vehicles. Last year, he'd catalogued every bit of it himself. Based upon the lists he'd brought with him tonight, nothing appeared to be missing.

Which meant that Ryan Hart likely had no evidence. It had been a bluff. Though the man clearly knew where this pit was located, he had nothing to show for it.

Then why had the Hart girl come out this evening?

It didn't matter, now that the debris was gone. It would be taken to the railcars Emerson had arranged at the Hanford rail-yard, and from there by special transport to New Mexico—as they'd always planned on doing eventually. The only catch was it was no longer possible to consider simply closing up the white train cavern again. It had to be collapsed—as Greg had rigged the charges to do. And with the explosions, they would also disintegrate and obliterate evidence of the scientists' bodies.

And now, the girl's too.

He had no choice about the Hart woman. It was impossible to let her go now. Of course, her disappearance would lead to a search—and form the basis for her father's demand that this site be excavated.

If they were very fortunate, Hart's demands would not be met. After all, he would have to acknowledge illegal access to the reservation grounds to even explain them. Then he would have to weave an involved story justifying them—after already having caused a reaction at LB5 by his incessant and off-base insistence on inspecting *that* location.

Even if the authorities agreed to dig at this site, there was a chance they would not excavate a full thirty feet of rock to the level of the white train before concluding there was nothing there. And if, in the last extremity, they dug all the way down, they would find the white train demolished and crushed—and the remains so reduced as to be unnoticeable in the depths of the excavation.

Adam had made a final set of contingency plans if he was wrong: new IDs, money in multiple foreign accounts, everything that access to almost unlimited Project funding could buy. Plus, his ultimate bonus should arrive eventually. After all, the lab and successful trigger prototypes were already on their way to other Covington labs. Cameron Foote valued loyalty and success; he'd keep his promise to Adam. Given Adam's knowledge, Foote really didn't have any choice in the matter.

Adam took the flashlight off of the girl's frightened eyes. There was still one piece of evidence he had to deal with himself—one that neither the security crew nor anyone else knew about.

He walked to the locomotive, half buried in the nose of the shaft, and took the half a dozen steps up to the cab. There he pulled a key from his pocket, one that opened the heavy padlock and chain that sealed the cab door. Adam heard the girl cry out—in fear, he presumed—as the padlock released. Then he pulled the chain free and opened the door.

The bagged body of Lewis Vandervork lay on the cab floor where he'd placed it last October. Inside the bag, at his side, Adam knew his rifle lay.

If this man could have been silenced in any other way, Adam would have done so. But he knew in an instant of interviewing Vandervork that that was impossible. The idiot had even called his girlfriend the very night of the explosion, ignoring orders. This was the only silence possible for a person like Vandervork. Now he had to get the body onto the cavern floor with the others.

Setting the flashlight on the floor of the locomotive, pointed to the ceiling, he grabbed the end of the heavy bag and began to drag it to the door of the cab.

He heard the sound of metal on metal.

Adam twisted in his suit. A figure stood at the bottom of the stairs, faintly visible in the moonlight through the pit opening. Someone in a hazmat suit like his own.

Adam leaned across the body bag. He cursed his trembling fingers within the Demron gloves and the limited vision of his mask. He finally grasped the zipper and pulled it toward him— revealing Vandervork's black shoes. Alongside the shoes lay the rifle butt.

Adam slid the rifle out and stood. The mask, already sweaty, was filling with a faint sheen of fog. Adam grabbed and yanked it off his head—then turned to shoulder the weapon, struggling to steady his hands.

❖❖❖

Ryan took the metal steps as softly as he could manage in the foreign hazmat suit. The flashlight was in his pocket. The rifle he held at his waist.

The space below was illuminated in a ghostly white reflection. Halfway down the stairs, Ryan could see the source. His eyes followed a light that was moving from left to right, its glow illuminating the side of a train car painted white. It was held by a man in a black suit and hood—an image so bizarre that Ryan felt disoriented, as though he were watching a priest tending a modern Pharaoh's tomb.

He slowed to a stop. The man and his light began to climb up the steps of what appeared to be a locomotive. The figure bent over and for a moment grew still. Then Ryan heard metal and the sudden rattling of a chain.

In that same instant, an anguished cry of pain and fear emerged from the darkness to his left. Ryan's heart was pierced with recognition.

He fumbled in his pocket for the flashlight, turned it on, and pointed it to the source of the sound.

Emily was illuminated, kneeling on the ground beside the open door of another white railcar. At her feet lay four gray body bags, interlaced with wiring and a dozen cubes of what had to be C4.

Ryan turned and pounded down the remaining steps. The flashlight bumped the metal banister, slipping from his hand and clattering to the lowest step—just as he reached the floor of the cavern and looked up.

The figure was above him now, the light steadily pointing toward the ceiling of the pit. The suited figure must have heard him, because he was turning, rising from a crouch to a standing position. A rifle was suddenly in one hand. His other reached up and pulled off the covering over his head. Then he raised the rifle to a shoulder, pointing it in Ryan's direction.

Even in the weak reflection of the light against the railcar,

Ryan instantly knew the face. It was Larry Mann. It was Adam Worth.

Ryan raised his own weapon and dropped instinctively to one knee. He barely steadied the barrel at the figure before pulling the trigger.

The explosion of the rifle fire echoing in the confined chamber was ear shattering. Then Ryan realized there was more than one, that *two* echoes were overlapping, the gunshots chasing one another in a slowly fading rhapsody of sound.

Ryan felt a stinging in his side, but he ignored it as he prepared to pull the trigger again.

Except the standing figure was gone. In front of the light, Ryan could see that it had dropped again into a crouch mirroring his own, the weapon drifting down. Then it crumpled to a still mass on the floor of the cab.

Ryan picked up the fallen flashlight and turned frantically toward the source of the painful cry as the twin echoes of the rifle shots slowly faded away.

Epilogue

SEATTLE, WASHINGTON

Emily looked across her temporary desk and out of the window from the second floor of the Queen Anne house. The contractors would be there tomorrow to begin converting her father's upstairs study back into a corner office for her. Then they would convert the rest of the second floor of the building into office space as well.

She closed her eyes and for a moment was back in the cavern. She could feel the cool air on her skin that raised bumps on her arms, see his eyes in the reflection of the flashes off the ghostly train cars, then hear the footsteps of her torturer on the dirt floor as he retreated down the side of the cars. And all the while, there were the four bags lined with explosives at her feet.

Adam Worth is dead, she reminded herself. He could never hurt her again. She forced herself to focus on Kieran's arrival in half an hour. She imagined them looking at furniture for her new office before joining her father and Laura for dinner tonight.

The dark memories retreated. Her body began to relax.

It was so much worse at first. Now she could usually avoid the full onset of panic when the sensations returned. Her therapist was pleased and optimistic.

She'd almost worried more for her father at first. He blamed himself for that night. He shouldn't have. It was her idea to go back onto the grounds with Heather, she reminded him. The entire case had been her idea.

But her father was getting better, too. It had really begun when she'd told him of her plan to join his practice—if he'd have her. The smile that he'd returned had hardly left his face since.

Of course, there had been a price. "I want an upstairs corner office," she'd told him. "And new furniture."

He'd made a show of hesitation, then agreed.

And how could he argue with her? He couldn't pretend money was an issue. Even after reverting back to a one-third contingency with Kieran's case, they were . . . flush. After that night on the reservation, and the capture of the security guards with the debris evidence at the rail station, Covington had offered a significant sum to settle the case—with complete confidentiality. Kieran had turned them down. "Not in a hundred years," he'd said. "Not in a thousand." So they'd offered more. The third sum finally came with an offer of no confidentiality. Kieran had accepted.

The Feds still hadn't figured out everyone involved with Project Wolffia, beyond Adam Worth and the core of security guards out at the site that night. Red Whalen, probably. Hank, their guide, certainly. Most of the rest of the people who worked at LB5 the past seven years. The problem with these guys, though, was that the extent of their knowledge about the Project was still unclear. Nobody had the stomach for putting away a bunch of Hanford lifers who thought they were loyally working for the government all this time.

It would help to put all this to rest, of course, if they could recover the testing equipment for the nuclear trigger—and the chemical trigger itself. "Give it time," Ryan had counseled Kieran and herself. "They'll find the trigger. And they'll get up the food chain eventually."

A part of Emily still feared that the nuclear trigger might surface as a bargaining chip to protect the people behind Project Wolffia. But it wouldn't if she or her father had any say about it. And though Ted Pollock and his family had managed to stay out of sight through all this, she was sure the Yakama wouldn't remain silent on the subject if it came to that.

All of this was helpful to Emily's recovery. Even more so was Kieran's move to Seattle with his mother and sister. Plus the assurance from Dr. Trân that the deeper access to Covington's inspection data ordered by Judge Johnston had led him to conclude that Kieran had a low chance of serious health effects from the October explosion. Just as Emily had been assured the same after radiation readings were taken in the white train pit.

She looked out the window at the azure sky and the distant outline of the Olympic mountains, wreathed in broken clumps of white clouds. She still hadn't asked her father today if he'd reached Poppy Martin to discuss Covington's offer of settlement. The offer had come despite the fact that they hadn't even filed the lawsuit yet. That was good. Despite everything he'd gone through, Poppy still had a love of Sherman and an abiding pride in Hanford. He'd be pleased that a fight wouldn't be necessary.

Emily forced her gaze away from the horizon and turned at last to the most recent file that had arrived at her desk. Business had been pouring in since Kieran's settlement. Some came from the publicity surrounding the Hanford case. Much was driven by Judge Freyling's praise of their new firm. And her father's reputation was still very strong, especially now that he'd signaled his full return to practice.

A file summary from Melissa was clipped to the top of the folder. It was a property dispute. A claim against an owner of an orchard. She read the summary carefully. Then she looked out the window again, grateful for the sunlight on this late September day.

A property dispute against an owner of an orchard. Her mother's words came back to her from the day that Emily had announced her decision to go to law school. Though already stricken with the early stages of her disease, Carolyn had smiled warmly and with obvious pride. Then she'd taken Emily's hand.

"Never sue a teacher," she'd said. *"Or a farmer. And only take on the fights truly worth fighting."*

Emily set the file aside. They'd pass on that one. She was sure her father would agree—or if not, she'd convince him.

After all, Emily thought, there was plenty of other work to do.

Acknowledgments

Thanks to my wonderful wife, Catherine, for drawing on a lifetime of reading to share insights on character and plot; to Libby, who always has a ready ear when her father asks; to Ian for continuing to cheer me on; to Susan, who listens and reads and encourages through the many months a book takes form; and to Scott, for allowing his brother and law partner the writing time he needs.

I also wish to thank my friends among the Yakama Nation, and my consultant for his advice about the nuclear industry.

Thanks as well to my editor, David Long, for his extra work on this second effort.

And finally, a special thanks to the many readers of my debut novel, who graciously took the time to write and ask for more.

Todd M. Johnson has practiced as an attorney for over thirty years, specializing as a trial lawyer. A graduate of Princeton University and the University of Minnesota Law School, he also taught for two years as adjunct professor of International Law and served as a US diplomat in Hong Kong. He lives outside Minneapolis, Minnesota, with his wife, his son, Ian, and his daughter, Libby.

Visit his website at www.authortoddjohnson.com.

Also From
Todd M. Johnson

To learn more about Todd and his books, visit
authortoddjohnson.com.

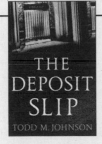

$10,000,000 Is Missing.

Erin Larson is running out of options. In the wake of
her father's death, she found a thin slip of paper—
a deposit slip—with an unbelievable amount on it.
The trouble is, the bank claims they have no record
of the money, and trying to hire a lawyer has brought
only intimidation and threats. Erin's last chance is Jared
Neaton.

Jared isn't sure Erin's case is worth the risk, especially
since his recently established law firm is in such dire
straits. But if the money is real, all his problems could
vanish. When digging deeper unleashes far more than
threats, both Jared and Erin will have to decide the cost
they're willing to pay to discover the truth.

The Deposit Slip